THE SOUND OF A
BROKEN
CHAIN

THE SOUND OF A
BROKEN CHAIN

J.D. CORTESE

Opportuna Libri, LLC
Timely books for every time
Durham, North Carolina

ISBN-13 (paperback): 978-1-7325590-0-4
ISBN-13 (ePUB): 978-1-7325590-1-1
ISBN-13 (Mobi): 978-1-7325590-2-8

Library of Congress Control Number: 2018958764

Cover Design and Interior Formatting by Tugboat Design
Author's cover photography by Portrait Innovations Professional Studios
Edited by Word Works Editorial Services
Published by Opportuna Libri, LLC (North Carolina, USA)

For any further information about specific rights and the copyrighted use of this book, please contact Opportuna Libri at info@opportunalibri.com. Mail should be addressed to Opportuna Libri, LLC, P. O. Box 52406, Durham, NC 27717-2046.

*To my wife Laura Voglino,
who has journeyed with me
until our paths became one.*

"...Oíd el ruido de rotas cadenas..."
...Listen to the sound of broken chains...
Argentine National Anthem

"To tell the truth," answered Altisidora, "I probably didn't die completely because I didn't enter hell, and if I had entered it, I couldn't have left it by any means, even if I'd wanted to. The truth is that I reached the gate, where up to a dozen devils were playing with a ball [...] but this did not amaze me as much as seeing that, although it is natural for players to feel happier when they are winning and sadder when they are losing, in that game everybody was growling, everybody was quarreling, and everybody was cursing the others."

"That's no wonder," said Sancho, "because devils, whether they play or not, can never be happy, whether they win or lose."

Don Quixote, Miguel de Cervantes

CONTENTS

THE SOUND OF A BROKEN CHAIN

PART I

Time Unfamiliar

1

I used to think there are reasons for everything that happens, and I wanted to understand each and every one of them. I have paid a price in blood and pain to learn that logic doesn't always lead to the truth. What little of me has survived, I've kept in my journals and managed to turn into a story. Some will see in these pages a warning about the tyranny of destiny. Others, like me, will finally accept that there's hope in embracing it.

As a teenager, I spent my afternoons walking the streets of Buenos Aires, stopping only to tie my shoelaces. I wasn't very concerned about them, so it's no surprise I would miss the exact moment when the threads of time started to slide out of their eyelets.

My last peaceful trek started, as usual, at school after someone had decided I was misbehaving. I am, unfortunately, too bright for my own good, cursed with an IQ that falls out of any chart. My supposedly grand mind, pride of my father, was what got me in trouble that morning. Let's say it's not appropriate to answer a math problem just as the teacher writes the equal sign. She sent me to the principal's office, thinking I'd spied on her notes.

Sandra, the still-quite-sexy secretary of Mr. Fernández-Souza, received me with a nagging frown. I had been spending so much time there she was teaching me to touch-type and had started to clock my progress.

"Here again?"

"A little incident with the math substitute."

"Caused by a hurt ego?"

"Not really. Well, maybe."

I liked Sandra, and she did get how bored I was with the mindless memorizing of what my teachers wanted to brand in my brain.

"Distracted?"

Sandra's smirk of disapproval tried to make me feel guilty about my misdeed. She was acting again as my pretty step-aunt, but, given that she was also prone to flirt with students, I blushed, thinking my eyes had drifted to the wrong parts of her figure. "I was," I said, "when in class."

"It seems your brilliant head gets lost in the clouds a lot these days," she said. "Have you been distracted anywhere else?" Her smile hinted she was thinking about girl problems.

"More like everywhere else, these days."

No matter what I'd say in the open, I did share Sandra's concern about my lack of focus. The city was worrying me more on my second year in Argentina, as the actions of its military government had become ominously clear by 1978. But I didn't say that to Sandra. I didn't know her well enough to know whether it was safe. I had given some of my own money to her church—a gesture so rare there as to be forever thanked for the gift—and her acquaintances seemed a little too conservative for my taste. The wrong kinds of connections to the government were very dangerous back then.

"You know what will happen," said Sandra, still entertained by looking over my a-little-less-than-up-to-school-standards ensemble. I became conscious of wearing a velvety blue sweater, its round collar illegally covering too much of my regulation burgundy tie.

"Yes, I do," I answered, planning to add some of my own standard argumentations against any oppressive rules, but that suddenly turned superfluous. Sandra's boss showed up, sporting a ferocious scowl and swinging around an attaché case. With a brief hand gesture, he summoned me to his office.

Mr. Fernández-Souza entered his sanctum so fast he was already watching me from behind the desk when I got in. "I'm not going to keep wasting my time with you, Mr. Weston," he said. "This is happening way too often, and we do take seriously the behavior of students. And...." He stopped, his eyes on mine. I kept quiet, having decided not to say more than five words in each visit to the principal's office. I had already said three of them— "Yes, Mr. Fernández-Souza"—and was prepared to carefully count the rest.

"I won't suspend you, out of respect to your father," he added, looking for an answer he wasn't going to get. I knew that the respect due to my absent father involved him paying twice the fee of other students, so my principal's silence was almost as certain as mine. "This isn't public school," Mr. Fernández-Souza continued, "and we'll send you home for the day, again and again, until you learn how to behave. North Americans, we know, aren't well educated." He thought he'd said something profound, but his views of America came from our TV's police dramas and the worst places in New York and Chicago. I still said nothing, now confident that my father was paying enough to keep me in the roll no matter what.

Mr. Fernández-Souza, finally losing patience with his solitary expounding of the school rules, pounded the desk and signaled the door; his straight arm was shaking like a compass pointing north. It also seemed like a Nazi salute, and it reminded me of something else I immediately forgot, when the reality of my life sunk in and my eyes teared up.

I was being sent home as if I had a family there to punish me.

He couldn't possibly understand how alone I was.

I had been orphaned from my own country by my mother's death and my father's job, and adopted by Argentina while I finished high school. Living abroad, I lost many things—like my relatives, so scattered in my country up north as to make it too expensive to contact them. And I lost my few friends from before I started to travel with my father's projects, mostly because they had turned less interesting after undergoing puberty. I even lost my name, Edgar Weston, as I was quickly renamed *Edgardo* by my peers, and even now I feel awkward saying the English version.

But there were also things I got in the trade for a country that wasn't my own and shared our freedoms only in appearance. I became fluent in Spanish—inspired by stories about an Argentine grandmother—and didn't look too foreign in a city full of tango-thirsty tourists and third-generation European immigrants. And I was free to roam the world alone, a street Kerouac, thinking by myself without the weight of nearby elders. Some would say this was dangerous, but I relished the new adventure of each day.

I accepted my punishment with a sense of being in the wrong, something the principal clearly loved, and which made him smile, and I left his office trying not to smile too much myself. After bragging for the tenth time about my knowledge of everything, a reprimand was in order. What I didn't know was that the punishment for showing off my brains was going to be much greater than being sent home.

I was going to be presented by destiny with a puzzle no human IQ could solve.

2

Out on the streets and walking aimlessly, my mind was free to work on one tangle of reality after another. The posters papering most windowless walls reaffirmed the insanity of a city getting ready to host the 1978 World's Soccer Cup—although it was best for my body's integrity to say football, not soccer. I saw a taxi driver leaving his seat to help an elderly woman get out. A kiosk manager smiled as she gave me change from a larger-than-appropriate bill. The streets were clean, and free from the usual wrappers, chewed gum, and dog excrement. The soccer tournament was behind everything I saw, heard, and smelled.

None of this made sense in a city where its people—the *porteños*—were as self-absorbed and confrontational as New Yorkers. Everybody had been told, over and over, to prepare for an invasion of tourists—just keep smiling and don't worry about the long-standing, city-wide curfew. I had decided to follow the recent disregard for this mandate and come back to my apartment quite late, after making a couple of stops to savor the great local coffee with a dollop of whipped cream.

I was trying very hard to extract meaning from a world that, under the surface, was all chaos and danger. Any tall man in a suit—or any well-built guy with a mustache—could have been a policeman out of uniform and up to no good, on his way to carry out an assignment involving kidnapping and then torturing the opposition to the governing military Junta.

But the most outrageous mystery on my mind was a paradox the radio served me for breakfast. As I woke up, I'd heard a story I was having trouble believing. A huge meteorite had crashed recently—on Friday, May 5—in some forsaken mountains way up north, near the Argentine border with Bolivia. The explosion was heard as far as 200 kilometers away. The next day, another smaller meteor had hit, close by.

What are the chances that two meteors would hit Earth, on two consecutive days and around the same place? That was impossible, or possible only if we could twist both time and space.

I spent my last afternoon of normalcy thinking about the meteorites.

* * *

It was dark by the time I started to make my way across Plaza del Congreso, the park next to the Argentine scaled-down version of the Capitol that—under yet another round of military dictatorship—was becoming a fossil of the country's extinct democracy.

And then I stopped, suddenly afraid.

There was a reflection shimmering at the edge of the park. It could have been a swath of fog, but in the evening's colder weather it would be unlikely. It was too clear to be fog, and it seemed to be made from infinitesimal crystals. And I had to cross it, if I wanted to reach my bus and go home. I have to say—because of what it means for my story—that the cloud, or wall of fog, or whatever the phenomenon was, was intensely, luminously purple.

After mustering the courage to pass through the wall of glassy mist, I rushed to get to the bus stop behind the *Congreso* building. My bus—or collective transport, Buenos Aires's ever-present *colectivo*—always arrived at the corner of Alsina Street at nine thirty. That day it didn't, and it was enough to unnerve me even more. I kicked a small ball of paper near my foot, which perhaps contained the ultimate secret of existence. But if I had to kneel and unfold that piece of spiral-bound notebook to read it, the secret would forever remain secret.

As soon as I turned back to face the street, I felt as if I had seen the *colectivo* I was waiting for rush past my stop and turn the corner far on my left, disappearing between the blurry lights of the two pharmacies which stood at opposite sideways of the avenue. But it wasn't as if I'd seen it but as if it was a dream I was having trouble remembering.

The bus had turned the corner without trudging its way along the street where it should have normally stopped. Just disappeared around the corner ahead without any trace memory of how it had gotten there.

And the paper ball had reacted with a similarly impossible recess and was lying again near the heel of my right foot.

Then, another bus turned the corner far from the avenue. I saw that bus, and another, and a third one. In some incomprehensible way, I saw all of them at once. Each had the same color but a different shape, as if belonging to other times, some past, some yet to come.

Time was discombobulated, and I felt fearful again.

When my bus finally arrived, I couldn't bring myself to climb its high steps. Wasn't sure anymore if I was climbing the one that had left or one that hadn't really arrived.

* * *

Whenever I didn't take the bus home, I used the old but reliable subways. I'd never done it so late, but my night was turning quite eerie and I entered the warm passages of the *Congreso* Station without a second thought.

The subway late at night was an exercise in not paying attention to others, but the girl immediately caught my attention. She was almost as tall as me—that is, really tall for an Argentine—and dressed in black, with a battered leather jacket. I wouldn't normally stare at women in the subway, but something about her was entrancing. It wasn't just the nice legs and broad hips, showing clearly in her tight black jeans, or the also very black hair, falling almost to her waist; not even her oval face, which resembled the angels in medieval paintings. There was a mystery about her, true darkness, and I tried but couldn't see her eyes, as she kept them turned down.

When she suddenly looked straight into my eyes, I shuddered. I'll never forget that first time I saw those burning brown eyes. Eyes of dark gold from an angry cat.

In most cities, this encounter in the late hours of a weekday would have ended with her getting ready to leave as soon as we'd reach her station. But Buenos Aires's subways are unpredictable, and the driver decided to apply the brakes just at the point between stations where we were moving at a decent speed. The girl almost tumbled and, grabbing her purse, sat on the empty seat next to me. The subway car had plenty of other seats, all as uncomfortable as mine, and I was startled by this.

She was looking away, and I wanted to say something to her, anything. Then, I saw her purse had opened and something was sticking out. A gun. A large black gun, both opaque and shiny in its various parts. A dark object that shouldn't have been there and I shouldn't have seen.

The girl turned, and she saw that I had seen.

3

I started to talk first, even though I knew my accented Spanish could make me a target if the girl—pretty and all—was a thief and ready to use the gun. Nobody there was going to leave their magazines to save me.

What I managed to say to her was, "What are you doing?"

"Who are you?"

I probably started blushing at that point. "Is that important? What are you doing with this...the gun?" My voice turned into whispering after guessing I was the only one who could see into her shoulder purse.

"It's not anything you should worry about. Keep your eyes on your stuff." She had the most delightful voice, her intonation having a hint of the Argentine inlands my precarious language chest could not place.

"It's just that...you know, the police," I said, uncertain about what we might each know. "It's dangerous, so late at night—they stop people and search them all the time."

"Yes, I know that. I'm not new around here like you."

For a moment, I wondered if she was an agent from the military. But she was just a girl, too young and beautiful to do the rough and dirty work one expected from the secret police. She also didn't fit the type of a prostitute seeking protection with a gun—in those days, a crime for which punishment would have been great. She wouldn't have risked getting lost in the city's destitute juvenile prisons.

I kept talking, sensing the probability she'd run away as soon as we reached the next station. "You have to be careful, that's all I was saying. Do you need help?" I said. And right there, I was offering help to a stranger who carried a gun.

"Who are you? I've asked already."

"My name's Edgardo. I'm living here in Buenos Aires while finishing high school. My father works in the United States." My accent worked through the kinks of that phrase as well as possible.

"Is he a spy?"

"What?"

"The CIA, you know, the Yankees."

I laughed, and for the first time she relaxed a little. We were all Yankees—and maybe CIA—to them. Her teeth were so white and she had such a frank smile, but her right hand was still grabbing the purse. "It's amazing you can live here," she said.

"Why? It's a nice city." Stupidly, I thought about how I could see Buenos Aires's world-famous opera theatre—El Colón—from our balcony, and the city's broadest avenue—9th of July—from my bedroom window.

"I mean with this government—the shitty military that keeps us under their boots."

She was right, but I couldn't explain to her that my father wouldn't care much about undemocratic power if it gave him more money than democracy. "Yes, I know. But I'm stuck here."

My face might have been expressive enough, because she smiled again and released her hand from the purse, landing it over mine. That gave me goosebumps.

"I understand," she said. "We're all stuck here. But, it will get better."

Her hand was still resting on mine. It was cold, and I swear I felt the contact of each finger distinctly. I had kissed a girl back home once, after a party where she'd taught me to dance, but there was a much greater intimacy with this stranger. We were alone in the universe, in a subway full of the ghosts of violence.

At this point, the lights of the approaching station enveloped our train, and I thought my stranger was going to leave without saying another word.

She stood, again hugging her purse. And then she smiled, losing a couple of years and making me wonder if she was even in high school. "Tomorrow, at five o'clock," she said, still smiling, *"Café Las Violetas."* And she added, probably seeing my surprise. "You pay, and I'll get to drink good tea and eat lots of pastries. *My aunt was from England, and I do speak English too."*

In an instant, the girl was gone, and the door closed with a screeching sound that needed a lot of greasing to be right.

I immediately realized a couple of things. She had said her last words in clear, if weirdly accented, English. And she'd left without telling me her name or why she had the gun.

4

I floated the entire next morning, thinking about the subway girl. I was surprised about not receiving my normal dose of harassment at school—being the despised *gringo*, I had a white-and-red target on my back. But I don't entirely blame my school classmates for this.

I was a foreign kid, jumping into their third year of high school with slightly-above-average-level language skills and getting better grades than the top students—even in Argentine History. These spoiled kids, sent to private school by professional parents, couldn't understand how tough the intellectual competition abroad was. The government kept lying to them—all of them, parents included—about the potential of Argentina becoming a world power and spent money it didn't have in building up Buenos Aires for the World Cup.

My friend Julian kept telling me that there were secret concentration camps and a Nazification of the entire country, but I took him with a grain of salt—after all, he'd also told me about the hidden death of the Beatles' Paul McCartney, and the guy's still singing.

Julian Neimeyer was a typical Argentine, both affectionate and arrogant, and my best and only friend in school. I call him here in the accent-less form of *Julián*, to save me trouble and because I kept calling him Julian. Our endless chats always ended in one of his mind's alleys, where conspiracies reigned supreme—whether staged by Argentina's military, or our big corporations and the CIA. For Julian, there was always a great evil power trying to control the world. And of course, only he could figure out where they were hiding the bodies.

Julian had saved me from a dangerous beating in one of those long midday breaks. I was enjoying too much my recently gained knowledge of Argentine soccer—please, say *football*, repeat a hundred times.

"No, guys, River Plate can't win any tournament this year," I had said.

"And what do you know?" Suddenly, a blond-and-blue-eyed son of the land was grabbing my jacket by the lapels.

"Hey, I'm just saying that the best players are sequestered... training for the World Cup." I moved one step back and realized I was surrounded by five guys, two of them noticeably larger than me.

"You can't possibly know how that works," said one of the small ones, trying his best to be menacing.

"Guys, what are you doing?"

It was Julian—at the time, just an introverted, broad-shouldered student who'd never said a word in my presence. He towered over everybody and looked quite Argentine—that's to say, very European—with his dark hair and brown eyes. In a movie, he would have been perfect for the role of a young Italian soldier.

The guy who'd started the argument tried to push Julian away and he, without a second of doubt, smashed the bully's nose against a very large set of knuckles. The braggart fell to his knees.

After the stunned group retreated, I was left alone with Julian, with nothing to do but to become friends, our two-year gap in ages notwithstanding. It was supposed to be his last year of school, and he was slated to graduate in December.

* * *

As soon as I saw Julian that day, I couldn't resist telling him about my subway encounter. I should have predicted he would go bananas.

"A girl with a gun? Are you crazy?"

"She was just...she had the gun but didn't..."

"Didn't what? Use it on you? Just wait."

"We don't know, Julian. She might be just..." But my father-certified IQ of 187 wasn't enough to concoct any story where the girl was doing something incidental and innocent with a gun big enough she'd need both hands to lift it.

"She might be a terrorist, one of those *Montoneros* who are killing people just to shake up the country. You know, we're all in this big mess because of them."

"Montoneros?"

"Yes, the leftists who want to make us into a second Cuba."

It was hard to follow Julian when he swerved through political minefields of his own making. What he said next proved my point— "You should be careful who you talk to. The Junta is watching, and prowling in the night."

As usual, I had a hard time figuring out Julian's politics. He might have been blaming a band of Peronist extremists just to make people believe he was pro-government. In those days it was either way to the right or to the left, with no middle ground. Only the late Juan Domingo Perón had managed to play both sides at once. Without him around, and with the ultra-anti-Peronist, ultra-anticommunist military in power, any political leaning was a mortal sin. Truly mortal.

In character, Julian kept talking alone and adding threads to a diatribe against the Montoneros, now including his prejudice the girl was one of them. Also in character for me, I proceeded to oppose him, developing all kinds of arguments about how improbable it would be to find a Montonero—worse, a teenage girl Montonero— riding the subway at night and with a gun at hand.

I tried to exit my failing arguments with a final bet. "I won't know if I don't see her again."

"You just liked her long legs."

"Well, yes, she's cute, and to meet her in a fancy café like Violetas won't be a problem."

"Not a problem? With the military spying on all of us? You don't know what you're saying."

"Julian..."

"I've been telling you this, and I know you won't believe me, but soon I have proof that they are doing...I *will* show you."

I interrupted again, stubbornly repeating how I was going to see the girl no matter what. I didn't know I had just pushed my friend over a line he wasn't ready to cross, forcing a series of decisions that were going to affect our lives. Greatly.

When I left for my math class, Julian was pacing in a circle, still talking, but now only to himself.

5

As I approached the entrance of subway B, trying to reach *Medrano* Station and the famous Las Violetas café, someone stopped me. He was keeping distance from me, not with his hands but with a series of requests. When I tried to advance, the man put both hands in front of him, as if pushing the air to contain me.

"Just wait," he said. "Stay a few minutes. I should...we need to talk."

I swerved around him and rushed to the subway's multi-level staircase.

It wasn't uncommon to meet talkative strangers and beggars in the city. But the man didn't dress like a homeless transient— although I couldn't remember how he'd dressed. I looked up from the subway stairs to see if he was still there. He wasn't, but that was not the weirdest thing.

I couldn't recall his face at all. It was as if he'd had no face.

As I finally started to descend the subway stairs, an icy thought climbed from somewhere deep in my memories, the time when both my parents still were alive and took me to church on Sundays. A time before my mother headed to Africa, to fight multinationals and discover her cancer; before I'd decided to follow my father to Argentina in hopes of finding the roots of my grandmother.

I had remembered those texts in the New Testament, where the apostles keep meeting Jesus over and over not realizing it is him. It was a ridiculous thought, but it made me shiver all the way to the opening doors of an iron-and-sweat-smelling train.

* * *

I reached Las Violetas and she wasn't there. I looked both inside and outside, and all over the sidewalk along Rivadavia Avenue. Owing to my overexcited state of mind, I ran all the way to each of the corners of that block to see if she was coming. And when I was ready to give up, I almost bumped into her.

"I didn't think you were the type that comes late," she said.

"Sorry, there was this guy..."

"Or the type that makes excuses when it suits him."

"I—I'm sorry. I wanted to see you."

Sometimes, the truth works. I did want to see that girl, now dressed more like one, with a beautiful purple sweater and pleated gray skirt, and wearing a bracelet made with huge gold beads. My interest in her might have been showing, because she calmed down and walked past me to enter Las Violetas.

We took a table near the windows and facing the front. The café's name—the violets—belonged to the long-gone *fin de siècle* Buenos Aires, the late Victorian era when the city hoped to turn itself into Paris rather than Madrid. The café had small tables with cast-iron chairs, delicate *vitreaux* gracing its doors, and waiters in fancy white shirts; it made me feel as if we had time-traveled to the early twentieth century.

I had the persistent feeling that this girl—Mariana Venturino, who turned out to have a lot of Italy in her genes and a year of school on me—couldn't possibly be traveling nightly subways with a gun. It was impossible to bring up the issue, and our conversation resembled more and more a date as we talked about our tastes on weather, food, and movies. It turned out we'd both started to read *Carrie* and wanted to watch *Close Encounters of the Third Kind* when it finally came out. Mariana was sweetly into crafts and proudly explained how she had put together her bracelet. Football wasn't our thing, and we didn't talk about it. We were seemingly enveloped by a culture we didn't understand, and when we did, most times, wouldn't approve it.

Implicit in our conversation was the point where things would start to slide downhill.

She said it first— "You want to know why I was carrying that piece last night."

"I don't." But I wanted to know.

"I'm involved in something, which is good, but it makes me do some awful things. Like arming people in our defense."

Son of a bitch. Julian was right.

"You don't have to tell me," I said, sure that my words had come way too late. I looked at her lips and wondered how, in a better world, it would feel to taste them.

"I am a Montonera," she said. The silence before and after those words had been long enough for her to review her entire life.

"You—what?"

I was stunned by her confession. But after Julian's comment, I'd learned a little about "those Montoneros." Montoneros was an outlawed organization, stemming from the left-wing of the Peronist party. They'd become an armed insurrection—a true urban guerrilla—and were fighting a terrorist war against the government. Their name came from nineteenth-century bands—bunches, or *montones*—of *gaucho* rebel fighters. And the military was trying to kill each and every one of them.

Mariana's mouth had stayed open, as if trying to catch back her words. "I have seen some people disappear," she said. "Right in my neighborhood. Coming out of church. I can't stand for that." Her cat eyes shone with a bright hue, like a topaz. I understood that, if threatened at home, she would for sure use her gun.

There I was, having an impossible conversation with the most unlikely revolutionary. It was one of those rare moments when I didn't think first; I grabbed both of her hands and stared into her eyes. "I don't care. I like you."

Suddenly she was somber and struggled for words. "I can't be with you, with other people...they won't let me. This has to be it." My hands were left behind as she stood, again ready to leave. This time there was no doubt I'd never see her again.

I did something that in retrospect made no sense, but perhaps was a desperate grab of other hands. I spoke, weighing every syllable, in my own language.

"Why did you talk to me in English?"

She answered also in English. Hers wasn't accented by her Spanish and sounded clearly British. *"I like to speak English, from time to time...sometimes."*

"Why?"

"It reminds me of my aunt Clarice...she taught me when I was little. I kept learning."

There was something more; we both knew that, and I said it. *"But why to me? What does it mean?"*

"I'm tired of this country. Of the big lies. I'd like to talk...like I'm not here anymore."

"And?"

"They killed her. My aunt. She didn't do anything, just teach Philosophy at the university. They took her from her home—and her daughter too. Ana María was six."

Mariana was crying, unable to go back to her earlier, better world, the one she'd shielded with our common language. And I knew why I was there, why she wanted to be with me.

I stood up and hugged her, caressing her hair—smelling her hair—and holding her body.

She couldn't notice it, but I kissed her head just as I began to cry.

6

Our high school—in Argentina, the secondary school or *el secund-ario*—was named "José B. Gorostiaga" after a little-known north-erner who helped to write the Argentine Constitution. Everything about it was little-known, except that it was expensive and exclu-sive. Only the children of the extremely well-to-do and those in cahoots with the reigning military were accepted. Of course, I got in because of my father and the green paper he brought to the coffers of the government officials who managed most pharma-ceutical boards.

But I wasn't so sure how Julian Niemeyer had joined me, as his family was in the lower floor of the Argentine middle class, hang-ing in there with lifesavers made from the wreckage left by their family business. Maybe Julian had some powerful godfather or had attended a select church where mustached higher-ups knelt for no particular reason.

I went to the large patio for the long midday break; Julian wasn't around to answer my questions. In fact, he hadn't shown up for the last two days. It was already Wednesday, and I had agreed to get together with Mariana and some of her friends. I needed to talk with him.

I drifted all the way to the back of the school's patio, a large rectangular space carved in a neighborhood expensive enough to have cost a fortune in red tiles and bribes. I looked at my face on the back wall, made of thick glass windows dark enough to resemble a black mirror.

Still no beard and sandy hair too unwieldy to comb. I did look like my father, one of those American faces with small features that would have merged inconspicuously with others in an Army recruitment ad. I'd seen a picture of my father in Korea where he looked like me. I hated having his grayish blue eyes. As for my father's German ancestry, it seemed dirty to me, as if all my relatives had been Nazis.

I didn't get to go over the rest of my long body of grown-too-fast sixteen before I found myself lying on the floor.

When I stopped watching the sky and sat, I saw Ricardo, the leading bully of my class, followed by two of his acolytes. Where was Julian (and his big arms) when I needed him?

"Hey, *gringo*, what the hell are you doing here?"

I knew where the moron was going but needed time to think about how to get out of that recurrent daytime nightmare. "What do you mean?" I said.

"Idiot! What are you doing in this country?"

"Same as you, studying the crap they write on the blackboard." I wondered if I was being agreeable enough.

"It's not crap. It is stuff about Argentina—my country. You'll see it when we bust your asses, you, who poison us with garbage and multinationals."

Ricardo was obviously hearing some propaganda at home. I couldn't possibly be agreeable enough to compensate for an entire family of morons.

Ricardo took another step, casting a shadow over my eyes. "Hey, what are you doing still there, coward? Stand up and fight for your country."

"I don't want to..."

"You are a big coward, like all the Yankees. We're going to show you how we fight in Argentina."

As if they'd rehearsed it, the other two started to chant "Argentina, Argentina." There were few people on the huge patio, and the ones I could see as I raised suddenly changed direction like fish scared by a shark. I was alone, and these guys were stupid enough to punch me dead over some misunderstood national pride.

I don't remember exactly what I thought, but I later thanked my father for taking me to judo lessons, so I could discharge the anger over my mother's illness.

I wasn't much for attacking anyone, especially when outnumbered, but Ricardo grabbed my shoulders and pushed me back. Not once, but a couple of times. I stumbled and lost my leather journal in the process; with the next push, I hit the glass wall, banging the side of my head and hurting my neck.

Apparently, Ricardo had decided to keep pounding my head against the wall with his punches, but first would attempt to shake out my breakfast. He should have gone straight to boxing.

The second time he grabbed my shoulders, I held his wrists—he was busy laughing and didn't notice. And, at the precise moment when he tried to push me again, I rotated and placed my hip on the space between his and a forward-moving right leg, with my right hand firmly placed on his back.

My Japanese *sensei* would have had trouble detecting that I was trying to perform an *O-Goshi* projection on Ricardo. The other kids probably thought I was trying to act gay, putting my ass near his crotch. But their disapproval would have only lasted a second.

Ricardo suddenly twirled in the air and hit the glass wall with a thud forecasting grave consequences for his future steadiness. My personal defense move had not been quite professional; on approach to the wall, I hadn't controlled well enough with my left arm the downward rotation of my opponent's body, leaving it to spin away from me at high speed, just like when releasing a yo-yo.

He ended up hitting the windows and their thick metal frames with his face.

Ricardo lay on the floor, his body contorting in pain and his nose dripping blood. I couldn't see the other two guys, but I imagined their unbelieving expressions. I was truly alone, in another country, in a dangerous world whose rules I only half understood.

And I was sure as hell I was going to get a suspension.

7

Mr. Fernández-Souza was somewhat forgiving and only gave me (again) a three-day suspension. It was obvious he felt sorry for me, a virtual orphan and transplant from a different country. I was also the school's best student—no matter how ridiculous I felt carrying the Argentine flag at public ceremonies.

I accepted my punishment without argument, thinking on how I needed a few days to plan for the next, certain ambush from Ricardo—his nose less harmed than his ego—especially since now my *O-Goshi* had been revealed. I didn't have any other significant move for a second round, which was surely going to be much worse than the first. Luckily, my suspension included an extra day without school—Thursday was going to be a big national holiday, May 25, celebrating the country's first independence revolt against Spain.

After the stressful morning at the Gorostiaga, I found the streets invigorating. Buenos Aires was approaching its winter, and it was cold, but not so much so that my class attire (gray pants, blue blazer, and a stained burgundy tie) would be insufficient. I thought how to best invest a free afternoon; after all, I had no family to notify of my misdeeds, and I doubted the director would contact my father through an expensive long-distance call.

Before going home, there was one place I needed to check. I was worried that something was not quite right with Julian. Maybe even something serious.

The city was immense, and half of the country's twenty-five million inhabitants lived there, stretching it far into the grass flatlands. It took three *colectivos* to get to Julian's house in San Cristóbal, an old neighborhood with a bad reputation going back to the birth of the tango—times of knife fights and whorehouses. My friend's house was surprisingly modern, a brick-and-glass apartment building; it towered over the others.

My favorite writer, Tolstoy, had said that all unhappy families are unhappy in their own ways. Our two families were broken in their own, interesting ways.

* * *

Julian's mother showed up at the apartment's door covered by a short, buttoned dress that looked like a long shirt. She was obviously still enjoying the effects of a few glasses of whisky; I could smell the last of them. Doris Niemeyer—known by the not-classy-at-all moniker 'Dorita'—was young for a parent, and I surprised myself looking inside her dress to a couple of very large breasts, which formed a thin dark line in between them. I went into a maybe too strenuous explanation—trying to keep my eyes from wandering around her figure—about why I was there and what vaguely academic thing I wanted to get from Julian on that afternoon, which couldn't wait until tomorrow.

"Would you like something to drink?" she said. "Let's go to the terrace." She was observing me with hungry eyes.

I sat on one of four chairs set around a table near their balcony; it overlooked a park with big slopes and even a fountain. Julian's mom sat across the table and started to serve me from a half-empty Coke bottle. Distracted and anxious, I almost looked under the table and then shuddered, wondering if she'd have on any underwear. From then on, I kept my eyes above the table's level.

"Do you know where Julian is?" As soon as I closed my mouth, I realized how stupid my inquiry was. Julian would never tell his mother whatever it was he'd decided to do—his latest crusade, where he was likely trying a new pair of binoculars.

"No, I haven't seen him since yesterday morning," she said. "You know, he doesn't tell me much about what he does...I do spend a lot of time alone."

"I'm sorry. I just want to know where Julian is. I need to give him the stuff from school."

"It's hard to be so lonely. My husband comes home late at night, and I don't work anymore. Julian tells me you're also alone in Buenos Aires—that your family is abroad."

I was going to clarify the situation of my family, and perhaps rant about my father's many faults. But I sensed how the conversation with my friend's mother was straying in a direction I certainly didn't like. Her eyes were red and wet, and she wasn't really paying attention to what I was saying.

"Do you want to try a whisky, Edgardo? Maybe we can drink it on the sofa, inside. It's too cold for me outside...I want to relax a little."

That was my cue to get as far as possible from my friend's mother. Without saying a word, I stood and moved back into the apartment, in the space between one breath and the next. Dorita followed me, also in silence but close enough I could feel her body almost touching mine.

In a series of short strides, I covered the perimeter of the living room, checking every picture on the walls' shelves and trying not to look back at the very loose clothing of La Señora Niemeyer. Meanwhile, I considered, driven by treacherous hormones, how she couldn't be more than thirty and maybe not even Julian's birthmother. By that time, she'd figured out I wasn't interested in whisky or any kind of interpersonal relaxation, and I asked her to let me leave some stuff in Julian's room.

* * *

My friend's room was more disorganized than what I'd expected from a guy who dressed neatly and talked as if he was a historian collecting the records of a fading civilization. His desk had piles of paper that reached my shoulders' height. It all seemed school-related, but soon I saw how his projects and other meaningless homework tasks were only coating deeper layers of glued newspaper clippings and spiral notebooks full of what appeared to be transcriptions of legal documents. Where and when he had the time to do this boggled my mind.

Reading over Julian's paper treasure (and sorting out the garbage) could have taken me hours, and I was duly worried that, by the time I left the room, Julian's mom might be wearing even less clothing. I decided to focus on deciphering a series of maps stacked in a separate pile.

There were huge ring-bound *Filcar* neighborhood guides from the city's previous three decades, where some pages had been marked and buildings circled in thick, red ink. Crowning the pile, he had set two recent citywide *Peuser* maps, with places both high-lighted and named in the maps' corners. In the few minutes I spent reading them, and weighing my friend's real state of insanity, I saw perilous correlations of his markings with military offices and clubs.

One circle was drawn so perfectly Julian must have done it with a compass. It was the School of Naval Mechanics, north from Palermo, and its acronym, ESMA, had been written in bold capital letters.

I remembered thinking what kind of mechanical knowledge seamen would learn at that school. *Do they need to fix their boats' engines?*

Although I didn't know the notorious role ESMA played in a history that was unfolding but we weren't seeing, I would regret the joke more than anything I've unthinkingly said in my life.

Another place Julian had recorded was seemingly at odds with my friend's obsession with the military; it appeared repeatedly in his maps and in a stack of notes containing only lists of streets and intersections. It was a café known to be a hangout for tourists, right there, in San Cristóbal. And dates written for that place were mostly from the last two months. My mind, quick at calculating calendars, soon found out these dates were all Mondays.

It was Wednesday. And Julian had first missed school on Tuesday.

On my way to the door, I went past Julian's mother fast enough not to see she had unbuttoned her blouse a couple of stops more.

8

By the time I'd reached the intersection of San Juan and Boedo avenues, deep in San Cristóbal, I was breathless and still rushing to escape from the encounter with Julian's mom, which I was struggling to interpret with meanings other than the obvious one.

Then, just across the street, I saw Julian sitting near the corner-most window of the Homero Manzi Café. He commanded a large table that, like his home desk, was stacked with paper. I wanted to see him as a writer hunkering down in a café to write but knew I was observing an aficionado spy at work.

I went into the tango-themed coffeehouse feeling a growing sense of paranoia. I was seeing my friend in a different, more worrisome light. He wasn't just a researcher of the strange, but someone possessed by it; perhaps a dangerous person I should avoid. I also realized why Julian was dressing more and more in monochromatic colors and had been cutting his hair shorter every month. He was doing what he'd said he wanted to do to prove his theories about the military's secret police.

Trying to become one of them.

In a moment of rare maturity, I briefly stopped and considered how maybe it wasn't such a good idea to interrupt Julian in his bunker and observation point. But some form of brain inertia made me continue, and soon it was too late. Julian had seen me and, after a second of hesitation, invited me to sit.

* * *

The other side of reality is just like this one, but less dull. And nobody tells you that you're crazy; at some level, you already know. A meandering conversation ensued between us and lasted at least two hours—hours during which, every time Julian talked about aliens behind ancient world events, I had visions of those two meteorites in the Bolivian mountains and believed him a little more.

I will summarize only the good parts. For the rest, you may want to just picture a crazy world where you can't trust anyone and everything that happens is the product of a very secret organization—the word "synarchy" was popular in the seventies to name a secret worldwide government, and Julian might have used it twenty times through the afternoon. Unlike Hitler, who'd thought the Jews were in charge of the world's economy, my friend favored a secret pact between world powers stemming from the Yalta Conference at the end of World War II.

"You don't expect me to believe all of this," I said, grabbing my head with both hands after one of his endless monologues.

"Why not? The evidence is clear."

"You know—if you weren't my friend…"

"And why do you think I'm your friend?"

I didn't have an answer for that. I was struggling to speak Spanish at length with him and had not managed to collect myself and bring up the subject of Mariana. There were plenty of barriers between us. "You…you helped me when I needed it," I said.

"You mean saving you from those thugs? I do it every time they fight with some new kid. Ricardo has a scar collection with my name—he's the worst fighter, just big."

And suddenly, I had nothing to say. I stayed silent for a very long minute, reassessing whether I had any friends—in Argentina, or back home.

"Hey, don't take it so seriously, *Edh-gard-ouh*," Julian said, mimicking an English speaker badly pronouncing my name.

We laughed to tears, just to be friends again.

"I don't understand why you don't want to tell me what you're doing," I said, trying not to be specific about my worries.

"It's simple—I want to see for myself."

"What?"

And he finally said it— "I want to see the concentration camps, those detention centers everybody's talking about."

"That's crazy; and even if there are any of those, they'll be guarded, and no one could enter if they aren't members."

"It's not a club, Edgardo. And I have friends of my own, very powerful friends of my father. They will vouch for my allegiance to the cause—and about my curiosity on how all of this works."

"Friends? What kind of friends?"

"My father knows well D'Agostini, the city's archbishop. He'll tell the upper echelons that I'm going to be studying military technology in the United States. I've told him I want to specialize in counter insurgency techniques, to fight the new urban guerillas."

I was confused. At the time, I still didn't know about the involvement of the Argentine priesthood with the ruling dictators. And I was a few days short of learning that D'Agostini should have been the subject rather than performer of an exorcism. "A bishop? And why will he help you?"

"Ah, those are old stories of my father and his car business. Stories of bungled cars repainted and made invisible."

"You can't do this. Those camps might be far away, and you can't...leave school." I was being idiotic in considering that having to attend school could stop Julian from demonstrating he'd been right all along in something so big.

"See? That's where you're wrong. Do you know what I'm doing here?"

"Studying the subject?" I realized at once that the two days he'd spent nesting in a bar wasn't what Julian was doing. A not-so-surprising miss, as I'd been showing my dumb side the whole afternoon.

"No, this isn't study time. I'm scouting one of the dumping stations for the people who are disappearing."

"Here, in the city?"

"A couple of blocks from here. You can see cars coming and going all day and sometimes trucks late at night."

Julian pointed across the street to a car parked near the corner. I followed his hand and—like a true magician—Julian transformed my world and made the old one disappear.

I didn't know much about the ongoing disappearances of political enemies and revolutionaries, but I had heard comments about how Amnesty International was using the world press to destroy the country's efforts to show off the glory of its born-again government. The term "dirty war" hadn't been popularized yet by that same international press. But Julian had provided me with details time would validate, stories about unmarked cars running around Buenos Aires and making stops late at night to collect the people to be purged. He'd theorized—nowadays, such fundamental knowledge people had exhausted the jokes about it—many of these cars were Ford Falcons, a harder-lined, toned-down, poor-man's sedan version of (maybe) a Ford Thunderbird.

There was a dark gray Ford Falcon parked near us, new but not flashy, and its two occupants tried to busy themselves with conversation. Guys dressed in business attire, of the gray-suit-and-blue-tie kind, maybe bankers on the way to an early dinner. Or maybe not. They were scanning the street, looking around with piercing eyes. And occasionally they stared forward, to a point Julian knew very well.

I had uncomfortable stirrings in my stomach and wanted to get out. The sky had also turned gray and ominous in a second. "You can't do this, Julian," I said. "You could get yourself killed."

"No."

"No, what?"

"Not just me. I could get *both of us* killed."

9

I waited near a poster for a tango show while Julian collected from our table reams of paper full of his slanted calligraphy. I wanted to dart across Boedo Avenue and get as far as possible from the car still parked outside. Again, I was being naïve and counted on the light of day as protection.

We didn't speak as we left the café, but Julian kept glancing back. I turned and saw the gray Ford Falcon taking San Juan Avenue away from us, heading to the riverside. The encounter with alleged paramilitary subjects had left a mark and I felt distressed, even somber. I managed to start a mindless conversation with Julian about the World Cup.

We began to walk along Carlos Calvo, a street parallel to San Juan. I considered telling my friend I had learned that Mariana was a member of Montoneros, but, since I was going to spend an evening with her friends, sharing didn't seem a good idea anymore.

Then, we both stopped at once.

The gray Ford Falcon was back and advancing toward us, one block ahead in Carlos Calvo. No doubts about it; this wasn't a conspiratorial fantasy. Only that, perhaps, when you see one of them, they start to pop all around you. Anyway, we were solidly trapped.

Julian reversed direction and started to walk past me, back to Boedo's early evening lights. I saw how pointless our backtracking was but followed him. I had to assume the Falcon kept throttling in our direction, while its driver checked his teeth in the mirror for leftover lettuce.

In one of those strange moves action movies won't include for their intrinsic stupidity, Julian decided to cross the street—an empty, one-way street, where the only car was the one with two professional killers—and left me alone. The Falcon immediately accelerated, and I imagined how far Julian's pile of papers would spread around his horizontal body.

Another car came out of parking, ahead on our sidewalk, and tried to cross the width of Carlos Calvo almost perpendicularly. Its driver didn't seem to see the Falcon coming, and the two cars got stuck, almost touching. I used the lucky break to run toward Julian, gesturing him to keep going.

Always the contrarian, Julian decided to stop and watch the altercation. I kept tugging his free arm, while the two suited guys got out and started gesticulating vividly. The offending car—a white Dodge, modern and compact—was now interposed across the street in such a closed angle it was going to be impossible to move it back to the street's center. And its owner was a big guy, blondish, who didn't look like he was from Buenos Aires. Perhaps it was a rental, I thought in those few seconds Julian and I idly stood on the black cobblestones.

"Wow, that guy's crazy," said Julian.

"Him? *We* are crazy—those guys in the Falcon, they are after us. Let's get out of here."

"I meant the driver, Edgardo. You know what? He looks like... like your father."

"What? I..."

I glanced back and found that Julian was, again, right. The interloper was a tall man, somewhat heavier than my father, but he had an odd familiarity about the way he stood as he talked the incognito policemen into helping him rearrange his vehicle, while ostensibly leaning and checking both cars for marks. We might not have been the most important of subjects for the secret police, because the two guys decreased the speed of their arm movements and started to help the man, both pushing the white car.

We walked away from them but, before we finally got far enough not to keep turning back, the man raised his head and looked in my direction. And then, I finally saw him.

I saw that this was the same man who'd tried to stop me from taking the subway, the one whose face I couldn't make out. Even then, it was as if the air around him were wobbling, subject to the effects of nonexistent heat—it made his features disappear in a beige-pink blur.

10

I asked Julian a hundred times to call me before doing anything rash, but I was also stressed out and couldn't calm down. After reaching my father's apartment, I still felt every single one of my heartbeats.

Perhaps because of the moment's intensity, I looked at the place as if for the first time. We were in a high floor of an old building, built in a French style that would have fit well in the upscale parts of Paris. Set on a large avenue—Córdoba—and near the sixteen lanes of Buenos Aires's monstrous 9th of July Avenue, we could see from the balcony a slice of the world-famous Colón Opera Theater.

From the street, anyone would have thought we were rich; inside the apartment, it was another matter. My father had kept the place sparse in furniture and abundant in books—a debatable treasure of English contemporary literature he had collected in a thousand airport stops. He'd acquired the entire opus of Bradbury, lots of Asimov and Arthur Hailey, plus mystery novels ranging from Agatha Christie to George Simenon. Lots of books, but my room wasn't painted, and the bed's mattress lay on the floor.

I wasn't sure what I was going to do. Julian's adventure with the military seemed like a Quixotic quest where he'd made me his Sancho without asking (had Quixote asked Sancho to go with him?)

and, even worse, my knight was now planning to make a run into a set of machine guns rather than windmills.

My stay in Buenos Aires was getting increasingly strange and dangerous, making my first impulse to get out of the country. It was, after all, what I usually thought when the loneliness started getting to me. The times were bent on reminding me I was just sixteen years old. Even though my mind might have been working exceedingly well, the world around it was wild—no matter the setting—and incomprehensible to my logic.

Back then, I still thought the world had to be logical to make sense.

I grabbed the phone three times to call someone, and on the fourth called Julian's home—his mom's voice was hoarse, as if she'd just awakened from a hangover nap—and found out that, as I feared, he wasn't there yet.

At some point the phone rang, hidden in the shadows; outside, a gray sky was camouflaging the intensity of an early evening rain. It took me six rings to get the heavy receiver.

"*Hola,*" I said in Spanish but, confused between languages, didn't know what to add.

"It's Dan—your father, Edgar." My father would always call me Edgar, but I was getting used to being *Edgardo*, the last vowel a touch more empowering.

"Dad, what are you...?"

"I called to see how you're doing. I'm sorry that I am spending so much time over here."

I had a vision of my father in a large office, with lots of glass and a view of the small town his company had enslaved, bribing its citizens so they wouldn't escape to the plains of Indiana. It was a ridiculous idea, as the sun had already set up there, and he had likely arrived at home and was sitting in another half-empty large house or surrounded by the many bottles of his bar.

"Are you hearing me well?"

My silences always annoyed him. "Yes, sorry Dad. I just got home and was trying to prepare dinner." A non-truth, as I was alone in the living room, in almost complete darkness.

"You should go out and try some of the restaurants nearby. It's a large city, you know, and you can have fun...walk around." My dad's voice was like our houses, half-empty and devoid of lighting. Just saying whatever would make you feel good until he smoothly hung up.

"I know, Dad. But I don't like to eat alone."

"Invite a friend. Don't you have a girlfriend?"

I wasn't going to enter a long-distance, far-reaching discussion about how hard it had been to get close to an Argentine of the opposite sex. I knew his was just a formal call, and he'd finish it only to write on his calendar its completion and the next tentative date for a follow-up. A woman—any good-looking, twenty-years-younger woman—would elicit a lot more of his handwriting.

His practiced selling voice startled me. "Do you think we just talk when I call you? I worry about you."

"You worry about me? And then what? Wait until the next time you feel like calling?"

"No, it's not like that—the work here's still intense. I want to see you, but can't leave, at least not right now."

"Sure, Dad. Don't worry; I'll be okay, right here. If the policemen don't take me, or..."

"Edgar, don't worry about that. It's just a government like any other. I will..."

"What? What are you going to do?"

"I didn't want to tell you before, but I talked with one of my friends, so he'll visit you. He'll bring you some money...he might already be in Buenos Aires."

I was going to say something but then said another thing. "A friend? What does he look like?"

"What? Well, he's tall and played football for Rutgers. A big guy.

Why do you want to know?"

"Just a thought. Maybe I saw him around."

"You saw him? What are you talking about?"

Unusual for our conversations, it was my father who finally hung up. Not an angry but rather a disappointed ending, just a click and a dysphonic noise. I heard it for an unusually long time, wanting.

I don't know when I finally put the receiver back on its hook, but I did fumble it a little. It was already night and the lights and sounds of cars announced the beginning of a weekend. I was used to sitting in the dark, seeing the reflecting flashes of passing cars on the living room's ceiling and thinking how these people were on their way to real lives involving dinners and agitated discussions with relatives.

I also remember thinking about that man in the subway's steps, who might have been one of my dad's friends, trying to explain himself in a mumbling, undecipherable Spanish. And how he'd later unwittingly helped me get away from the cops.

The guy was still on my mind when I decided to heat up some leftover pizza in the oven. I'd had my fill of Argentine streets for the day.

11

Saturday came, and I found myself at a large soccer—again, I mean football—party, which had been vaguely designed to celebrate the World Cup to start the following week but was really an excuse for getting together with friends. I wasn't there as a friend—in fact, I only knew Mariana, and even that wasn't factually true. Most of the people attending were older and much better acquainted with each other.

Mariana said hello and pretty much disappeared for the evening. I hung around with a bunch of guys who chatted loudly about the Argentine team—the National Selection, as it was usually called—and how it could win the whole thing. In retrospect, I should've noticed that none of them said a single word in support of their outspoken government, which was bent on making the tournament into an issue of national pride.

At some point, completely bored, I wandered near the apartment's balcony. I'd seen Mariana approaching it before, and now she was reclined against the metallic balustrade while staring into the distance. She wore a beautiful green dress, so simple and loosely fit, but also perfectly revealing of a figure much more rounded than what I'd imagined. Her long hair, tight at the back in a thick bundle, made her into a Diana who carried her spears in a dark tube.

She was there with Aníbal Reinoso, but I didn't see him until I got close to the balcony. I had met Aníbal (and let's kick down his annoying accent on the "I" from now on) earlier at the party, and his closeness to Mariana made me jealous from the outset. He was an older guy, tall like me but with broader shoulders and strong, large hands. He unabashedly flaunted a big beard—he looked like a young and handsome Rasputin—and a mane of long, unkempt hair. In the States, I would have thought of him as a hippie. But there, in a world sterilized by the dictatorship, he was an obvious outcast; the type of goons who ruled Argentina would assume was an armed leftist. Even now, I can't argue with his wisdom about hiding like that, in plain sight.

They were talking, and, from the room's corner, I heard and still remember every word they said.

"You don't have to worry," Anibal said. "We have everything covered."

"It's too dangerous," Mariana argued with a whispering voice, "and they can find out easily."

"You don't know enough, Mari. We have a good plan."

"And why don't you want to tell me, you know, what we'll do when it starts?"

"I can't. Too risky."

"This is all risky, and I am also involved. Don't lie to me—what's going to happen at the end?"

"You don't—shouldn't—know everything. Nobody does."

Anibal stepped near her. I couldn't see his eyes from the side but knew he was trying to get closer to her. Likely all the way. I decided that I had to leave the party and forget Mariana and her dangerous friends.

I had taken one step away from them when she said, "I don't want to do it; they could kill me."

"No, we will protect you." The way Anibal said this frightened me. It was the same selling voice my father used for his matter-of-fact lying.

"I don't, Anibal. I really can't do this job."

"You should do it. For us, for your family. Don't you remember?"

"I *do* remember. Every day I remember it...we lost six of us to them."

"And then, for what? Do you want to quit?"

"I'll do it. For them."

I should have intervened then, shouted at her that revenge is never worthy, whether you serve it warm or cold on the plate. But we talk a lot about democracy and freedom in my country and then act poorly when fear overtakes our reason. That's what tyrants want, and many times get, the hiding, the acceptance.

Mariana was different from most of us and lacked any fear. This could kill her.

I jumped into the frame of their scene like an actor who's coming for his shoot. Mariana's most significant line had just been said—I'll do it, for them—and the climax was gone. At least, I reached them before Anibal got any consolatory touching. I'd had a taste of that and didn't want him to have any.

"Edgardo," she said. Her eyes were bright as if she had cried.

Anibal looked at me with the eyes of a killer. "Didn't they tell you not to listen to private conversations?"

Mariana waved him to stop, and I, like a good actor, knew it was time to leave the stage.

* * *

Mariana caught up with me when I had collected my jacket from the bedroom and was already opening the apartment's door. "What are you doing? Do you need to leave?"

"Yes. I have a lot of math to do for school tomorrow."

"Math?"

It was a great sin to reveal my penchant for studying mathematics to any girl, but I just wanted to get away. I was having visions of

Mariana and Anibal kissing on balconies and didn't want them to evolve into an unwatchable sex duet.

"Edgar," she said, and my name hung in the air until I realized she'd said it in English. "Why don't we talk outside?"

I was pushed by two graceful, naked arms into the hallway between the fifth-floor apartments. I realized that I didn't even know if the apartment where I hadn't partied was hers. "I'm sorry we didn't have time to talk," said Mariana, and I finally encountered her eyes. There was a great deal of sadness in them. I wanted desperately to hug her.

"I did want to have some time with you," she said. "But the party, these people, some are friends and some partners." The word "compañeros" clearly did not mean "partners" or "colleagues" but rather implied a deep political connection, the kind involving people you plot disasters with. That much had been clear from Anibal's speech.

Was everyone in Buenos Aires trying to oppose the dictatorship? Obviously not, as I would soon get to experience. But most of the examples I could come up with supported the theory.

"Well, they are your friends. Not mine."

"What do you mean?" Mariana's temper flared quickly, with the sort of defensiveness about one's own clan that was getting the entire country in trouble.

"I meant you do have friends. For me, it's more difficult."

I turned and put my hand on the elevator door. She grabbed it, and I was paralyzed by the contact and her proximity, our bodies parallel and our arms converging on the wooden door with a ridiculously small window.

"Don't go," she said. "I want to be your friend."

"Why? We just met—in the subway, don't you remember?"

"I need a friend," she said. "Somebody that's outside all this mess."

"I understand, but..." Then, I woke up to the fact that she'd been speaking partially in English.

I joined her in English I swear was accented with Argentine tones. *"Why do you keep speaking to me in English?"*

"Learning English was—is—the thing that ties me to the past, before everything got screwed up."

I understood immediately and took her hand. We all have had a place in the past we thought was safer. But our early world with close ties to a family—or a beloved country—had been corrupted by others into a faraway land that didn't make sense anymore. That much was true for both of us.

I finally interrupted the silence, while our eyes stayed tied together with intolerable pressure. "Why don't we start over? We had coffee and a party, and that wasn't so bad, was it?"

"Yes...sure. What do you want to do?"

I didn't know and said it. My mistake.

"Let's go to the movies," I tried, a second time.

"Good, let's do that..." Her voice trailed off, and I felt she wasn't sure either.

As if moved by alien forces, my hands opened the elevator's door and I slid the metal grid that served as its inner door. Before I realized what I had done, I was inside the cage and she was out of my world.

"Thanks for coming," she said. A little pause, just long enough for me to want to open the elevator door and kiss her.

Life is full of things we didn't do and would have changed everything, if we had. This one will forever stay with me.

Her hand came through the opening between the metal bars. I was afraid she could hurt herself if the elevator started, which was a dumb thought as the outside door was still propped open by her body.

We came so close across those rails, so much more so than any time before. She approached them, and I tilted to her, trying to listen as if I were a priest and she was beyond the meshed window of a confessional.

"I'm sorry that I have this life," she said. "Try to understand it."

My mouth came to rest on her cheek, and we bounced away.

There wasn't much more I could do to break the metal shield that separated us. She was in a prison, and those were the bars.

The elevator door closed, and I saw its little glass window depart upward.

When I got to the streets, I wanted to howl to the skies above. To the impassive stars.

I wanted to cry, and my heart was full of something. I felt both free and prisoner in a way I couldn't understand back then.

I still have that feeling today, and my eyes are tearing up.

12

It took me the better part of the next morning to level off. I didn't seem to be able to do anything completely, not even taking a shower. Our bathroom's shower always made me a little dizzy and claustrophobic; it was covered wall-to-wall by so many tiny white tiles that I felt as if I were walking at the bottom of an empty swimming pool.

I needed to talk with someone. A couple of *colectivos* later, I was again at the door of Julian's building. This time, I'd preferred to meet him downstairs and avoid any further conversations with his mother.

With Julian, there was no defined setting for our meetings, and soon we were moving across the city. We avoided the buses and just walked and talked until we reached the farthest boundary of our arguments and the eastern limit of the city, the coast of the endless Río de la Plata. We'd fought many times over whether its English moniker should be The Silver River or Argentine River, as both the country and river were named after the chemical element. But standing at the city's edge, it was easy to be in awe and feel like astronauts watching the waves from the brown ocean of an alien planet.

Julian had just finished analyzing well-known presidential

assassinations—including Lincoln's and the still-too-hot-to-handle case of Mr. Kennedy—and dissecting the recent warring African revolutions that made our school's maps obsolete by year's end. For him, most international events were premeditated and had been carried out by secret international groups vying for world power.

Back then, I dismissed Julian's ideas as borderline crazy. But his views will always have a strong hold on me. His was a universe where no death was senseless or unplanned, where there was a reason for everything that happened. There was always a compass, if invisible. The same kind of want forms the basis of all religions, and it gives us peace by rendering the world meaningful beyond its savage carnages.

Some of Julian's misdirected hope for the future would stick with me and guide my own life.

"Are you there?" Julian was snickering at my absentmindedness.

"Sorry, just thinking on what you said."

"What in particular?" He smiled, as that was one of my classic moves, trying to get him to repeat his last digression.

"The last guy killed by an assassin."

"The last...?" And then he laughed, with a huge laugh not expected from a bookworm who was spending so much of his adolescence studying in libraries and—now I had proof of this—staking out war criminals who before he'd just imagined to exist.

"I want to know what you will do," I said, "with those notes you're taking. What's your plan?"

"I told you last time; I'll have a meeting with the archbishop. D'Agostini, do you know him?"

"Know him? The guy's all over the newspapers parading with the Military Junta. His cassock must be turning green, like an army shirt. You should not see that guy."

"I will. And it is Archbishop. Have some respect for the Church, my friend."

"I don't have to... *you're joking, aren't you?*"

50

"Do you realize you are mixing English and Spanish all the time?"

"Yes, I do, but I'm not confused now. The priesthood is not as innocent as they look. There has to be more to their collaboration than showing up all the time next to the Junta."

"I'd assume so, but I need a hinge to open the door and see what's inside."

"Mechanical tools aside, what you're doing is very, very crazy. They'll know you are not part of their...and then what?"

"I need to see by myself, because I want to be the Great Whistleblower. Blow up the whole thing in the international press."

"Isn't it the same thing Amnesty is doing? And the people here couldn't care less; they think it's all propaganda against the country. *Nothing* is going to change."

I was right, but it didn't make me any happier. What Julian was doing, giving it all to an insane cause to save a country's almost nonexistent honor, was the right thing to do.

I wasn't yet ready to understand this. And I was going to pay a large price in pain to acquire that knowledge.

13

I left Julian back home and I continued aimlessly walking the streets, enjoying the pleasure of keeping my mouth shut. I finally took the subway, far away from home.

I emerged from the ride at Lavalle station, at the opposite end of the rectangular plaza I could see every day from my bedroom, and proceeded to walk the last few blocks to my building in a state of daydreaming bordering hallucination. I was reinterpreting Julian's fantastic stories as a vision of Argentina becoming a later-day Third Reich, a fourth such reign being built in South America. The cathedral-size synagogue near our building begged to disagree, but I chose to ignore it.

I was stuck in Julian's world, and it wasn't much fun.

Reason prevailed after repeating quite a few times that I was, like most Argentines, waiting for a time when democracy will return, when another unexpected recess of the tyrannical tide will foster the arrival of a new, more fortunate government.

Contradicting my reasoning, I now had two friends (was Mariana a friend or a romantic interest?) who were bent on risking their lives amid an unstable, secretly violent society.

As soon as I entered our building, our doorman Don Manuel reinforced my stereotypes for the city's numerous immigrants from Northern Spain; they were frequently pictured as being short, stocky, and with conjoined, brushy eyebrows. I was sure he had been the butt of a million jokes during his lifetime. But the man was responsible and did help, at times.

"I have a letter for you, Don Edgardo," he said, straightening up from a varieties magazine.

"A letter?"

"Yes, from a friend of your father. He came to see you and left it for you."

I had been half expecting a contact from the mysterious man, surely a drinking buddy of my father who shared his strenuous efforts to look ten years younger and trick well-exercised, thirty-year-old divorcees into his bedroom.

"Oh, yes, I knew I was going to get something."

Don Manuel delivered the letter to my hand with a sharp pirouette, like a casino's card dealer. The envelope was thin, and I guess it disappointed me so much I didn't open it right away. I first waited until I reached the privacy of our elevator and then waited a little more, until I got to open the door and leave my bulky set of keys in the Ming-like Chinese bowl.

I should have waited forever.

The envelope contained only one page, with a single statement written in large, open block letters, which would have seriously annoyed my classically-oriented language teachers. It was strange to read something so short and understand it less and less with every reading. I wasn't familiar with the kinds of emotions that would make people faint, but after a minute I had to grab the marble table that supported our expensive fake bowl to avoid hitting the floor head on.

The note just said:

YOU CAN ONLY SAVE ONE

14

The impact of the unfathomable note was so great that pushing reality into its bottle took a lot of energy, much more than I could muster. I remember trying to do some homework—it had something to do with the Argentine Constitution being a straight heir from other Latin American countries, while denying its obvious connections with the French and North American versions. When learning from the teachers my school selected, I would just swallow whatever medicine they offered.

Monday arrived after an almost sleepless night. Trying to twist that note's single line into something meaningful—reasonably connected with my father—had given me first a headache and then, later, the feeling of losing my mind. I also had unremembered nightmares and the beginnings of a sex dream involving Mariana. But before she got naked and my dream progressed into wetness, I woke up as if from another nightmare—with a heavy chest and sweat threading my forehead. I walked around the empty apartment until the sun managed to come up.

I got to the Gorostiaga's presumptuous grounds worrying about Julian, ready to try and calm down his increasing paranoia. In the first long break, I talked with his class preceptor, a thin guy with very long hair and who behaved like he was a sexy rock star. My friend wasn't in class but had called to say he would be late for the day. Well, I was happy to know he was coming.

I can't say I was prepared when it happened. One can think on something as a probability; it doesn't mean being ready to confront it. Ricardo seemed to have put on a few pounds during the weekend, and he stood ramrod straight and eye-to-eye with me. I was no vampire, but I could see the arteries on his neck pumping blood in a rush.

Ricardo again showed his preference for shoving people around and pushed me backward, hard. His entourage—two big guys this time, a bad sign—stayed a few steps behind.

I tried to stand but fell all over a pile of cleaning supplies. A bucket flipped, and dirty water started to penetrate my clothing—so the cleaners would have to remove both dirt and blood from my imported blue blazer and matching gray trousers. This, if I stayed alive.

I stood up but then couldn't move, completely frozen by fear. I was going to die, my face and the brain behind it pulped by Ricardo's big-knuckled hands. He had adopted a boxing posture and sent a right hook that, luckily, my head decided to evade before I saw it pass by with my eyes. The next time, his heavy hand hit the surface of my cheek and broke the corner of my lower lip into a tooth. I fell again, this time on all fours. At least my tooth was all right.

Ricardo was saying something about me being a homosexual—a *maricón*, in the lexicon of the times—and his friends transformed it into the more appropriate feminine, *marica*.

"Marica, marica, marica," they chanted.

Oddly, I rose wondering whether that moniker, which could now follow me for the remainder of my school years, could be connected with the name María.

María. María Ana. Mari-Ana. Mariana.

It was thinking on her name that saved me—I needed to survive, for Mariana. Others would say that I was suddenly very angry and reacted with a bit of luck. I could agree with everybody and felt reassured I wasn't going to be expelled. This because Julian's preceptor had seen the altercation and was coming toward us, yelling at Ricardo to stop. Everybody knew this was his sport.

I experienced a joint wave of peace and war and had a second or two to think intensely. I thought about something Ricardo wouldn't want to hear. It involved cutting his balls and strangling him with them.

I actually thought about how one would go about doing it.

He saw something in my eyes, in my shaking fists bloodied by having touched the red on my lips. And he took a step back and adopted his boxing stance again.

I kicked his crotch from the front, so hard he fell forward as if pushed. He stayed on his knees, mumbling some complicated insults and hoping his friends would come to his aid. Nobody moved, and the preceptor's run slowed as if he was coming down to a stop.

Before reality resumed, I'd taken a large mop from another bucket, and wet and heavy as it was with bubbling soap scum, swung it like a baseball bat into Ricardo's head. He spun like a kid playing on the floor and hit the same glass panels I'd crashed him against the previous week. This probably stopped his groupies from attacking me, especially because Ricardo was in serious pain and had adopted a fetal position while visibly crying.

I think my blood testosterone reached its all-time high right at this moment.

When I turned around, the entire patio was silent, and people now watched us from the upper floor's corridors.

And Julian's preceptor was smiling.

I didn't get a suspension, and I swear that, as I was leaving the director's office, a senior administrator winked at me.

15

Making arrangements for a night at the movies with Mariana took effort comparable to a military campaign. The phone number she'd left me was from the friend's house—Luisa—where they'd held the football party. I met at first some opposition from Luisa, but then she vaguely remembered me from the party and gave me a few tentative phone numbers, of a house in the downtown of the state capital, La Plata, and a ceramic factory in the suburban town of Lanús.

A more experienced guy would have given up when confronted with these indirect contacts, thinking that Mariana really didn't want to see me. But I had the crush of all crushes, and who wouldn't, after meeting an exciting girl, an outlaw in a secret mission to overthrow an evil government; a girl of contrasts, with brown eyes that would burn the back of your head. It was the stuff of adventures introversive guys like me—the words "geek," "dork," and "nerd" still lay undiscovered in the river of time—would only get to experience in video games yet to be invented.

Mariana was surprised I had managed to reach her, and perhaps out of respect for my tenacity, accepted my invitation to go to the movies on Friday. She was going to spend the next weekend in the city—she didn't say why—and we could thus meet at Luisa's place.

We chose to watch the just premiered *Close Encounters of the Third Kind*. Mariana had said she loved science-fiction, but I think she was just following my excitement with the movie.

When I hung up the phone for good, the radio was spilling more news about the early-May meteorite impacts in Northern Argentina. Apparently, the chickens had not been laying their eggs and local phones had been strangely disrupted since the phenomenon. Nobody was talking anymore about agents from NASA—or the CIA—investigating the crash in black helicopters.

Argentines didn't seem to be thinking much about the event, worried as they were by the World Cup. I guess our experience in the States with Roswell wasn't so familiar back then, and only fringe-obsessed aficionados like Julian Niemeyer would have tied those impacts with aliens and their UFOs.

The years have brought me a larger perspective about religion and the cosmos. In light of this wisdom, I would consider our choice for a movie to be fateful enough to reflect on a Designer.

* * *

The movie was basically a take on the aliens-coming-to-Earth formula, twisted to make it heartwarming. We enjoyed it and exited to the streets in good spirits and talking about cosmic ideas—it turned out Mariana believed in astrological signs, but I wasn't going to show my usually nasty reaction to any nonscientific theory.

She was dressed again in one of those all-black outfits, with a new winter jacket made from shiny plastic. I just loved to be near her and didn't make a connection between her dressing and dark clouds on her mind. But as we walked along Corrientes, getting close enough to my place to consider inviting her in, she seemed to become less communicative.

In one of those silent gaps she'd opened in our conversation, I noticed a Ford Falcon parked on one of the small side streets. I couldn't make out its occupants in the shade that covered the world away from the businesses' lights, but the periphery of my consciousness detected people sitting in the front. Dark people like the black shadows.

Mariana had to stop at a pizzeria to call home. Her family was quite worried about where she went and how late she'd be coming home. While she made the call, I waited, planning to entice her with some slices and a less-scattered chat about who we were and what we liked in the world. The kind of thing I assumed people should talk about on a first date.

When Mariana came back to our table, she just said that we should be going back. Someone had called Luisa with an urgent message for her but wouldn't explain particulars to anybody but Mariana. She was shaken and took my hand, if only to guide me into the streets.

* * *

One hour later, we were in Luisa's apartment, where Mariana would stay while in the city. Luisa turned out to be Mariana's best friend from elementary school, and now I could see why she liked her—at the party, I'd been so enthralled with Mariana I didn't see any other girls.

Luisa was a very sweet girl who talked ceaselessly but entertainingly about music and celebrities of the time. I stayed with her while Mariana kept trying to reach her family again on Luisa's bedroom phone.

When Mariana came back, her face was pale.

"Sorry, Edgardo. I'm not sure what happened. Nobody important called." She said "nobody" as if there were a precise list of people who would call in an emergency.

"No problem," I said. "I should go. It's getting late, and you're already home."

Mariana just nodded, but I could feel the shackles closing around her ankles. We were reaching the parts of her life that she wanted to keep from me.

I stood and walked toward the door. It was Luisa who opened it for me, making a pained expression for whom I was the target.

The door remained open—and Luisa steadily on its margin—as I waited for the elevator to come.

A hand on my shoulder stopped me from entering.

It was Mariana's. "Aren't you going to say goodbye?"

I turned around to see two wet eyes, from which tears could pour anytime. "I—I thought you were worried," I mumbled, unable to stop staring at her eyes.

"I'm always worried. That's my problem, not yours."

"I can't...it's so hard to understand what you want. We had a good time, didn't we?"

"Yes, we did. I loved to go out...but my life is complicated. Maybe when all this mess passes, we can go out again."

"All of this? What is it that you don't want to tell me about?"

"I can't. It is too much...it's dangerous."

I surprised myself by saying, "I don't care. I just want us to spend some time together."

"Together?" A smile floated to her face from some deep place within, and it pushed away the tears into two vertical bright lines that crossed her face.

"Yes, together. Why not?"

There might have been a million answers to my question, but she just kept smiling. "Give me some time, just a little more. It'll get better soon."

This time I didn't like the plea for time and started to slide the cage-like door.

She stopped me and, in a moment that hesitated before flowing into the next one, our lips came together, and I felt the warmth of hers.

We crashed into each other.

I was now desperately trying to satisfy a new thirst, a need for wet warmth from another body. Like a desert animal, I had found a pond and was trying to drink it all, all of the waters coming from a dark, dangerous depth.

Our kiss might have lasted just a minute, but as it always is with love and time, it was a minute that couldn't be measured by clocks.

Immortal time.

16

It happened so fast I didn't have time to put it all together before I was running at full speed, back from my bus stop on Rivadavia Avenue. A comment from Julian, suddenly remembered, had triggered the fear, a fear so clear and precise it felt as if an icy knife had penetrated my back.

"They call people first," Julian had said, "to be sure they're at home, when they come."

When they come...

The Ford Falcon parked near Corrientes, the strange call that had brought Mariana back home on a late Friday evening.

I was running, but as I approached the second street's corner, I knew it was too late. I could see it from afar, like watching a wide-angle view in an old newsreel, the kind showing the peaceful prelude to a well-known catastrophe.

The people who took Mariana Venturino didn't look like the man-in-black-suit spy types most people would expect, even those who lived in Argentina at the time. They were just guys, a group of men in sweaters and jeans who were escorting Mariana to a car. It could have been just a girl and her friends from a rowing team—broad-shouldered and tall—getting ready to drive her to a party. But the two who flanked Mariana were too close, and the two waiting while reclined against the Falcon's trunk too eager to leave. And the one who'd kept an old lady captive against the entrance door, he was just too serious to have good intentions.

I made it to the corner across from Luisa's building and started to cross diagonally to the parked car, disregarding the visible size— and the likely invisible guns—of the members of my opposing team. Then, something pushed me forward.

I was airborne and saw a large—supernaturally immense— motorcycle running deafeningly on my right. Saw asphalt and then hit it hard as the world jumped on me.

I might have been stunted, almost unconscious, for a few seconds. By the time I was able to stand on a weak right leg and check the streets in both directions of traffic, there was no one there. No cars, no people, and no Mariana.

It felt as if the world had turned upside down. And I was also upside down, a man sustaining the enormous planet with the soles of his feet.

The real world extended around me like an apparition, the kind that haunts those who have peered into the darkness.

God had never been very real to me. But Hell now was.

PART II

Time Unremembered

1

I had been pounding the wall of my shower for a while and considering also bouncing my head against it. I took consolation in my tears being so hot that they would become part of the fog around me.

Julian was at the door. "Edgardo, are you all right?"

"Yes, don't worry. I'll be out soon."

My legs were shaky—especially the one making me limp—and I kept having flashbacks of the disappearance. Yes, that's what I was already calling it, even though I hadn't been able to find anyone who believed she was truly gone.

I had enlisted Luisa Bacile to help me with asking around in her building, but everyone we'd reached out to had been dismissive, saying that Mariana was always out late at night and we shouldn't worry about her; that she'd be back soon. There was a studied steadiness in them, but also falsehood in their calming words. We couldn't find the old woman who had been cornered by the assailants; there were too many old ladies in the building, all hiding behind more than one set of locks. Age and wisdom, I guess.

But what got me the angriest was Luisa's mother, who kept repeating that the military—our government, she insisted on correcting me—couldn't be involved in a kidnapping. It was all lies the left was making through its gossips' grapevine, attempts from outlaws to undermine the flourishing democracy that awaited them in a not-so-distant future.

I got so upset that I left, but not before yelling to the woman what kind of democracy theirs was, if the Argentines couldn't even decide when it would come back. Luckily, my curse words came straight in English, and they didn't notice them.

When I reached my apartment, I couldn't calm down. I called Julian, and he caught something in my voice because he told me to wait and rest until he made it to my home. He showed up so soon, I looked at my phone as if I'd just hung up. I had been sitting next to my floor mattress for most of an hour and couldn't tell him—even myself—what I had thought, if anything, in the interim.

Julian made some scrambled eggs and toast—his idea of an American breakfast—but was much more Argentine when setting the coffee's concentration, which remained well above the American range. I didn't need any stimulation to stay awake; I thought I'd never sleep again.

After tasting the eggs and drinking the heavy coffee, I realized that the sun was coming up and my ordeal was already several hours in the past. Julian completed his work of physical contention by encouraging me to take a shower. He would have undressed me if not for my strenuous objecting that I could do it by myself.

But now I finally had to explain to him what had happened. And I was scared that he, of all people, wasn't going to understand.

"All right, why don't you start again from the beginning," said Julian, adjusting his body into the only comfortable armchair we had. He had gotten me to sit across him at the coffee table, arguing that my pacing was making *him* nervous.

"Again?"

"Yes, again."

"I told you that I'd put two and two together. I figured she was under surveillance of some sort, and I ran to catch up with her. The police, the military—whoever those people were—took her into a car and then they were gone."

"Did you see if she was going of her own will with them? They could have been, you know, Montos like her." When one uses a nickname for an armed organization, a country is in real trouble.

"They couldn't be," I said, and lost my certainty. "Why would they take her in the middle of the night?"

"One a.m. is not the middle of the night. Not here, in Buenos Aires."

"What are you now, Sherlock Holmes?"

"I'm just trying to figure if there's a real concern, or...well, we don't want to get too paranoid about the military."

Julian didn't understand my laugh. I think it went well beyond what's acceptable and, as I had been crying, he couldn't decide if it came from hysteria or grief.

I suddenly stopped laughing. "It's always about you, isn't it? The great Julian Niemeyer, who is going to expose the military and its criminal activities. Wake up, Julian. Nobody cares. They can take you, or Mariana, or me. They can take any of us."

"First, they came for a friend..."

"Yes, that thing. Then, for a neighbor, and finally, for you. That's the kind of world we're living in here. I should have, I..."

"Leave?"

"Yes, when I had a chance."

"And why don't you leave now?"

"What?"

"Yes, why don't you call your all-powerful father and ask him to take you back to the United States?"

"I can't."

"Why, because you hate him?"

I considered this long enough for him to smile. "No. It's not that. I need to find Mariana, help her."

"You just met her...so, why bother? She got herself into the mess she's in."

"Julian, you're starting to sound like those people at the building. Like everybody, with their heads hiding in the ground."

"We all live like that. There's always a hole to put our heads in and not to see."

"I do...I want to find her."

"Oh, my friend. You're in love with that girl."

"Why do you say that?"

"Don't be defensive; it's a good thing. You're finally appreciating the products of our land."

"Julian, you are a son of a bitch. A great *hijo de puta.*"

"And finally, you've insulted me in well-pronounced Spanish. I'm really proud of you."

I felt that Julian wasn't understanding how bad I felt. "What can we do? Please, tell me there's something."

"Well, I'm going to expose these sons of bitches for all the things they are..."

"I'm not going to wait *that* long. We need to do something right now."

This surprised Julian, and for a moment he weighed his secret mission in life against my risky budding relation with a stranger. All that I value in mankind, the reason I hope there's a future for all of us, was contained in his next words.

"All right, let's get the phone and make some calls," he said. "We are going to find her."

2

It was amazing to prowl the invisible web of people that connected the neighborhoods of Buenos Aires. Mariana wasn't even living at the address she'd been taken from, but there was knowledge about her wherever we looked. Every store owner knew the pretty, tall girl, or at least someone from Luisa's family. It wasn't a conscious memory, but the kind that could be exercised after a prolonged conversation and a few probing questions.

Julian was a master of this protracted art, almost like the young version of a *noir* detective. As he held a pack of potato chips or tweaked with the candy strewn on an open display, he would ask a first question that necessarily led to a more significant second, and then add a third one, which revealed some hidden link between one of the store's clients—or even a relative from the management—and Luisa Bacile's household. Twice, someone was promptly called into the store, and it turned out that person knew who Mariana was.

This seemed a somewhat pointless exercise to me, and also an expensive one, as we'd collected enough snacks, candy, and varieties of coffee—even dwelled over buying a large piece of meat—that we now had enough food to feed us for a week. But then, after all of that, one lead did pay off.

"People at night?"

Julian turned back from a shelf full of coffee cans. "Did you see any?"

"Yes, a few times, when I was closing for the night. You know, there were three or four guys in a car, sitting still. Strange, being so late. They'd just parked just across from Luisa's—her building. I didn't want to stare too much, you know, weird stuff could happen if you meddle in the affairs of the military's friends."

And of course, you wouldn't dare to intervene, I thought, *even if they were taking someone by force. Whistling and looking down would be your approach.*

The bodega manager continued his story of almost nothing, or at least of a nothing that contained only obvious information we already knew—guys at night, a Ford Falcon. Some of his guys were short and dark, whether coming from the Northern provinces or a racist imagination.

But then Julian asked an irreverent, but also brilliant, question. "So, you saw them, but did they do anything other than wait?"

The manager took a long time before answering. "The last time," he said, "they were leaning on the car, and eating pizza slices. I'm sure it was pizza."

Julian's follow-up was to the point. "Do you know from where?"

"Sure, the pizzeria that's at the intersection of Rivadavia and La Plata. I know their box, with the big red letters, and was surprised they didn't get anything nearby. So many places just two blocks away."

"Thank you, Don Ramón. Thank you for helping us, and give our best to your wife." Julian was at the door before the owner had time to conclude his mumbling parting remarks.

"Let's go, Edgardo. We have something."

"The pizza?"

"Yes. If a bodega owner is like a dentist who can talk about his patients, a pizzeria's boss is like the town's barber. They know everything and everyone. We'll get something."

I was thrilled with my friend, the sleuth. After throwing all the junk we'd collected in a street trashcan, we started to walk so fast I almost stumbled on some broken sidewalk tiles.

3

The pizzeria was such a classic place it defied qualifiers. La Gran Pizza de Onofrio e Hijos looked like an old business, but only in appearance, and it had large red letters clumsily hand-painted on its windowpanes. It was the kind of pizzeria that was a perfect hangout for businessmen on their lunch break and young guys waiting for a date with just a few bucks in their pockets. Good pizza, coming piping hot and fast from a huge wood oven, a stream of discs that could satisfy large crowds at lunch on a workweek day. But now it was the weekend, and there were enough beer glasses around to make you think twice whether it was a German restaurant. The smells of Italy's heart would soon convince you otherwise.

Julian apparently had had enough of his interrogations and held himself on the counter with a stance so unstable I touched his shoulder to assure him I'd take it from there. I wanted to try and see if I could match his skills.

I approached the likely owner—a big man who'd been sampling too many of his creations—like we were just two guys in a quest for good pizza, with a tip about his joint from some fellows who'd come late at night and drove a Falcon. Don Onofrio (or one of his grown-up children) turned out to have a memory of the consistency of his mozzarella cheese—or perhaps resembling the holes of some outlawed fermented Gruyère he had been testing. "Your friend seems in need of some of our heavier stuff," he said. "What about some garlic pizza with big tomato slices?"

I wouldn't have considered it prudent to give garlic to a half-way fainting Julian, but the pizza-man was showing interest in us and I let him make us a custom pizza. He sang some opera tunes as he twirled, high in the air, the dough of our unborn pizza; he soon had it placed on his oven. When he returned to the counter, the heat and some inner revelation made him look like a crazy scientist from a movie—one where the director had gone in the direction of large, fat evil.

"Now, I remember," he said.

"What...what do you remember?" Julian's face was a little bit flushed, and I wondered if he would topple over; I reached out to hold him.

"The guys. The ones with the Falcon. Now, I remember them. They come often, and always buy a double-mozzarella-with-ham to go. They're usually in a rush to get to work—maybe they are the night security of a hotel."

"Why do you say that?" Now, I was the one posing as the great detective.

"All of them look like police, you know, with short military haircuts and plain clothing."

Yes, those are our guys.

"Do you know where they live?" I was still trying to seem on a quest for leads on other awesome, perhaps extra-strength garlic pizzas.

"No, I don't know, but they mentioned a house in El Tigre." The Tigre—a locality named after tigers, who knows why in Argentina—was just north of Buenos Aires, crowded by the small islands of the river's estuary. "His boss, now I remember, his name was Martínez. They'd mentioned him a few times."

I had to use both hands to capture Julian's back before he collapsed flat on the floor. He became visibly upset, and our conversation with the Onofrios pizza's representative was over. We took our slices to go.

When we were back in the streets and Julian spoke, his insanity was flaring. "I knew it," he said. "This is bad...*they* have her."

"They who?"

"The torturers...Martínez."

"And who the hell is *Marteen-neh-eehz*?" My English slipped and the surname Martínez gained some extra syllables.

"A big torturer, the worst. They call him 'The Hammer' because he likes to smash fingers one by one with a small hammer...and finish people off by breaking their heads open with a big one."

I felt something nauseating that couldn't be attributed to smelling seasoned pizza for over an hour. I couldn't get much more out of Julian and soon developed problems of my own. I felt dizzy, and my vision started to shift; the night sky took on a deep shade of violet. The streets, infected by that same unseemly color, grew purple stars in each reflection.

When I turned back to have a last look at Don Onofrio's pizza place from across Rivadavia Avenue, something even eerier left me breathless. The letters on the business's windows were no longer bright red. They did have a red outline, but the core was now dark green, a glaring difference I should've noticed.

As if running away from a revolting dream to enter another, I looked down at the box I was carrying, which contained our still-warm slices. Its block letters were also green.

I shifted my gaze back to Rivadavia and saw something even more unsettling, an impossibility that reminded me of my late-night encounter with the purple mist and those shifting *colectivos*.

Something large—large as in Tyrannosaur Rex's size—was moving quickly, high above the avenue, and heading to the night sky. Something shaped like a bunch of grapes, purple grapes. It wasn't a clear reality but rather a shimmering hole within it.

I can't explain it, but an entire city block shook and wobbled all the way down to its atoms. And I was sure to be the only one feeling it.

A wave of change and color had passed like a whale through a large city's thoroughfare, unnoticed, and then ascended to the skies like the immense, invisible wake of something monstrous.

The thought frightened me to the core, especially since I was fighting hard to keep remembering what I'd just seen. And I was afraid, very afraid, because there could have been so much more of that time unremembered.

4

The afternoon went by without any news about Mariana's disappearance. I stayed in bed for what seemed like an hour but was several. Julian was also distressed, even maniacal, and from time to time he would come to my room with some crazy idea about how to gather a secret address in "*the* Tigre" or whispering a fabricated name of "a friend who knows a lot about this business" and who could intercede for us to recover our obviously innocent and very dear friend.

Archbishop D'Agostini came up several times on his verbal excursions. But I remained unconvinced that any priest could help me—and it was just me, as I was being selfish trying to completely own Mariana's predicament. I should say up front that I've never been a good Catholic and, after my First Communion party at my grandparents' house in St. Louis, I swiftly drifted into deep agnosticism. Although occasionally I felt it necessary to soften my views, especially when visiting the ultra-religious circles my father traveled in Argentina's capital.

I was getting immersed in some sort of self-justifying mental argument about the non-necessity of God when Julian reappeared, looking like a transfixed saint straight from a Goya painting, sweaty and sickly wide-opened. The contrast between his ecstasy and my godless existentialist reverie was remarkable.

"We forgot something basic," he said.

"Elementary?"

Julian was going to answer before he snickered at my pun. "Edgardo, please, be serious. I have an idea."

"Of course, like, why don't we read the minds of her captors?"

"No, we can read the minds of her family."

"Her...family? *Dios mío.*" Strange I'd said that while considering the lack of a real God. But God and the Devil were both in the drinking water in that forsaken time and place.

Julian couldn't contain himself— "Her family runs a ceramics factory in Lanús. She told you this, didn't she?"

"Yes, well, Luisa Bacile gave me a phone number for the Venturinos in Lanús."

"Well, I looked them up in one of your directories—not sure why you'd keep so many around—and it also lists an address in La Plata. Maybe it's their family house."

I was going to argue with him but then reconsidered. Mariana's parents could know something more and help us in the search for their daughter. I faked being very excited while imagining dungeons hidden within the lush vegetation of *Tigre*.

Being young means you sometimes do the exact opposite of following the straight line between A and B. Going to La Plata was seemingly the wrong thing to do, but, in the absence of any shortcut to find where Mariana was being kept, I agreed.

I also didn't want to lose sight of my overexcited friend and wasn't feeling rational enough to be left alone in an empty apartment. Just looking out by the window was making me anxious.

And remember, this time the monsters were real.

* * *

At some point, Julian left, and I continued to stay deeply compressed into my precarious floor bed. Don't even remember whether I said goodbye to Julian or let him go in silence. I couldn't sleep and thought an awful lot about Mariana. But I was lacking the level of worry I should've had about the fate of my new friend—the pretty girl with beautiful, earthy eyes—after so many hours without news. My worries didn't measure up with the dark maelstrom we were circling.

We weren't aware of the scope, the vast destruction of the Argentine society being carried out by its military Junta, a ruthless government that could be fairly compared on its carnage to the Third Reich or to later evil regimes in Africa and Eastern Europe. It's possible that as many as 30,000 Argentines, many uninvolved with politics, lost their lives horribly and pointlessly. Thousands of citizens were tortured with electric shocks in their genitals, by pulling out their teeth and nails, or peeling away most of their skin. Less fortunate ones have had scared rats sent to crawl into their intestines. If I knew this back then, I would have died from heartache.

I wanted to believe in God, so I could believe in Hell, not in Heaven. I understood those who wanted a better afterworld that will grant them the goodness this one lacks, but I was rather hoping to find out if there was a punishment for perpetrators of Big Evil. Those who carried out such atrocities in my borrowed country should have been punished so much and for so long that, to feel that any justice has been done, all time left in the universe would come up short. Only an infinite punishment would counterbalance the many planes that flew over the Atlantic to dump thousands of drugged human beings into the ocean. Friends and coworkers, daughters and mothers, fathers and sons—a whole, grand human family who had only sinned by wanting change and freedom.

My heart was in the right place, while still innocent about what was going on and what was to come. In hopes of finding a cosmic Justice, I had joined those who want to believe.

5

The Constitución train station spread its iron tentacles to the south side of the country; it was a dark, immense building made in the style of London's old train stations. This wasn't so far-fetched, as many of the Argentine railways had been built by the British. A golden *colectivo*—from the "60" bus line, renowned for having the longest route in the city—left me near the station's entrance arch.

Julian was seated in a corner café, and he waved me in, while splashing his face flat on the surface of a large glass pane. I somnambulated to sit with him. Croissants and very hot *café au lait*—Argentina's ever-present *café con leche*—sounded great at seven thirty on a Sunday morning.

"You look worse than I feel," he said. "Are you ready for this?"

"No, and I'll never be."

"Fair enough. Let's order something for you—waiter!"

The waiter—could he possibly had been another Don Manuel?—came to our table following a drunken sailor's path designed to monitor the business of all his other customers. Argentine waiters were famous for never using a notepad, keeping tabs of a dozen tables in their memory. The next round of standard *café con leche* and croissants we ordered wouldn't occupy much space inside his broad cranium.

"We better rest the mind a little," said Julian. "We'll need to be in our best game when we talk with your girl's parents...do you know who designed the diagonal streets in La Plata?"

I did know about the predesigned city, endowed with an optimal—though unbelievably confusing—path for cars and trucks that they'd thought immune to traffic jams. But I let Julian have his turn at explaining this and drawing it on a napkin, which soon looked like a cathedral's *vitreaux*.

Passing time was a skill that teenagers instinctively make into an art.

After a while of that authoritative exposition, I felt envious and jumped into a crusade of my own—the science-inclined proto-geek—presenting him with a puzzle I'd read while learning about surface tension and the physics of bubbles. I was still entranced—rather than scared—by shiny, rainbowy spheres.

"The thing is what would happen if you make two bubbles at different pressure. The equation for pressure and surface tension would make them take two different diameters but then, you connect both halves of your experiment with a spigot. What happens? Would the small bubble get bigger, or the large bubble get smaller? What do you think?"

Julian acquired one of his insane asylum's smiles and I thought that, with an adequate supply of coffee drinks and croissants, we could have had an Argentinean-strength discussion for the entire day.

This time, we had to ask for more napkins.

* * *

Our train to La Plata left Constitución Station at eight forty-five, and we'd boarded it while still unsure—even more unsure than before—about the destinies of people and bubbles. Perhaps everything would burst and dissipate into nothingness. Perhaps life itself was just a bubble of time, floating uncertain until it joined an infinite space of darkness.

I have come to think that the philosophical mind of teenagers many times wanders close to the ultimate truths.

The train car we were assigned to—something had possessed Julian to buy first-class tickets—was clunky, noisy, and very much in need of repairs. My seat seemed to have lost half of its screws, making the horizon outside the window shake as if the largest earthquake on human history were embracing the infinite plains that sprung away from Buenos Aires.

Julian couldn't stay still, and he wandered back and forth to increasingly long strings of train cars. I lost sight of him and, if he was looking for a functioning cafeteria, probably would never see him again.

I started to fall asleep, soothed by the train's now-even vibration, when a noise—or the sudden lack of one—woke me up.

A large man was sitting next to me, on the opposite site of the aisle.

I experienced a resistance to look in his direction, as if my neck had suffered a spasm.

He waited, smiling broadly, until I realized it was the same man from the subway. The same one who'd interposed a car to protect us from a Falcon patrol.

"*Good morning, Edgar,*" he said in English.

6

The man stayed silent long enough to worry me. I noticed that he was big, but without broad shoulders, and slightly overweight, with gray hair on the temples overtaken by poorly-kept sandy hair. I was lying against a window and couldn't see his eyes, which were also turned away while he fidgeted with something in his pocket.

I had to say something. "Who are you?"

"Are we going to start with the hard questions?"

"Did my father send you?"

"In a way, you all sent me."

I noticed he had an impeccable American accent, but with some familiar undertone I couldn't place. "I am okay staying here," I said.

"No, you are not. This is a dangerous place."

"Every place is in danger from something," I said, still trying to avoid the man's eyes.

"But not in every place you're trying to fix it."

I don't know why I answered the way I did. "It's Julian, not me, who wants to fix...this, the tyranny, the kidnappings."

"Yes, *los desaparecidos*." His Spanish was also excellent.

"I—I just want to get Mariana back." I wasn't handling the conversation very well and looked down the aisle to see if Julian was returning to our seats.

"Don't worry. He's detained and won't be here for another twelve minutes."

"How do you...? Are you stalking us?"

"Yes, of course."

He said this so matter-of-factly I didn't have an answer, and it took me a second or two to recover. "Why? It's not any of your business, whoever you are."

"It is my business, and as for who am I, the world is a more complicated place than what you have figured so far."

"I want you to stop following us."

"And to stop helping you the next time the police jump on you two?"

I remembered how he'd blocked the police's Ford Falcon. "The... how did you know?"

"Don't you want to ask me why I am helping you?"

"It's something my family does sometimes, send help when it's needed, without being asked."

"Not this time. And not for long, *Edgar*." The tentative way he said my name was unsettling. "I won't be able to help you for long," he added. "It will be all up to you."

The man had a silver-looking coin in his right hand; he flipped it very fast and high, so he could clap it between his hands as it fell. Even when his hands closed very hard on the falling disk, they made no noise.

"Life's a series of random choices," he said, watching his open palm holding the coin. "And everything you do affects everything else that's going to happen. Like this coin. See, how it's mangled and curved? I found it on the street and have had time to figure it lands heads 63 out of 100 times."

"Just a trick coin."

"It has been banged up by life, like all of us." The man smiled sadly, and I thought on the philosophizing that was a way of life in Argentina. Perhaps this man was another ex-pat like my father, moored in Buenos Aires for long years while closing deals for another pharmaceutical joint.

"It's not that simple, Edgar."

"What?"

"Not even your father controls what his company does with him."

"How do you know that?" I was going to say out loud that he'd read my mind but stopped after thinking up another question. "Are you following us to...?"

"La Plata? You can say that. It's kind of obvious since you boarded this train. My problem is not this trip, or what you—or your friend—might do over there. Things are going to get very complicated, and as I said, dangerous. And you are not prepared to make the right choices."

"And you are?"

"No. Not really, nobody is."

"Then leave me alone," I said, turning to my left as if I was ready to take a nap.

"I wish I could," he said, likely still staring at me. "But I can't. I'll never leave you alone until.... Just remember, be careful with your decisions, as you can cause a lot of harm to lots of people. It would be best if you forget the whole thing after this train ride, and let life take you back to the States."

I started to watch the railway, upset about having to deal with someone who clearly was not inclined to ever leave me alone. When I turned back, he was standing ahead of my seat, awkwardly leaning on our car's interconnecting door—but I could have sworn his voice was still coming from the nearby seats across the aisle. For a moment, my eyes caught his, and the fog that surrounded him dissipated long enough to see.

Those eyes, possessed by an inhuman resignation I'd never seen before.

The eyes of a haunted ghost.

My heart might have skipped a bit and caused me to black out, because when I reacted and opened my mouth, he was already crossing the gap to the car behind ours. A second later, he was gone.

I looked over his seat, as a tracker trying to detect signs about which way this insufferable guy would go. Something made me lean over my armrests and peek at the plastic green surface of his still-depressed seat.

Someone—of course, it had to be him—had written in red marker and big block letters: "YOU CAN'T SAVE EVERYBODY."

Reading this made me immensely tired, and I reclined back for a moment to recover my sanity. I might've closed my eyes again—I'm not sure about that. But as soon as I leveled back from my stressed-out state of mind, I stood and grabbed his side of the seats.

There was nothing written on the well-worn sitting cushion. Not even scratch marks on its surface. And the seat had recovered its flat, cold surface, one not recently visited by heavy buttocks.

Julian startled me from the other side of the car. "Hey, Edgardo."

"Yes, what do you...?"

Still three seats away from reaching our row, Julian was already telling me his story. "I found two guys playing guitar on the last car—great musicians. You should have been there. It was amazing."

I wanted to have been there with him. Hear the stories these vacationing rock musicians had told.

I never got to tell him about the man's visit.

7

We left our train under a large glass enclosure that was slowly falling apart like most of those provincial railways—most buildings in Argentina seemed to come from the largesse of an undefined, prosperous past. The La Plata station had a huge, green-striped dome and several exit archways reminiscent of an opera house.

Julian got directions from a newsstand, and practiced high-level synchronized gesturing with the owner, while I glanced over the first pages of the Sunday's newspapers—*La Prensa*, the press, and *La Nación*, the nation, not the most original names. These two, and many others, did not waste any time on international, national, or genocidal news, and got right from their titles to summarize the upcoming football matches. War World III could start, but we wouldn't know about it until the last game of the World Cup was played. The only planetary reality for June 4, 1978, was that Austria would be playing Spain that night.

As we left the train station, we crossed paths with a couple of short-skirted girls, who could have been teen models in European magazines. This being my third trip to La Plata, I knew the women there were even more beautiful than in Buenos Aires, and that was saying something. I already regarded Argentine girls as the most stunning ones a transplanted teenager could be lucky enough to find in a new country. And if it sounds strange that female images would busy the mind of a guy who was invested in a dangerous search-and-rescue mission for his love-at-first-sight beloved, I can say that I was relishing my luck on meeting Mariana, one of its comely children.

"Yes, they are distracting, my friend."

Julian had one of his small notebooks on hand, probably already scribbled with detailed directions to the Venturinos' residence. I smiled, thinking on doodles he might have also made there, of known sightings from super-secret, military UFOs.

For a moment, I thought to ask him about the meteorites, but he was still focused on those neighboring short skirts as they were being blown around by the wind. And—I'm ashamed to say this—I was also distracted and forgot to ask my question to the greatest possible expert I could have found.

We men, our minds are cursed by the existence of women.

* * *

I pulled rank over Julian and got him to call a taxi to take us to the Venturino estate, insisting on how it was a little out of the way. The truth is that I kept seeing Ford Falcons at every corner and assuming all of them were after us. These were common cars back then, and not just exclusive of the secret police, so I could've been confusing similar sedans with them. I was having a fear that many Argentines had endured since 1976, when the military took over the country for a second time in a decade.

As we traveled around the roundabout opposite to the city's Cathedral—a building which always reminded me of New York's Saint Patrick—Julian created layers upon layers of a masterful story about the Venturinos I didn't want to hear before meeting any of them. By the time our taxi stopped, I was having visions of an old, decrepit factory in Lanús, where generations of Venturinos had been hiding as they fought a private war against successive governments bent on destroying the near-socialist imagery that descended over the country during Perón's reign.

In line with the ingrained social isolation my friend described for Mariana's family members, I imagined how Kafka could have written one of his best books about the gothic place my friend summoned: *The Factory* would have been the perfect title for it.

The simple, rectangular, stone-brick house—one floor, just like all the others on the block—dissuaded me from the moat-guarded vampire castle I'd been putting together in my mind. It did have a door with bars, and opaque glass panels in place of windows, but that was as common then as it is now. And there was no picket fence to protect the residential door or the small, almost perfunctory garden in front of it. Just a small intervening space separated the house's door from its garage's double doors and from the street.

I had to give it to the Venturinos. Their house would have been invisible to an Argentine, so average a four-year-old would draw it without even looking at it, and anyone older than ten would forget it as fast as an unwritten phone number. The same bars and glasses and gardens and bricks could be seen several times a block, in every block, like infinite reflections in a mirror.

"Are you sure we are in the right place?"

"Yes, this's their home in the city."

"Maybe we should have gone to the factory."

This time, it was Julian who wanted to tell *me* that I was crazy. "Not on a weekend. Today, we'll have better luck here."

8

The doorbell from the Venturinos' residence was apparently connected to a sound-producing device in another universe, since we spent what seemed to be hours pushing the button of the doorbell and waiting for a ring. I started to get nervous, and my resolve to go ahead waned to the point of slowly backing away from the door, one step with each of Julian's failed attempts to ring. But he kept his cool; I should thank him for not letting me turn around and go back to the railway station.

My reaction also came from an inner revelation: I was finally acting like a rational human being, finding the many reasons for not doing what we were trying to do. What stopped me from leaving was a basic sense of justice and freedom, instilled by my teachers in elementary school, back in Pennsylvania. The stupid idea that we were leaders of the Free World—whatever the meaning of that word was—and we will defend the human right to freedom until our last breath.

Yes, I was that idealistic. But suddenly Mariana represented for me all of us: our fight to be heard; our right to say our peace without coercion. I would love for her to be free again—it was the clearest idea and the deepest pain I'd had in my life. And, to say something good about that early form of myself: I was sincere, and my love for humanity was pure.

My inner fight about going back home ended when the door quietly started to open.

"Who's this?" It was a hoarse female voice, loaded with uncertainty. It seemed to come both from near and away the door.

"We are friends of Mariana," said Julian. He was leaning on the glass but quickly retired his body, I assumed fearing the woman would go back into hiding.

"Yes, we want to know if you have seen her," I said. I approached the door's edge in two quick steps.

"Please, leave. She's not here."

"I know. I was there when they took her."

Silence again. A minute passed, filled by thinking on the other side of those wrinkled glass panels.

The woman spoke again. "What did you say?"

Julian gestured me to come forward. "I am her friend," I said. "I want to help."

"Nobody can help now."

"We can..." Julian started and then stopped.

Could we have helped anyone?

"We will take care of this. You should leave."

"I won't, *Señora* Venturino. I've met your daughter, and I want her to be safe."

Maybe because my English accent and clumsy Spanish phrasing were weird, or perhaps after a hint of contained emotion managed to cross the boundary between us, but there was movement and shuffling of chains and the door started to open.

I saw eyes like Mariana's. Not exactly like hers, but what they would be after decades of sadness and loss. Two brown stars on their way to extinction.

"I am Pocha Venturino, Mariana's mother. Come in."

The glass doors closed after us, and the castle's snaking chains promptly secured us from the hostile world outside. We were in.

* * *

The house was spacious. At first, and while Mariana's mother kept driving us deeper and deeper into her place, I thought she'd direct us to the other side of that block and then wave us out before closing an identical glass door behind our backs.

There were two patios, and many rooms leading to them. Large houses sometimes held generations of a family and, if the people became poorer—not unusual in Argentina's economic carousel of many decades—the whole dwelling could be fragmented in smaller clusters and sold as a kind of flat condominium, connected by narrow corridors running deep into the city block.

I smelled pasta—its sauce, actually—and remembered it was Sunday and noodles were as holy as to be a bread-like continuation of Mass. More bread and wine for the afternoon. The richness of the aroma suggested lots of spices and tender meat slowly being cooked. But there was also staleness and a languorous smell that talked about few people around to fight the humidity of a subtropical climate.

As we were being led through the second patio, I saw the largest room so far. It had many foldable wood chairs and looked just like meeting rooms in our old church near Philadelphia. I stood across its door for a second, staring at a large green board on its back, ghosted by chalk clouds and crossed by small lines that had survived the erasing of a street map. I didn't know what meetings Mariana's very political family conducted there, but they might have been the kind those policemen in Ford Falcons would've loved to know about.

The last room was a living room—*el comedor* in Spanish, their place to eat rather than ours to live—complete with a long table suitable for Argentine-style family feasts. The Venturinos were from Italian extraction and no doubt would meet every Sunday to eat pasta, drink wine, and watch football. Or had met, as I wondered how much of a normal family life they could have after years of secretly fighting Argentina's military governments.

We were standing, uncertain as to whether we'd be allowed to sit and restart our conversation. It wasn't the afternoon yet, and lunch could begin as late as two or three.

"How's that you know her?"

"I met her..." I said and then reconsidered, remembering our gun-on-the-subway story. "Recently, but we are very good friends."

"I told my daughter to be careful, not to be seen with strangers."

Pocha's comment annoyed me. "But she's free to talk with any people she likes, isn't she?"

"And then, she chooses someone like you?"

I didn't know what to say, and Julian intervened. "You mean a *gringo* like Edgardo?"

"Yes, she shouldn't be talking to foreigners. It's dangerous."

"But she speaks English," I said. "We talked...she knows the language."

A forced smile, not something my girlfriend's mother would frequently use. "My sister. She taught her. Mariana's very bright, but like all of us, unlucky."

And right then, she started to sob. It brought us back to what was behind our visit, the awfulness of what had happened.

"Don't worry, *Señora*," I said, "we will help."

She looked at me and smiled. "You are a good son," she said, "and have a good heart, but right now you can't help anyone."

"*Señora*," I started.

"Pocha, please call me Pocha." And she touched my shoulder and then hugged me, still coughing and sobbing for her—our—lost child.

When I turned toward Julian, he had an expression like some-one who was witnessing a miracle. And he was right, as we had been granted safe passage to Mariana's underworld.

9

Pocha said few words while we ate with her mother, a very Italian, thin-as-sticks old lady, who silently served us pasta with a thick sauce and delicious meat; later, she delivered a bread pudding with clumpy cream. Oddly, it was food without wine—even children would drink some wine on Sundays. The stories Pocha told us throughout the meal were only meant to illustrate the fact that they had lost a dozen family members, and thus grown accustomed to the waiting and not knowing what tomorrow would bring.

Pocha's mother was soon gone with small, frail steps, but not before I got to observe how much Pocha resembled her and how little Mariana looked like these two women. Pocha had the harsh features of her mother, swollen high cheeks and a nose a bit too long for a woman. And her eyes were of the darkest brown, unlike Mariana's, sunken eyes that had seen too much and sought in their proximity to the nose the strength to go on. Perhaps Mariana looked like her father, but there was no mention of the absent male components of her family.

It was like a sad scene taken from a painting, and it reminded me of how shadows were the most significant part of a Caravaggio. There was something very Italian on that family's tragedy, these solemn, prematurely aged women trapped in a life that was an eternal wake for relatives taken by force. It was a truly Caravag-gean world, where blackness suggested the impending death of our flesh.

As I contemplated the place's collective helplessness, I might have shown the sadder side of my nature, which called into play Pocha's maternal instincts. She couldn't believe my father would leave me alone for months on end and in a foreign land. And even though she was restrained by the prevalent anti-American senti-ment—we were quite the imperialist pigs back then for South Americans—Pocha ended up offering me her help and hospitality. It was sweet of her, having a kidnapped daughter and wanting to protect me.

She had already accepted her family was doomed. And I hadn't, at least not yet.

* * *

On finishing his second serving of pudding, this one with the tradi-tional sweet spread made from milk—*dulce de leche*—Julian started his own brand of probing.

"Do you know if Mariana is involved in anything dangerous?"

"Why do you ask?"

"We're here, at your home, so you can be sincere with us. What I'm asking is—was she hurting people?"

"No," Pocha almost yelled the word. "I'd never let her get involved with...the violence." But it was as if she'd said too much.

Julian waited for a minute to end the ongoing silence. I appre-ciated this, as the room was full of the dead we hadn't known and paying them respect seemed the right thing to do.

"I'm sorry," he said. "It's just that I want to know if she's in danger. Maybe if she doesn't know anything, they'll let her go."

"They...they don't need you to know anything to torture—to kill you."

"Well, some people came back." Julian seemed to be talking to himself.

"Do you know anyone who did? Who's telling you this idiocy?"

I was in the middle of a verbal war and didn't have any ammunition. Julian had blushed and was looking at his shoes. For a moment, I thought it was all over.

Pocha smiled, probably taking the upper ground to humiliate my friend. "You know," she said, "lots of people are talking about this order the military are supposedly bringing to the country. The trains that run on time—like Mussolini used to say—and how the university is now clean from political signs and aerosol writings on the walls. Sure, it looks better, and clean, but it's as if someone had used a flamethrower to clean it. Many now look the other way at the violence, and most would act carefree for as long as they don't lose a son...or a daughter." Pocha choked for a moment, but she wanted very much to finish her words. "It's all great unless it happens to them. Well, this has happened to us, because we spoke up and defended our rights."

"But the Montoneros are also violent," Julian said. "And they use their guns to kill."

Julian's comment bothered me. The Montoneros organization had collected people with strong antimilitary persuasions—activist Christians, atheist Socialists, and disenchanted Peronists—to wage a protractive war against the entire military complex. Sure, the "Montos" had guns and explosives, but the other guys had tanks and planes, and controlled an army—troops, policemen, and mercenaries—twenty times larger. It was a fight they couldn't win.

I didn't want Julian to continue, but it would have been impossible to silence him. My friend was trapped between what one day would be called "the two demons" and he saw only a conflict between forces—the military's imposition of social order and an armed insurrection. That was the reason Julian wanted to infiltrate the military. To make them see the error of their ways.

I knew, at that very moment, the truth contained in the man's short letter.

You can only save one.

* * *

They kept arguing from both sides of the fence for an hour, and I kept trying to contain the verbal fighting by throwing them off course with broad questions about Argentine politics that annoyed them both. But their disagreements were a battle, and, just like a game of chess represents a real battle, we were considering consequences that would produce real dead people.

It wasn't, unfortunately, a bloodless board game—they were playing with the precious time left to save a life.

It was the eve of winter and, before Julian and Pocha reached any kind of truce about their entrenched positions, it had turned completely dark outside.

10

The day had ended fast, so we said our goodbyes empty-handed. We hadn't even left the Venturinos' inner luncheon room when we heard from Pocha's mother that we had a visitor. It was the last person I could imagine showing up. I immediately recognized him from the party—Anibal Reinoso, the bearded Montonero with the physique of a medieval warrior.

Julian didn't know who he was and walked closer to the presumed family member to shake hands. I would have rather wanted my friend to jump on the guy and extract from him why he'd mixed up Mariana with his organization. But Julian was already extending his hand—very formally, with an Argentine distancing—while I tried to near the door's edge and keep going.

When he recognized me, Anibal went from smile to snarl.

"*You,* what are you doing here?"

The tone was harsh, and Julian froze, but he regained composure in an instant—I was still paralyzed—and put his body between mine and Anibal's. Still, the Montonero's long hands could have reached both of us and grabbed our necks.

Sensing trouble, Pocha gave a couple of steps forward and gestured haltingly toward Anibal. "I know them," she said. "They're trying to help Mariana."

"Them? *Him?* He's the one Luisa told me had gone to the movies with Mariana when they got her. He should have done something to stop them."

Before I could explain, Pocha rose her voice to a deafening level. "Don't be a dumbass, Anibal." Somehow, and even though Pocha was a great deal smaller than Anibal, he seemed to shrink in position. It was clear who was the head of that wolf pack.

"All right," said Anibal. "I'm sorry guys, but things haven't been going very well...can I talk?"

Pocha authorized him to speak with an almost undetectable nod.

"Mariana is very important for us," he said. "For the organization, well, nowadays we call it just '*la Orga.*'"

"They know it's the Montoneros," Pocha said, nodding. "Go on."

By this point, Anibal sounded like a child whose parent was nagging him about the proper way to address visitors. I caught a funny look in Julian, as if he were witnessing a Papuan ritual no Westerner had ever seen.

"Well, you know that she's gone," Anibal said, "but I assure you she wasn't really doing anything violent with us. We only put her to transfer arms between safe houses and to organize an event. I won't talk about *that*, Pocha, no matter what you've told them."

"It's all right," said Pocha, "tell them."

"No, I won't."

"I want them to know more—they've been talking big risks to find Mariana. It's best if they know what's going on."

I sensed an imperceptible change in our position after the implicit contract that had taken us into Pocha's world—and thus, the Montoneros' world—but it could have far-reaching consequences, more than anything else that had happened in our visit.

"I'm not sure they should know anything," Anibal jumped in, but then they went through a dozen variants of the negative, until Pocha's mother interrupted. "Did you leave your truck outside? That's dangerous."

"Your truck? Did you bring it here?" Pocha's admonishing tone sounded out of place.

"It's no problem, Pocha. I'm collecting stuff for next week—the guys at the house in Florida need some plastic, and I'm going to drive late at night up there."

"You brought the truck *with* explosives? And left it at our door? Are you nuts?"

I looked in the direction of a visibly pale Julian. Our accidental learning of the ways and means of Montoneros was putting us in even more danger. Things were getting serious.

Pocha turned to me, as if I'd become again the outsider— "Can you give me a few minutes? Please, wait on the front patio and don't leave before I get a chance to...chat a bit more with you two."

Julian and I quickly crossed the door, and I would have continued all the way out and into the streets if his hand hadn't have closed around my shoulder. "This is a terrific opportunity," he said.

"To do what? Didn't you have enough?"

"We need to get into that truck."

'What?"

"I want to see what they're moving around...the explosives."

"Julian, we need to get out of here. We're way too deep into something we can't handle."

"That's the fun part."

My voice was deflated enough to betray how afraid I was. "I just want to find Mariana."

"We won't find her if we don't take some risks. Come on, let's see what these terrorists have under the hood."

Terrorists. The word wasn't so common back then.

Mariana was a terrorist. And that, rather than scare me, was a little enticing. Me, the science guy, was in love with a terrorist.

We scurried away without another word.

11

The truck was parked in front of the house, and it was just as average and thus invisible. Big, boxy, worn out, and several decades past the time to be archived in a dumpster, that run-of-the-mill transport would still last another thirty years, if the owner had had the good sense of befriending a competent mechanic. The truck's cabin was covered by lavishly twisted writing—standard lettering like those illustrating most *colectivos*. Subversive Argentines were yet to discover the beauty of unmarked vans and worked at the opposite extreme. It was impossible to know which of all these business and last names belonged to the driver.

I could see inside a small figure of the Virgin Mary and, over the small instrument panel, a handsome picture of Tango's grand-master singer, Carlos Gardel, who perhaps would offer a complementary opportunity to ask for forgiveness based on the meaninglessness of life. I considered what kinds of wishes the Virgin and Gardel would receive from the users of that truck.

"Hey, Edgardo."

"Yes. It's locked."

"Help me to open this. And hurry."

When I made my way around the vehicle, Julian's ingenuity surprised me. The truck was locked front and back, but this was an old Chevrolet, old enough to have one of those little triangular windows on its front doors—usually only useful to tip out ash from cigarettes at red lights. And Julian had managed to almost open the driver's side one with a long key.

I held the window while he finished propping it open. Then, we got inside with a reverse-elbow move from Julian that reached and dutifully opened the door's handle.

"Nice truck," said Julian.

"Are you serious? This thing is ancient—looks like the trucks they used in *Lassie*."

Julian smiled, as he'd also watched the old black-and-white shows that would fill the gaps in TV programming.

He was quick to move inside—quick enough to suggest it wasn't the first time he had illegally entered a parked car—and inspected the glove compartment and the gaps between seats. "Let's try to get to the back," he said. And just like that, Julian opened a sliding panel behind the front seats and slithered into the blackness.

I wasn't feeling like following him in there, but soon a wobbling light suggested he'd found a flashlight. I breathed in, like I was going to submerge in a lake, and jumped, falling in the dark to a very hard floor in the truck's rear box.

"I can't find anything," Julian said, likely to himself.

"Where are you, Julian? I can barely see—that's a very weak light." I was taken by the redolent smell of grease and a garnish of mold.

"No money for batteries. Maybe the Montoneros like to work in the dark."

Some Montonero ghost likely got angry, because the flashlight went out and fell, and we both tumbled in the black chamber where we were momentarily trapped.

"Ouch," I said, stumbling on a couple of very solid objects.

"Be careful—Agh!" Julian crashed into the truck's unseen cargo.

After a few seconds of more standing and falling, I got hold of the flashlight and illuminated a grotesque face—Julian's.

"Get that thing down," he said. "Better, point it here—right here."

Stored between a couple of boxes containing ceramic tiles were several large bags that, considering their assorted styles and states of integrity, had probably supported several generations of anti-military revolutionaries. Julian took from the pile an ancient black duffel bag and started to examine it. I pulled out a black-striped white Adidas bag much like my own.

"Look at this," said Julian. "These are the explosives they were talking about. They'd use them to make tube bombs—the Montos love to put them at police hangouts."

I could see that his bag was filled with small bunches of newspaper wrappings, each tied with a hemp cord. He held the one he'd opened; it contained a small brick of a weirdly colored material.

"I don't know if this one has anything of value," I said. "I guess it's just documents and money for..."

"What's up?"

I extracted a heavy black gun from my white bag. It was stylish—for what I could imagine a gun to be, thinking of cowboys and their Colts 45s—and it had a wooden cover for the handle, and a barrel that was almost perfectly rectangular; its straight lines gave it a manly character, the kind of gun a professional killer would use.

"That's great. Take it."

"The gun?"

"Yes, the gun. We may need it."

Julian took the gun from me and, to my amazement, swiftly carried out a safety check of its lock and removed the magazine to verify whether it had some bullets left. "We need to get out of here," he said, and started to head back to the front seats, before I got to ask him where he'd learned to handle handguns.

Getting out of the truck took less effort, as we didn't return it to its original state. We were just closing the truck's door when the one from the Venturinos' home opened.

It was Anibal, as irate as usual.

12

We were trapped on the street's side and behind Anibal's truck. Pocha was chatting with Anibal, while they stood idly at the house's doorsteps. I could hear Pocha's hoarse, deep vowels— "Are you planning to do the church thing anyway?"

"You mean without Mariana helping? We need someone on the inside."

"Well, you need to get *him*, no matter what," she said. "Perhaps then we can negotiate a release for her."

"You're getting this the other way around, Pocha. We need the guy to have leverage, and we cannot get him without Mariana. We are stuck. And I had to break ranks with my old unit, so this is now my own thing. I'm alone."

"Patience, that's the best weapon," Pocha said. "We've waited long enough—there will be other chances."

"Not as good as the World Cup: it's public, and everyone's watching it. It will shame them into leaving...they won't be able to govern."

"Ah, Anibal. You haven't seen enough—*they* always come back. And they don't need a reason to stay around, one as weak...they aren't going to leave just out of shame."

I missed the next exchange as Julian seemed ready to tell me

105

something, while I was going to ask him what he'd done with the gun. We both stopped cold on hearing the commotion.

Across the street, someone was taking a metal pan or some other kitchenware and clanking it very hard. It was a huge noise-making stunt; and it had rhythm, as if from a song, but one I couldn't place.

Without paying attention to what was happening, Julian dragged me along the truck's side and to the farthest point from the Venturinos' door. I turned around and heard Pocha arguing with someone in the distance.

I could see a tall guy across the street, banging two circular pieces looking like the tops of some metal pans. Pocha had increased the volume of her arguing, but that didn't seem to affect the crazy neighbor.

I was watching the developing scene from the truck's edge but couldn't make out any of the features—even the contours—of that large, presumably male figure. He was surrounded by reddish fog, limited just to him; a blurred man, hitting those things with every sliver of his strength. At times, the objects resembled two saucepans; other times, a saucepan and a casserole, or two trashcan tops. And at yet other times, he wasn't even there. It was as if someone were editing reality with different versions of the same event.

I can describe so many other things about that scene it's hard to believe it only lasted a couple of seconds, until Julian pulled my arm and made me land on the sidewalk. It felt as if I'd been trapped in a carousel of images for days.

What was going on with me, with my reason?

* * *

"A crazy guy," said Julian, smiling as he approached Pocha and Anibal.

"Where were you, guys?" answered Anibal, curtly.

"We went for a walk," I said. "Just around the block." My voice sounded like I was whistling near a graveyard.

"It's not that safe at night, you know," Pocha said, cutting off Anibal and saving us from more explaining.

"Not so bad, but of course you have people like..." Julian stopped, as now the street was empty and quiet. The crazy man was gone.

"Kids, you have to go home." Pocha had recovered her tough stance and was ready to bark orders.

"We don't know much more than when we came," I said.

Pocha smiled. "Don't we all?"

Incredibly, the woman still had an inner supply of warmth and offered suggestions for the trip home. It was too early to encourage us to stay for the night and not late enough to make taking the train back to Buenos Aires an unreasonable option. I assured her that I'd share a taxi with Julian right off the station, promptly taking him back to his home while on the way to mine. The military-imposed, city-wide curfew had been loosened up for the football championship, so we wouldn't be stopped by police as it was customary at night.

Before going, Pocha pulled me aside. "Thank you for coming," she said. "I know how difficult it is to take sides and fight for someone."

"I just want Mariana to come back."

"Me too. It's making life unbearable, and...I'm not ready to lose another child to them."

"You won't," Julian said.

"We will help," I added.

"I will hold you to your words," Pocha said, staring at both of us with burning eyes, just like Mariana's. "I will tell you things, but you will be bound to help us."

We nodded in silence. We had been sworn to their secret society.

Suddenly changing tone, Pocha turned her eyes down and added a softening comment, something conciliatory that was as Argentine as wishful thinking— "For now, we'll have to just pray they let her go," she said, closing her eyes. "There's little she's done, and maybe that will help her. She might come back all right."

The plain sincerity and hopeless hope in those words would stay with me for some time. It was a strange time, where strange things happened to everybody. There was hopelessness and hope, lovelessness and love, lifelessness and life, and they were all unnaturally combined.

13

Julian had said something about a meeting on that Monday to see a professor at the School of Medicine. And I, like the sleepwalker I was those days, made it to the austere conjunction of buildings containing the medical branches of the University of Buenos Aires, without giving much thought to what we were going to do. Julian was two years older than me, a little behind in his schooling and always saying he wanted to study Medicine. But I couldn't imagine my sleuth friend with a white coat and a stethoscope.

The city's medical school was a large building, and it seemed even larger from the inside. As we climbed the stairs—there were no functioning elevators that day—I saw the great hall from above, painted in grayish tones and lacking all those political posters, aerosol wall-writings, and hanging flags everyone was still talking about. Such overloaded activist decoration of Argentine universities had been common years earlier, before the Junta took over after a brief window of political freedom. Now, study halls were quite clear, but there were police on every entrance, checking bags and coats for weapons and explosives.

I don't remember anymore what department we visited, perhaps an aftereffect of the secrecy Julian had instilled in me before our meeting with a well-known scientist who was—he'd said—connected with Montoneros. The characters who opened the half-windowed door (did every door in Argentina have opaque, wrinkled, or otherwise non-transparent glass?) and led us into the inner sanctum of science appeared to have escaped from comic books. Or possibly horror novels, as they resembled vampires, like the pale, tall, bald, self-important man who opened the door; or werewolves, like the housekeeper who was cleaning the floors; or other forms of the undead that remain so far unwritten, like the slug-like creature who was carrying two large flasks filled with a nasty-smelling yellow soup.

After such inauspicious entry into Argentina's science world, nothing could have surprised me. Except that Julian's revolutionary professor did exist, and he seemed like a normal academic, with thick glasses and a blue sweater low enough to show a nice tie and an Oxford light-blue shirt. Some hair lost on the front of his head, and some turning white over his temples, but that could be expected of someone who was trying to think hard in a collapsing world.

I couldn't believe the guy existed, and even less that he was a disciple of a Nobel Prize winner—Bernardo Houssay, a past glory of Argentine science—and had travelled all over the world teaching Physiology. There was something both formal and rebellious about him—a middle-aged man, slightly overweight, who smiled constantly—and I pictured him as an adventurous kid whose parents had made sit for dinner dressed-up in a tie and a jacket.

I was going to interrupt the unending introduction of Julian and his way-too-preliminary kissing-up game targeted to facilitate a future job for him when he graduated with an M.D. But then I saw the photograph on a cabinet and understood how this guy had become a protected specimen of tolerance. The picture showed him, and a couple of suit-and-tie guys, chatting with a priest. My little knowledge of the attire of Catholic prelates was enough to decipher that priest was a cardinal. Another priest was standing in the image's background; that second one, none of us could have known back then one day would be the Pope.

Maybe there is such a thing as enough protection to survive anything. Doctor José María Acevedo, whether by luck or intent, had acquired enough to survive in his scientific fishbowl.

* * *

Julian and the professor were at it like two excited Ping-Pong players. Julian served, fast. "You know we're here to get some info about Montoneros."

I don't know what exactly Doctor Acevedo had thought we were doing in his office, but the word Montoneros unleashed a series of spontaneous movements that individually might've been missed, but together were suggestive of an adrenalin rush, and not of the good kind. His right leg shook independently of his body, and a silver pen twirled between his fingers as if ready to take flight.

"I shouldn't have said anything to you last time," the professor said. "I can't tell you much more now. The last year has been bad, really bad for us. The leadership escaped to Europe, and many here are imprisoned...I don't want to risk any more of us to be captured."

Julian pressed on. "You're the one that doesn't want to be captured, isn't that so?"

"I worry for me and my family, sure, and who wouldn't? I've been very lucky. Now it's a little bit easier. With the World Cup, the military are distracted, but we wouldn't want any information to leak."

"Information about what? Are you guys planning something?"

Professor Acevedo was a bright guy, brighter than us, and he knew what he was doing. But he had once been an idealist, and it was apparent that he was living his relatively safe life with regret. For a moment, he looked toward the shelves, the laboratory record books and photographs documenting his success.

Julian reacted, just before the professor waved us goodbye. "My friend, Edgardo, came with me because his girlfriend, Mariana Venturino, has been taken by the police."

Professor Acevedo turned pale, seriously affected by the comment, and started talking. Apparently, Mariana's family was quite famous in the Montoneros organization. Pocha's husband had been a founding leader—until he and his brother were killed in a shootout with the police. Afterwards, Pocha had continued his involvement with the leadership, acting as adviser and in general as a voice for reason that fought the more extreme elements. A remarkable woman, the professor said, and a tough one.

The talking had loosened up Acevedo, and he continued as if remembering good old times. "I am going to tell you something," he said. "I still know a few things, as some of the elite members talk to me—no matter that they know I'm here, totally exposed. There are going to be some big operations, timed to coincide with the World Cup."

This was the first piece of real information we had obtained.

I was stunned, but Julian didn't lose sight of our goal. "Are you sure about this?"

"Yes, of course. I've heard it from a reliable source, 'El Pepe' Firmenich."

"*The* Firmenich? The one who runs the Montoneros?" I now believe that Julian and I both said the same thing at once.

"Yes, guys. The bastard himself confirmed it for me. There'll be some activities during the World Cup."

"What kind of activity?" Julian said.

"Serious, conclusive."

"Conclusive? What are they trying to finish?"

The game was now between two deaf Ping-Pong players. Julian had his idea of what he wanted to know and the professor a short list of words he was willing to say.

"We're starting again the big fight, boys." Acevedo stood ramrod straight, as if his stance were belligerent. "We were decimated at the start of the Junta's government, but we'll come back, soon."

Julian was triumphantly smiling. "So, is it going to be an all-out combat with the Junta?"

The professor broadened his smile even further, into the "humoring-you" range, maybe to the "don't-be-such-a-pair-of-idiots" range. "No," he finally said, "we don't have enough people to do so much damage, not anymore." His voice quickly dropped to depths of baritone mourning. "They've killed most of our original resistance. I can't say more—this's getting risky for all of us."

Julian turned silent, as if rethinking his approach. I tried playing the innocent.

"Doctor, I'm worried for my friend Mariana," I said. "She might have been involved with something; something that could be happening this week."

"I am sorry about her. They're returning almost no one these days. But what I'm aware of is not happening this week; it has something to do with the broadcasting of the Cup's matches—maybe taking over a transmission. Your friend, is she involved with a radio station?"

"No, not that I know," I said, deflated.

"And *who* may know more?" Julian's voice came out as whiny when he meant it to be inquisitive.

The professor looked in the direction of his trophy cabinet and made a small gesture that dissipated in the air.

"I don't understand," Julian said.

I knew which of the pictures he was pointing at and said it. "The church?"

Professor Acevedo looked straight into my eyes with unabashed pride for me. "Yes, you've got that right," he said. "Some churchmen know and can help you. Do you know someone?"

"D'Agostini," said Julian.

"Ah, the old fart. I hope he's not still blessing both the troops and the dying captives. But he might know, and maybe he'll tell you who's holding your friend."

"We'll talk with him," Julian said. "He could help me—us."

"Be careful." The professor sat down, tired of saying dangerous things for no real good reason. "The bishop likes to play double-games—I wouldn't be sure about getting involved with him."

"We don't have any other choice," I found myself saying.

"Well, you may be right; not, if you'd like to get your friend back." The professor was trying, in his own way, to be supportive. "It might work," he said. "I've known of a few people who are let go. This can happen, but only if she's not much involved."

I thought of Mariana carrying that gun on the subway and something acidic started to gurgle deep in my stomach.

14

I was turning a little more philosophical about our quest, perhaps a consequence of having spent the last hour sitting idly in a café across the medical school, watching my friend so immersed on collecting notes from our meeting I was doubting he was still breathing.

Julian stopped the note-making to address his annoyed friend. "What do you think about Acevedo?"

"The guy is strange—that's all I can say."

"But he gave us something solid, isn't that so?"

"Well, he was insistent with the broadcast thing, but I'm not sure that will help. It might not have anything to do with Mariana."

Julian continued thinking out loud. "He said we should talk to D'Agostini."

"No, what he said is that someone on the curia might know something. Not necessarily D'Agostini."

"If he doesn't know, nobody does."

"He may have the wrong kind of knowledge, the kind that could get us killed."

"We need to see him—I *am* going to see him. Tomorrow."

I knew better than to start a long cycle of "we-will-or-we-won't" with Julian. I would always lose those. Soon, he was again back to his notes and I was left alone to contemplate what the hell we were

doing. Saving Mariana—if that was possible—meant risking everything for someone I barely knew. And after two days of wandering and asking questions, I was starting to doubt that it was what I
really wanted. Like fog, my interest in her was evaporating on this
new light; even the memory of our warm kiss was fading.

But just as I was ready to give up on her, something happened to
turn the tide.

I couldn't stay idle while Julian ignored me, so I started to engage
in people watching. The café was large and had windows on two
streets, but in the early evening only seven tables were occupied.
There was a pretty girl, dressed in an immaculate white shirt
and a pleated blue skirt—she had made a good drinking choice,
a double-size coffee topped with a pile of cream and assorted
pastries on the side. A balding man—too old for a student and
perhaps too elegant for a professor making little money, but not
for a banker or a business type—was eating a large ham sandwich
that seemed to contain an entire pig's leg. The waiter was crossing
the bar bearing a coffee cup, making a beeline to a young guy in
a T-shirt—that one was surely a student.

When I'd turned all the way back to our table, Julian was staring impatiently across the table. "I forgot," he said, "that I need to
pick up something at the counter." I watched him walk away and
start talking with a lanky young man behind the cash register, who
reached down and extracted a small box. Julian brought it back
to our table and placed it between us. It was clumsily sealed with
wads of adhesive tape.

"What's that?"

"The gun."

"Are you crazy? Did you bring it with you?"

"Don't want to leave it at home—and we may need it."

"And why did you leave it here?"

"The police." Julian pointed across the street to the School of
Medicine, a dark gray ship shaded by the early winter night. "You

know, they do check bags and sometimes pat you down. No reason to take risks."

"And you think that keeping it here, with unknown people, is much better?"

"I know the bar's manager very well." Julian made an O.K. sign to the guy behind the counter, who smiled noncommittally.

"Still, it's so...it's the craziest thing you've done lately."

"Watch me. I'm going to improve on that. Now, let me take this box to the bathroom so I can open it. Can you keep an eye on my things?"

I was tired of arguing about what Julian was doing—I was tired, period. Just to entertain myself, I started another round of bar-people watching. This time, it didn't go so well.

I am trying to describe something for which we humans don't have any sensory experience. Best I can do is to say that we're used to seeing time move forward, and thus expect new seconds to arrive regularly and build on what's behind. It's like driving on a road at night, watching ahead to where the headlights reach.

But, as I turned around a second time to watch the bar's tables, something inside that instinctive perception broke down. It was either me—tired, perhaps sleep-deprived—or the world around me that had ceased to obey the normal rules. I got to watch the other roads, the ones not taken by me but perhaps taken by other Edgardos. And something else was different, something so abhorrent I experienced sudden nausea—physical, spiritual—and powerful emotions that were intensely dark and full of despair. Not sure how to even get to those.

The girl in the white shirt was now drinking a tiny cup of espresso. The businessman had not even started to eat his sandwich, which stayed untouched while he got deep into the sports section of a newspaper he didn't have before. The waiter was bringing again the same coffee cup to a student, who now wore a jean jacket I hadn't seen before. None of the seven occupants of the café's tables remained the same as two minutes earlier. And there was a new table—right at the bar's center—with another gentleman who was starting to read another newspaper.

It wasn't just another businessman but rather the insufferable man who was stalking me.

My eyes collided with his, and he smiled. He pointed to the seat across from him and nodded.

I reached the spot and didn't wait until he opened his mouth to talk. "I want you to go away," I said. "Don't want to see you anymore."

The man smiled. "That's not going to be so easy."

"Why? What do you want?"

"What's best for everybody—and I really mean everybody."

"And what's that?"

"That *is* the grand question."

"Can you stop being preachy? Please, I'm having enough problems as it is."

"That, I know."

"So, please, do leave me alone."

"Let's don't go there again—not now. I've told you, you should stop this stupid search with Julian."

I noticed he had said "Julian" in English. He'd said it exactly as I would. There was something unsettling in his pronunciation, more than the actual words.

"I won't stop searching for Mariana," I said, firm but unsure of the reason.

"There will be consequences if you don't. I can't control..."

"Are you threatening us?"

"I'm not particularly concerned about Julian." Again, the name said in smooth, mother-tongue English.

"Then, you're threatening me."

"Yes, but I'm not the one doing the threatening—there's a lot more going on, and some of it, neither I nor you, nobody really, would be able to control."

"What are you doing there?" I heard Julian's voice and turned to see him, just as he was sitting again at our table, a hand crossed over his body to cover the handgun hiding inside his jacket's pocket.

"I was talking with..."

When I turned back—it had been at most five seconds—the man was gone. Not only he was gone, but his small cup of coffee and the spread newspaper were gone too.

I had been talking with a ghost.

Finally, all that was happening, and I was trying to forcefully hide under the rug, collided with me, with unstoppable force.

Either everything was a hallucination—and then Mariana was the smallest of my problems—or I was seeing something real and transiting an area of reality best described in episodes of *The Twilight Zone*.

My inner world, or the outer world, or both, had been replaced by a version where everything was possible.

I might have resembled the state of my mind, because as soon as I sat Julian touched the back of my hand and squinted, likely trying to ascertain whether I was going to faint— "Are you all right?"

"A bit shaken."

"I understand. But you should be sure that..."

"Give me the gun," I said, hearing myself say it.

"The gun? Why?"

"I want to have it with me—need to learn how to use it."

This sounded as dumb and impulsive as it was, and Julian realized I was near a breakdown. He didn't want to give it to me. I insisted, twice actually. "Sure, Edgardo," he said, "but let's take it out in a safe place. I need to show you how to use it—and remember, it's just for protection."

I was going to say something defensive of my position but thought Julian would worry about me starting to shoot around like a madman. I did look like a madman.

I wasn't even sure if I was a madman.

15

I have a vague recollection of exchanging the gun with Julian in the shaded turn of the subway's stairs, just before reaching the station's platform. I put it in my jacket's inner right pocket, which was almost to the point of bursting.

"Are you sure you want to keep it?"

"I'm out of sorts—want to know if it gives me some confidence."

"They have been known to give too much confidence to some people."

"Even with a lot of added confidence, I'll feel barely passable as a human being."

"Just hung on. We're going to do better from now on. I will arrange a meeting with the archbishop for tomorrow. Okay?"

"Yes, we'll talk..."

At that moment, I saw someone in the station, behind the other three people who were also waiting for a subway late on the workweek evening. It was the man, strangely dressed in black—I couldn't remember if he'd been wearing black at the bar. He seemed heavier, even stout, but it was probably an effect of his wearing a thick, very black wool sweater. Without a jacket, in winter, and with his unkempt hair, he resembled a homeless man.

"Julian, I'll see you tomorrow at school."

"You are not coming with me?"

"No. I'm going to take the train the other way, going to...don't worry. I'll see you tomorrow." I realized, knowing those subways by heart, that I had lied, and we could have traveled together. Julian was going to switch subways to Line C, at the 9 de Julio station; I could have gotten out there and walked home. But for some reason—maybe he was also tired and wanting to go home—Julian wasn't in the mood to reinterpret directions.

He took the next train, clutching his blue paper-wrapped notebooks while trying to accommodate two spiral-bound notepads between them. The other passengers climbed to the same subway car in complete silence, like animated cutouts of real people. And I was soon alone on the subway's platform. Not alone, as a black outline ahead had become animated and was walking toward me. I wanted to argue again with that man, see if I could get him out of my life permanently.

Unfortunately, he was thinking the exact same thing.

* * *

I didn't get to say anything. As soon as we were close, he revealed a long crowbar he was hiding and swung it around and toward my face. Even with the surprise, I moved back and away, and the weapon only got to graze my forehead. I felt something, like burning pain, probably the bar cutting skin. Then, the inertia I had acquired from my movement matching the bar's momentum hit me hard, as if an explosion was blowing me away slowly.

The excavated throat containing the subway's rails was behind me; I wasn't sure how close I was to the platform's edge. I fell sideways, trying to spread my body so it didn't fall completely into the gutter. My right leg, however, decided to test the open space and started to drag me down. And the gun in my pocket seemed to have turned magnetic, and its attraction to the rails was also pulling me down. I put my face close to the floor, as if listening to the coming steps of the man, who was readying himself to push me off the platform.

I tried to grab his foot with my left hand, but on raising my back I started to slip away. He saw it and turned to kick my abdomen and make me fall backwards. He missed and fell on his side, crashing on the platform. I used the small break—while he was sitting and starting to stand up—to recover my equilibrium by sliding forward, crawling as if I had people standing over my back. My face felt wet, and it bothered me to the point that I swabbed my forehead with my free hand. I saw it come back smothered in blood.

We stood facing each other. The man still held to his crowbar and was blocking my access to the stairs; we were too close to the platform's end, and there were no other exits left I could use for an escape. I only wanted to get past him and run—if I could do that, I was considering giving up my life of secret detective.

I also had the crazy idea of saying this out loud. "All right, that's it. I'm out of this, isn't that what you want?"

"Too late, you know too much already."

I was going to add something, while fighting my agitated breathing, but I realized what he meant. He was going to kill me—it was in his eyes, their slight over-extended aperture exposing too much white around the irises, and in a fisted free hand ready to carry out the final act.

For once, I got a lucky break and, when he advanced to push me, his lengthy stride allowed me to kick him right in between his well-spread legs. He fell—his crowbar flew and made clanging sounds on the platform—and I jumped over him while watching the nearest exit, the one I thought could be my way to freedom.

Something went wrong, whether that I entangled my foot with one of his, or that he put an extended leg below my right knee. I fell and hit hard on that same knee—a very painful contact—and the move left me on all fours on the floor. I looked up, but the station was empty and the yelling I'd planned wouldn't bring any help. Some guy was watching us from the station's opposite end—I could swear he was also dressed completely in black, like the man.

Whatever break I'd had was over, and I was suddenly in the air. The man had hauled my body up with his arms crossed across my stomach and was trying to throw me away and into the rails.

I could see the next train coming, still just a pointy light deep in the tunnel.

Right then, the man made a costly mistake that would weigh on the final outcome. He didn't secure my arms but rather lifted me up from my belly, like a sack of potatoes. I used the balancing weight of my arms—plus a dose of fear-driven energy—to swing them together and in a long counter-clockwise circle, thus pushing both of us backwards. I fell, painfully again, first over his body and then on my back.

Maybe he had hit his head and was momentarily woozy, but whatever stopped the man left me able to remove myself from him, kneel on my good knee and try to stand up. The train was now closing in on the station, and I could hear its wheels jumping on the old railways. Before I could move from the spot, I was in the air again, falling, and the man was coming down with me.

It wasn't as bad a fall as I'd imagined, but, as I tumbled down the rails, they hit me hard where I didn't have the protection of ribs. I couldn't move from the pain. The man approached and took my head between his hands, ready to smash it backwards against metal.

Fear took over in an instant, and I lifted my right hand into his face; on its way up, it took out his arm and broke the pressure. With that same hand, still bloody, I hit him hard on the right temple.

He moved backwards. I moved sideways. The train was starting to threaten both of us, probably less than three hundred feet from entering the station.

In one of these acts that will sound rational only with the passing of time, I extracted the gun from my pocket and pointed it to his face. It had the safety on, but I didn't have time to change that.

"Well, that's some improvement over the last time," he said, and walked backwards to approach the platform's edge. I was still in mortal danger, my jacket against a rail, the train still coming.

Using a move that seemed well-practiced, the man turned, grabbed the border of the tiled floor and swung his body in a lateral movement that put him over the platform.

I didn't see much more, as I had the pressing matter of escaping a collision with the slowly-stopping train. I stood over the rails on the opposite side, where two people who'd just walked onto the platform watched me in disbelief.

At some point, the subway train started again its course toward the dark tunnel. Luckily for me, the one on my side was delayed or had given up for the day.

By the time I'd managed—in many more steps and falls than the man—to climb over the platform and stand there, my attacker was gone.

16

It took an hour of waiting crouched at the station's stairs to muster the strength to take another train. By then I was worried that the subway would stop running and I'd be left alone in a dark station until someone came to rescue me. I was also hurting—diffusely on my right knee but with more precision on areas of my low back—and had a superficial cut over my left eyebrow, which was still bleeding.

When I entered the subway car, I was so tired that I lunged forward to sit on the nearest double-width seat. I couldn't have stayed upright when the train started to move again.

The entire passenger's car was empty, with the rush hour already past and most people now watching the exciting soccer games—or their repeated analysis—in their living rooms, the luckier ones in pioneering color transmissions from the brand-new state channel—Canal 7. But that night I wouldn't have been able to feel excitement about anything.

I watched the empty seats across the aisle, fearing someone was going to materialize there. Maybe a ghost who'd escaped the underworld just to keep me company. I felt all alone in the entire world. Or maybe I was alone in a new world, one that was being shifted into something unfathomable.

And now, I was the one riding the subway at night with a gun.

PART III

Time Unseen

1

That night I dreamed about my encounter in the subway. The man was now dressed in red, with a winter jacket that was too tight for him.

My defensive battle went down more or less as it did in the real world. But the more I worried about staying alive, the less coordinated was the passing of time. As I climbed over the platform's edge, the man vanished in front of my eyes.

I then noticed an illuminated area on the arched walls of the tunnel. Red paint was dripping heavily, and a message had been smeared over some old, fragmented movie posters.

YOU CANNOT SAVE YOURSELF

As soon as I read it, the text blurred and went away like smoke. The train was entering the station. It was empty. The station was also empty.

I found myself lying in my father's bed, still dressed like the night before. There was enough light outside my room to see the gun on the night table, a dead black-and-white bird.

Even before I made breakfast, I was desperate to get in touch with Julian. It felt as if we were in substantial danger, but I hadn't figured out what it was. Phones were all hard-wired back then, and answering machines weren't common, so it took some time to be reassured his phone was ringing in an empty room.

I wasn't thinking particularly straight, even after two cups of coffee. So, I called the direct line of my school's secretary and announced I was sick (stomach bug) and couldn't go to class. But then, I did exactly the opposite of what one should do after calling in sick—I took the bus straight to the Gorostiaga School for Lost Souls. Owing to my worried demeanor, and the very pale face I had, nobody argued with my showing up while sick. The section preceptor who received me probably assumed that, first, I'd wanted to find my friend to get help with the homework, and, afterwards, I would want to go home and keep vomiting. People had started to reinterpret my life according to my own lies.

Unfortunately, Julian hadn't shown up. I was asked if he'd eaten the same spoiled fish I had invented, since he had failed to call and excuse himself. Too bad, the whole trip had been in vain and now I had a growing queasy feeling in my stomach, as if I'd really eaten a sickening dinner.

I went to Julian's home, hoping he really was sick and hadn't undertaken his stupid adventure of hitching a ride to the military underworld. His mother answered at the door's intercom and asked me to go upstairs, which activated even more my ongoing stomach sensitivity—this time, the fear of confronting another attempt at seducing me. Luckily, Dorita was distracted, getting ready for a job interview and trying to look her best in a long skirt and white blouse—pretty in a sexy-librarian kind of way. When she turned and reached down for telephone notes, I tried not to look at the plump curve of her butt, so noticeable with the tight skirt.

It looked as if I wasn't going to get anything out of my trip. But Dorita unexpectedly came to the rescue and said something about Julian hanging around places he liked the most. To calm himself down, she said, and because he needed to meet someone nearby.

That random statement suddenly narrowed down where Julian could be. He didn't have any preferred walking grounds other than

Parque Lezama, a park near the corner of Buenos Aires's famous riverfront neighborhood, La Boca. Julian would spend entire afternoons at the Café Britanico across the park; it was famous as an early hangout of the legendary Argentine writer Julio Cortázar, where he had written his first novel.

I asked myself, Why not? and What do I have to lose? I said goodbye to my friend's slutty mother with my best job-hunting wishes.

When I got to the street I felt that the sun was very bright. Reality finally collided with fiction, and I sustained myself against a tree while vomiting imaginary fish.

2

I got off the *colectivo* at a stop too many blocks away from Lezama Park. It had been months since I'd taken a stroll in the San Telmo neighborhood. Some of the alley-like cobblestone streets intersecting Defensa Street resembled what the city must have been at the beginning of the twentieth century. A street thug of the times—later known as a *guapo*, a word meaning courageous—could have appeared at any time, ready to dance a tango or knife someone over priorities concerning a woman or a corner's ownership.

By the time I reached Café Británico, at the park's northwestern corner, I was worrying that my friend might not have been there. I didn't have many more options, so it was either that or nothing.

But Julian was there. Across the street and in a corner window, I could see him talking with a man hidden beyond the window's frame. I couldn't risk crossing the street, or Julian would see me. Unfortunately, I wouldn't be able to hear them from afar.

To solve my problem, Julian decided to call the waiter with a gesture broad enough to come from someone drowning. A minute later, he was opening the bar's door for another guy, who smoothly passed him by and got out.

I had no doubts the middle-aged man—dark hair with graying temples—who followed Julian to the street was D'Agostini. Dressed in dark gray as a sign of his profession, but with a black sports jacket, the archbishop could easily blend in anywhere in the city.

Arnaldo José María D'Agostini—Archbishop D'Agostini—had gone to incredible lengths to hide his human name from the masses. Even Julian, obsessed with detective work, was especially proud of having uncovered it. I was more partial to the idea that the archbishop was used to hiding things from the limelight, so his self-disappearing was merely practice for him.

He was a wiry man and may have been involved in sports when young. For some reason, his muscled body reminded me of Bruce Lee. There was a lot of energy in how he moved, and a youth saved at the time and put in motion later to support goals of power. If only ten percent of what Julian had told me about the archbishop and his tight connection with the military was true, power, evil, and spying were second nature to him. Faith was only to be used in the service of these goals.

I was already afraid of the man, although it would have helped me to know that one day D'Agostini would meet his match in another mysterious character—Alejandro, a secretive vigilante who would appear out of nowhere to clean up the ranks of the torturers—and, like many of his victims, the archbishop would forever disappear in the Atlantic Ocean. But this is another story, better to be told by someone else.

Julian was in his best subservient personality, at times looking down at his own shoes, and, even though I couldn't hear their conversation, seemingly on good terms with the archbishop. D'Agostini kept smiling, with whites even paler than him, and a couple of times lightly touched Julian's shoulder. Whatever Julian had said was working.

I decided to cross the street diagonally, looking away to hide my face. I wanted to hear Evil speak.

I hid at the entrance of a building, close enough to see them. "I just would like you to say it again," the archbishop said. "Just to be sure."

"Why?"

"It's a perilous trip, the one you want to take. And we don't like our work to be public."

"I've told you I won't say anything."

"That might not be enough for my friends in the services. They're kind of protective of their facilities."

"I can't tell you more of what I've said already, Father. I need to see for myself how you're taking care of those traitors. They've done a lot of damage to the country."

"Let's save the nationalism for Martínez and *his* friends," D'Agostini said, his sternness visible even from where I stood. "They'd like to hear about that—I, on the other hand, I'm a man of faith and care only about the work of the Lord."

I saw Julian flinch, showing teeth at the archbishop's comment. That was what I'd been afraid of—the hate could show at the worst time.

D'Agostini was too bent in his own brand of social propaganda to notice the brief clinching of Julian's fists. "I will allow you to come with me and see what we're doing," he said. "I hope you will understand how it serves the Church, to show our compassion in front of evil—the worst kind, that, like anesthesia, numbs people into atheism and chaos. You'll see, my child."

"Yes, Father. I'll be there."

"Remember, eight thirty tonight, at the corner of San Juan and Boedo. Be there, or we could have a problem."

D'Agostini touched Julian's shoulder again; Julian, in turn, lowered his head as if seeking forgiveness. The archbishop mumbled something I didn't hear, maintaining my illusion of watching a public confession with the background of Lezama Park.

Without saying goodbye, D'Agostini turned, walked around the street's corner, and disappeared. He'd left Julian staring into the vast greens of the plaza, right in the direction where they sank into the low housings and tiny harbor of La Boca. I was sure my friend was imagining a future where he became history's great instrument for change and justice. A superhero. Or a savior.

Dangerous, dangerous ideas. The priest—whether the archbishop, or anyone who knew Christianity—could have warned Julian of what people do to saviors.

3

I almost crashed into Julian as he started to rush back along Defensa Street. His face told most of the story about his past meeting—elation mixed with anxiety, and the pressing need to keep what he had done secret from me.

"Edgardo? What are you doing here?"

"Didn't you tell me you were meeting with D'Agostini?" I was trying to skip the part about searching for the location of his meeting. He noticed it.

"So, you saw me with him."

"Yes, I did. And what did you talk about?"

"Well...he didn't say much," Julian said, still juggling in his mind how I'd made it to that particular corner without him telling me anything. Perhaps the student was surpassing the master.

"I...wanted," Julian spoke again, stopping after each word, "to see...those places, you know."

Nobody back then would name the military's detention centers as the close-enough copies of Nazi concentration camps they were.

During the next few seconds, I caught a glimpse of another Julian and I didn't like him at all. I was seeing the conflicted person who could think, in another pocket of his mind, that what the military—and perhaps the Church—were doing with the country could ultimately be the right thing. Clean the imperfection; destroy another kind of opposing conspiracy. A human conflict coming from untold generations of genes trying to isolate themselves from others.

I knew it wasn't just him, his own confusion. It was the worst of us, what had always managed to come back in new forms. I remember thinking then that we were doomed as a species.

Since I knew Julian was lying, I pressed on. "So, you aren't going to go...there, I mean to their prisons. Is he not taking you?"

"No, my friend. He's not—this's over."

"I'm sorry." By then, we were both lying, and I didn't care much.

"Don't worry. We have a lot to do if we want to find your Mariana."

It was the first time he'd used her name—and it sounded fake, as if he was talking about a geographical landmark. Let's go and find the Mariana Trench.

I was going to have to revise the terms of my friendship with Julian, but not right then. He could still help me, and so I tried to go back to what I cared about. "Did you ask D'Agostini? About her."

"He said he'll ask around."

That part of his conversation with the archbishop I hadn't heard from my hiding spot, so I gave him the benefit of the doubt. "We need to get an answer, and soon."

"Yes, don't worry. Would you like to get coffee and talk?"

"Thought you just got some."

"This place inspires me."

"Like Cortázar."

"So, you know about it. Let's get coffee—I can always get another espresso—and I'll tell you what I have learned about what he was secretly doing while writing at the Británico."

Julian was all smiles again, but I had crossed a Rubicon of sorts with him and would need more proof of his trustworthiness. It was a sad recognition.

As I opened the café's door, the same one D'Agostini had gone through minutes earlier, I decided that I'd had enough of lies and misdirection. I was going to find out what Julian was doing, also see the truth by myself.

It was around five in the afternoon, about three hours from when my friend was going to have the meeting he wasn't telling me about. A meeting with those D'Agostini should have considered as Satan's own angels. But the priest—like apparently all of us—had been telling too many lies to know that.

4

After a round of espressos, Julian left without saying much. The two hours I'd have to wait for his meeting with D'Agostini would have been an eternity if I'd spent them walking the boring streets of San Cristóbal, so I started to meander back and forth along Defensa Street. It was the equivalent of pacing around my living room.

There was an antique market in San Telmo I liked, and I tried to buy there an old shaving kit for my father. First, I reviewed the Gillette type, mechanical shavers that held rectangular razors, but I was disillusioned by their mediocre quality. Then, I remembered that my father was used to shaving military-style, with those straight razors one swipes on a leather strop. I found a Solingen set in decent shape and at a reasonable price. While I was paying for it, I wondered why I wanted to give my father a gift while I was spending so much time criticizing him. I concluded that I didn't have any real family, and he was fulfilling the roles of likeable and unlikeable members of a more extensive set of relatives.

Before I left the stand, something odd happened. The seller— an old woman with thick glasses—mentioned that someone, who looked just like me but was quite a few years older, had asked the day before for the same shaving kit. I didn't make much of it at the time, as most Americans would seem alike to a pair of old Argentine eyes; I was sure the gentle lady was trying to trick me into paying more for my purchase.

* * *

I was having one of those days when I was distracted and got late to all my appointments. Night had fallen before six—it was close to winter—and I had dumbly tried to reach San Cristóbal by *colectivo* just when most people were getting back to their homes. Bad idea, at a very bad time.

Julian and D'Agostini were at the corner where the Café Homero Manzi stood—from before all of us had been born, and probably destined to remain long after we are all dead. I had no choice but to follow them from way behind, barely getting to cross San Juan Avenue before being crushed by a stampede of evening traffic.

Wherever my friend and the priest were going, they were taking their sweet time. They finally stopped at the front of a warehouse, and a man in dark clothing showed up; he started to wildly gesticulate towards a sliding metal door.

An old Mercedes-Benz truck suddenly came to a stop across the driveway, and then lurched backwards to point straight to the street, its rear near the entrance's side. I noticed that a Ford Falcon was parked just one car away from my watch point; it was all part of a well calculated choreography. The place's distance from the street lights and the cave-like entry of the facility, plus the broad avenue that thinned itself right there, all allowed those policemen to keep complete control of the surroundings. Another Ford Falcon was parked across the street—more eyes, more guns, all ready to defend against Montoneros or whoever would try to take over their post.

They all knew each other well and, when it came to the rest of us, there were no great secrets between them. Everybody was hiding the mess from the prying eyes of the multitude.

We were the sheep and they—all of them—were the wolves.

* * *

The warehouse's sliding doors opened with a chirring noise, and the truck backed down into the dark. Its weak front lights turned off, and darkness enveloped the entire sidewalk. One of the Ford Falcons crossed the street and parked behind the truck, sealing the shadowy driveway. Two men came out from the car and started to watch around in preplanned patterns.

For a moment, I worried that in the commotion someone was going to see me; if they did, I was sure no civilian would intervene to save me. If anyone passing through saw something—anything—that person would quickly cross the street to disappear into the better illuminated avenue.

After what felt like an eternity but was no more than ten minutes, D'Agostini and Julian approached the entrance. The archbishop was holding Julian's shoulder and showing him something behind the truck, pointing with his free arm; I'd swear I could see Julian's surprised expression even from the opposing sidewalk.

Collecting all the energy I had at hand, I walked toward the side of the Mercedes truck that was farther away from the car and all those visitors, hoping their attention was now focused on the truck's cargo. There were two large trees on the half of the block closer to the bustle of San Juan, and they created a very black spot where I could hide. I reached it like a soul lost at sea, breathless and shaking under what understandably was major fear for my life.

I was close enough to the truck to be able to peek inside the dark entrance to the warehouse. What I saw was what I'd expected to see, but it still scared me even more.

A row of people was slowly making its way out of the truck. Flanked by soldiers in civilian clothing, they were being helped one by one to get down, and then endorsed to another soldier, who took them inside the cave-like area further ahead. At first, I thought they were hurt—or blind, so much were they stumbling—but then realized they'd been hooded and handcuffed, so they couldn't find an exit from their wheeled prison.

Stupidly, I wanted to see more and forgot why I was there and how my friend—and D'Agostini—were standing on the other side of the truck. I took a couple of steps and then realized I could be in serious trouble. I was in the line of sight of at least three of the policemen.

Before I could do anything else, someone grabbed me from behind and I thought my life was coming to an end. I stopped breathing without much air left inside and felt pain in my deflated chest almost immediately.

A hand, thick and strong as a large piece of wood, pulled me toward the face wall of a house, sequestering my body into its receded entrance. The hand belonged to a huge guy—at least a head taller than me, and with shoulders as broad as a dinner table. If he were to hit me, with those hands or really any significant part of his physique, I wouldn't survive it.

"I'm Rafa," he said, trying hard to be heard just by me. "Anibal sent me."

"Anibal?"

"Well, you know, it was Pocha. You've both got her interested in getting D'Agostini to help get Mariana back."

There I was, with another Montonero, and not ten steps away from their worst enemies. My world was indeed a very strange place.

5

"I need to see what happens to my friend," I said, trying to speak as lowly as I could. Even that whispering was tainted by my nervousness.

"Don't you worry about your friend."

The big guy spoke with soft, worn words, and even a few of them told me he came from the lower classes. Although Montoneros had started within Argentina's middle class, the movement preached a Peronist gospel that appealed to the oppressed working class. And it had gained many members from workers who sought to help the country by arming themselves to fight for their rights, dreaming about the day when socialism—or communism, although I don't think many knew the difference—would rescue them from poverty and from the right-wing dictatorships always ready to get hold of the reins of power.

I finally collected enough courage to speak in a normal voice. "Why do you say that? Look, he could be taken."

"He's with D'Agostini. He likes to first play with his mouse."

"His? What do you mean?"

"Shhh, don't be so loud or *we* will be in trouble. Don't want to have to grab my 45."

Again, the solid hand grabbed my shoulder and pulled me

closer. I could see a shiny edge to the guy's eyes, even in an almost complete darkness.

"This is something he does often. Take candidates for a tour—to test them and decide if they could be of help. Or to scare them into silence."

"But he could also kill him—my friend, Julian."

"Sure. This is a dangerous game. See?"

"See what?"

"The bishop is taking him away from the entrance. It's the usual way he does it—he doesn't take them inside the first time."

"Would he bring him here again?"

"Yes, once or twice more. Maybe make him hold the communion cup while he blesses the...condemned."

"Do they kill all of them?"

"Why don't we get a little farther away? You're worrying me with all this talking."

We slowly retreated, walking very close to the street's old rowhouses and jumping to take refuge in their inner entrances whenever possible. We went about half a block's distance before Rafa felt relaxed enough to stop and light a cigarette.

When Rafa talked again, he sounded calmer and his words didn't betray his upbringing as much. I saw a good-looking, big guy, with heavy facial bones that would withstand a blow with a wrench. I was tall but felt tiny against a body twice my size. This was the defense of the Montoneros football team—here, our American football. And he knew to be a disposable, the kind of soldier they send to charge at the frontlines after wishing him well and letting him say goodbye to all his buddies.

"Don't worry about...*Julián.*" Rafa's Spanish accentuation of my friend's name was so strong it reminded me how many times I'd forgotten to say it the Argentine way.

"You keep saying this, but we've left him alone."

"With D'Agostini."

"You seem to believe that the priest is some kind of saint."

"No, not really." Rafa had a wonderful smile, natural and clear.

"What are we going to do?"

"Hope he's scared enough not to want to see D'Agostini ever again."

I couldn't have said it better. Obviously, Rafa had street smarts compensating his being a goon for what we'd now call a terrorist organization.

Although that night I was having doubts about who the terrorists were.

I had to try one more time. "Aren't we going to do anything about this?"

"Let it go. It's...it won't be the best night for me to try some rescue operation."

"Why? Is it your day off?"

Again, the disarming smile. "No, and don't be a smart ass. We have some things going on, and I don't want to alert the troops about tonight being an 'active' night."

I didn't know what he meant, but I knew he wasn't going to tell me more.

"Let's go," said Rafa. "We have to go to Cristina's."

"Cristina?"

"My girlfriend. She's Mariana's friend."

Apparently, I was going to meet one by one the entire Montoneros organization. Like the Mafia, they were checking me out too, just as the military were checking Julian. New people, a growing end for their organizations. And the potential for more killings. From either side.

I turned around to look back at the warehouse's entrance. The truck was now gone. Julian and the archbishop were gone. I had obviously lost my chance to peek inside the mechanism that was destroying the country. The war that was being fought against the citizenry was for sure dirty—as it will be forever known—but it

145

managed to hide its dirt very quickly, out of sight but never out of mind.

I wished a mental Godspeed to my friend and took Rafa up on his offer. Sometimes, seeking alliances is the best approach. And I had the feeling I needed as many friends as I could gather.

The brightly lighted corner of San Juan and Boedo welcomed us. From the times of knifing *guapos* and a newborn tango, when San Cristóbal was a most dangerous spot of Buenos Aires, that corner had seen the worst of the city pass by.

The current times were no exception.

6

The ride with Rafa took me to yet another part of Buenos Aires I didn't know—the Flores neighborhood, midway between downtown and the city's north boundary. He had a beat-up Fiat 600, an impressively minute two-door compact, the kind of car that could barely cope with such a giant in its front seat. We made it, but I could count every bump in the intervening pavements.

We were two blocks from a large park, and the street was submerged in darkness under the blossoming canopies of old trees. Cristina's house was an old cement-front house, recently remodeled but still showing its original, very baroque frontispiece decorations. As we entered the long main hallway, it was clear this wasn't single-occupant housing. There was an ancient segmentation, forming a row of apartments that probably grew out of the misfortune of a previous owner, who'd parceled the property into a multi-family housing.

Most Argentines rented—we, the Westons, were no exception—as the purchase cost for houses was outrageous and credit had become extinct with the faltering economy; a great deal of the middle class didn't even have a bank account.

"Are you scared?"

Rafa was smiling and might have misinterpreted my meditative silence for fear.

"No, it's not that. I was just thinking about these houses…"

"Yeah, it's a neat place. Each apartment has a big patio against the main corridor; well, it's just on the other side of the wall."

A long, tall wall ran on the right side of the open hallway that connected the apartments—all were on the lower level, and the two I saw first had small rooms upstairs from their patios. These were large containers for city people, who believed they were living alone, as if on a countryside home in Italy or Spain. But it was a pauper's version of those houses, designed just to keep the illusion of individuality.

* * *

The girl who opened the painted metal door—after carefully peeking through a small glass window—was so beautiful it shocked me.

I could barely say hello and, instigated to repeat myself by Rafa, tried to complete a single sentence as if I suddenly couldn't speak at all in Spanish. Cristina had long hair like Mariana, but it was lighter and wavier, not what I was accustomed to seeing in Argentine girls. And her face was very smooth, with big, bright green eyes. She didn't have the animal intensity of Mariana, but there was such peace and beauty in my rescuer's girlfriend I wanted to have a few minutes of silence to contemplate her like a classic painting. I also began to remember my kiss with Mariana, and my lips felt a little twinge of interest in comparing Cristina's perfectly shaped mouth with hers. All of this happened in a few seconds, while I was trying to recompose myself and talk as a supposedly almost-fluent Spanish speaker.

If Mariana was an attractive girl who accidentally had been turned into a vampire, Cristina was the story's good witch. Just like that.

* * *

Rafa left to try contacting Anibal, but not before asking Cristina to stay with me. If he knew that I'd been fantasizing about kissing his girlfriend, I'd probably be in urgent need of a dentist.

We sat in two garden chairs, incongruent in the middle of a block in one of the world's largest cities; the patio's corners were crowded by pots with flowerless plants. Something, whatever it was, plunged us into deep conversation. The twenty minutes we spent together seemed to stretch into days. I had never talked so much, so soon, and with such uninhibited pleasure, with a girl. I didn't know if that was the way she was with others, or if I needed to be comforted by a female figure, but my delight was its own reward, and we flew over subjects like we'd been friends for ages.

Cristina Contiglia was from a poor background; her mother was a seamstress and her father an unemployed machine operator. They had come from the interior provinces to the country's capital, back when Juan Perón was in power and enjoyed moving masses of immigrants to Buenos Aires. Her mother now felt they owed everything—the little they had—to Perón and his wife Eva, forever known as just Evita. Cristina was cruising with difficulty the first year of university, trying to study Economics, but she first had wanted to be a writer. As for how she got involved—and in what sequence—with Rafa and the Montoneros, she was uncharacteristically vague.

Somehow, we got into a conversation about English literature. She loved D.H. Lawrence and William Blake—had read them in translations—and was tackling Aldous Huxley. We were still talking about the complexities of *Point Counter Point*, which I had read fully in English and mostly in Spanish, when Rafa came back and did a double take, probably after noticing how close our faces were as we spoke and gesticulated.

Cristina went inside to look for something, and the big guy cleared his throat before speaking. He looked even more impressive in the patio's lighting—I could now see a thin scar running down his left cheek, probably from a forgotten fight before he grew into a giant. "I talked with Anibal," he said, "and he says we did the right thing, not intervening with your friend. Too much is going on."

"Too much," I said. "What's too much?" I didn't want to sound angry, but I was.

"You understand that, if I tell you, you're compromised."

"Compromised?"

"Yes, Edgardo," Rafa said, looking away and trying hard to think what to say. "What we're doing is dangerous, and they could..."

"It has already cost to Mariana a lot, hasn't it? And what about what my friend, Julian, is risking?"

"Julian got in this mess all by himself. And Pocha wants to know if he can get some useful information from the archbishop."

"Agreed. But, what about Mariana?"

"She also knew there were risks. Anibal thinks that maybe it's not too late for her."

"Why?"

"She's a small fish—they're really after Anibal."

"But they can torture her to get to him."

That did annoy Rafa, probably because it was both true and broke the logic Anibal had been selling to him. "I know," he said. "But I'm sure she's not..."

"Dead?" That single word from a returning Cristina stopped us from talking.

"Cristina, we can't be sure." Rafa's tension was visible as he tried to diffuse the real problem. He wasn't a bright ideologist, and it seemed he mostly did what he was told, which brought me to the question I had been asking myself: What could Cristina possibly see in that guy? A good lover? The nice guy I was sure he was?

"We do have a plan," Rafa said, after reflecting a little longer.

"And Mariana is part of it. We need her, and we're going to find a way to bring her back."

"You need her? Why?" I couldn't stop arguing for a better plan to rescue Mariana.

"We have..." Rafa was going to repeat himself but stopped for a few seconds to regroup. "Well, I'll tell you. We're going to intervene in the World Cup's transmissions—several times—and tell people our side of the history. Really, it will be more than..."

His next silence was very thoughtful, and I thank Rafa for thinking before crossing a line that could make me the potential subject of kidnapping and torture, or even get me killed. But it was too late; I'd crossed that line the first time I met Mariana.

"We have already interrupted some of the transmissions—Argentina versus Poland, and today we did it for our game against France. It's not perfect; one was in Mar del Plata, so they heard it only in the coastal area; the one today could reach only around La Plata. But it was our leader, Firmenich himself, who spoke for more than ten minutes at halftime. And now..."

"No, Rafa. Don't tell him *that*—it is a secret just for Montoneros." Cristina approached me from the side and grabbed my back. I felt the warmth of her body against mine and shuddered.

"He needs to know why we do this, Cristi, so they don't do anything foolish with his friend. Know why we're going to do anything to get our Mariana back. We are going to interrupt the last match of the World Cup, Edgardo, when the whole world is watching. And it would be amazing, because..."

"He doesn't need to know everything. *Please.*"

"He does need to know this: Mariana would help us to make our point, finally and totally."

I exploded with all my accumulated anger— "Why Mariana? Can't you get Firmenich to talk again —he's the chairman of your organization, isn't he?"

I had said too much, and Rafa's face twisted in a half-angry, half-condescending smile. "No, it won't be Firmenich," he said. "We are going to kidnap a top official, involved with the torturing, and *he* will give the message. Confess his crimes in front of the world. Mariana is the one who can get him for us. Martínez, that son of a bitch."

The last words caught me unprepared— "Martínez?"

"Yes, we'll take him and show the Argentine people what's going on."

I realized that I had been speaking to a group of people who could have been living the last few days of their lives. And I was one of them.

We were all doomed.

7

I made the journey back to my apartment again in Rafa's tiny car; it seemed more comfortable on a second seating. Rafa was unusually talkative—he obviously liked me—and kept stressing the nobility of a foreigner who'd suddenly decided to risk his life to save a girl he had just met. Since Rafa would often risk his own life to rescue people—during his adventures as a Montonero—he related well to that sort of impulse. And he said something to that effect, hidden in the hyperbolic style many Argentines used, which always reminded me of those patients who asked their doctors for advice about hypothetical friends—friends who were most likely themselves.

All through the trip, I'd kept playing with the surprisingly small package the market seller had made from the straight razor and its bulky strop. It looked like meat wrapped in a newspaper by a butcher. I thought the razor would be a good gift and my father would enjoy it—a reminder of his rarely-discussed years serving in the American military.

I was exhausted but tried to be polite with Rafa, saying my goodbyes to him in the repetitive manner the locals would say until next time, sometimes for half the length of a short meeting. Also, I didn't want to eliminate the possibility of seeing Cristina again—so taken I was with her—and thus I behaved like a good friend who wants to organize the next outing with his in-group.

One thing we did talk about remains distinct in my memory, perhaps a byproduct of having behaved so carefully in Rafa's company. He said again something he shouldn't have.

"Don't you worry, we'll find Mariana."

"You apparently believe you guys have everything under control."

"We never do, and that's the best part. But..."

"But what?"

"We have a...an important meeting this week. Nobody's supposed to know."

"And? Are you going to tell me?"

Rafa thought for a second, and I could see a thought—*Why not? He's almost one of us*—as it crossed his mind. "The *action*," he said, "is going to be this Saturday. We'll meet on Friday to discuss it—I can't tell you much more, but Anibal is sure we'll be able to rescue Mariana."

"How's that...?"

"I can only tell you this for now—be patient."

I gave up. I had gotten as much as I could from my accidental protector. "All right," I said. "I trust you. And please, keep me informed of what happens from now on."

"Sure. Don't worry. We will topple the Junta, get rid of these assholes for good. You *have* to trust me on that."

And there I was, parked with a terrorist in front of my midtown Córdoba Avenue apartment, and just a short walk from the Colón Theatre, an endearing symbol of the ultra-conservative Argentine elite. We were also across from Lavalle Park, at the edge of the city's lawyer district, where there was a whole universe of legality that on some days could even look real.

The irony of all this was amazing; there we were, a professional and a budding revolutionary, plotting the overthrow of a military government.

Just a few days before, I had been the shy kid that bullies would target. Now, I had a knife—sort of—at hand and a gun stored in my bed table's drawer.

* * *

I had barely made it to my apartment and left the jacket and the package with my dad's gift over a corner chair when the phone rang. It was the doorman, immediately bragging about being at his job at 2 a.m. He said that someone was coming to see me, a friend.

In my state of exhaustion, I thought it was Rafa, not remembering I'd seen him depart in the direction of Flores.

My door opened almost on its own, revealing a Julian still dressed as he was when meeting D'Agostini. His face was so pale, it seemed color had been drained not just from his cheeks and lips but also from all his internal organs.

He looked as if he'd narrowly survived an encounter with a vampire and had only a few drops of blood left in him.

8

I started to make coffee and sat Julian in the most pliable of our armchairs—my father's favorite—leaving him alone with repeated encouragement to take it easy and relax in silence for a while. He seemed ready to have a panic attack—his tension was so contagious it made me jittery.

Coffee worked its strange magic of both awakening people and making them more relaxed and sociable. Still, Julian bore remnants of his nightmarish night, and I wondered if I should have spiked his drink with some of my father's whisky. Julian went from a stuttering, monosyllabic acquiescence to a more continued narration of his adventures with D'Agostini.

I decided not to interrupt him, as I usually did whenever he was explaining something. *Only talk when it's essential, when you can learn something new*—I kept repeating this thought like a short prayer. But it's hard to keep one's private promises.

That night, it was hard for Julian to stop talking. "I told you that before," he said, "and I tried to do it just now...but it's hard to clear my mind. I've met D'Agostini a few times, as he's a good friend of my father—from his business dealings, but he never says which ones. Every time I had a chance, I told the archbishop that I sided with the government and its quest to clean up the mess of people like Montoneros...those armed beasts." The word "beasts" was charged with such emotion I felt how much Julian despised the counterrevolutionaries. He was searching—just like me—for clarity and logic in his world, and the Montoneros were a source of confusion.

I mentally scratched out any mention of my recent dealings with Rafa.

"The archbishop," Julian said, "he eventually thought it had been *his* idea to let me see what's going on behind the curtains. I had just met with him at the Británico when you showed up early...today? Or was it yesterday?"

"Yesterday," I said, raising my watch.

"Well, yesterday it is. He told me to see him in one of their locations, I mean, one of the centers of detention; I guess he picked a very small one, in the city. I tried to be excited at my meeting with him, but I was so scared—it's easy to research these things on paper, but when you are actually there, it's scary." Julian looked for another sip of coffee in his empty cup, but I didn't want to leave him to get more coffee. If his story's thread broke, it might never get restarted.

"What was I saying? Oh, yes, the place. It seems they still have many of those detention hangars, hundreds all around the country. People are taken to them daily—from very long lists that a committee makes and updates."

"With torture thrown in the middle." I couldn't resist interrupting him.

"Well, sure. But D'Agostini says that's a necessary evil; that it will all stop when they've collected enough information about these...groups. The Montoneros, ERP, MOR..."

"The MOR was a political party, you know." I had started talking and now couldn't stop.

"*Was* is the right word. All these leftist parties are violent and have no place in a democracy."

"Democracy? What kind of democracy destroys anyone it doesn't like?"

"D'Agostini says that we'll go back soon—in a few years at most—to a better, more solid democracy. President Videla told him that."

"*Presidente* Videla—that's just how he calls himself. And you believe him—do you believe any of these people?"

"The military is just continuing what started during Isabel Perón's years...she was a democratically elected president."

Julian had been hypnotized by D'Agostini. My friend was sometimes just a mirror for other people's views. And my role as friend was to keep waking him up from those trances.

"No, Julian, she wasn't," I said. "It was Perón who made her his VP, and, when he died, she had to assume the presidency. Her excesses were the excuse for the military to take over. And now they say that they're just following her orders?"

"You are becoming quite a historian, my friend, the American."

I blushed, taken by surprise as I expounded a passionate—and progressively irrational—argument, worthy of a true Argentine. Julian laughed, as there was a little ridicule in me advising him about the true course of his country's recent history.

"I'm tired of arguing the archbishop's points," he continued, finally more conscious of his unconscionable arguments. "He *will* show me more of what they're doing, how they extract information that's useful. He says it's all very humane."

That was my turn to laugh, but underneath, I was very concerned about my friend. He'd absorbed too much of the military's propaganda, distilled and concentrated by an expert sorcerer, so that the potion was precisely compatible with his physiology. I could lose him in the darkness of the other side.

"Let me continue, Edgardo. They have to be rough—these are, after all, rough people. D'Agostini compared the process to a tooth extraction without anesthesia. He'll take me to a small facility..."

"Dentists without anesthesia? Are you hearing yourself, Julian?

This is crazy."

"I want to see, with my own eyes. No more researching newspapers and the news. I've got to see if what these people are doing will change history. If someone can make a better future."

If someone can make a better future. The most prophetic words Julian would ever utter.

I propped myself up from the armchair and finally got the strength to shake Julian's shoulders— "Are you insane? You're letting them brainwash you...I thought you wanted to expose their crimes."

We sat in silence. Julian was upset with me for intervening in his fabricated world, which he was keeping rational with a great roll of duct tape.

At the end, friendship prevailed. Julian made a joke about my soon-to-come honorary Argentine citizenship. And I laughed, feeling ridiculous for taking in so much of a country I was just visiting. I reminded myself how I could leave any time I wanted. But I knew that wasn't true.

I had understood, on that desperate night, how much I loved the country of my grandmother, that dysfunctional and malformed society which, after over a hundred years of independence, didn't know the first thing about freedom.

9

This time, I was the one who sent Julian to take a shower and get rid of his nerves. I wasn't doing so well myself and received the first hints of daylight sitting on my bed. My life had fallen into disarray. Perhaps it was time to start packing my emotional bags—and the real ones. I couldn't be living like that—halfway between everything, and nowhere close to being settled—when a simpler life waited for me in the States, boring but preferable to the violence that was erupting in my expatriate stay.

In that desolated state, I wandered out of my bedroom and opened the sliding glass door to our balcony over the Córdoba Avenue; a nice breeze penetrated the somewhat stale air of the apartment. I came back to the living room and hauled several weeks' worth of newspapers I'd taken from our doorstep over to its dark wood table.

For some reason, I immediately zoomed in to the scattered news about those meteorites in Southern Bolivia. Apparently, people were already dismissing those news, and talking about only the first one of the two as possibly real.

"A presumed artifact fell in Orán last Monday, on May 8, in Argentine territory."

"On May 9 and 14, airplanes were spotted in the remote area

of 'El Bolsón de los Fantasmas'...the ascension to The Valley of the Ghosts takes about 2 days...."

"Mount Zaire was partially collapsed by the impact, and the object is now buried under hundreds of cubic meters of ground...."

"A meteorite, not a flying saucer, would have fallen in Salta, Argentina."

"The US Embassy denies any involvement of NASA scientists."

A colorful magazine my father subscribed to carried even more contradictory information about the meteorite. It mentioned that the impact happened on May 8, but then it said that "since May 6, Mario Posadas, a telephone operator, has been detecting regular interference in communications." And, although the more recent newspapers reassured the public that NASA was not involved at all, one of them added, "Two NASA pilots toured the Zaire Hill surroundings and collected fragments of the object."

After finishing my quick scan of the confusing stories, the facts were still dancing in my head. My reading speed increased, together with my heart rate.

"A meteorite of singular proportions hits the southern slope of Mount Zaire, in a remote region of Bolivia..."

"A metallic object fell on May 6, at 16:15 Bolivian time..."

"...an elongated object, spewing colorful rainbows."

"...a gigantic cylinder, clearly visible and of a very bright white color, expelling dark smoke."

"...the explosion was heard in a radius of more than 200 kilometers."

Comparing these articles about the meteorite affair, I reached the conclusion that, yes, something extraordinary and unexplained had happened. But I still couldn't understand how two meteorites could fall roughly at the same point, on a fast-rotating Earth, on consecutive days.

Then, it hit me. The impossibility made its own answer.

The meteorites, separated in time. In spacetime.

My mind sometimes did things like that, frequently enough to drive me crazy. It pooled separate events together, and then jumped to form a new, logical order with them. That's how I'd earned an incredible IQ score on that ill-fated test—only one in ten million people would have an unwieldy brain like mine.

Sometimes, two separate events are not separate at all.

I had been considering the problem all wrong. There weren't two meteorites but a single object that crashed—breaking in pieces—in that remote mountainous area.

A single object, crashing in the geographical neighborhood of Argentina as it was travelling through time.

Someone had travelled in time to our world, to that time and to a southern corner of the world. And their machine—their *time machine*—had crash-landed in linear time.

Crashed at two different times, but at the same place.

It was at that precise moment that I became a physicist.

But I couldn't stop and took the next step—putting together two other disconnected events. I remembered that, in the last day, two people—Rafa and Julian—had told me that what they were trying to do could change history. At least Argentine history.

What if those changes won't be for the long-term well-being of our species?

Was there any better reason to travel in time than to change what ultimately went wrong?

This thought horrified me so much I left the table and went back to the balcony, hoping for more cool morning air.

It was possible, not likely but possible, that one day we'd attempt to correct whatever had gone wrong with humanity. Something so bad it might justify the need to go back, pull the eraser, and start all over again.

But who would do it, and worse, why?

I had always thought that the present was just a narrow slit, unassailable and ever-changing. But if the future—such future where time travelers existed—was real, it lay on a continent of time that couldn't be seen from the present. Only there could I find the answers to my questions.

If there was an answer, it was to be found in time that was unseen.

I was still distressed by my bout of dangerous musing when my sight wandered down, to the sidewalk just underneath our building.

And then I saw the man again—that same man who'd tried to kill me.

He was there, looking up. Straight at my window.

I could swear he was smiling when he nodded and made an OK sign to me.

10

Whatever stress had been drained from Julian by taking a restful shower, it had seemingly migrated like an angry spirit to me. My face probably told him that in a flash.

I tried to find a distraction. "Julian, we need to go to school. We haven't been in class for days."

"Nobody cares these days. Everybody in this city is just waiting to go home and watch the Cup's matches."

But I had found a reason for keeping us, especially me, away from thinking about serious issues: I couldn't figure how close I was from the magic number of twenty-five missed class dates, beyond which I'd lose my status of regular student. And thus, I dragged Julian to our hated Gorostiaga School for the Dumb.

I left Julian outside the building, as he didn't seem too preoccupied with his own class departures. He looked like a dog that needed a leash; I wasn't sure if I was going to find him there when I came back.

The school principal's assistant was a fox-eared, greasily combed guy, who always tried to show empathy toward students but consistently felt short of it. We knew him as El Señor González, but nobody was sure of Mr. González's first name, or even if that was his real last name. I luckily looked the part of the sickly teenager, but wasn't sick enough to be completely forgiven. El Señor González consulted a large black book and came back with a diagnosis of intermediate danger—twenty-one-and-a-half absences—bad but still survivable by exercising caution. I wouldn't want to be labeled as a "chronic absentee"—he'd used the vernacular, *ratero*. Why Argentines referred to playing hooky as if it had something to do with rats escapes me.

After this, I had to attend, even perfunctorily, a couple of my classes for the day. I was in a dark mood, and Ricardo and his boys stayed away during the main break. Even a moron like him could sense when the guy he's usually bullying would gouge his eyes at the least provocation. I had to escape from my classroom for the last two hours of school. At some point, I walked alone down to the patio's back—the only student outside of class, invisible to all—and leaned against the glass wall to put my forehead in contact with the smooth, cold surface.

I didn't even notice I was again crying for Mariana.

* * *

When I finally reached the street, I found Julian mumbling incoherently. I worried that the word salad coming off his mouth was symptomatic of a stroke, but my knowledge of the world was—as for many adolescents—based on unearned confidence and not real acquired information.

I finally forced him to stop talking, breathe in a few times, and repeat the parts I wasn't getting of his scattered speech. That worked a little better for my understanding but wouldn't for anyone who didn't know my friend.

"Hey, Julian. Can you tell me this again? And this time, word for word, without skipping."

"They are—I saw one of them—and he looked at me. He was a big guy, and he looked a little like...someone I knew, maybe from when...from when *they*...but he was different. From afar he looked...I thought...but he was older."

"What are you saying?"

"Someone is following us."

I had enough candidates to run out of counted fingers. "Maybe it's a colleague of your friend D'Agostini, checking us out."

"Don't know, not sure...maybe you're right. But *that* face. I saw him. He looked at me...I felt something. And first couldn't even make up his...like, he had no face. It made my stomach curl."

He didn't have to tell me who that stranger was. I knew the feeling of not being able to make out a face that's staring at you, the awful sensation when your brain screeches to a halt because it can't process a certain bit of information. I was now sure this aftereffect of sighting the man meant we were being exposed to something not of our world.

Whatever was after me was now trailing Julian.

"Is he still around?"

"I think he left. But, Edgardo, you have to understand..."

"Understand what?"

Julian's face was contorted like whatever was going on inside his head. "He is...scary-looking. Maybe so much it's screwing my mind and I can't see him. Like the Gorgons."

"Come on, Julian. Don't speak Greek to me. It turns me on."

A little smile and a sign there was hope for Julian. I would just have to take him through another day. Maybe if I could stop him from attending that fateful meeting things would get better. Or maybe not, and I should let him get inside the cave of the monsters again. I truly didn't know.

One day at a time. I repeated that to myself. Again.

I kept patting my friend like one does with a well-behaved dog, or a misbehaving baby, until he calmed down and claimed he needed a cup of coffee. It was Julian's normal way of saying he was fine.

11

We made it to Julian's apartment by sunset. My sense of time had been shaken, and I have only a vague recollection of the afternoon and of Julian complaining about us drinking too many cups of coffee.

Julian's mom was at home and, after she saw our sorry state, took it upon herself to offer us even more coffee, any available cookies, and perfectly toasted ham-and-cheese sandwiches—Argentine *tostados*—she made for us in an instant. We would have eaten anything in close proximity to our mouths.

For once, the woman helped us, and I saw how well she could treat my friend when he came back in one of his downward moods. It was a mixture of pampering and consolation that took away ten years from him and left a little hurt boy in need of maternal warmth.

I might have remained my own age, since I couldn't help looking at her—this was a woman from whom even her everyday nickname, Dorita, smelled of man-hunter—and wondering why she'd constantly show herself in such a lustful light. I also guiltily considered how she could be twenty-some years older than us and remain so sexually attractive. Perhaps it was the unbelievably tight pants, which from some angles appeared painted on her skin.

She was a woman with edges, corners, and curves, in all the senses of those words.

After dealing with her needy son, she approached me as if I also needed comfort from a motherly figure—and I did; that much was obvious. She gave me another toasted sandwich; the bread was spongy, the cheese had melted but was crunchy at the edges, and the ham was barely wet. I took it as if it were water given to a man just out of the desert. And probably from the first time since I'd met her, we both smiled at each other.

Motherhood, like love, is a powerful force of nature.

* * *

I accompanied Julian to his point of encounter with D'Agostini, and he got more and more tense as we approached a corner of the Patricios Park, a large field that had survived through the city's history by changing hands between private landlords and public administrators. The park was in a chronic state of abandonment, common in other corners of the city. The military liked to paint walls to erase political graffiti, but they either lacked the training or weren't very interested in planting trees and watering grass.

The streets we were walking were well lit and full of shops, but, as we reached the park's edge, a dark wall of poorly lit spaces appeared across the large avenue. It made me feel as if we were reaching the coast of an ocean at night.

D'Agostini had given precise instructions to Julian, warning him he might not be there to receive him. I let my friend go, staying near the protective lights of a shoe store. He crossed Caseros Avenue in the direction of the park.

A Ford Falcon—another green one, or the same green one, or the only green one in the entire city—advanced to the point where Julian's jaywalking was going to intercept the park's sidewalk.

Even from a distance, I saw a gesture from the driver, pointing

Julian to sit on the car's empty backseat. And then the front passenger turned around and brought an offering to my friend—just as the car's backdoor closed.

I know I couldn't possibly have seen the object from where I was, but its image is so clear it's more likely I have superimposed it from the memory vaults of an unfortunately more knowledgeable future.

It was a black hood.

12

Time didn't move forward much during the next few hours. The night kept getting darker, and the park turned even more invisible without that many cars transiting *Caseros* Avenue. In great contrast to the night, the closed stores had left their lights turned on. I sat in a café and had breakfast—coffee with hot milk and two old croissants—even though it was close to midnight. Repeated the *café con leche* and added a sandwich with sweet Spanish ham. Occasionally, my eyes wandered down and I felt the weight of my body and the need to sleep.

But most of the time my eyes were fixed on the spot where the green Falcon had parked for a couple of minutes. The deal with the archbishop had been that Julian was going to be returned to the same corner after his infernal visit.

I waited. Thought about my encounters with the strange man, how he was dressed differently each time, and whether there was a rationale that could connect him with a race of super-intelligent aliens, who'd send such an emissary to another time. When my theories failed to make sense, I kept going back to waiting.

I was only semi-aware of time, and the waiting became the only thing I was aware of. Having some experience with the chronic lateness of a sizable portion of Argentines, I'd learned to sort of hibernate in the wait, moving only to ask for more coffee—this time, espresso—and another croissant, this one so stale that it had probably waited for me several days.

At first glance, Julian was walking very slowly and ramrod straight, as if he were crossing an invisible hanging bridge above a black abysm, which only resembled asphalt from afar. I'd already paid for my collection of empty plates and was out of the café in seconds.

Julian was a ghastly sight and his eyes were sunken and dark. It was cold, but he looked sweaty and his shirt's collar was soaked.

For a while, we floated together staring silently at each other, but then Julian did what he'd never done before—he hugged me, cradling his head on my shoulder. For once, I was the rock and, even amid all my uncertainties, I felt a little stronger. I was grateful and emotional that my friend was back; my body shivered, and my hands shook uncontrollably.

We remained on a street corner until we found the strength to start walking back to Julian's home, so very late at night it would have been quite concerning in a normal time. But nothing was normal, and nothing could match the horrors I assumed—and soon would know firsthand—were happening in that city.

Everywhere. Even nearby.

13

Julian's story was one many Argentines could have told, if they'd witnessed it and survived. He was both lucky and unlucky enough to have done both.

"I don't know how many people were there, in the detention center. At the entrance, they took me to an office—very official looking, with file cabinets and phones on each desk—and I had to wait there for D'Agostini. The people didn't even care I was staying near them; they said their names to me and made phone calls as if I wasn't there. I felt that I was being held at a police station for some traffic infraction, and it felt cold, but it might have been me. I was afraid, even more when D'Agostini showed up."

"Did he tell you anything useful?"

"Not really, the man's stiff as a piece of wood. He showed up in full gear—cassock and a big crucifix—as if ready for an exorcism."

Although I never saw that crucifix, I have a clear image of the priest and his cross. I kept talking, trying to slow down my walking before we got too close to Julian's neighborhood. "Did you talk to any of the military people? Maybe we can get some names, people who can help..."

"I know. To get back your Beatrice."

"Mariana."

"It was a joke. Dante, you know."

"I do know about Dante and his beloved. We studied it last year. But, what did you see? Tell me."

My friend was so good at rewriting and embellishing his memories that this was my only chance to get something closer to the truth.

"I walked with D'Agostini to an open space in the middle of the warehouse. It was noisy out there—I'm sure the place had been once a car repair shop, a *taller*. They had turned an air compressor on and two people in overalls were painting a car—bright red—and talking loudly. I'd think the neighbors would know what was going on; they should've called the police for...What am I saying? Calling the police is never a good thing. Either they wouldn't listen to you, or would mark you, so you would end up in a place like that."

"How could they have possibly known?"

"Let me talk, please."

I stopped, resting my back against a house's wall. We benefited for a few minutes from the yellow clarity coming to us from some weak street lights. Then, I nudged my friend to walk, and we took the next corner to the left, toward San Juan Avenue. I was worried that Julian would soon put on mental blinders and let his flexible mind forget—this time for his own good—what had happened. I wanted to get him to sit in any café still open so late at night, so I'd get to hear the whole story.

Julian was mumbling to himself. I paid more attention— "Yes, I told myself. It could be this or that, but I know what it was...and D'Agostini took my arm, like we were taking a stroll—the bastard— while we got across the illuminated part. There were several parked trucks covering the back, so you couldn't see inside. I recognized the blue color of police trucks, but those didn't have a single written mark of..."

"What? What did you see?"

"As we reached the back of the...it was horrible. There was a large box, like a cage; it was metallic...metal, I'm sure of it. People crowded inside, they had hoods like the one they'd put on me. Two guys in overalls walked around and pushed inside a guy who had a hand hanging out."

"God, that's awful."

"Yes. I asked D'Agostini, why so many. The son of a bitch smiled; he was so proud. And he kept walking, dragging me into the dark until we reached it."

"Reached what? It's hard to figure out what you're describing."

"It was dark; I couldn't see well."

Now it was Julian who stopped, a block short from the illuminated avenue. I swear that I felt monsters crawling in the dark, all around us.

He finally continued, "There was an enclosure way back. A brick house, something put together in a rush. D'Agostini took me inside—no windows, and two doors with rugs over them to soundproof it." Julian was trying to be journalistic in his description, probably thinking about the notes he was going to write. "We entered a dark room, and..."

"Tell me, you have to get it all out."

"The smell. Shit, urine, and something else—like burned meat. There was a table in the back...and two people. One was dressed in a gray lab coat and held down a thin guy, in underwear and with the head covered by a hood. He was shivering all over."

"Julian, what the hell were you doing there? This is crazy."

"I retched, and almost threw up. And they laughed—it was a demonstration, just to see how strong my stomach was. And D'Agostini, he got close to the captive and asked the men to take the hood off. He blessed him and started to pray, even tried to get him to touch a Bible and read a passage. Then...then, I saw his face."

Suddenly, I felt my own age, young and stupid as I was. I touched Julian's shoulder, and we quickened our pace to reach San Juan.

"It was a kid," Julian continued, "he looked barely fifteen. They probably did it in purpose, to show me they could do it to me too. They used one of those electric *picanas* on him, to put electricity through his body—it was a small unit, connected to two car batteries. They took his pants off and punched his balls first. He tried to yell, and when he did, they covered his mouth. The kid had red scars all over, couldn't move one arm, and..."

"What, Julian? What else?"

"They didn't ask him a single question."

* * *

It was too early for cafés to be opening for the new day, but one was receiving its fresh baked goods from a small white truck that apparently shuttled between all the neighborhood's coffeehouses.

I was exhausted and cold, and I welcomed having something hot. My overactive brain had already consumed my unappetizing midnight breakfast. At that point, I had a single, lone thought left in my mind: what these degenerates would do to a pretty girl, especially if they had to extract information from her.

I was shivering. It was a chilly morning, and the fires from the city's secret Hell weren't doing a thing to warm up the windows of our café. They were fogged by the morning's icy dew, and the blurred cars outside were followed by ghostly afterimages.

The sun would come up soon. For all those who were free enough to see it.

14

The entrance to my building was poorly illuminated and Don Manuel was a folded shadow behind his usual counter. "Don Edgardo," he said. "Someone is waiting for you upstairs. I let her in...she was insistent. Sorry."

"Don't worry," I said, but could already feel adrenaline cooling off my arteries. I considered and discarded names at great speed. It couldn't be police, I thought stupidly, because they were all men. I forgot to ask the age of my visitor, who could have been Pocha. And I didn't think it could be a Montonero delegate, as Rafa or Anibal would had come themselves.

I was so stunned that I jumped when the elevator's door closed and it started to rise. I couldn't think clearly, as so many of the people I'd thought could come didn't have my address—not a great obstacle for the police, though.

The door opened with a chirring noise. I stepped out trying to show some courage, having decided to confront whoever would come to my doorstep at dawn.

There was a female figure silhouetted by the hallway light. Sitting astride on the floor, her back against my door. One arm between her legs.

For a second, I feared that maybe she had a gun. But the arm was limp and poured like a stream to a hand. It was as if someone had left a puppet with its strings cut, right at my door.

Then, I saw.

It was Mariana.

15

I kneeled, trying to figure out whether she was hurt and how to lift her body.

"Edgardo."

"How's that..."

"They let me go."

"What happened? Did they do something...?" I was talking about more than her arm.

"I twisted my shoulder trying to get away. They kept me in a house—don't know where."

"Did they torture you?"

"No, someone came every day and kept them in check, told them not to touch me. Never saw him."

I was on my knees, hugging her. She smelled of earth, as if she had been buried. And she had been, but now was resurrected. "Don't worry," I said. "You're back."

"It's my family...they want them."

"I will protect you."

"They just interrogated me. About them."

I was finally holding her from below her good arm. Even standing up, she was heavy as if ready to faint, but kept mumbling something about saving her family—and about a boat, the noise of its engines.

"It's all right," I said to stop her. "All right."

"The police wanted to know about my family. Only that."

Mariana's eyes were closed, and I got to scan her face, which was covered by leftovers from blows, blows that had not been hard enough to be more than a plea for silence and obedience.

She kept talking, barely making sense, repeating that they'd only wanted to know about her family. Why her family? And why now, when it'd been reduced to a few mourning women?

"Let me open," I said, leaning her body against the wall. Held her arm while I unlocked the door. "Get in."

I closed the door with a thud. As soon as we were inside, I hugged Mariana, surely too hard for her state.

This time our lips found themselves in the dark. The street windows were closed, and their curtains lowered almost to the sills. The house was cold.

We were in a cave, and the only fire was coming from inside us.

I closed my eyes and made the little glares of daylight disappear. I was so tired, so ready to give up. Mariana's body was soft, barely steady, but now I could touch it. She was, finally, a real person.

At least as real as she had been before I'd lost her—already halfway to becoming a ghost.

* * *

I woke up and saw her lying next to me in the bed. I tried to remember, very hard, if we'd had sex. I got nothing from my body. I couldn't sense even a slight change in the rhythm of my heart.

I was as sad—with that body so near—as I had been before, when I could barely imagine her. Mariana was as much an unknown continent as she had been before. And I was less of an explorer than she deserved.

Her body seemed longer now, and it got lost in the ends of my

179

bed. But she seemed very small when I covered her with a puffy down blanket.

I touched her hair and my finger slipped, landing on her cheek, very close to where she had been stricken by a heavy hand; two purple lines continued over a mound of swollen face. My lips found her skin and her eyes twitched, just a little. Eyes that were not awake, and not dreaming, but resisting the light of consciousness. And I couldn't blame them—our world was full of false light, and if these eyes got to see any, it would be full of waking nightmares.

16

While Mariana slept—and occasionally snored—I managed the strength to call Cristina, so she could alert Pocha and Rafa that *they* had let Mariana go. I arranged to take Mariana to Cristina's home that same night, so she could meet her family and decide how to best hide from the police.

Since I was holding the receiver of my big rotary phone, I decided to reach Julian. I had left my friend so distraught I was uncertain about how, and if, he would be recovering from the previous night. Perhaps because of this concern, I wasn't going to tell him—no matter how much I wanted to—that Mariana had been released. He could interpret the event as a positive sign, and I didn't want him to improve his view of the military.

I was lucky enough to get him to answer by the third ring. "Well, I'm glad you're awake," I said. "What are you doing?"

"Keeping up with my investigations and trying to record yesterday's meeting."

"Do you still have any energy left?" I yawned to show what I'd meant, or maybe because I needed it.

"It doesn't matter. I have to be ready."

"Ready for what?"

"For my next meeting with D'Agostini."

"Are you going to go back? You can't—it's crazy."

"Not to the detection center."

"So, where then?"

"D'Agostini will introduce me to a leader."

"A leader of what?"

"You know him—Martínez."

"No—you can't."

"I will."

"You shouldn't."

"Are we going to keep playing this game?" Julian said, with an unfriendly voice.

I knew I'd been pushing him too hard— "I'll stop if you recognize that you're totally out of control."

"I can't stop. Not now."

"That, I can see. But, when are you seeing this...leader?"

"D'Agostini will introduce me to him tonight. He said he wants me to get involved. And Martínez wants me to attend a family function this weekend—he will be there."

"This is too much, Julian. What are you now, a member of the family? A permanent employee of the Junta?"

"It's not the Junta. Martínez is Chief of Operations."

"You mean Torturer in Chief."

"Can you stop, please? I will do it—it's too late."

"Too late for what?"

"To change my plan. I have a chance now to expose Martínez."

"No, you don't. They'll kill you."

"I will do what I can—and what I should," Julian added, trying to tone down his sourness. "Maybe you can come with me. Again."

"That would almost assure we both get killed."

I was trapped in a standoff from which there was no escape. I couldn't be in two places at the same time—protecting both Julian and Mariana. And I didn't want to use my ace—Mariana—with

Julian. I ended the call knowing it would be pointless to keep trying to stop him.

* * *

As I entered my bedroom, I saw Mariana's naked back in the lighted bathroom, just as she was using her good arm to pull a bath towel around her body.

There were three long welts crossing her back, diving deep into her left hip. And another mark near her shoulder—the raised seal of a belt buckle. Her back was so white the markings looked like a Chinese character made with deeply red ink.

17

The rest and the shower had made Mariana seem corporeal. She had borrowed a sweater of mine, which reeked of the lavender cologne my father had sent me for my birthday. For the first time, and forever after, I would love the smell of lavender.

She sat on the bed with me, covering her pained arm with the other. We both needed each other, and I wasn't going to leave her alone. Never again.

And she, she had managed to find my apartment from a joke I'd made after the movies. I had sung my address to her as if it were the most famous fake address in Argentina. From a tango about a second-floor apartment—mine was on the fourth—reachable only by elevator.

Corrientes 348, Segundo piso, ascensor.

A joke, and a subtle hint. She'd followed it, like a lifeguard, all the way back to me. Not to her family or the Montoneros. To me.

Something great had passed through us. I know it because, when I remember that day, I get emotional and feel my eyes burn.

* * *

"How did you get involved?"

Mariana looked at me. Those brown eyes, the way they shone. They were hypnotic. "There was no choice for me," she said. "They killed my father, my older brother, and took my aunt and her daughter...I couldn't stay still."

"Your mother—didn't she stop you?"

"Her? No way; she will go down with the ship," she said, and smiled. "But maybe the ship is already underwater, and we're all dead. Though, we still think we can come back."

"So, it's a vendetta."

Mariana smiled again, and I forgot for a moment my own seriousness. "With so many of us being from Italy," she said, "sure, it's a family vendetta."

That was true enough and I didn't know what to say. I put my arm behind her head before saying what I was thinking— "Why don't you come with me?"

"I am with you, Edgardo. I came to you."

"I meant to the States. My father can get you a passport—a visa, something."

"Me in the United States? No, this is my country." The way she said *"Estados Unidos"* had a hint of anger, enough to reveal the ever-present ghosts of the Left behind her revolutionary quest. We, the capitalist pigs.

It was sad, but I was the enemy too.

"You don't understand why I've done this," she said.

"Understand? They almost...they could have killed you."

"I can't leave. My life is here."

"Your family will be happier if they know you're safe."

"I don't know. Many have left, but I can't. The movement...we need to keep fighting. We can't let them win."

"For what? To bring socialism to Argentina? That's never going to happen."

"I didn't get into Montoneros for that...some people did." I noticed

185

how much trouble she had with the arm and helped to accommodate her back upright on the pillow. "It's confusing," she said. "I was involved with the church, and many in the organization were believers; for them, it was all about fulfilling the promise of the Gospels."

"The meek will inherit the Earth?"

"Yes, that."

I understood. I wanted to follow her, even into the realm of the twisted history of her country.

"It was all about getting everybody their share," she said, "solving the awful disparity with the rich. But the country was now poor—more than when Perón was first president—and he also lied to us. Well, he didn't lie; he was just himself, seeking power any way he could. We wanted to believe...we were idiots."

"No, you weren't. It was a noble cause."

"I'll do my part, go back to the field. That's my place—being a foot soldier."

"You are not just a foot soldier. And your part in this war is over." I'd finally remembered that I shouldn't agree with her when it came to Montoneros.

"You know it is not. And I don't want you to take more risks. Didn't you have enough danger the last few days?"

"You have no idea."

And the moment when we could have told each other the truth passed.

I came over her, like another blanket. I wanted her to forget; forget both the dreams and the nightmares.

I turned the lights off and we tasted a little of each other. But we could only do so much—her body was as hurt as her soul. I did kiss her neck, and my hands felt comfortable under what used to be my sweater and now smelled of her.

I explored her skin, shy of the deeper crevices but confident I could mold the larger surfaces to fit my own.

We needed the heat. We couldn't find enough of it.

We were both dead and alive, subject to immeasurable danger like Schrödinger's cats. But for us the poisons and the threats were too many to count.

We slept through our last afternoon of comfort. As a pale sun hid behind the city, we took a taxi to Cristina's house in Flores.

18

Cristina and Rafa were all over Mariana as soon as we crossed the patio's threshold.

Rafa kept repeating her name— "Mariana...Mariana, we tried, we tried to find you."

"They let me go. Apparently, I'm useless." Mariana looked down, as if she had trouble keeping her head up.

"No, girl," said Rafa. "You're not. You were very brave. This—this was just a warning. It's all there was."

Mariana smiled, as one smiles with a lot of sadness. "A warning," she repeated. "Like we needed to be warned this's dangerous."

A few minutes later, Mariana excused herself and Cristina took her to rest in her bedroom. I hadn't realized the extreme effort she was making to stay awake. The day had been a gift to me.

Cristina chased me as soon as she left the bedroom. "How is she?" she asked. Cristina's stare was intense; I felt like a child being interrogated by a parent.

"All right," I said, still feeling a pinch from Cristina's expression. "Is there anything you want me to do?"

"There's...a meeting of the leadership. Tomorrow. I want you to go with her."

"You mean the Montoneros?"

I still couldn't believe Cristina was working for that violent organization, always one step short of wholesale terrorism. But at that point, I wasn't sure anymore who was terrorizing who.

"Yes, they're meeting tomorrow," Cristina continued, undeterred by my confusion. "To discuss the kidnapping."

"Kidnapping?" I said, although Rafa had told me about their plans. My memory was fuzzy, impaired by days of no real sleep and a barrage of events I hadn't finished processing.

"I can't tell you, Edgardo. Sorry. It's best if you don't know a lot about what's going on."

"Rafa told me you guys want to disrupt the World Cup transmissions. Get a guy to confess publicly the military's crimes."

Cristina nodded but pursed her lips in displeasure. "I guess Rafa has an even bigger mouth than I'd thought," she said.

And then again, that great smile and its pull on me. Another beautiful girl, one who was also connected with dangerous people. Was it the violence that attracted me? Was I even more attracted to Mariana because she was closer to the archetypical "bad" girl?

"It doesn't matter," Cristina said. "You need to go with her. She worries me."

"Well, I don't know what that would do for her."

"What you have to do for her is to *be* with her."

And that was that. I was going to the meeting, and Cristina spent a great deal of time giving me very detailed instructions about it. From how to dress for the event to the peace of mind that would entail being paraded blindfolded in a car, so that I couldn't know where they'd be meeting.

Just like Julian.

But I didn't tell her that.

* * *

I was so overwhelmed—by being allowed to follow Mariana into the lair of a revolutionary organization—that I stepped into the semi-illuminated street without thinking which way I should walk to find one of the many bus lines running along Rivadavia Avenue. I had started to walk in the wrong direction when I was startled by something.

Millions of years of evolution kicked in. I was being watched.

I turned around, one way, and then in the street's opposite heading. Couldn't see anyone.

But the feeling was there, powerful. I kept going back with my swiveling sight to a shaded corner on the opposite sidewalk. In the jungle, even the subtlest of movements can be felt, and I was sure a shifting patch within that almost-black shadowed area contained a human being.

A little black cloud was born from the darkness, and it scuttled away in the direction of the street's corner. I was far away but, in a moment of insanity, I sprinted out of my spot, having decided that this time it was going to be me the one doing the following.

My insanity was telling me that marauder was the man—*the* one man—who was trying to catch me.

19

I pursued the man a few blocks, but soon his quick turns at corners lost me. I didn't know the Flores neighborhood well and soon ended up leaning on a tree, thinking how I would have to wait until daylight to find my way out of streets lacking the parallel grid they kept near Rivadavia.

I felt strange and remembered the night I'd met Mariana, when all those *colectivos* passed over and over in front of my eyes—the same one many times, or its alternates in as many different worlds. I'd seen one man but was sure there were others, right there, moving under the surface of my vision—unseen but present. Some of them wanted to kill me.

The man had moved fast the last time, cruising away and into the night. I walked a couple of steps, and then my sight caught the lights of a bar, so bright in the very dark street.

I had seen once a painting by Edward Hopper of people sitting at a bar's counter, its magic light contrasting with the darkened street outside. That corner was similar, but the man was the only customer at such a late hour.

I didn't think twice and entered, walking the few meters that separated his table from the bar's entrance. An empty espresso cup laid on the table, which could have been his or a remnant from a previous visitor.

I wanted answers, and, driven by anger, I tried to grab the man's shirt collar. I missed, and my hand landed flat on his chest.

It was the first time I'd touched his skin.

It has been said that if you travel back in time, you shouldn't touch your old self.

Apparently, it works the other way around too.

As soon as my hand made full contact with the man's chest, something changed. I couldn't tell what it was other than saying it felt as if I, and everything else, was falling away.

I was standing on a pedestal that had started to climb higher and higher, running from a receding world.

But it wasn't space that was changing; it was time. Time was reorganizing itself, forming a deck of cards containing every single instant that had ever belonged to our universe. Time was there, all at once. And I was somehow out of it, in an indescribable country.

I saw myself, studying Physics at MIT.

A discovery impossible to comprehend with my uncouth teen-ager's brain—how particles can be tagged to a point in spacetime and then later returned to that earlier state. To another time and place.

People talking on TV about an assured visit to Stockholm to collect the Nobel Prize of Physics. Joking that my precious subatomic particles would miss the ceremony, delayed a whole year in the past.

Strange typewriters attached to small TV sets, with screens full of unfathomable equations. Immense machines and tiny men. And finally, time machines, being built by robots. Time won't be more of an obstacle than distance for our distant descendants.

Imperfection in our future.

Desperation at not being able to get out of the Milky Way. And disappointment, like that of a player who realizes he'll never make it to the big leagues. By not being able to build an extra-galactic civilization, we were destined to be squashed by more powerful contenders.

We were not humans like us any longer, but the errors of our ways came from the very start, when we were still biological.

We will go back in time, some day, eons from now. To correct our past failures. All of them.

I saw something in motion, indescribable as a vision of Heaven. We think in terms of spaceships born from our aerodynamic transports, the tiny things we built and must fight against air to fly. What I saw was more like a three-dimensional city, with buildings thin as needles pushing away in all directions. It was a loose arrangement of ill-defined parts, many of them incorporeal, and it was moving between the stars like a fast comet, bordering the edges of the galaxy and ready to jump into the vastness of nothingness between them. The first step to becoming a cosmic civilization.

The space-city didn't end anywhere, and it wasn't in any particular time. It curved—if that was the word, as it just vanished at the boundaries—and showed up in other places.

My primate brain had reached the point where it couldn't see or tolerate any more.

* * *

I woke up from my trance. I was now sitting, and the man watched me with knowing understanding. And with something else that resembled pity. He stood up and passed me by, saying into my ear—"When you see the red box... *jump!*"

He said it like he was giving me a gift. Smiling.

I turned around to see where he was going. I was now alone in the bar. But I was sure I hadn't been alone.

The man was real, and now I knew who he was. He knew too—that I knew.

I stopped breathing when I finally understood.

I had seen the great Time Unseen.

I should have known. It was so simple.

If you want a job done well, do it yourself.

There it was. The even-more-improbable truth, if there could be such a thing, even for me.

I had been sent back in time—maybe even built my own time machine to do it—to fix the past or kill myself.

20

My eyes were finally free to see. Apparently, the Montoneros didn't like hoods and had some leftover eye masks from a past Carnival. The eyeholes on mine had been sealed with black electrical tape.

I was standing on a patio, which was covered with a tent-like roof made with green sailcloth, so damaged it hung like a drape. I couldn't see the sky or any of the surrounding buildings. It could have been an old house anywhere in the city. The absence of any bearings was irksome.

Everyone around was silent, and more people were coming out to the patio with the apparent intention of surrounding me. It took me a few seconds to realize it was because they had no idea who I was.

Anibal Reinoso, tall and bearded like a Persian warrior, stepped forward and out of the circle of Montoneros to extend a hand I shook off, both out of fear and to show I wasn't a prisoner or some spy. There was palpable relaxation of the group when he smiled.

"You do follow your girlfriends anywhere, don't you?" He spoke jokingly, but it was obvious he didn't like me. "Don't worry," Anibal added, looking around to seek other eyes. "He's a friend, and he is concerned about Mariana's well-being. I can understand that, considering what she went through. Do you, people?"

It was clear, seeing the collective nodding, that Anibal was a leader for the group and his word enough to grant me safe passage.

Instructions for my behavior had been spelled out during my previous conversation with Cristina Contiglia, but Anibal relished explaining how I was supposed to only stay for the beginning of their meeting, including, only as a show of camaraderie to me, a general description of the kidnapping to take place. But afterwards, I'd be locked away in a back room while they discussed the specifics of their operation. I couldn't object to that and thus nodded countless times, trying to show my complete agreement with the proceedings.

I kept glancing at Mariana, a beautiful apparition in an unlikely blue dress. She had come with Anibal, presumably without blinders, but she was acting as if she couldn't see me, barely raising her eyes from the floor. Everybody but Mariana looked like truckers enjoying a rest stop—many jeans and jean jackets, dark clothes and light-green workmen's shirts. The other two women there wore pants, smoked constantly, and apparently had never visited a hair salon. Mariana was the lonely princess in a dark children's story.

I just wanted to take her away, grab a train, and hide in Argentina's southernmost country. I imagined us staying at a cottage in the Andes, where the mountain range turns into a patchwork of snow and lakes. We would be together on a constant honeymoon, fishing trout in hidden lakesides and collecting wild strawberries on mountain slopes.

Maybe it was that light-blue dress, so out of place there.

Anibal started his harangue to the troops as if he were a decorated general— "No dictatorship, no matter how powerful it might look, would be able to resist the power of the insurrected masses of workers, the unrest of our whole country. The revolution, nurtured by the workers, will be our cause, and we'll help with the fight."

As I heard him talk, I corrected my assessment of Anibal to

a Cuban-educated general. "We're disengaged for now from the leadership," he said, "but not powerless. We are an autonomous platoon and, even if the National Conduction doesn't know about us, we will carry our mission and succeed. The Second Counteroffensive will start with our cell, early, even if the organization isn't ready." Cheers broke the speech, a little too loud for a secret party. I was still considering the word *"descolgados"* Anibal had used for his Montoneros, who were now working outside the hierarchy. It sounded like they were a disconnected phone—as if they'd lost their connection while trying to reach their central command.

Anibal imposed silence with one of his general-like stares. "Let me tell you about our plan," he said.

If I needed another reason to escape that place, the plan Montoneros had for their kidnapping of Martínez was insane. Apparently, Mariana worked for a large church in the Almagro neighborhood, which Martínez frequented as a parishioner. And, incredibly, the great torturer had a large family and many friends; even more surprising to me, one of them had chosen him to be the godfather of a child. The next Saturday, that family was going to have a baptism rehearsal he would be attending. Mariana's task was to lead a small team of Montoneros to a sideline room inside the church—she was given its keys during ceremonials. From their hideout, the team would enter the rectory during the service and sequester the military man. She would also help them to escape using the church's lateral entrance.

The rest of the plan was supposed to be kept secret, especially from me, but someone asked a question—probably not what Anibal wanted—and a mention was made concerning a later TV transmission, at a time yet to be disclosed, where Martínez would be forced to explain the true scope of the military-driven disappearances, which had been expanded to include many uninvolved, unarmed civilians. Anibal cut it short before any dates were included—although he didn't know that I was already aware of most of their machinations.

He then made a single gesture, pointing to a hallway, and it was the cue to take me away—two guys, the biggest ones, were consigned with the deed. I felt a little proud that they had sent them to escort me out, considering how scared I was. I would have gone by myself to hide in any room they'd open for me—that far I was out of my element. This was a real illegal operation, with lots of people carrying guns and an aim that would make all of them traitors in the eyes of the Argentine government.

And I knew all about it, and was now in the middle of the action, privy to how they had planned their moves. Worse even, I knew that I'd been singled out by fate to screw up the future of the entire human race.

* * *

The room I was sent to was that of a youngster, one who apparently loved to build and paint scale models of cars, ships, and planes. I wondered how he'd kept them so clean, and what gift of patience it took to paint with so many colors the countless details of a large galleon-like ship—its base revealed it was Lord Nelson's HMS Victory—and to do it so perfectly, down to the cannon turrets inside each of the tiny square windows. I fantasized it had been Anibal, who had a secret personality and would hide from the world to build memorials to historical wars.

Of course, I had no idea who that kid was, whose house I was in, and even if it was a house that belonged to one of the Montoneros. Cristina had made it clear they'd try to protect the movement's helping non-members, who at times lent their homes for meetings; this was especially important in case they were taken and tortured to access their human networks.

She'd said that there had been enough innocent people killed, and this was a thought I couldn't shake off my mind.

I was holding a luxurious red convertible—a Cord, an automobile

I'd never seen before—when the room's door suddenly opened and someone outside said my ride was ready and I was supposed to go.

I left the modern-looking classic car next to a submarine, oddly noting how it was so mismatched in size with respect to the ship that it seemed the Cord could fit people coming from the same world as King Kong.

21

After the mind-bending encounter with the man—who, according to my own bent mind, was an older version of myself—I had made a simple but profound decision. From then on, I was going to do the opposite of what I'd normally do.

If my actions would unleash some future disaster, threatening enough to mankind's fate to get the attention of all-powerful time overlords, then the very best thing I could do would be to act unpredictably—and for sure, uncharacteristically.

In that vein, I decided to go and see Julian as soon as the new day broke out.

It was Saturday, and my showing up just before seven in the morning to Julian's home was patently weird. I couldn't explain it with our usual mid-week's excuse of getting together to march across town to the Gorostiaga, and I entertained the idea of saying we were going to a Palermo park to run for our Physical Ed program. Considering how little we did together other than talking, the idea of us in shorts, in winter-like morning weather, running through the coastal woods, was plainly ridiculous.

Dorita was even sleepier than me, and she just opened the door to me without question or surprise. As I entered the apartment, I saw how her lack of care extended to not bothering to cover herself well to answer the door while wearing a short nightgown. I averted my eyes—out of trained politeness—but couldn't help to catch a glimpse of her anatomy.

Apparently, Julian's papers had metastasized into his bedroom. His bed was now buried under an amorphous pile of newspaper cutouts and what looked to me to be parts of a manuscript consolidated with scissors and tape.

"Don't you have anything else to do?" Julian's eyes were almost shut, and he propped himself up just enough to have his head vertical.

"Well, I couldn't sleep."

"And you don't want me to sleep either."

"Something like that."

"Is there anything we should be doing?" Julian pointed to the window's yellowish sunlight.

The Montoneros had given me a seat at the baptism rehearsal—with the mission to keep an eye on Mariana, but more likely to make her feel more comfortable before their plan was triggered. "I'm going to see Mariana today," I said.

"Yes, you'd said she's back. That's...incredible. But, how is she?"

"All right, but I don't think she should be walking, or..."

"Walking? Where will you go with her?"

"There's a plan..." I said and stopped.

Suddenly, I felt exposed. I didn't know what Julian had learned from his meeting with D'Agostini—and possibly with Martínez. Whatever I said could spiral out of control and cause ripples in time, the kind that could make many lives, even yours truly, expendable. I tried to think quickly—as quickly as possible on a Saturday morning and with two hours of sleep—and attempted a poorly planned counterattack. "Did you get to see Martínez yesterday?"

"I thought you were telling me about a plan...yes, I saw him."

"With D'Agostini?"

"Sure, I guess I've already told you. The archbishop was there; it wasn't a secret meeting."

"How's Martínez? Did you talk to him?"

"Are you even interested in my answers?"

"Yes, of course. Sorry, you were saying…"

"I met Army Colonel Martínez, Juan Aurelio is his name, if you want to know. Good looking son of a bitch. And he was dressed in such tight uniform you could see his pecs."

"So, you're attracted to him."

"Shut up."

The tone in Julian's words ignored my faked playfulness. I waited before continuing—"So, what did you learn?"

"A lot, actually. They want me to participate in what they're calling 'The New Youth Movement'—I will be creating messages for distribution to the general public. Explain how to bring about a 'new' Argentina, free of aggressive unions and the communists that are robbing the middle-class of its prosperity."

"A fascist Paradise."

Luckily, Julian didn't slap me and just continued. "No, it's not that. Some of their people are really bright and have a proposal to take the country forward…"

I counted to ten, very fast, and said nothing. I still had hopes Julian wouldn't be permanently brainwashed and would continue with his dream of revealing the crimes of the military—the same dream I now knew the Montoneros had—but in my friend's counter-spy version.

He kept talking. "You have to understand why I'm changing my mind. I don't like those communists…"

They are not all communists. I kept counting.

"And I think Argentina will be great again, the best in the world."

Could I keep counting to more than a hundred?

"D'Agostini and the colonel were very nice with me. They invited me to a baptism ceremony."

I was reaching eighty-seven when I stopped— "Baptism what?"

"Yes, Martínez is the godfather of…well, not sure, a daughter of the daughter of a cousin. Who cares? It doesn't matter; I'll be there. And you can come with me."

The roulette of possible tomorrows stopped, and I lost. Perhaps I couldn't change the final outcome. I felt trapped but had to say yes. I was going anyway.

22

There were enough people attending the baptismal rehearsal in an inner church room to fill all the seats available. The narrow room apparently served as a spill-over for the types of ceremonies a church doesn't normally carry out in its main nave—too big for the Last Rites and too small for confirmations. About half an hour of waiting made me familiar with the decorative wood panels and ceiling lamps.

By then, it was clear there was no sign of Martínez, and the young family waiting on stage for the rehearsal was getting concerned—perhaps worrying that the high dignitary might get (dangerously) upset if they went ahead without him.

Since it was a church, and Julian had been educated in a predominantly Catholic culture, he stayed silent and didn't complain. I was much more antsy and kept thinking about the Montoneros and their now inapplicable plan.

Finally, Mariana appeared, spent five minutes pampering the baptismal family, and then came to see us. "Please excuse the mess, Edgardo," she said. "We're going to start the rehearsal...but cancel what we were going to do. I've been told he's not coming. You can go, if you want."

Julian was stunned into silence by the extraordinarily pretty girl coming to see me—I hadn't told him Mariana was there, fearful he might leak the information to the wrong people. I ignored Julian and reached for Mariana's hand, putting my face near to hers. "I'll stay with you," she said, "*if* you want."

Mariana smiled, but then rushed back to the small podium without saying anything. Julian had a sour frown and started to collect his stuff. Something dark was possessing him, and I realized that I had failed to help him find the truth he wanted, as much as he'd failed to help me find mine.

And, after we left that church, I would have to explain lots of things I hadn't told my friend. There was no way that what had just happened couldn't lead to more serious trouble between us. But soon I was distracted by other events; as soon as we got outside, Anibal showed up at the doorstep and took Mariana with him to a taxi that was waiting at the church's corner.

I had another salty pizza with Julian that night but couldn't enjoy it, my mind busy thinking how it was possible that Mariana was now both so close and far away.

* * *

The second round of the attempted baptism occurred the following day, Sunday, and was more disorganized—for all of us, including the baptismal family and the Montoneros. The real ceremony was being carried out in the main nave of the Basilica of San Carlos Borromeo, sometime in the middle of the noon Sunday Mass, with an attendance in the thousands.

It was a huge church, part of a complex of edifices built by a religious order. I couldn't find Julian before the mass started, with herds of parishioners pushing to enter the nave as if a people's dam had broken. I had to sit in a corner and almost behind one of the immense arches that flanked the church's central pews.

The church had been beautifully decorated in striking colors—

golden altars, blue ceilings, and red-white Romanic arches. It was large enough to contain a small stadium's worth of parishioners. Sneaking around in this vast open space would be a nightmare for the Montoneros, and, if sane, they'd cancel their operation. In my mind, I concluded they should have and probably had done that already. But then my soul cringed when I saw Mariana climbing the marble steps to position herself where she could guide the young couple and their child, plus a godmother who was a little too heavy for any sudden movements.

Even in the large walkway at the center of the massive church, D'Agostini was a distinct figure and I recognize him immediately. He was walking away from the altar with disregard for its holy contents of consecrated wafers—not kneeling or making the Sign of the Cross first, unheard of in a conservative church like that one—and the way his body swaggered suggested this was not only his turf, but he owned it.

I followed the priest with my eyes, just like so many others. Dressed in full archbishop's regalia, he was an impressive sight.

He stopped at the end of the pew's rows, where an amorphous mass of people was still making decisions about standing, leaving, or trying to find an acquaintance and thus a seat. D'Agostini shook hands with a tall guy in a gray suit; behind the man's shoulders, two much bigger men in overcoats ostensibly stayed at arm's length. From a distance, the man in the gray suit resembled Frank Sinatra, perhaps more a Sinatra who had come to church with a couple of his friends from the Mafia.

As D'Agostini took the man forward along the church, his acolytes followed him with their heads down.

I was now completely certain that man was Martínez.

Both the mass and the baptism were uneventful. D'Agostini didn't do the main homily and left it to the church's priest, a portly man who went on and on about the reign of God on Earth but loaded each of his words with contained anger. I attributed this to an unconscious reaction to the visible power of the archbishop, his absolute control over him.

After making families suffer with so much preparation, the two baptisms lasted no more than four minutes each. Even from half a block away, I could see the practiced smile of Martínez, a man who resembled more an American politician than a Special Forces colonel. But he stood his ground, did his part, and joined his protective detail as soon as the water, oil, and baby crying had served their purposes.

Mariana stayed with the child-bearing families, her back turned to me as she watched the conclusion of the Mass. A stranger to Catholicism, I didn't partake of the communion and thus had to keep moving in and out of my spot, as people came back and tried to reach the mid-row seats. Maybe because I didn't know the ritual that well, and expected much more music at the end, I was startled when the stout priest told us to go with God and into the world.

But what surprised me even more was seeing Mariana leave the front area, and then sprint to catch up with Martínez and his entourage, as they tried to make their way within the crowded exit lines at the church's entrance.

I knew what that meant and instantaneously worried. The Montoneros' plan—in whatever modified form it had survived the stump suffered the previous afternoon—had been green-lighted.

I lost all semblance of belonging to Christianity as I tried to get out of that church, pushing and shoving people at either side.

* * *

Outside, the concentrated humanity made any quick movement impossible, and I glanced at Julian, way too far away to be heard or yelled at. Mariana had disappeared and, since the steps descended to half-opened metal doors, I couldn't see much of what was going on in the street.

I pleaded with a family to move over, so I could pass between them. They were completely deaf, and I felt like a ghost.

A couple of people collided with me and I drifted even closer to the entrance's iron fences.

There was a crashing noise ahead, and then a sound my brain recognized before I did. It was a gun going off. Everybody started to run.

As I was reaching the steps, I stepped into something and stumbled, almost falling down the short stairs. I saw that I'd banged a large gift box with my misstep. It was a surely a gift for the baptized, lost by the family's friends during the commotion.

And it was bright red.

23

As I had been told to do in the most fantastic way possible, I jumped.

My body immediately hit the back of someone who was moving across the entrance. I fell backwards, taking someone else down with my fall. I heard more gunshots and could see from the floor the waves of people rushing into the streets.

My elbow was on the stomach of a stunned guy, whose legs were trapped under my body. I saw another man on the floor beyond him, his extremities twitching and flailing.

Then, I understood.

The guy under me was Julian; the one twisting nearby had taken the bullet my friend might have caught otherwise. For whatever higher design things had gone the way they did, I had just saved Julian's life. It didn't escape me that—at least in some versions of reality—I would have been left alone to deal with my destiny.

The man lying next to us had stopped shaking. I raised my friend by grasping under his armpit, while trying to make sense of the barrage of movement outside.

Two cars and a truck were parked at an angle in front of the church's entrance, the truck large enough to spill over the lateral street. Across the avenue, two other cars had parked in double-line, well into the asphalt and blatantly against the traffic's stated direction—both were Ford Falcons, and one was green.

The truck near us had its rear wood-door open, and two guys inside held Martínez—one was Anibal Reinoso. The other had his left hand in close contact with Rafa's head.

Two other men in overcoats shouted from behind a black car—a limousine, large and slick. One had a gun pointed in the direction of Anibal.

And someone was driving a car in between those groups, moving it back and forth, as if deciding between parking and running away—it was the kind of driving one does when guns are pointed at you from either side.

People were spreading along both sides of the avenue, a few of them oddly crossing the street toward the shooting. And four men in police uniform tried to stop traffic so they could cross the street.

I should have been doing something to take cover with Julian. But what I did—even with my friend not totally conscious and weighing over me—was exactly the opposite.

I walked toward the confrontation rather than seeking protection behind the thick walls of San Carlos.

I wanted to see where Mariana was. Be sure she was all right.

It was not a smart choice.

The two doors of the sandwiched car opened at once, and the guy who had been trying to drive it stumbled out. On the passenger's side, I could see Mariana trying to get away, in the worst possible position between the limousine and the truck, corralled by the broad street and the four thugs behind her.

She could have run, perhaps making it behind the truck and the cover it offered. But she unfortunately saw us—saw *me*—and started to gesture that we should get out.

I didn't make it to remove my arm from under Julian's body before she was taken. It happened so fast, I would elaborate later it wasn't by the policemen who were now crossing the street—a *colectivo* had just passed vertiginously in front of them—but rather by one of the overcoats. I couldn't tell for sure; my eyes were completely on her.

In an instant, she had disappeared inside the limousine.

I took a couple of steps forward, but it was way too late. A member of the group of policemen still trying to cross the street had seen how Mariana had signaled me, and he and his partner began to move in our direction.

The Montoneros' truck roared and started to move, its tires screeching; Anibal had managed to take Martínez inside. His pale face was the last thing I saw before the door was closed by a solitary arm coming out of the shade.

The truck quickly disappeared at the other end of the block.

The limousine guys started to get back inside their car, perhaps to start a pursuit. And our two policemen were approaching the sidewalk, having some trouble getting past the scattered vehicles.

I pushed Julian, and he understood without words. We started to run into the church's side street and toward Rivadavia. If we made it to the big avenue, we could manage to lose them.

I thought as I ran how we were not even two blocks away from where Mariana had been taken the first time. And I was now running from other people bent on capturing me, with the whole world turned against me, and no understanding of why that was happening.

24

We climbed into a *colectivo* just as the street light went green. I could see through its rear window the shrinking silhouettes of the guys who were after us, moving their arms desperately and probably expecting that the bus driver would care enough to stop.

In principle, we both felt safe, Julian even more than I did. I was still obsessing about Mariana and her all-so-very-bad luck with the police. Being Sunday afternoon, there were enough seats for our bodies to find rest.

We didn't know which bus line we'd boarded, and we didn't ask. It took us quickly across the Almagro middle-class neighborhood, full of tree-lined streets, and in a path that seemed vaguely river-bound.

We might not have known where the bus would ultimately take us, but the police did.

After twenty minutes or so in our cheapskate ride, we had cut across a good swath of Buenos Aires, always going eastward. Our bus—whose line number I've since learned and then forgotten again—hadn't changed its quick pace or the level of occupancy. We were now nearing the city's edge, and getting ready to cross another big asphalt gap, Libertador Avenue, when the *colectivo* came to a hard stop.

We were about one block from the multi-lane avenue. We'd been stopped because three police cars had obstructed the street ahead; a truckload of uniformed policemen was now circulating between the detained vehicles, making people descend and produce their documents.

On any other day, we would have started to search our pockets for the Argentine's universal ID document—our DNI, or *Documento Nacional de Identidad*. But we knew they were after us and quietly decided we had to get out of that particular *colectivo*. Julian grabbed my shoulder as he stood, and we both moved like Siamese twins to the back, simultaneously and loudly asking the driver to open the door.

Bored, the driver opened the door and didn't even look back.

We tried to avoid running and thus risking being seen by the wandering battalion of policemen, but if they knew our *colectivo's* license plate, the probability of leaving unnoticed was slim. A few seconds after we'd descended by the backdoor, two policemen— one in full gear and the other in civilian attire—barely stopped by the driver's window before starting to walk in the direction we had taken.

Since the police troops were moving so slowly, at a stroll's pace, I thought that they hadn't picked up on us. But I forgot we were just kids, and they were part of an organization accustomed to taking people from their homes with total disregard for normal police protocols. We were two teenagers, in daylight and on a lazy Sunday afternoon—gazelles surrounded by a pack of lions.

Perhaps what saved us was the lack of modern communication technology back in those days. Other than verbally alerting their partners, those two officers would have needed to resort to their primitive walkie-talkies, which few of them normally carried. Rounding up people like cattle with their Falcons, maybe they'd do that with ease; but chasing on foot and carefully checking each aisle and entrance in a neighborhood full of palatial houses and shaded corners was more difficult.

Our luck, however, wasn't all that great, and two other police-men soon joined the first team. I saw them first—two on each side of the street, and, in each pair, one of them watching the road while the other entered and checked any open hallway. They were about a half-block away, approaching the street's corner, and we were hiding in one of the first houses of the next block.

I took the lead when I saw that a car was parking on the old cobblestone street—I remember it as a sky-blue Peugeot 504, a classy though inexpensive sedan of the era. I dragged Julian with me to hide in front of the car; the owner saw us but was too busy trying to get someone to come out so he could leave. For him, we were boys playing on the street, hiding from their friends to make a practical joke. But that afternoon, those boys were playing a dangerous game.

The policemen were talking to each other across our street. I couldn't hear them well, but I assumed they were trying to decide which way to go. I guess having the intersection between them and us was what saved our lives.

After a long minute of police deliberation, which I'd spent watching for the car owner and his passenger, two of the police-men decided to move into the street that ran perpendicular to us. The other two were coming our way, and on our side of the street.

The driver of the Peugeot we'd used as a hiding spot kept check-ing our backs. He opened a large glass-iron door and a young girl appeared; she started to walk toward our car.

Our luck was running out fast.

As Julian was getting ready to run along the street, I stopped him so fast he crashed back against the Peugeot's shiny fender, hitting his head against its flat grille.

"It's best if we go across the street," I said.

"No, we can't. They'll see us."

"They'll see us anyway. We can get across and run around the corner...they won't have time to see it's us."

My next pull almost threw Julian into the street. We stood and ran.

I think we should have looked first in the direction the traffic was coming, but we didn't. And we likely spent several cat's lives worth of luck while crossing between at least three cars and a madly-driven delivery truck. Part of our good luck was having so many vehicles between us and the policemen. My right arm could testify about it; after being swatted forward by the impact with a car's side mirror, it miraculously didn't break in two.

Whatever the cost in cat's lives, we reached the other side and soon were skirting the corner to enter another side street.

We random-walked the neighborhood without checking any street signs, our attention focused behind us, trying to watch the blind area one can't scan with the eyes fixed ahead. In war, they would have called them our "sixes."

The enormous open spaces of Plaza Italia extended in front of us. We had there the shaded, crowded botanical garden; and, across the avenue, the wandering paths of the zoo and the sprawling setting for the city's agricultural exposition, which hosted annual festivals full of prized bulls and farming machinery. Just near an angled intersection, Santa Fé Avenue started to run back toward the downtown. It was a great combination of directions to get lost in the city.

25

We didn't want to risk going back to my apartment and thus wandered north, deeper into Palermo. Its inner streets were shielded by enormous trees, whose roots escaped from the ground and made the sidewalks irregular. We didn't talk much, and I thought some of my own desolation had moved telepathically to Julian's brain. Everything was indeed lost, and it was no longer possible to go back to our lives of school attended or skipped during the day, and music and conversation filling the nights.

I don't remember when the rain started, and I'm not even sure if it ever happened. When researching that period, I haven't been able to find any evidence of rain in Buenos Aires on that evening. But it was raining, and we sought refuge at the threshold of a house's steps. The rain soon turned heavier, and my shoes made splashing noises as they coughed up a liquid load they'd extracted from the puddles that had taken over the streets.

There was something alien about that rain, and when I looked further back along our own street and closer to its farthest visible point, some intersections didn't seem to have had any of it. There was though, here and there, a little more sunlight in the spreading twilight. Those curtains of water and light did not belong to the same slice of time as ours, but to other plays with other actors.

I felt goose bumps, sure that I'd witnessed a flaw in the Creator's design. That might have been true.

I don't know whether Julian felt the same, and I didn't ask him. Something distracted me. What made me aware that the rain had ceased and realize that my shoes had been unexpectedly rendered dry, was music pouring over us, sound made into invisible water. Someone was playing the piano above and had left a window open.

It was a strangely violent piece, primal music that, on any other night, I would have found difficult to hear. But it was the same violence of its order, fought against the randomness of a waning storm, what would fix it indelibly in my brain. It was us, humans, searching for redemption by beating our own tools, just like ages earlier, when we first understood that the other side of consciousness was death.

I've never forgotten that harsh melody and, many years later, I finally identified it as a famous piano concerto by Prokofiev.

PART IV

Time Unbeknownst

1

We didn't have a plan for what to do next, and as it got darker, the city seemed to be composed of blotches of light stuck together, coming from the stores, and corners where the world fell into a yellow-green darkness. We jumped between those lighted puddles but soon worried—we said that much to each other—they would be coming after us, no matter where we went.

Julian's answers to my questions became shorter at first, but then turned very long and incoherent. I thought he was surrendering to exhaustion.

"Edgardo...can we stop?"

"Yes, sure."

"I'm not...the things I want to...before them, you know, even if we don't come or if they can get what we wouldn't say otherwise, if they..."

I can't reproduce exactly what Julian's speech was like, but soon I was at a total loss to understand him.

He extracted a key ring from his pocket and started to fumble with it. "I had a key made for you. I'd made a...wanted you to have one...for if you need to come when I am...when I not..."

I wasn't expecting him to faint, but as he turned to me his body continued its rotation and fell away. When I reached for him, he was splattered on the ground but still speaking to himself. His words were coming out of order, meaningless.

* * *

Dorita had put Julian to sleep and closed the door, perhaps a little too forcefully. While he was with us—recovered from the spell but still not totally himself—Julian hadn't talked much and slowly calmed down.

"I need to tell you something. Let's go to the living room."

Julian's mom walked ahead of me and I was reminded of my adolescent attraction to her. It made me both angry and shy whenever I tried to talk with her.

Soon that thought was drowned by a tsunami. "Julian is sick," she said.

"No, it's just that we've had a tough time, and..."

"He's not fainting from stress. It's his medication."

"Medication? For what?"

"Julian was diagnosed last year, and the pills make him sick sometimes."

Argentines have trouble dealing with overt sickness and would hide it until it either disappeared or turned hospital-serious. It was clear that for Dorita there was a great deal of shame attached to whatever was affecting Julian. I quickly considered a range of possibilities for such concealment, from syphilis to cancer.

Still, she surprised me. "They call it a dissociative disorder, or traumatic psychosis. Each doctor has a different name for it."

Psychosis. The word triggered interconnected images of my friend—his irrepressible obsession with paper collection, those conspiracies he always saw afoot, and the unscientific relationship Julian had with the truth.

I lacked back then my later knowledge of science but luckily asked one pertinent question. "What are they giving him?"

"First, they gave him...Haldol, I guess, but it made him sleepy and untalkative. Now, he's on chlor-something, maybe chlorpro-madine? A new drug. It doesn't make him sleep so much, but he can't see well; and there's the fainting, especially when he gets up from..."

Dorita started to cry, and I couldn't refuse to hold her. I ended up cradling her head and touching her hair. I didn't want to be so close to her, smelling that strong perfume and feeling large breasts against my chest.

* * *

I can recall only fragments of my stay with Julian that night. He read me some poems from Borges that tested the limits of my understanding of Spanish, and he slept for irregular stretches of time—I had the suspicion Dorita had given him a sedative.

He got excited again later and played music a little too loud for 3 a.m. on a Monday. I especially remember a ballad from Sui Generis, a then well-known and later immortal rock duo, who sung softly but added strong existential overtones to their lyrics.

But what really got forever stuck in my mind was the song's coda...*aprendiendo las lecciones para ser.*

...*learning the lessons for being*

For me, those lessons had gotten harder.

2

It was a foggy morning in Buenos Aires, one of those days it took a menacing appearance. I don't know what it is about those streets, but sadness with the power to corrode your soul takes over the city as the farthest views disappear in the white numbness of a cloud. Perhaps it's just a perspective thing, and the ubiquitous low housings make you feel as if you're in a small village that can end at every new corner. Or it is something about the draining of all colors, which are necessary to convince you of the reality of this town. When depressed, I tend to think it's because the city takes the lividity of death from the skies, and perhaps also from the mistreatments its citizens have perpetrated against her, when, and if, it was ever alive.

My meditations on that morning were as sad and colorless as Buenos Aires. I was swallowing hard my ongoing personal jokes about being the Sancho for a Julian Quixote. It was no longer a joke. And Julian was like Quixote in the worst possible way. His quest, his big aim in life, the adventurous things he wanted to do to expose the military, were all truly quixotic.

Because my friend, like Quixote, was crazy.

* * *

We arrived at my apartment after stopping by our high school. Since I was feeling angry, I had managed to kill my mother again.

One could say many negative things about murdering your parents, but death works like magic as an excuse. The principal not only allowed me to stay away from class—as much as I needed, and for as long as I could keep up with the homework from home— but, seeing how bad Julian looked, extended the waiver to him as custodian of my misfortune.

My lie would also work because I was confident my father had never mentioned he was abandoned by my mother, just before she started a crusade against the clinical trials his company sponsored in Africa. There were days I'd doubted I ever had a mother and thought I was just the result of one of my father's genetic experiments—a failed one at that.

Having exhausted our energies—and minds—we decided, incoherently, to visit my apartment and grab some things. We skipped any conversation with our doorman, and I rushed to the elevator. I wanted desperately to take a shower and get away from Julian's bouts of incoherence. I rushed to open the door and turn on the lights.

"Don't," yelled Julian.

I stopped short of turning on the lights. "Can you stop...?"

"Don't you smell it? It's gas. There's a leak."

My mind worked better than my sense of smell, and I found the culprit immediately. We had no doubts there were people who wanted to kill us.

But it wasn't the military; it was that man.

Or one of the versions of the man.

One of my own selves.

Julian sprinted to action with such speed it made me doubt the catatonic state he'd displayed just a couple of hours prior. He made me open every window and quickly found the electric box at the end of our floor's hallway—handily cutting the supply to my apartment. Julian even unearthed the short ladder I was certain we'd lost during my very confusing first day in there.

Julian explained, with the confidence and gravitas he admired so much in Sherlock Holmes, how someone had prepared the explosion for when we arrived. I couldn't look up to meet his eyes and let my disbelief be seen. I was sure that—other than not knowing the name of the perpetrator as I did—Julian was, as usual, correct.

I said little because if I told him who had really done it, I would lose him forever. And, in all truth, I was having trouble keeping my own sanity from slipping away.

I was surprised by the deviousness—and proficiency—the other Edgar had shown setting up the trap. A shunt cable surrounding the base of the big lamp on the living room's ceiling, perfect to create a big short-circuit. Tape around the leaky windows over the street side, to ensure gas would accumulate enough in the main space. And a handkerchief soaked in gasoline to capture the electric spark and cause a large enough fire to ignite the gases.

A job carefully done, taking all the time in the world. For Julian, the confident work of a professional; but for me, of someone who knew how to finish it just in time. After all, the gasoline was still dripping from the light's fixture when I climbed the ladder, when Julian finally let me take a look. And why not take all the time needed? The saboteur had had knowledge of when we were going to come back; in effect, he'd had access to our plans.

After all, I had all of them stored in my brain.

* * *

We did some cleaning and organizing, restoring the living room to a less dangerous state. At least, we could now turn the lights on without blowing up. I was happy that Julian had recovered a semblance of normality, probably because his mind was now busy studying the work of another conspirator. He might have been feeling reassured that, finally, there was abundant proof we lived in a dangerous world, and, behind each door, there were others, who were listening and plotting.

I was stressed by recent events but had the strength to find a storage place for a set of pills Dorita had given me for if Julian was away—something in her manner suggested she knew our adventures might mean going into hiding for a while.

I spent most of that afternoon trying to figure out how to find a lead, any lead, to where Mariana might have been kept. And after Julian's hellish tour, I had all the worry of the world about her being tortured by the military. I also knew that the Montoneros had Martínez and—for good or bad—they weren't going to let him go.

Both groups of fanatic, violent people had—or believed they had—enough leverage to tilt the other's hand. It was an untenable situation.

The only strong memory I have is of us together, looking out the living room window. An awful fog had compressed our world to less than the length of neighboring Plaza Lavalle.

It was like being in a ship sailing into scudding masses of low clouds. And Julian was still the elder captain, best for dark waters. I was sure the world he saw was, as the fog, amorphous, inchoate, and above all, threatening.

3

Perhaps it was a premonition, but I was walking nearby the phone when it rang.

"Hello, Edgar."

"Oh, it's you." The switch to English had become so easy for me I could get confused about what language I was speaking. It must have been English because it was my father and Julian was frowning.

"Apparently, it is me, son, but not being well-liked."

"It's not that, Dad...I'm having a complicated time over here."

"It must be, I imagine. I have been getting calls from your principal at the *Gouhr-rous-tee-ahgah* School." My father's Spanish, even a single word here and there, had never taken off, and his pronunciation, having picked up some Bostonian accent while at Harvard, was downright awful. "I haven't returned his calls," he said, "not before talking with you. So, what's going on?"

"Nothing."

What I meant to mean everything but was sure my father would understand literally.

"I thought so. I'm going to tell him you're fine."

"Yes, you can..." And then, I remembered my unconfessed matricide and decided to change directions and avoid that call at any cost. "It's best if we leave it as it is," I said. "The principal is very protective; he thinks he has to help me adjust to living alone here—I hate him."

"You have to be more understanding, with grown-ups."

"I am, with you."

"No, Edgar, you aren't."

A less troubled and more rational young man would have accepted that was true. But I wasn't any of those things and went into a pointless attack. All the while, I was examining the last box of books my father had sent me.

"I *have* been understanding," I said. "Do you think it's easy to be left alone in a foreign country? How often do you check on me? A month would go by, and I don't hear from you. I'm alone, going to school with no friends..." I waved dismissively to Julian, who probably wasn't following even the basics of our conversation. "You don't really care, Dad. As long as you travel, go out with your friends and have..."

My father, who'd been carefully following my words, and was far brighter than I was willing to accept, stepped in before I used words like "girlfriend" or "sex"— "Edgar, I'm alone too. And I understand you better than you think. Remember that it was your decision to remain there rather than come back with me. *Your* choice."

He paused. I extracted a book—Joyce's *Ulysses*—which I couldn't possibly finish, even in English. Cultural showing off from my father.

"I'm here, working to build a future for you...for us. You might think it's selfish, but work in drug development is hard..."

Another pause. More lies to come and *Point Counter Point* by Aldous Huxley. Another snobbish choice, but one I had already read twice on my own and bragged about with Cristina. But I missed noticing how we'd both agreed it was so worth reading.

"Edgar, I will soon be at a point where I can travel and spend more time with you."

It irritated me to no end when my father used my name to start sentences. "I don't care."

"Don't you want to see me?"

The Double Helix by James Watson. My father wanting me to be a scientist like him.

"I want to be here," I said. "I need to."

"Are you sure?"

The face of Mariana flashed in front of my eyes. I was sure.

"Yes. I'd like to finish school here."

"Edgar, we need to talk a little more about this."

"As I said, Dad, we can talk when and if I go over there." I wasn't sure anymore who was talking on my side of the phone line.

"I wanted to tell you this, son, thought it was going to be a welcome surprise...I'm going to be there in a few days."

"What?"

A copy of *The Glass-Bead Game* fell to the floor. Herman Hesse's last book would one day be my favorite of all time.

"I'm going to see you soon. I will be there to see the Cup's finals, maybe stay for a few days."

I don't know how the conversation ended. It had been doomed from before I'd said my first word.

4

After the agitation that followed any more-than-a-minute-long conversation with my father, my day was pretty much over. We made sandwiches with thick prosciutto and cheese, drank lots of café au lait *à la Argentine*, and discussed—trying to distract ourselves from other problems—the possible progress of Argentina to the finals of the World Cup. I'd kept my faith on the local team, which was undoubtedly the world's greatest in the mind of a foreign kid immersed in a culture that hammered its leather-balloon glories at every opportunity. Julian, contrarian as always, was a fan of the Dutch team, and he argued that the orange shirts were technically superior to other teams and the most likely to reach the finals.

Little did we know, we were both right.

Nobody from the future had had the courtesy—or the smarts—to tell me that a miraculous event would lead Argentina to winning the World Cup.

And, also unbeknownst to me, these events were at the core of my future troubles.

After all, future time is, in its essence, and usually forever remains for most humans, unbeknownst.

* * *

I went to bed in a state of intellectual disarray that was becoming usual for me, and I had a night of nightmares and sweats. Woke up a couple of times, desperate to drink water; probably just the after-effect of dining, yet again, on pizza that was seriously salty.

The only dream I do remember was the last one. I was running between trees at night and knew the man was after me. Fog was hiding most of the tree trunks, and it made me fall every other step.

The man was trailing me, close enough to make sounds I heard echoing in my ears. One doesn't think much on sounds while dreaming, and many dreams are like silent movies. But this one was full of crackling, splotching, and the indescribable rushing sounds two people make when running through the enclosure of deep woods.

There were gaps in the dream, and perhaps I stopped for a while, but, as I started to run faster, I jumped over a small creek and fell.

When I stood up, I was confronted with a dark, rectangular pit, a grave someone had prepared just for me. I couldn't move, even when hearing approaching sounds behind, and experienced a terrible, heightened sensation of fear.

That image was burned in my retinas when I woke up in total darkness.

And, unfortunately for my peace of mind, I did remember my last thought in the dream.

Who am I to judge if I should live?

If I had been already judged superfluous by those who knew everything—our future god-like descendants—why should I wait so many years to go back and destroy me?

Maybe ending it all would also end the nightmares to come.

But the dream also gave me an idea about how to contact the man and get some answers from him. If I was so affected by what I'd dreamed, I would likely never forget it. When some fear took hold of me—something I knew well of myself, and he would know of himself—I usually tried to exorcise my demons upfront, to destroy them. That usually meant finding a place where I could relive the experience.

There was only one place in Buenos Aires where the dead met the living, where death surfaced to coexist with us.

The old city cemetery. La Recoleta.

5

I started my hike to the underworld by crossing between the immense Doric columns that supported the temple-like entrance of Recoleta. Saying it was foggy would have been a big understatement. A horror movie about a cemetery couldn't have been shot that day—you couldn't see anything. Most of the marble buildings crowding the huge campus disappeared into a cloud. I think few would have entered the city of the dead on a day like that.

I walked the main venue trying to orient myself, as this was a place where I have gotten lost every time I'd visited it. The story of Recoleta was like that of other above-ground cemeteries in the Americas and Europe: interments excavated by floods, leaving corpses floating in the streets; empty tombs that were rebuilt above the earth; great epidemics of yellow fever or malaria and the sudden need to expand capacity; and finally, a great competition for space, pushing the poor away, so they could not find rest anymore in the same grounds as the patrician few.

It didn't take long before I didn't know where I was. Domes crowned by angels—some raising their hands, apparently angry with their permanent assignments. Crosses big enough to topple their tombs. A huge condor set atop a pyramid in a popular tomb—with countless commemorative plaques. The afterlife equivalent

234

of a middle-eastern bazaar.

The corridors got narrower, and it was foggy enough they all ended in the same white wall. I was wandering like a pained ghost and had passed the same corridor at least three times. I tried to go around the place and found myself almost crashing into the walls that separated the drawers atop drawers containing the non-living from other larger stacked containers, the ones holding the living in the cemetery's neighboring buildings.

Again, I didn't know where I was, and, to some extent, it didn't matter.

I was taken by a strange, stylish green statue of a girl next to a dog. She reminded me a little of Mariana in a long dress. I knew there was a popular story about her death but couldn't remember it. She was like a child goddess watching the passing of souls. I tilted to read the inscriptions in the plate below. It was a poem to the dead daughter, by her father, in Italian. For some reason, I was able to read it.

...Perché? Credo al destino e non a te, perché?

Why? I believe in fate and not in you, why?

...Perché solo sò che sempre sogno conte, perché c'é di che?

Because I only know that I always dream about you, why is that?

I read the lines again—it was so much like my plight with Mariana, how I felt about wanting to be with her.

"Perché? Solo il destino sà il perche e mi domando perché?"

I realized I'd heard, not thought, those last lines. And I turned around to find the man, now dressed in a black jacket and a burgundy turtleneck sweater. "Why?" he said, back to English. "Only Destiny knows the reason, and I ask myself why."

The weirdness of my life. I was standing there, watching myself watching myself. "What are you doing here?"

"Are you joking...?" He didn't want to use my name. "You practically screamed you wanted to see me. Aren't you worried that I'll try to kill you?"

"I think we're past the point of trying to stop me. I know who you are."

He smiled. "Who *we* are."

"And why you are here," I said. "Me, trying to kill myself, yourself."

"That *is* the question. But let's get away from here; it's very crowded."

"Crowded? This place is almost empty."

"In time. Crowded in time."

I didn't say anything and just stood there, seeing every little wrinkle in a face that one day would be mine. "There are points in space and time," he said, "where many...possibilities exist. Like different universes. You and I have been in this particular spot, at the feet of Liliana Crociati's statue, many, many times—hundreds, thousands of times this same day."

"Us? You mean we've done this before?"

"Not before—now. It's just that...each time was different, and it wasn't really us. I have—not me, but other travelers—tried to kill you here. You must have escaped, or I wasn't very good at it." He paused, and the illusion of his height being greater vanished. My heft had grown with the years, and, with the puffy black jacket, the man's body seemed a lot larger than mine. "We better get away," he said, "before one of us finds us."

"One of us?"

"Don't play dumb. You know enough..." He started to walk, like Julian when he'd try to stop my annoying interruptions. Apparently, I would carry some of Julian with me.

I tried to catch up with him, before he entered one of Recoleta's identical, narrow corridors. Tombs on the right; tombs on the left.

He was speaking again. "I was told..."

"By whom?"

He turned to me. "Can you let me talk? Forget the aliens and all that crap. It's more complicated than that, you know, *our* problem. You might think that I know exactly what went so wrong here, but

I don't. Nobody knows, not even them."

"*Them?* It's either you or the aliens."

"I can't tell you who. And there's a lot even I don't know. This is... an educated guess."

"Only that?"

"A very educated guess by intelligences far more advanced than ours. Non-human intelligences."

"Robots?"

The man smiled, knowing that I didn't know back then what a real computer was. "Well, more or less," he said. "Machines, with machine brains a million times smarter than humans. *The Machines.* One day, we will also call them *The Constructs.* They'll run the show, in a future...can't tell you more. Let's stop here."

We hid in the steps of a tomb's entrance. It had a large front panel of black marble, and one of its glass windows was broken. I didn't want to look inside.

I tried to keep talking. "Why can't you talk? And what are we doing here, together?"

"I'm protecting you."

"Thought you wanted to kill me."

"I have been told you should die. But now, I think the machines might be wrong."

"The machines that are a million times smarter than us?"

"Anyone can be wrong," he said, looking away. "And I'm a little strong-headed about it."

"You mean *we* are."

I can't describe how weird it was when he smiled, the sense of not knowing where my reality was. "Yes, we are," he said. "And now, before something goes wrong, let me tell you what you must watch for. Something will happen, and you will have to make a decision that's so hard it's a given you'll take it one way. But it's wrong, and the fate of humanity hangs in you doing something else."

"That makes no sense."

"It would be really easy, if I knew."

"You don't know?"

"No, and as I'd said, *they* also don't know."

"Then, why all this? Going to so much trouble. Traveling some-one else through time."

He stopped long enough for me to notice my belabored breath-ing. "They thought I'd be able to figure it out," he said, "or kill you, if I couldn't. I have a good reason for your success."

"If you kill me, you're gone too."

"Exactly."

"But you can't figure what to change."

"I see that I *was* a bright man," he said, smiling. "The problem is that what you have to do—or avoid doing—is something happening so fast, there might not be enough time to act. We have to go, now."

"What? Why? I need to know more."

"I saw people back there—my kind of people. They're walking farther down the halls. Our time is over. Come."

We started to walk, rushing between twin alleys and long corri-dors. I thought I saw shadows in the fog, moving in the parallel alleys. After ten minutes of wandering around almost sprinting, we stopped, both breathless.

"I will be leaving now," he said. "But I won't be far."

"Did you set up the explosion at my home?"

I couldn't fathom the expression that fixed his face. "I told you," he said, "by now there are dozens of copies around. Failed trips where I'm trying to either help you or kill you. Can't easily tell who is who."

"Great," I said, and then thought about the best question I could ask him. "How do I find Mariana?"

He smiled. "You've missed a clue. You were very close."

"Where?"

"In La Plata."

And he moved away from me, quickly disappearing in the impenetrable whiteness.

6

Somehow, I'd ended up sitting in the pews of Our Lady of the Pillar Church—*Nuestra Señora del Pilar*—the extremely old white church next to the Recoleta Cemetery. I knew the church dated from the eighteenth century and his name had something to do with a pillar and its visitation by the Virgin Mary. But that afternoon, as the fog slowly cleared outside, I was distraught enough not to want to know even what I knew.

I was still seeing a pair of eyes. I could recognize them as mine, with their little brown imperfections, radial lines over a background of bluish European irises. But these eyes were not in my head, and they resided in another person's orbits. These eyes had been watching me as the man talked to me. I felt like one of those people who'd traveled out of their bodies during surgery, seeing themselves from above.

I had thought it'd be good to see *the man*—the now euphemistic name I was still applying to my pursuer—but miscalculated the effect an encounter with my time-travelling self would have on my resolve. I now didn't know what to do, and worse, truly worrisome for my sanity, I didn't know who I was.

Copies of me traveling back in time? To kill me but perhaps also to help me?

Twentieth century's Physics had not advanced in the 1970s to the point of theorizing publicly about parallel timelines. And I had no way to understand what artificial intelligences might do or what kind of power they could have. There was no Internet, cell phones, digital photography, or tiny devices with entire music collections. To someone forty or fifty years in the future, I might have seemed like a caveman.

Still quite antsy, I changed seats and got closer to the altar, re-sitting on the left side of the church's main nave, close to the pulpit. It was a contraption resembling an elevator in Captain Nemo's *Nautilus*, decorated in gold and a light blue approaching the color of the Argentine flag. Tourists were all over the place—many surely visiting for the World Cup—and I kept my head down to avoid being seen.

I might have passed for one of the faithful, even more so when, in a moment of indescribable heart-heaviness, I kneeled on my seat's rest and put my face between my hands.

At that moment, I could understand why people believed in God.

I was a natural atheist, the kind that abhors all organized religion. But I was there, in a centuries-old church, and engaged in thinking that was normal for the legions of believers.

Do I have free will?

Is my destiny cast in stone?

Can I erase my ultimate sin?

I was confronting a reality that, for most, would belong in the realm of the supernatural. It wasn't a reality with a real God, but God-like minds that could do things only He was supposed to be able to do. Predict the future, see time outside its course, and intervene to make the world the best that could exist. And what these beings had done with my life were, like many things the Bible's God had done to mankind, actions to be more expected from the Devil. The subtle torture I was being subjected to denoted the sort of super-human mind only a god (or a demon) would have.

I had started an inner dialogue that disgusted me because it was hiding a plea, and thus it had transformed itself into prayer.

I was praying to Fate, but a Fate that had a fallible mind and was trying to improve its knitting of the threads of destiny.

I suddenly stopped caring, and a voice hollered inside my mind. Its intensity gained the power of true praying. Either the deity then listened, or I'd calmed my mind enough with a pinch of silence, but my impossible problem revealed its nature to my infinitesimal primate brain.

There was no solution. I could act, and whatever I did would be my own call and my doing, even if it resulted in my undoing.

I wasn't much of a football player—either American or Argentine—but knew that the ball was in my court and I should run with it.

I was going to save Mariana or die trying.

And if the universe came to its end with me, so be it.

An Edgar Weston I could barely recognize stood up, inches taller, rose above all possible worlds, and decided to be the hero of his story.

7

I went back to my apartment in a state I felt was determination but approached fury. I stormed the place, checking for messages with the doorman, going through my mail like it was a deck of cards I needed to shuffle, and pressing my friend for news he couldn't possibly have. It was a fundamentally unreasonable position— we knew nothing about Mariana's whereabouts, and we were trying to stay hidden from others—and it eventually led me to feel depressed.

It was Julian who suggested I call Cristina to see if she'd heard anything. I found the idea refreshing, exactly for the unsaid reason Julian had suggested it: Cristina was lovely, and I had a crush-like affection for her. But I had the suspicion Julian was engaging in preventive matchmaking—logical if one considered that both of our partners, Mariana and Rafa, were missing and in danger of never being heard from again.

Whatever my friend's twisted ploy was, it worked, and I was soon on the phone.

"Yes, hello? Cristina?"

"Who's this?"

"Edgardo."

"Edgardo...Oh, yes, Mariana's friend." Cristina's voice was so tired it seemed to crawl out of my phone and down to the floor.

"I was calling...do you know anything about Rafa?"

"No, I'm sorry, but we haven't..."

"I'm sorry too."

She spoke again, tilting up her tone but failing to convey any positive emotion. "We will know soon. I mean, they can't hold them forever."

I realized we were in the territory of pacifying lies, but I pressed on. "Do you think anyone knows?"

No answer. The silence prompted me to launch a series of ridiculous questions. I even asked her again where she went to school—couldn't remember her chosen career—and started to make small talk, which sounded like I wanted to invite her to a dance. It was clear I had a need for pampering a male friend couldn't satisfy; I was, after all, a motherless child.

I went back to my questions, remembering the man's last comment. "Do you think Pocha might know anything about them?"

Silence suggested a yes. "We can go and see Pocha," I said. "To La Plata. I mean the three of us."

Julian showed me a sheepish smile that was easy to crack.

"Good," said Cristina, the Argentine equivalent of "Okay." "Why don't you come when you get out of school?"

"School? No, sorry, today we have no classes."

Julian mouthed "never" and I tried to sound confident—I don't need to go to school, I said, high school is so easy—while only succeeding in emanating a desperate vibe, as if they had kicked me out.

Cristina agreed to the awkward plan with silence, and I finally managed to end the call. For a conversation that didn't produce any real leads and went nowhere, I felt strangely exhilarated.

* * *

A few hours later, the three of us were riding another train to La Plata. At first, we didn't talk much—out of our worries—but then engaged in the kind of mindless talk that had characterized teenagers from the time of the Pharaohs. I failed to find common ground with Cristina in TV or movies, mainly because Cristina disliked science-fiction shows and their reruns. Julian, apparently showing off to our beautiful partner, bragged about his knowledge and theories of everything. He then unsuccessfully attempted to shift the conversation to the World Cup and the prospects of Argentina to classify for finals—we were now in the preliminary Group B, together with Poland and Peru, but also with a very dangerous Brazil—but soon we found little more to say.

The conversation picked up as soon as Julian decided to go on one of his fake errands and disappeared through our car's connecting door.

Cristina gave me a complete report on her chosen career—it was economics, I should have remembered. She talked about how hard it had been to enter the country's best university—of course, the one in Buenos Aires—in times when the entry exams were starting to toughen up again. She was forgiving when it came to my high-school-student status and sought to talk with me ignoring our obvious age difference.

I remember when she went into a different line of questioning. "How did you meet Mariana?"

I was stumped, as I suddenly couldn't remember; it seemed I'd known Mariana all my life. And when I thought about the gun in her purse, I was even more paralyzed. *"In the subway,"* I finally said.

Cristina smiled. In my distraction, I had spoken in English.

"Sorry," I continued, forcing myself back to Spanish. "It was like that, a meeting in the subway at night. We decided to have coffee."

"Love at first sight."

Her comment was obviously true, but I kept trying to explain.

"We just...we liked to talk. Spent time together and went to see a movie. And then..."

I knew that was pretty much all of it. Our story, before or after, had been shaped by violent interruptions, courtesy of government thugs. And I had become the knight who meets a damsel once and then tries to rescue her from the dragon.

8

I entered Pocha's house with the same internal struggle and spiritual prostration I'd had when visiting Recoleta's Pilar Church. There was also a similar darkness, and a moldy smell of dampness that made me uncomfortable. Inside, it appeared nobody had cleaned up the rooms after our last visit. Maybe all the available energy was being consumed by worry and desperation.

But one wouldn't see any of this in *Doña* Pocha Venturino's face. She was as stern and uncommunicative as I remembered her, and we couldn't get more than monosyllabic retorts to every question we posed.

It was getting late in the day, and Pocha was trying to run down the clock and force us to leave. Luckily, we were three and she was just one—with grandma mostly a butler-like figure around us. Over time, Pocha started to talk, especially with Cristina, and we soon found ourselves holding cups of coffee and staring at pieces of a stale cake, while we all sat at a round table whose edges had seen better times.

Pocha was apparently unmoved by the taking of her daughter at *San Carlos*, just as if she were denying it could've happened a second time. She said, over and over, that she had known nothing about the Montoneros operation at the church and was as worried as we were. Such a perfect story of denial convinced me that she was lying. I didn't need to consult my expert friend to reach this conclusion.

The day was going to end with another round of fog and a monochromatic afternoon characteristic of wintertime in Buenos Aires, and by extension, neighboring La Plata. And so, we stood after having carefully finished our barely eatable cakes, seemingly ready to leave. Pocha also stood, in the middle of our group, with her head very high.

I'd just noticed how large and battered the charcoal duffel bag Julian carried was when he said—for the tenth time— "I can't believe Anibal didn't call you."

"He's not very good at calling," said Pocha.

Cristina had been getting angrier, likely feeling betrayed by Pocha. "And what about Rafa? They're very good friends. I don't understand why the Montoneros don't try to rescue him."

"If they could," Pocha said, "they would." She then fell again into one of her silences.

I decided to break it. "Do you think that Montoneros would trade Martínez for one of their own?"

Again, silence we didn't know how to break. Too many questions and a few bad answers.

"He's right," started Julian. He was pumping his right foot on the floor, the vibrations climbing his trousers all the way to the waist. "They could trade her, Mariana, for that son of a bitch. Maybe they could then find Martínez again...they were following him, weren't they?"

"It's not so easy. We—they'd found and lost him many times. He does hide well." Pocha's smile was the definition of creepy.

"If they found him once," Julian said, "they can do it again."

Pocha held a piece of silence like a dog's bone. "We're running out of time."

I had to say it— "For what?"

"The eyes of the world are on Argentina." Pocha's voice was oddly emotional, as if that one-liner, coming from the military's propaganda, was a heartfelt expression of her soul.

"And?" Julian raised his tone, covering another "and" question I had uttered under my breath.

"Whatever we do now," Pocha said, "everybody will see."

Cristina didn't waste time going back to our lone issue. "Pocha, do you think that *that* is more important than the lives of your friends? People will forget soon what happens during the World Cup."

"No, they won't. Not this time." There was something on Pocha's face that reminded me of witches. It was getting dark, and it seemed as if we were acting a scene from a horror movie.

"I want to see Rafa again," said Cristina, and she let her words hang in the next silence. "I don't care what Montoneros should be doing, or what history would say about you, Pocha. Is there any way to contact Anibal and talk with him? I want to explain..."

"I don't know," said Pocha. "I really can't help you."

More silence, and this time I noticed that Pocha had never mentioned Mariana by name. Not once.

Cristina kept trying, but it was enough for me. Julian also realized our play was finished and we should go. Surprisingly, after some hard-to-calculate time beating around the bush, Pocha said something remarkable, given the circumstances. "I don't want you to go back so late to Buenos Aires. Why don't you stay here for the night? Is that well with you?"

We were so surprised that we said yes.

9

In the early morning, the train station was freezing cold, as La Plata was characteristically much colder in winter than Buenos Aires. The hangar-like iron ceiling above us had enough glass to create a diffuse clarity; there were so few railroads departing from its open end, I had trouble thinking this could be the main station for the true capital of the richest province in Argentina. We could have been in a station way down South, high in the Andes, although those were so naked and solitary they resembled train stops in the middle of Africa.

I held Cristina's hands—so cold and soft—while we waited for her train to come. Julian and I had decided to stay behind, so we could investigate further, in the parlance of my friend. I wanted to have more time to be with Cristina; she was very sad, and I didn't want to lose sight of her.

It had been a long night as, after I'd left the lights on in my room, Cristina had knocked and come over to see me. We'd spent two hours—maybe more—talking and trying to calm our nerves. We found a deck of cards in a drawer and played a few hands of *Chin-Chón*, the Spanish cards' version of Gin Rummy. Even in the middle of the night and under stress, she was the better player and won every time. I didn't care much, and there was also a little of that intoxicating quality about spending the night awake with a remarkably pretty girl. Cristina had dressed in a borrowed night-gown—her legs would occasionally show themselves too much. When she left, the sunrise couldn't have been far away. I'd stayed in bed waiting for the light to climb my window, trying not to think of her.

The train finally arrived from Buenos Aires. We said our good-byes to Cristina, and I enjoyed the South American custom of kiss-ing and hugging people with real affection. I could sense a change in the duration of our proximity; it was not customary to stay close for so long, resting on each other. I guess we both needed it.

I didn't know what to expect from my future, even the one for just that day. The so-far-undisclosed plan Julian had mentioned would keep me in La Plata, but I would have gladly followed Cris-tina to Buenos Aires, trying to collect more crumbles of her warmth.

Truthfully, I didn't have anywhere to go.

* * *

What Julian wanted to do was sheer madness. Coffee and crois-sants at a bar across the train station wouldn't soften me enough to take again my usual position as his sidekick and partner. He had decided we would stage a stakeout of the Venturinos' home, as they do in cop shows.

Basically, we'd keep monitoring the house to see if Anibal showed up. I argued with Julian that Anibal might take days to appear, and, a little less effectively, explained how during our current absence—we'd already been gone for hours—he could have already been at the Venturinos' home. Julian countered that the times were dangerous and Pocha would take some time to contact the Montoneros about her daughter. It was a talk between two deaf guys, and we didn't exclude how, rather than meeting face-to-face, Pocha and Anibal could have easily communicated via telephone.

My friend was many things but the one I was most sure of was his being the guy who's always ready. I never asked him if he'd been with the Boy Scouts, but he could have been a leader there. The rugged bag he carried—made from tough sailcloth and dyed almost black—contained a cornucopia of food and supplies that could have lasted us days. He also had a 35-millimiter camera, a Minolta 7s roughed up by use. Julian proudly took it off its leather holster and displayed for me the exposure settings and lens controls, explaining how he'd created a developing lab in his bedroom's bathroom.

I didn't know much about cameras back then, but his camera's short lens suggested that Julian wanted to take pictures from up close, and this worried me, even before I saw the gun I'd left in my apartment briefly surface between spare notebooks, rope, and an extra sweater we might be sharing at night.

We easily found an outpost for our stakeout in a run-of-the-mill café—across the street from Pocha's, and thus not so much of an outpost. Soon, with more coffee and toasted ham-and-cheese sandwiches, I got Julian's extended lesson in photography, including the, according to him, relatively easy-to-understand concept of exposure as the fractions of a second the shutter opened to expose the film. Not so easy to understand was the role of the Minolta's diaphragm—which I kept trying, incorrectly as it were, to compare with a human eye—and how one could use it to get both good focus and blurred layers in different portions of the same image. When Julian tried to explain the reasons behind the high DIN/ISO sensitivity of the professional-grade *Ilford* black-and-white film *we* would be using for night-time shooting, my so-called brilliant brain finally gave up.

Every once in a while, we looked up and checked the door of Pocha's house, maybe one-third of a block away.

We obviously felt invisible.

10

It was a day that taught me the nuances of the dictionary's etymology of the word *excruciating*. We kept our post for hours, under the increasingly critical watch of our waiter. Argentines would hug a cup of coffee for a while at their cafés, but our not leaving at any cost triggered conversations between the behind-the-counter likely owner and the sole waiter of the place. Being the subjects of their gossip was fine with us, but after four hours, the repeated insistence of the guy charged with bringing us a dozen of total cups of coffee beverages—espressos, *café au lait*, and my favorite, dark coffee topped with whipping cream—plus a sampling of their pastries led to a breaking point.

I knew this as soon as the manager made his way around the counter. We were told to leave as per some old—but probably just invented—city ordinance, which considered it illegal to stay in a restaurant for extended periods. He said we might've been taking seating space away from new customers and reducing the take-home pay of waiters.

Julian argued with the guy, but his increasing agitation didn't help our cause, as the ultimatum was really motivated by the prevalent fears—of terrorists, leftists, or any other forms of non-governmental ruffians. Maybe if we had been two or three years older and sported buzz cuts of the sort that scream young police, the discussion would have taken a different turn, or never happened, driven by another kind of fear.

The owner insisted—and the waiter nodded—that *they* had the right to exclude anyone from the premises. A few minutes later, we and the duffel bag were again in the street, just a block from Pocha's place.

Our departure from the first café started a nomadic existence, favored by the presence of similar establishments in every neighboring block. The city appeared to have been built as a just a spacer for its coffeehouses. We visited four other coffee-providing places, each allowing us a sometimes distant but nevertheless continuous observation of Pocha's front door. We only had to choose the right table at each establishment and be sure to order enough food to pacify our waiter. Even more food than what we were eating, as if we were waiting for someone.

A day like this probably inspired the famous play about waiting for Godot.

* * *

Time passed by without any of the differences that make it distinct. It got cloudy at times, and light played games with the shadows, surprising me when, in the darkest moments, I could actually see better into the house's entrances, all the way to lights at the end of the tunnels that granted entrance to private worlds.

I nodded off a few times, and Julian encouraged me each time to stay awake. But I finally surrendered to the lack of sleep, and my friend probably thought I needed the break more than his conversation.

I watched a dream from the outside, seeing through a big eye while stuck beyond its curvature, in the dark.

I saw the same street at night, illuminated by sodium lamps. I was standing on the sidewalk, just across from Pocha's front door. I didn't know if I could cross the street. Or if I should.

What I most remember from the dream were the spheres. Purple balls, tall like buildings, and patterned by swirls of other colors, like toy marbles. There was a certain glass-like quality about them, and they resembled transparent worlds rolling toward me. They stopped in the street's center, wobbling a little, like the glass beads in one of those games where they would move around until they snugly fit on a depression of the board.

I was still staring at the parked spheres when I woke up. I didn't notice that one of them remained outside the café, ghostly as a gigantic soap bubble, and disappeared only when I was completely conscious.

Night came, soon enough. Not all at once but in patches of lagging daylight and in the growing company of car's headlights. Dark was well advanced by the time businesses turned on the yellow-green fluorescent tubes in their display windows. Still, light was light, and I welcomed the intrusion.

I had by then lost count of the stories Julian had told me. They put him in places all along the South American continent and in adventures where he thwarted marauders and got praise from strangers. He was—to himself and increasingly to me—like one of those Cervantes' characters, sailors of the Earth who collected adventures in each town they visited. Half of them were true, but with Julian the fun was that one didn't know which of the halves were true.

Without knowing why, I felt goose bumps when the sodium lamps finally awoke, still weak, no more than pinpricks to the night.

11

A few hours of darkness went by without any sign our wait would ever end. Cars passed by, and other cars parked for a while and left. But one of the parked cars, an American-looking compact, drew my attention—his occupant stayed inside for a long time after it came to rest between a truck and an old sedan. Maybe he was setting up a stakeout that was destined to us. Maybe there were nested stakeouts all the way to infinity.

I was concerned about the car but hadn't yet raised enough internal worry to disturb Julian from his afternoon-edition newspaper—*Clarín*, I think, as he distrusted the pro-military writings in *La Nación*—whose pages he'd used as a curtain to stop all conversation. But then I saw something.

The compact car's door opened, and something came out. I thought it looked like a rifle and panicked.

A man grabbed the edge of the open door and hauled himself to stand. Big guy, but in the dark, I couldn't see much of him. From where I was looking, the object and he were only a silhouette.

It was a man who held a couple of crutches to move about.

I opened my mouth in archetypical disbelief. It was Anibal Reinoso, strenuously making his way to Pocha's doorsteps.

I dragged Julian out of the café in seconds. We had devised a system of periodic payment of our bills, so the waiter didn't even turn in our direction when we hastily escaped his domain. I had to come back to pick up my friend's not-so-surprisingly-heavy black bag and caught up with Julian as he crossed the intersection toward Anibal in a tangential direction.

I should thank La Plata's City Hall for the old trees gracing Pocha's street, thick enough to hide us both behind a gnarled cylinder of wood. Also, I'd thank Anibal's crutches, which kept him reduced to single steps as he crossed the gap between sidewalks. The injured Montonero managed to skip—or be skipped by—at least three vehicles.

* * *

What follows is what I recall from the conversation we overheard between Pocha and Anibal. Their voices were loud, with enough contained anger to be clearly heard—no concerns about passersby or police walkabouts.

Maybe this wasn't the first time Pocha had asked him this. "Why didn't you come before? And what the hell is wrong with your foot?"

"Thanks for the concern. My foot decided to go left just as I jumped right off the big truck."

"You and that damned truck. It's going to kill you one day."

"There are plenty of guns already pointed at me."

"And I guess there will be more soon, when you reach the airwaves."

"Yes, soon enough. We're preparing *him* for the big event...he's really a hard-headed bastard."

"Are you going to recover my daughter?"

The next silence punctuated the question, and I swear I heard the ruffling of Anibal's clothing as he uncomfortably accommodated his crutches.

"You know she signed up for this," he said. "And there are risks, with our kind of work."

Pocha raised her voice and stood quite straight, as if trying to reach Anibal's eyes. "I want my daughter. *Soon.* You know she's only safe until the transmission."

A tug from Julian, hard. *Transmission.* For a moment, I forgot my anger with Anibal.

Anibal was talking again— "You know that nothing is quite sure when dealing with our friends in boots."

"You don't have much time, anyway. And I want this—I want *her.*"

The lowered head of Anibal was completely covered by his black hair. It looked to me like a hood. "I will do what's possible," he said, at the limit of what I could hear. "The cause is first."

Pocha approached Anibal, as if ready to strike him. "Don't talk to me like a damned Trotskyist," she said. "You know this is all about power and revenge. They killed us first, and now it's our turn."

"I don't care about your family's history with the military." Anibal had used the scolding term *milicos*. "I just want to be free from them."

"Even if it costs us Mariana. I thought you'd wanted her to be your girlfriend."

"You know she's not really that. I wanted to...but she's only talking about that kid."

Pause. Another tug from Julian. I liked it this time—felt good being *that kid.*

Pocha's anger, wound up to its core, exploded slowly, word by word. "What you'd only wanted is to have sex. With my daughter. She's also just a kid, and you, you are a disgrace."

I didn't see it but heard the huge slap on the face of *Mr. Macho.* Anibal's face twisted under the pressure, and he stumbled enough to struggle trying to regain control of his crutches.

Anibal was quickly back to his own warrior self. "Did you bring me here just to insult me?"

"I brought you here to tell you this to your face. I want my daughter back."

"I will do what..."

"Back! Do you understand? Want her back, and if Martínez is the problem, I'll drag his ass all the way to the office of his friend, that other criminal D'Agostini."

D'Agostini? I'd expected another tug from Julian, so when it didn't come I turned and my heart skipped a beat.

Julian was crossing the street, already being lighted by the yellow glare.

And Anibal had seen him, even before Pocha did.

Things happened quickly from then on. "You," Anibal yelled. "What the hell are you doing here, listening to us?"

Surprisingly, the next line was mine. "He is with me."

Pocha looked at me like a ghost, or a returned *desaparecido*— "Edgardo?"

"You are a pair of *metidos*," Anibal said, making his way to us like a tumbling snail. "You're going to get what's meant to you." We stayed in the middle of that street, while I pondered if *metidos*— those who meddled in other people's affairs—had a strict translation to English. I was going to have plenty of time to consider it while lying in a hospital bed.

Anibal got to Julian first, and, losing one of his crutches grabbed him by the throat. He was as much holding Julian as garnering support not to fall. I guess that Pocha was stunned, since I can't remember her saying anything.

"Please, we're here to..." Julian's voice was belabored, and I worried Anibal was going to seriously hurt him, or worse.

"No, you are not going to do anything," said Anibal. It was clear he was ready to squeeze harder.

It was one of those moments one has trouble believing it really happened. Like taking a long-shot to the goalpost, I kicked Anibal upwards, aiming straight for his balls. Two seconds later, he was kneeling and Julian was free.

I should have stopped, but I didn't. The black bag was at Julian's feet, and I picked it up, swung it and hit a disbelieving Anibal directly on the side of his head. Unable to escape the impact, he fell sideways and remained still, as if he were peacefully watching the night above the lights.

Goliath had fallen.

12

We carried Anibal into Pocha's house. Julian held the crutches, and I had the uncomfortable task of supporting him. He was in relatively bad shape, and I felt awful about having surrendered to my base instincts and hurt him.

Pocha wanted to put a frozen steak on Anibal's eye but he refused. He was showing off a macho cool, but his left eyelid and part of the temple had suffered serious sandpaper-like scraping with the glancing blow of the sailcloth bag.

I was trying to stay away from him, but when I brought some ice cubes wrapped in a wet kitchen towel, he grabbed my hand and forced me to look at him.

He didn't say anything, but his expression was clear enough.

It's okay. You came to the help of your friend, and I understand that.

Without a word, we decided to let it go for now. As for getting Mariana, I knew that I might need him, and it was best to keep the bastard around.

* * *

Like in a bad Italian movie, we all ended up spending the night in separate rooms. Pocha had assumed her role of Mother of the

House and forced us to wait for daylight with her, summoning the military and other monsters that crawled at night in Argentine cities of the time.

I spent my second overnight stay in one of the many empty rooms in the back of Pocha's house, which, judging by its flowery bed cover and the assortment of dolls we quickly stored under the bed, had once been occupied by a child—maybe Mariana.

Since I couldn't sleep and was in a heightened state of excitation after the fight, I started to follow every sound coming from outside my bedroom. Soon, I heard muffled voices downstairs.

I only heard fragments of a conversation, but they got stuck in my memory. It was the tension that made the exchange memorable.

Pocha sounded truly at the end of her rope, her voice trembling. "If you don't do anything, I *will* have to."

Anibal raised his voice. "I can't help her, not without risking everything. She's not essential for the plan."

"You mean she's expendable. Disposable."

Silence became part of the conversation.

Disposable.

I lost heart after this and decided to try and get some sleep. And I was soon sound asleep.

I dreamt again of those purple spheres.

And the man was there.

We were there.

* * *

Anibal had left by the time I woke up. The sun was not yet above the line of sight of Pocha's front window, so he had probably wanted the cover of night to leave the house. We had an oddly normal breakfast with Pocha and her almost-silent mother. The formal plates and wicker bread basket belonged to a neorealist Italian movie.

Pocha didn't say much but offered us a ride to Buenos Aires. She said she had some business to take care of in the city, involving a trip her company required every week, so she could pay the factory's providers. I thought she was supplying the details for my benefit—the foreign kid—but I did know how handling Argentine checks required precautions akin to radioactivity, including hour-long explanations of how and when they should, or could, be cashed.

It was funny that the classic Italian *Doña* Pocha Venturino would own a sporty two-door car. It was a brand-new, Argentine-produced Renault Torino TS, instantly recognizable as the country's equivalent of a Pontiac GTO. Back then, it was a sure sign of monetary status. Odd choice for a business-lady like her, especially in a shade of green the military would have liked. It had fancy big wheels, with five-point stars that screamed race car, and a big wood panel in the front, filled with unnecessary instruments. The Torino was a fake speed machine, all the way to its logo with a bull standing in the hind legs, mimicking the horse in a Ferrari's front plate.

I enjoyed the ride, sitting in the front with the window open. Pocha drove without talking to us, and Julian decided not to contribute anything, squeezed by his bag on the backseat. The city soon enveloped us, and we emerged near the south-bound railroad station, at Plaza Constitución. Pocha then left us—without asking much about where we wanted to go—on *Corrientes* Avenue, near the point where the city starts to slope down toward the river.

We simply left the car and said goodbye. She was looking away, trying to reenter the avenue's flow.

13

"Let's follow her," said Julian.

"What?"

"She's going somewhere around here, and it's not to pay any suppliers."

I knew he was right but still hesitated before following him, long enough to put the kind of distance between us and her that finally triggered a sprint. We moved forward along Corrientes while, even from afar, I could see the green Torino stuck at a turn that led into Reconquista Street and the city's bank district. Reconquista would then empty all these vehicles into the colonial square, Plaza de Mayo, just a few blocks away.

As if in queue to remain out of our reach, Pocha's car started to move into Reconquista. I thought we were going to lose her but, apparently, the experience of fighting traffic had been too much for her. She pulled into the first available parking garage.

I caught up with Julian at the sidewalk just across from the garage's entrance. "And now, what?"

Julian looked at me like I was an unbelievably huge idiot, having recovered with the chase his stature as the big brother. "We follow her," he said. "From a distance."

Although I had started to feel like that idiot version of me Julian hated so much, we followed Pocha closely for the next few blocks. We were approaching the plaza, visible but framed between two massive buildings. Pocha kept walking faster with each passing block, and she'd put some good distance between us.

We were at the edge of Plaza de Mayo and, on the left, I could see the house of government, Argentina's famous Casa Rosada—the "Pink" House—legendarily considered to be a hybrid between the White House and a red Kremlin. On the right and across the plaza, I could see what little was left of the colonial house of Spanish legislation, El Cabildo. And—not to forget the ever-present religious influence on every Argentine era—there was a massive Greek-like temple facing the square, the city's Cathedral.

I was wondering which way Pocha would go on foot, and specifically, why she was moving so openly into an area that was closely guarded by the military.

The answer surprised me. It was waiting on the nearest sidewalk of the plaza, dressed in appropriately professional, dark gray clothing.

There was a distant thundering. Strong, menacing.

The Devil was being announced.

D'Agostini.

* * *

It wouldn't have been possible for us to get close enough to Pocha and the archbishop to hear them talk, as the plaza had a chronic circulation of cars that would block any sound coming from its core. If we crossed the avenue to get closer, they'd see us; if we moved around the vast space—attempting a roundabout approach from the rear—enough time could pass for the meeting to have ended before we approached them. And if they saw us, they could have escaped separately in any number of directions, hiding between the tourists that were feeding a million birds.

I took a couple of steps ahead, confident that the traffic was being contained by a red light. Julian apparently hadn't followed me into the pedestrian crossing.

Pocha was reaching the spot to which the archbishop was heading. He'd been walking parallel to her, probably his way to be sure everything was going according to his plan, while still being able to deny he was meeting a Montonero leader.

I turned back, distressed by feeling alone while chasing the mysterious duo.

Julian was detained at the last sidewalk's edge. He was arguing with a guy who held his duffel bag. It was clear he didn't want to return it to him without some proof it was his.

It was also clear that the guy was *him*. The man. My aged doppelganger.

I wanted to run as far away as possible. And thus, I turned back to face the plaza, ready to run toward Pocha and D'Agostini.

The crosswalk's light was going to turn green. This was, I'd say, the least of my problems. Because between me and the end of the pedestrian way, a new obstruction wouldn't let me walk more than a few steps forward.

It wasn't a car failing to stop—like many did—at the painted white lines. What it was cannot be explained in simple dictionary words.

Tall as the plaza's pyramidal monument, a purple-orange glass sphere was stationary over the street. And I was sure to be the only one able to see it.

A normal human being, especially one who'd dreamed something like this the night before, would have run as fast as he could and forever away from that spot. But I'd had enough of problems, interferences, chases, and lies, and I didn't believe the thing could be a real obstacle. Or even a real thing. I thought I was just trying to trick myself—by incredible means—from acting like a true knight and finding my lost princess. A gigantic made-up excuse for being a coward.

Doing what any other day would have been unthinkable, I kept walking toward the object, even faster than before.

I thought the illusion was going to vanish just as I managed to reach it—it was even a little bit flimsier than in my dream, its edges like pink steam. But I was wrong.

I crossed the reddish film of that tiny cold star and fell into an abysm.

It was like being launched into the vacuum of space.

14

Being inside the sphere was like being under anesthesia—or dead—in that I felt like I'd entered a dark space and then, an instant later, found myself kneeling on the pavement. Nothing in between. Just a cold sensation in my body, as if something icy had grabbed my soul.

I felt that time was not running as silently as before. I could hear now time's engine running, and I felt how the wheels push past each other while propelling the universe forward.

I knew, without proof and for the same reason more forcefully, that, while in the sphere, I had visited the mechanism—or a mechanism, at the very least—that puts together the succession of our instants. With the same blind conviction, I knew my short trip outside time had changed me forever. My soul had aged a million years and now was burdened with unreachable knowledge of all the possibilities in the universe.

I was somehow certain that I had seen features of all my futures. Saw them in the dark corridors of the houses of time.

This had all happened in a second. A very long second.

I didn't turn back to see whether the man was still there. I stepped onto the sidewalk, the cars starting to move behind me. I kneeled again and picked up a street tile's fragment, just a little larger than the other broken pieces strewn over the park's poorly maintained walkway. Took aim and threw it ahead, above my head.

The wheels of the mechanism started to spin. Some would even say they started to calculate.

The fragment hit right in the middle of a large gaggle of birds. One of them shook its wings and scared another one. In an instant, the impact had transformed the peaceful landing into a frantic scene; the huge local pigeons, *palomas de la plaza*, were now flying in a swirling cloud all around Plaza de Mayo. The noise of flapping wings and the overexcited calls muffled all other sounds, and people started to move toward the surrounding streets.

I sneaked through the swirling mass of birds and people, placing myself near the May's Pyramid, *La Pirámide de Mayo*, a monument built to commemorate Argentina's emancipation from Spain. Pocha and D'Agostini were standing on the opposite side.

"I hate the *palomas*," the archbishop said. "They mess all over the plaza."

"Are we here to talk about *palomas*?"

"No. As I said, I came only because I was curious—you, Pocha, calling me, after fifteen years."

"I told you what I want."

"I don't care about what happens to Montoneros."

"You are a Man of God. How can you say that?"

"These are evil people. They will...suffer."

"My daughter is *not* one of them."

"She is, and guilty like all of them. But I'm flexible—and do care about the damage your people can do."

"They aren't my people anymore—I'm retired. And you know they have Martínez."

"Sure, we know that, but we have your daughter. And you and I, we both know that Martínez is more valuable—to us and the Montoneros. As for you personally, I think you'll give anything to have her back."

"Where do you have her?"

I could sense the archbishop was smiling when he answered— "She's is in one of our twin stations in Floresta. And she's fine, but only for now."

Floresta? Where the hell was that? I knew of the Flores neighborhood, not about this other one.

Pocha talked, a little louder. "What do you want?"

"To ensure her safety, I'd need to know where they're—you are holding Martínez. After that, I'll tell you where you can rescue your daughter."

And then, suddenly, it was raining like we were in the Amazon's jungle. Buenos Aires enjoyed a temperate climate most of the time, but there was a mean tropical streak whenever it decided to pour.

I heard Pocha, talking softly now— "They'll be moving him around a lot. But I can check, find out where the next holding house is. We have many safe houses to keep the prisoners."

"*Pri-sio-ne-ros,*" said D'Agostini, relishing every syllable. "You know, you guys are decidedly weak. Only capturing people when there's a specific reason....We are past that point. Everybody we're getting now is just a step to eliminate all of you. Crush you like cockroaches. He's just one man, you know, the colonel, and, whatever it is that you plan to do with him, you are no match for *our* movement. Remember this."

"What I'll remember is that you and your friends are great sons of bitches."

The last words, *hijos de putas*, took a life of their own and flew like dark pigeons in the silent esplanade.

It was now raining hard, and when I looked down from the menacing skies, Pocha and D'Agostini were already walking in opposite directions.

15

Julian was elated by my catching up with Pocha and the arch-bishop. Contrarily to what I'd guessed, the tiny bit of information I'd gotten from them made him jump with joy. I can't describe the expression on his face when I said— "He also mentioned that they have a couple of facilities, twin ones, in Floresta."

"That's it!"

"What?"

"I know how to find her."

"You do? You know?"

"I know everything."

"Julian..."

"Well, most everything about those sons of bitches."

My translation circuits broke down. Had I mentioned that I'd heard Pocha say they *were* sons of bitches? Or was it such a common name-calling—especially for the military and their folk—that everybody used it as a synonym? This was a frequent problem with speaking a different language: it was so hard to replicate the intensity of emotions and reasons behind how people used insults. It was beyond me.

"Hey," said Julian. "Don't be disappointed. We made great head-way with your tracking."

"How's that?"

"When they created their detention center in Floresta, someone surely selected real estate to rent, and then bought it, some large place like a warehouse. We can find out if they got more than one—to save money with a deal. I have some records at home..."

"That's brilliant."

"Thank you, Doctor Watson. The game's afoot; isn't that how he would say it?"

It was irritating when Julian imitated Sherlock Holmes, but I let it go. Before we left Plaza de Mayo I gave it a worried look, searching for the spheres.

If Julian was Holmes, I had turned into a character from one of Borges's stories about the impossible made real.

* * *

In the ungodly accumulation of paper crowding Julian's room, finding any particular record was very unlikely. His packrat's delight was evident in the way he moved from one piece of paper to another, freely associating potential connections between them. Whenever he broke open a pile of blurry photocopies, a penetrating smell invaded the area; I couldn't place it, but it was somewhere between rubber and cleaning fluid.

It turned out Julian had "interviewed" a few people in Floresta, including a night watchman who was hired during the year's end holidays to keep an eye on a building at that neighborhood. It was, eerily to me, another car shop like the one Julian had toured. The watchman had placed it close to the city's western railroads, the Sarmiento line, but he wasn't sure about the address.

Julian also produced records from neighbors who'd verified the place had been closed since 1976, when the owners had moved to another, unknown site. One of the interviewees knew the original owner and said she'd overheard someone talking about "another

Condor" not ten blocks away.

"Condor?" I said, dumbfounded.

"*Operación Cóndor* was the name of the mission for this center. They are detaining people from Chile, Uruguay, Bolivia, even Brazil. I guess they'd thought of a condor flying over the Andes—but don't really know."

I frowned and gave him a sly smile, since I didn't know that this time we were talking about a real international conspiracy, one that would be responsible for the deaths of thousands. A vast operation designed by South American military governments—with some serious help from my country in the North—to mutually eliminate leftist subversion.

I was a little miffed when answering Julian's short speech, "And what does it mean 'another condor'?"

"That would be *our* condor."

* * *

There were a few hours of post-discovery excitation. We didn't have a good map of Floresta—by then, I knew the neighborhood was like a westward extension of Flores—and so we were left with asking around in several stores until we found a recent *Filcar* Guide, a huge spiral-bound collection of Buenos Aires maps. It was a cartographic labor of love that covered the city's countless neighborhoods and suburbs with incredible detail. We also packed—repacked, really—Julian's blackish bag, adding an extra sweater for me and an umbrella, since the rain had reached worrisome, summer-like intensity.

Julian made a point about not taking the gun with us—so we wouldn't be confused with terrorists, he said—and, even though at the time I cringed at that, his paranoia might have saved our lives.

We spent the afternoon in the drowning rain, apparently no closer to finding the first condor than we were at Julian's home.

We only knew that the place was close to the railroads and near a certain Venancio Flores Street. About the second condor, we were clueless.

Night was quickly approaching when lightning began all over the skies. It was so bad you could see flashes of light and hear thunder every couple of minutes.

We were walking across the street from a series of two-story housings—this was the most common configuration of the city outside downtown—when I noticed how it was broken by a slightly taller commercial building. I pointed to the place's rolling metal curtain. In light-blue and white that would be perfect for an Argentine flag, a deft artist had drawn an immense silhouette depicting a bird, its wings spanning the entire width of the grooved iron panel.

The enormous italicized letters below the image clarified, somewhat ironically, what the place was...

Automotores Cóndor

There was light escaping below the barely open curtain. Above it, more light percolated between the narrow slits of wood-slated windowsills.

We had found the second condor.

16

I climbed the dividing wall with help from Julian but, after that, I was alone up there like a high-flying trapeze artist in an open tent set in the middle of a hurricane. The storm was raging, and water appeared to fall in swirling curtains; I'd learn later that city buses had been trapped by the rising waters in some underpasses. All the water available above me had decided to jump to earth.

The outside wall of *Automotores Cóndor* had been secured against intruders with pieces of broken bottles cemented to its top edge. That might have been a complete protection several years earlier—and even then, in need of better masonry—but only a few pointing glass bottoms remained. I was thus able to take one tentative step after another, not much more than that. I just kept moving forward, trying to skirt the wall and reach a hanging ladder, which was propped at the innermost point of the building's patio.

The wind suddenly picked up and I almost fell inside. Trying to recover my equilibrium put me close to kneeling over a dangerously pointy half-bottle that looked like a mouth with plenty of snaggletooth. After the misstep, fear took over and I decided to wait it out until Julian managed to reach me. I carefully leaned on the neighboring building's side wall while peering to see if Julian had climbed the wall. From my stressed-out point of view, this took him half an hour; time being relative as it is, it was probably short of five minutes, estimated by the progressive soaking of my jacket.

Rest assured, we hadn't worked out a plan for our rescue of Mariana. Clueless knights stuck in the castle's ramparts, we were only succeeding in getting into more serious trouble. Give us some courage points for our risk-taking approach; but do subtract a few more than those, considering our lack of intelligence in having taken the most exposed route.

Julian finally walked the soaked plank like I did, and he approached me with a face of extreme fear I had never seen on him.

We were never going to make it all the way to the ladder—it was impossible to walk the rest of the narrow, broken-glass-covered median. The cemented glass was unfortunately intact there, and putting our feet over it seemed unwise. And now the night was much darker, with enough rain and wind to make it hard not to fall.

We found a corner where a balcony from the nearest building crossed the wall's upper edge and decided to use it as an awning to wait for the storm to end. The next few hours were from the longest and loneliest I can remember; it seemed as if we'd been cornered on a mountain pass.

And the noises that came from across the patio made surviving that night even harder.

They were human screams. Somewhere inside the house, people were being tortured.

* * *

The wait started to do unseemly things to Julian. I noticed that he had put his legs on either side of the duffel bag—now shrunk to its minimal expression after we'd extracted anything we could use to cover ourselves from the tempest. His legs were shaking, not as if from fear or cold, but in steady preparation to turn fluid and

275

collapse; even his hands twitched fitfully.

I tried to talk him out of his spell. "How are you doing?"

I might have said "¿*Como te sentís ahora?* —"How do you feel now?"—as the Spanish inquiry was more specific about the worrisome now.

He looked up from his shaky hands, but his eyes failed to focus on me.

"I said, 'How are you feeling?'" I repeated. "It's cold and it'd be best if we move, at least a little, so our feet don't get numb. I see you're shaking..."

"We will be heroes."

"What?"

"When we rescue...everybody that's inside. They're going to name streets after us."

"Julian, please. We can barely help ourselves—look at us, stuck on a ledge like sitting ducks. We're going to be shooting practice in the morning, just a target exercise for the soldiers."

And I had been trying to be helpful.

"You don't understand," Julian whispered, now more aware that we could be overheard. "All the work—my work the last two years—is going to make a difference. They are going to remember my name, what I did."

I thought of lists of the disappeared their families were publishing in Buenos Aires newspapers. *Los desaparecidos*, the vanished people. The military knew what they had done. No streets or schools would carry our name.

Julian was mumbling now. "Massera will never be president. And Videla won't get to occupy Chile..."

I couldn't sort out the conspiracy mumbo-jumbo Julian was spewing. I was losing half of his words, but it didn't matter; for me, fighter of aliens and future people, nothing could be sufficiently logical anymore.

In a sense, we were both now living outside the rational world.

17

The sun hadn't come up yet, but some clarity was surging from the east. It was coming from a riverside we couldn't see, behind the building that had offered us protection from the rain. I noticed, in the middle a hypothermic daydream, shadows moving underneath us. There was a procession in the dark core of the patio. After a few seconds of adjusting my eyes, what I saw left me astounded.

There were bodies moving around the patio. Dark, amorphous bodies; bodies I could only see as conical shadows. And they were probably walking, although it was impossible to see their feet from up high—they were all covered by colorful plastic ponchos, and their heads were crowned with big hoods. I couldn't see anything under the waterproof capes that encapsulated them. Worse, the receding darkness had stolen their warm colors and left a leafless forest of gray and black.

Just shadowy figures, moving step by step. Their shackles couldn't be seen but their power sensed in the way they were stumbling forward.

A string of prisoners making their way around the open space of that long patio, sloshing over invisible puddles, sliding on unseen mud, and rushing to the point of lurching forward—as if they were being chased by the ones behind.

One of them could be Mariana.

Julian looked at me and I looked at him. We knew it would be impossible to tell if that was a break from Hell itself or an insidious form of torture, as the worst of those would surely mix pain with the promise of a taste of freedom.

18

My memory of my days in the *Automotores Cóndor* detention center has been shattered by pain. My mind decided at some point to only save the moments that were not enveloped in the suffering of those around me—or mine. This is not to say I don't remember what happened to us.

After all, there's only one day in a life when one becomes part of the missing.

Desaparecido.

I'd like to blame Julian for drawing attention to us. I can also blame my inability to properly tie my shoes, and I also lay fault on that damned black bag we'd been carrying with us for ages. It's true that I stumbled over the thing and fell on top of a bush, causing enough of a rattle to bring two armed fellows to the spot.

Julian was still up in the dividing wall, a well-intentioned knight caught while trying to go over the castle's rampart. The bag was down on the patio with me, pushing my knee against the ground.

But the true reason for my fall was trying to catch a glimpse of Mariana. I was so sure she was there, walking that punishing short march under the rain. I hate to say this, but what happened was my fault. The more time that passes away from that night, the clearer it is that I simply screwed up.

There was a false step, and I joined the ranks of the undead.

* * *

From the start, we were seen as just overgrown children playing a detectives' game—and we were that, of course. The policemen commanded us to produce our documents, and I didn't have any with me, as my passport was stored in the far away land of my apartment. In their questioning, we were asked for our full names at least three times. The two guards, both in blue ponchos and one of them sporting a very large automatic rifle, quickly decided we were going to be taken with the rest, and become presumed leftists, terrorists, urban guerilla troops, or whatever they could accuse us of being that was deathly illegal.

It didn't help our cause for freedom that Julian kept playing dumb, a favorite game in Argentina, already part of the vernacular as the all-purpose response— *"Yo? Argentino." Me? Argentine*, a phrase signifying that being a citizen of the land meant not involving oneself in anything. This shield-statement was supposed to keep people away from any conflict; at least, that was the conventional wisdom. But conflict was everywhere, and the saying wasn't going to protect us.

Playing the "pair of idiots" card was easy for us—we were them, visibly so—and it might've helped that we were teenagers and frightened in excess. My accent, present even in the few words I'd spoken to the guards, was enough to convince them I was one of those adventurous foreigners who goes around doing crazy stuff and might've dragged Julian into an adventure of sorts. They kept referring to us as kids who were trying to be smart-asses where and when they shouldn't.

Still, we had been lucky to be detained at the best time—if there was ever a best time—for being captured in the entire reign of the notorious Argentine military. The World Cup had created such a large international interest in the uniformed ruling elite that they had granted their enemies an armistice of sorts. The military didn't want to be seen in their open violence to civilians.

Having been taken during that brief cooling period, where the government was trying to hide its illegal activities—including torture and mass murder—decreased the chances we would be summarily executed after interrogation.

The government had been so confident about passing with flying colors the test of foreign eyes that, it is thought, they'd made a deal with the expatriates who were running most of the Montoneros from Europe. But apparently, not with some rogue Montoneros still in the country.

It was also an unfortunate truth that we had seen too much and now fell somewhere between the innocent—the few without uniform the military would be able to forgive—and those proven to be in cahoots with the armed insurrection. Enough for us to be tied up, hooded, and quickly confined to a holding cell, at least until the games were over and we could be safely disposed of.

Not a good future to have but still better than having been shot on sight.

PART V

Time Unrecovered

1

I knew that I was alone by the lack of any sound or vibration on the rough, unfinished floor. I would later learn I'd been placed in the first of a series of small jail cells, which resembled the draft blueprint for a real prison.

I lost track of time after the first few hours I was left to simmer in my doubts. I had been hooded, which I thought was an ominous sign. But I kept the faith, thinking that I should survive, that Mariana was somewhere nearby, and that I was going to liberate her and escape from that hellhole with her and Julian.

All faith is unreasonable.

No food was given to me during the first day. My stomach was anything but quiet and my brain desperate for answers. I went overtime into that place of our minds where all art is born, the one containing vast empty canvases of the mind. The beginning of this book is to be found somewhere in those spaces of dark thought.

I entertained my mind by filling it with stories, trying to avoid going crazy with worry. I didn't know at the time this was a common coping mechanism used by people in concentration camps to survive. It is surprising—perhaps also concerning—that I'd started to do this so early in my captivity.

I thought there was hope I would be spared, since I had a part to play in the destiny of mankind. My hope was that we'd be released, when the management realized we were innocent of any terrorism against the State.

All hope is unreasonable.

I wasn't alone in this silent prayer. Many thousands had fallen into the same trap of false hope.

* * *

There was music sometimes, and its sounds ameliorated the pain of my silent stay. It was very soft, distant, but after a while my ears got used to how it raised above the feeble threshold of white noise—together with shuffling bursts of other indescribable sounds—and I started to pick up one isolated word or a single verse from radio songs. The repetition of aired programs helped, and I got to recognize the most popular records, the ones played many times over the day.

Tú, siempre tú. Franco Simone singing "you, always, you," a long love song full of "I love you," which I tried to associate with Mariana.

Mi amor imposible. My impossible love. Another pop hit, this one with very Latin American rhythm. I grabbed these words as a secret prayer for my hope that love, in any form, would save the world.

My black universe also contained people talking in one of the rooms on my right. At first, what they were saying sounded like incoherent babble to me. They needed car batteries; their bosses weren't bringing enough of them. They were forced to fill more buckets of water every day, something they didn't seem to like and considered a waste of their time. I'd learn much, much later that they were referring to means of torture essential for carrying out their daily jobs.

The batteries were for the standard portable electric tool they used to apply big discharges in pain-sensitive areas—*la picana eléctrica*, quite famous in Argentine as it was created by a local policeman who came from a well-known literary family. They were also talking about the then-almost-unknown practice of waterboarding, probably something their bosses had learned in international conferences about up-to-date military technologies to combat terrorism. Many Argentine military leaders, including the Junta members, had attended and spoken at them.

It was a good thing for my mental health that I didn't understand much of my captors' chatter.

I was placed far away from the torture site and thus only heard the torturers talking on their breaks, when they dispensed small talk to each other and complained about the military administration. But, above all, they discussed every single kick made by an Argentine player on the green field. Some of these men were from the capital, with heavy *porteño* accents; others clearly came from the provinces, their intonations so skewed I couldn't place them. One said he was from Rosario and kept repeating that the best games were going to be played in his city's stadium.

From him, I learned about the most important game of the tournament.

To him, we all owe our freedom.

2

I passed time in my cell by thinking a lot about time. Could I remove the curse that had fallen over my life? Had I already changed the direction of my future? And, if I had meddled with my destiny, was whatever had made me come back in time still necessary to be done? There are hundreds of ways to go about this argument. I know, because I tried them all.

After a while, I could look at two of these paradoxes at once and not go crazy. *Or was I going crazy and hadn't noticed it by being so involved with my twin paradoxes?*

And then, to exacerbate my delirium, there was the phone. Its unexpected, frequent ringing could drive me insane all by itself.

At first, I couldn't comprehend why there would be a phone in a place where no prisoner could ever get out or make a call. But slowly, and because the thing was so close to my cell, I started to pay attention. Garbled sounds. The rush of the torturers to answer. A softer tone in their undecipherable talk, a signal of authority figures on the other end of the line.

The reality and monstrosity of the surreal calling finally hit me: it was the back and forth of the gained information, transferred from the captives' pain to attentive listeners up the chain of command. It was suffering being exchanged for new leads: names, addresses, and targets to continue the evil enterprise.

With that knowledge, the sound turned unbearable, as it revealed what was causing and maintaining Argentina's vast machinery of destruction. It was the repeated pounding with each new ring that became the symbol of my visit to Hell.

* * *

Suddenly, I was propped up and, since my legs now couldn't sustain my body's weight, raised by enough hands to be coming from two people.

They made me kneel first, and then took a long time to decide whether they'd remove my hood during the session. They argued that there were rules about it. For better or worse, I was sure to have gotten the rookies.

They finally took my hood off, and, while the two men in green workmen shirts and dirty pants—who did look the part of car-shop mechanics—decided if I was worthy of the *picana* or they were just going to beat the hell out of me, I had time to assess them. I was trying to calm my justifiable fear—I hadn't urinated myself but was close—and perhaps develop a description to have handy for the police. If there was another kind of police, an honest one.

The two torturers were probably policemen out of uniform, or their good friends in the military. One of them had drawn a swastika on his shirt's arm, but in a reversed orientation.

It took them ten minutes more to decide what to do with me. There had been some collective worry that I might have been an American spy, because of my accent. I wanted to tell them how a sixteen-year-old CIA spy would break some sort of record. None of us knew then that the CIA was behind the entire Condor Operation and thus one of the torturers' bosses.

From the idle chat, I learned that their command offices hadn't been able to find any connection between the name I'd given them and any known terrorist. They had brought a stack of papers—dropping some of them, mixing the others—to verify whether my name was on a list on its way to turning black from their greasy hands. They crossed out two people on the list, and, since they hadn't carried out an eraser with them, left it like that and without correction.

At least, my pain might save two other lives.

After having passed the preliminary formalities, I was administered a class-C beating. They kept saying it was just so that I knew what was coming to me, and how much of a bad boy I had been. I think they'd said as much, but by that point I was trying to summon the power of humor to lighten the load of my punishment. It was like I was synthesizing and applying my own laughing gas.

I was slapped, more so when I started to laugh at them. And then, I was punched in the face a few times, until I was bleeding enough I started to think I had some loosened teeth. It was just more of my luck that the guy hitting me was the smaller of the two, while the stouter one kept trying to set up the *picana* but only got measly pops when he short-circuited the ends. He was getting upset and didn't pay much attention to the weak treatment his colleague was applying to me.

In a gesture of terminal frustration with his equipment, the bigger guy stopped the small one, with some technical excuse I can't remember, and they both went into a verbal harassment mode.

They insulted me with such variety—and fluid language, so they weren't as uneducated as I'd imagined—that I missed more than half of their angry bursts. I got the gist of being a foreign homosexual, given to having sex with terrorists—for them, the basest form of consortium with the devil—and having had some sexual experiences with bulls, donkeys, and other beasts with large penises. My mother was apparently an experienced prostitute, and I should've found residence, perhaps even protection, inside her vagina. When translated by my brain into less than four-letter fare, it all seemed idiotic. But since it was replacing a more thorough beating, I took it serious-faced, as if I were really reflecting on the meaning of their words. I finally received my hood back, like a penitent ready for the procession.

As I'd said, I was a lucky first-timer and got the rookies. But I was in a dead-end prison for the damned, and it was only a matter of time before I lost some real teeth and got electric burns all over my body.

If the cat gets tired of playing with the mouse, it does not set it free.

3

The worst part of my first round of torture wasn't the pain or the punches—and a few sliding blows to my ribs—but the devious way I was left to sit astride and hand-tied on the floor while they went through the paces with Julian.

I knew it was my friend because they'd mentioned the median wall where we had been found just as they dragged him inside. They—it was the same two—were nastier in addressing him before the session, and even warned Julian about how much hurt was waiting inside that room. The door was left ajar just for me, so I would suffer with him at a distance.

I overheard a lot of agony during those endless days, but the time being so close to where they tortured Julian was the worst. Every blow reverberated inside me, as if an invisible snake had slithered over the floor and climbed all the way to my chest. And the now fully-functional *picana* delivered a string of sickening sounds, changing from whirring to scratching, in a way that brought memories of a dentist's drill, sounds that made me panic as I knew the lowest-pitched ones meant contact with my friend's skin. And then there were harrowing human sounds, which I've managed to disassociate from specific discharges, and now I only remember as sighs, laments, and outright screams, constantly surrounded by a veil of sobs and chocking.

Julian was portlier than I was at the time, so they took him for an adult. I'm not sure if he wasn't already eighteen, as he could have lost school years because of his illness. Whatever the reason, the torturers thought he had reached the age for a full treatment.

For me, as I'm sure it was for him, the time he spent inside that room lasted for years. And for the first time in my life, if I had been given a gun and freedom of movement, I would've entered the fetid room and shoot those two men until I was sure they were dead, but not before they'd suffered a great deal from their wounds. I was already soaking in the same overt violence that possessed them.

In a daze, I found peace by thinking about my predicament. Even after having gone in great detail over all the possible screw-ups time-travel can cause, a weighty doubt remained on my mind. Most paradoxes were based on theorizing that if one were to change the past, impossible things would happen. If you weren't allowed to change the future, no matter what I did to my grandfather he wouldn't die by my hand—although I might end up killing some-one else's grandfather. But if change were possible, and I success-fully killed Grandpa, I would immediately sever the connection with my personal future—there would be a brand-new one, where I didn't get to exist.

The problem is that there's a third possibility. What if I kill grandpa and we are still both in the same timeline—one in which I'm both dead and alive. A Schrödinger's cat world, where differ-ent courses of the same history coexist, and a little bit of pressure would lead you to jump into a world where Hitler did win World War II.

I was definitely starting to lose my mind, but I had a little hint about the existence of that multi-level universe.

By going back in time from my future, I'd created all these versions of myself, some trying to save me, and others bent on accomplishing my extermination.

I needed to stop that madness. And to do that, I had to get out of prison. It's strange how my unreasonable thinking made me find the courage to restart my quest to become a hero.

Now, I was the Quixote. And as Quixote, I believed in the reasonability of all that was unreasonable.

In Cervantes's words, I believed in *la razón de la sin-razón*. The reason of the un-reason.

4

I was escorted to my cell by a guard while in a state of complete desolation, not knowing if my friend was all right—and whether I'd be called back soon to the house of horrors. Only my renewed determination to find Mariana and escape held me together, partly because I knew that if I didn't regain my freedom, Julian, Mariana and I would be all soon dead.

Feeling courageous but being stupid, I argued with my guard that I was an American and had rights—he laughed, saying he was also "American" but from the South. As for my rights, he was four-letter clear I'd lost them by falling into their lair. An unintended consequence of our moment of conversation was that he treated me for a second like a human being and explained how to call so I'd get untied and be allowed to relieve myself in my personal bucket.

Back to sitting alone in my cell, my hands hurt badly, and my back was compressed uncomfortably against the wall. This led me to slide down and leave behind my hood.

I could now see, at least a little, from under my hood's bottom edge. It was a colorless world; walls with cracked, blotched gray paint, and a cement floor with dark stains I didn't want to ascribe to blood but surely were. There was a real door; my cell wasn't a precarious wood box but rather an abandoned room.

Apparently, I'd gotten the luxury suite.

Having regained a corner of vision, I contorted to see my hands. They were a little bloody—nothing serious, just chafing caused by friction burns and a few cuts. The coarse rope they'd used to tie me up went several times around my wrists, strongly wound but in such a clumsy way I could've used one of my hands to untie the other. My foot, however, was firmly chained to a ring cemented to the floor.

All of this was useful knowledge. I stored it in my mind's newly opened manila folder, the one labeled *Escape*.

* * *

I had a chance to see the silent morning march around the patio. It was another dreary day, a storm threatening though not yet over us. But this time I was seeing the show from below, as a new member of the crew.

There were two people supervising the walk. I couldn't see them—they'd kept the hood over my head—but could hear intermittent voices of discontent with our progress, forming a menacing litany promising more pain on the coming night. The voices were unknown, so I made a note that there were at least four guards in service at the *Cóndor's* last station for those who'd rebelled against the illegitimate authorities.

I kept my pace, sometimes bouncing against a surprisingly solid body standing just in front of mine. It was hard to imagine we had been walking in a circle, while blinded and restrained with rope. But, as I was finally reaching a steady rhythm, everything and everyone stopped.

Two people were yelling—probably at each other, a verbal confrontation that forgot the need for secrecy—and I could hear every word of it.

"No, soldier. They can't...we can't do that."

"Other places are doing it, sergeant—it's a national feast."

"A feast? Are you crazy? They are our prisoners."

"At the ESMA, some of them are helping with the official advertisement, writing magazines." I didn't know much then about ESMA, the city's School of Army Mechanics, or about its notorious detention center, which would become the lasting symbol of an era of madness. It functioned underground, just half a mile away from the "*Monumental*" stadium, where many of the World Cup's matches were being played.

The presumably superior officer had a well-thought answer. "Sure, they'd keep them in the 'fishbowl' at the ESMA," he said, "glass offices they should be putting to better use. But those were journalists, professionals. Here, at the *Cóndor*, we have the worst of the worst: '*negritos*' from other countries, dark-skinned half-breeds that are not better than stray dogs. They are useless—and many are not even South Americans."

Well, that was me, and at least I felt included.

"I thought you said they needed to be reeducated here." The presumably young and presumably low-ranked soldier was if anything persistent. He was getting close to being forced to join the other rebels marching around the patio.

The chief's answer surprised me. "You know, if we can reeducate them, we'll do so. If not, we feed them to the fish."

There was a pause, and probably some smiles. I didn't know how true the last comment was, the "naval solution" they would apply to us at the end.

"Please, sergeant. Let me do it. It's for the country, not them."

"All right, *Paco*. When is the game with Peru?"

I had already overheard that Argentina would now play Peru, and the locals should beat them by lots of goals, to outscore the other teams and progress to the final match. There were technical reasons for this, and it amazed me to hear these torturing thugs engage in subtle, sometimes even byzantine, discussions about the merits of competing teams. If Argentina didn't make the grade, it was all over, ending its hopes for a home-court win of the World Cup.

"Sergeant, it is tomorrow, at seven. In my *Rosario.*"

My Rosario? So, this was the guy I'd heard talking before, the one who'd expounded the mastery of his province at Argentine football.

"Well, *Paquito.* Let's bring them to the back room, the big one; I'll get someone to move the television back there. But you'll have to fix the TV's antenna, so we get good reception. And you're responsible that they sit, keep quiet, and don't bother us. I'll shoot the first one who moves the wrong way."

There was a silence of agreement, and a couple of comments about a Navy guy who was now openly running for office between the higher-ups. Didn't know who he was and can't remember much more of their interaction—after all, it had been heard but not seen.

I only remember that they had given me a faint hope that escape was possible.

5

During the next day, I kept the irrational hope of finding a way to get out of that hellish dungeon. Still, I was stunned by the sharp interruption, my door ostensibly forced ajar. My heart skipped a beat and it felt like I was being stabbed in the chest.

I was taken downstairs with the hood still on, but, helped by the combination of air drafts and wavering humid coolness, I figured I was on my way to the very back of the facility. Without warning, they pushed me forward and someone unceremoniously removed my head blinders.

It was a startling sight. I was in an unusually large room with high ceilings and a rectangular lunch table at the front. The room was big enough to be only poorly lighted by two incongruent—given the stoic setting—French-style standing lamps, which were placed near the back wall. A desk, set next to the front wall, supported a not-the-smallest-size-but-close-to-it TV, which was not more than a box surrounded by more cables than it should have, and topped by an antenna that resembled two angled paperclips. Two of the guards were repositioning the entire set for improved reception—in black and white, as color was mostly for export—while a third man sat contemplating their handiwork and giving them free advice.

The improvised watch-room looked like a cheap classroom, but one turned into a chapel for monks with a vow of silence. Slowly, prisoners like me were being taken to each row of seats, unhooded, and encouraged to scooch over, so more people could sit. It was like a crowd of penitents being carefully arranged in the pews of a church getting ready for a service.

I searched for Julian but only saw beaten men, some apparently having been starved for quite some time; a couple of them had awful, poorly-cared-for scars and swollen eyes in all the colors damaged skin can take. There were maybe forty men there—and three women, sitting in the front—but I didn't know if those were all the tenants of the evil hotel that operated in *Cóndor Automóbiles*. None of the women was my Mariana.

Finally, I saw Julian's face, two rows ahead, so pale his nascent beard resembled soot. He saw me too, and I was grateful to see that his eyes had enough shine to suggest the madness had not overtaken him—not only his own, but the one added by that place.

I tried to watch the game but couldn't, my mind floating between the prisoners, from hands tucked between nervous legs, to heads distractedly downturned and ignoring the Argentine attempts at goals. Only small upward nods were given after each new success, while the guards ignored us and kept yelling, following the endless cries of the announcers.

Gooo—OOOO—ooo—OO—ooool! Goooool!

The first goal was an overwhelming offensive run by Mario Kempes, twenty minutes into the game. He received the ball from Passarella and cruised over the Peruvian defenses. Even I knew the names of those ultra-famous Argentine players.

First goal on the road to victory—four were needed for the country to be a finalist.

But it wasn't a joyful victory, and being there only deepened the feeling that our captors didn't want it to be ours; that we were being shown a triumph of a country they thought we didn't deserve and were trying to destroy. Even I, heir of a different land, could feel the enormous contempt they had for us. Their hatred had metamorphosed into the will of winning over a poorer country, intimidated by the ever-present arrogance of the military rulers.

The TV screen up front was so small I couldn't follow the complex motions of a game I'd never played beyond the basics. I was just waiting for the right moment of distraction, anything that could come from the numbing effect of the guards' concentration on every play, and then hoping to use this gap to try something. I glanced at Julian, and knew he'd been doing the same, even though his eyes had barely contacted mine.

Perhaps because of the desperation, or as I started to consider maybe I had imagined Mariana being there—since she wasn't at our forced conclave—at some point I thought how the whole exercise could turn into a total disaster for us, or worse, the final one.

I was crazy enough to have decided to try and summon the bubbles.

I know this sounds truly insane, but I had no options left except performing a miracle.

Even as I tried not to doubt myself, I raised my hand and made a closing gesture, almost like an orchestra conductor shutting down the brass. I might've looked like a student wanting to ask a question in class, his face screwed in painful concentration; but nobody saw me, as the collective attention was concentrated on the game.

I'm not sure if what happened next really happened. I saw a small swarm of violet grapes, which flew and fused to build a curved wall between me and the guards, who were absorbed watching the brilliant Kempes in a narrow fight near the arch, ready to make a third goal—I'd missed the second one entirely.

Time stopped, or it seemed to, as if it were being examined with a magnifying glass. And across the spheres I saw many blurry images, and then just one face—thin, dark, and with an unshaven beard—a face with dark, intense eyes.

Unfortunately, something went wrong, and before I could see in my purple crystal ball how to escape the nightmare, the entire structure flickered and disappeared.

The gods had abandoned me.

6

I was devastated. Without the blueprint of my future the purple spheres could provide, I was left to my own devices. I realized that soon after the game, I would reenter the local chamber of tortures, this time to confront a functional electrical sparker.

Maybe the fear helped me, and as we approached the critical point in the game, I started to pay careful attention to our captors, like someone who's trying to escape prison should. I could see three guns in their holsters—they were the belt type, much like what street cops used—and how one of them, the nearest to our chairs, didn't have a belt or a holster. Four men and three guns.

The fifth man was leaning on the room's door, manning the entrance just so nobody could say they were derelict in their duties. His face suggested he didn't care—or fear—what we could possibly do.

Since I had been seated near a gap between two chairs, I could see all around the room; I could have easily stood and walked up to the gathering of guards near the TV set. I touched my chair and verified how it was unfortunately made with two wood plates and a twisted bar of light metal. No way I could unscrew a leg and use it as a weapon. The issue of the three guns—I couldn't see whether the door's guy had a fourth one—complicated any wishful progression to control the ensemble.

Ready to give up, I scanned the room for options. A tall guy, thin but muscular, was staring at me from sunken, dark eyes. I had seen those eyes—inside the bubble—and he had seen in me that we were both thinking the same thing. I would later learn his name was Jorge, and he had been a mid-level member of another insurgent organization, the ERP—the *Ejercito Revolucionario Popular*, an armed group that, just like the Montoneros, had wanted to start a people's revolution in Argentina. He was the closest to a real soldier I could have found in that room full of broken people.

We exchanged a few glances and nods, and silently developed a plan. It all happened so fast, I didn't have time to evaluate how unlikely it was to succeed. Julian noticed our non-verbal communication and joined the fun.

Rather than explain how we told each other of the steps to take, I'll describe the events as we put them in motion.

Play for the fourth goal: close to five minutes into the second half. Just after a goal Kempes made in the first few minutes, Tarantini gives the ball again to goal-maker Kempes, but things get very defensive and confusing for him near the goalpost. Finally, like a star basketball player, Passarella jumps very high over the crowded defense and, with a head shot that was taken by Luque into the net, finally consolidates the home-team victory.

The announcer started a record-breaking yell to mark the scored point.

A fourth goal. Argentina would play in the finals.

One. Two. Three.

I stood up, taking one step forward.

Jorge quickly moved toward the door. The guard looked at him quizzically, as if Jorge were trying to get out and use the restroom.

Julian jumped up and forward, clumsily pushing the unarmed sitting policeman, and, in the process, toppling his chair backwards. In a silent room full of absorbed watchers, I heard the guy's head hit the floor.

Jorge punched the doorman with violence and immediately grabbed his gun.

The other three guards stood and reached for their guns.

I swung around the chair next to me and threw it right in the middle of the group, the three men standing on my right flank. It hit two of them on the head and quickly drew blood on the closest one.

The guard still standing on my left extracted his gun and pointed it in my direction. But in the next instant, he jerked and flew back against the wall. Jorge had shot him in the head.

Before the two guards I had hit with the chair could do anything, Jorge advanced a couple of steps and pointed his gun straight between them, probably guessing he'd be able to kill one of them before the other one had time to shoot back.

The long syllable of Argentina's victory had ended.

Maybe fifteen seconds altogether had passed, but in those we and the country had earned the freedom to keep fighting.

7

After our rude crashing of the football party, someone found enough rope in a closet to tie the four guards who'd survived the fight. Jorge was quick in organizing things, and soon found another ex-ERP fighter—this one in worse shape than he was—and put him in charge of a group that would search for more weapons as we, meaning he, Julian, and I, managed to secure transportation. The other ERP guy rose to the occasion and kept shushing everybody to stay quiet, insisting that any noise could be heard from the outside. I agreed with him, since so far, the game's outbursts at each goal had masked the mess we'd made and even Jorge's gunshot.

We reached the front and saw a truck parked inside the building, dark and thus invisible in the shadowy entrance. There was a tiny ray of light filtering out from the entrance's office and someone was carrying out the night shift—an unlucky fellow for sure, forced by his peers to miss the super-game of the night. From the hallway's door, we could see his profile over the green frame of the glassless window.

Jorge approached the window, holding a gun he'd taken from the dead policeman. *"Buenas noches,"* he said, as if ready to buy movie tickets.

Without waiting for an answer, Jorge shot the attendant

through his hand—and the grooved old wooden desk—fast enough for him only to make a big sigh and then holler in complete disbelief at what had just happened. I remember the sudden smell of gun powder and of something else, which I assume was the guy's own tissue burnt to a mist by the point-blank detonation. He tried to cover the hole with the other hand, although I got to see it wasn't as big and crater-like as I thought it was going to be. Blood was wetting his sleeve and the desk's surface.

The guy only managed a constrained, thinned-out voice, appealing to our whore-like mothers— "*Hijos de puta*, what have you done?"

"This is so you know we're serious," said Jorge.

"You, assholes. Shit—it hurts...."

I understood why the guy had been left out from the action, sidelined on a desk job. He didn't have the stomach for blood, especially his own, and his head was now orbiting, like a plane getting ready to land. He was woozy enough to land face down in a pool of his own blood—this made me a little queasy too.

Jorge didn't commiserate much with the attendant and rushed around the counter, searching for the truck's keys. Julian and I were left standing on the other side, watching the attendant writhe—mumbling and crying his misfortune on being shot.

Julian grabbed a dirty towel from the floor and handed it to the attendant. "Here," he said, "use this as a compress." The towel was covered by black oil stains, as if coming from a real car shop.

"Where's the girl?" I said. "Her name is Mariana Venturino... *Ven-tu-ri-no*."

"I don't know."

"You're lying," said Julian.

"I don't...hear me out. I'm telling you the truth," the guy said, pushing hard on the towel now wrapped around his hand. "They took her. Two days ago. I have nothing to do with that."

"Why? Why would they take her?" That was Julian, his anger substantial for someone in such poor shape.

I knew the answer before the stupid policeman opened his mouth.

"Someone called," he said. "From the zone's command. They wanted a transfer to another side, because someone might've known we had her here."

Julian still didn't believe the guy. "You *are* lying, son of a bitch."

"No, she's gone. And I'm not lying—a monsignor called, from the curia. I would remember that. They never call here; they only do it for the prisoners who are well-connected. He said she was of the highest priority, you know, *prioridad máxima*."

It was us. We were the ones who had caused Mariana to be moved.

Ours had been a clear case of Heisenberg's uncertainty principle in action. We had affected the position of Mariana in the universe just by trying to locate her. Now, she was again indeterminate, spread out in a limbo all over the city. We were never going to find her again.

I didn't need to ask Julian if he thought it was D'Agostini. One didn't need Einstein, or Heisenberg, to figure out that the archbishop had anticipated our moves. He had figured out a rescue was coming as soon as he'd told Pocha about Floresta.

"Julian," I said, "I'm going to go and check anyway."

"There's no time."

"The truck will be ready soon, Julian. Go and get the people from upstairs. I'm going to check the cells on the other floors."

"No, don't do it. There isn't..."

But I was already going, though not fast enough to skip seeing Jorge as he hit the attendant on the head with the gun's handle.

It was no time to worry whether he was going to survive the night.

* * *

I had no idea what I was doing. I walked the floors incoherently, like someone who'd lost a car in an airport's parking lot. First, I covered the second-floor hallway, looking inside every cell from one direction; then, even more desperate, I retraced my steps and just peered into the same dark cubicles but from a different angle. At the time, I had the pressing sense of a clock ticking somewhere nearby and feared being left alone with an angry mob in search of payback.

The smell of urine mixed with other remnants of soiled clothing—plus mold and wet, loose ground, these two perhaps tolerable, but then topped up with an acidic overtone of decomposition—was burning my nostrils and brought back to my mouth the awfully muddy potato paste they'd given us to pre-celebrate our night of forced watching of the World Cup.

I was losing my ability to breathe, and the walls started to close in on me. By then, I was tottering like a drunk on the second floor, the one leading to the only balcony visible from the street. I saw something with my peripheral vision that startled me; it made me feel a rush, the confusing need to both come back and leave at once.

It was just a little glassy thing that shone under the rough touch of light coming from a naked hanging bulb, the sole light source in the hallway.

Mariana's bracelet, the one made with gold beads she herself had threaded together. The same one she had shown me on our first date. Now it lay on the floor, just a piece of useless beauty in the bowels of an unearthly hell.

It was both proof that we had found her and of how we'd lost her, probably forever.

But I did take it with me.

* * *

At the end, only fifteen of the prisoners were willing to make the escape. Some were just too broken to stand up and run. There was very little we could do for them—that anyone could do for them.

We opened the rolling metal gate, and eerie silence greeted us outside. The game was still in progress. The torturers, at least the ones we'd left alive, were tied up in a back room, and the attendant at the front desk was still unconscious. After hiding our people under the watch of Jorge and his ERP pal, we resealed the truck's rear with a thick panel of green sailcloth. Some of the prisoners were very skinny and babbled incoherently; it felt as if we were part of one of their psychotic episodes.

Like a black whale, the truck surged into a scary ocean of freedom.

Before we would encounter the first street crowds and honking horns celebrating Argentina's extraordinary—and forever suspicious—victory of that night, the only real noise inside the cabin was of Jorge's making, as he tried unsuccessfully to shift the truck's gears. The thing coughed up rattling noises, and I worried it was going to run out of gear-teeth to grind.

I had tears in my eyes, but my emotions were clouded by not having found Mariana. The escape, the people killed a few meters away, the beatings and the misery of the last weeks, they all paled against the time lost on trying to find her.

Precious time that had been lost in captivity, time we were never going to recover.

PART VI

Time Undiscovered

1

We ditched the black truck even before getting past the nearby *Flores* neighborhood, but I'm not sure about the specifics. The strangeness of having lost time—weeks, maybe many weeks—possessed us, and we floated from moment to moment like astronauts in space.

We spent a somnambular hour with the people we'd carried with us, while they were slowly departing. Some went along with the crowds sporting Argentine flags and matching T-shirts, quickly disappearing in the embrace of a motherland that was trying to be proud about something. Others had some residual social instinct and clung together to follow their new leader, Jorge, who was still the same revolutionary thirsty for revenge, and might've been unknowingly buying them advanced tickets for another theatre of horrors. A few didn't have any idea whether they had families to return to and started a march to nowhere in particular. We were the only two captives who were recent enough and intact enough to have the amount of leftover soul needed to head straight back home.

When Julian and I arrived at my apartment, we were in a daze, a deep and powerful tiredness that numbed my legs and counteracted the heights of our previous adrenaline-heightened time. But we found my place in such chaotic state it jolted us.

We had left in a big hurry, and the floors were strewn with clothing; the beds had exploded as if we'd flown away. The last coffee we had had grown enough mold to look creamy.

Julian verified that the police hadn't come to his house either, exerting himself by trying to talk details with a very sleepy mother. I heard Julian tell Dorita one of his spontaneous, while still perfectly consistent lies, something about suddenly having accepted an invitation from my family (one that didn't exist in Argentina, but he'd made large, entrenched, and prosperous) to spend time in a summer house we had in Rosario, this only so we could watch the game against Peru with them. This all sounded quite fantastic to me, still reeling from the images of our poorly planned heist and violent exit from *Cóndor*.

"They were still celebrating when we took the bus," Julian added for effect. I noticed he'd skipped any reference to the final score of the game—even his mother should know by then about Argentina's 6-0 win—since we had only half-watched the match. The banners we'd seen in the streets had been muted in the subject of the result, and the fans we saw busied themselves chanting about how much their team had violated the losers' behinds.

The call to Dorita reminded me of Julian's medications, and I spent my remaining energy finding them—I'd kept a couple of pills on my bedtable—and forcing my friend into downing them with water and some old crackers. He had done well, considering the harrowing circumstances, but I was worried about what could come next.

Our inner fog finally grew back, to the point we could have fallen asleep standing up, and we both collapsed on the living room's divans. With my last bit of energy, I stumbled around closing all the window shutters. I ended up on the same couch, or on another one in the bedroom; I really don't know.

The dark welcomed me with open arms.

* * *

I woke up with the certainty I'd missed something important and not a small measure of fear, as if my life were near a crashing end. Someone—the man, the military goons, or even the Montoneros—was bound to get me and end it all.

Julian was surprisingly, and eerily calm, like a philosopher ready to drink his poison, and he tried unsuccessfully to ease my worries. His logic was sound, but his scared eyes told a different story—one of a game we were trailing by as many goals as Peru had and for which there wasn't any way we could win. I don't know exactly what he said—perhaps my language circuits were overloaded—but the highlight was that I had to get out of Argentina.

Before you succeed in getting someone to kill you, he said. That was as close he'd ever gotten to reading my mind on the spot.

I soon learned that my U.S. passport had disappeared in my chaotic though easy life of the last few months. With my recently acquired knowledge of what was really going on, the loss was almost a death sentence for me. If I was ever detained and asked to produce an identity document, I could join again the ranks of the disappeared.

I hadn't checked for my original passport since I'd landed in Buenos Aires, mainly because I was of the idea that a wrinkled Xerox copy kept in my back pocket would be sufficient proof of my American citizenship. But I knew now that nobody, neither hired lawyers nor theoretically friendly police, would help me without my passport. I was moored by the stupid loss to Buenos Aires, like a quarantined ship under an American flag.

It was Julian who finally suggested I call my father to ask for an expedited passport. I had forgotten that he was a well-connected man, with higher-up friends in Washington he could ask for favors. The kind of friends who'd ask him for massive amounts of illegal drugs to be sent to Vietnam or other places where soldiers needed highs or lows made to order.

The conversation with Dad went well at first, when the main issue was my "lost" passport and all the troubles it could cause me when visiting him. I didn't want to foster paranoia in him, so I didn't tell him about how buses and taxis were being stopped for document verification. I knew of Gorostiaga students who'd been detained, unloaded of any ID they had, and then forcefully asked—in front of a crew of guys with automatic weapons—to recite the numbers of their Police Department's ID, National Document of Identity, or, but probably also and, any other piece of numbered identification they had carried with them. Having and knowing these official documents by heart could be the difference between being and not being anymore.

But Dad went in another direction I didn't predict. "Do you remember what we talked about last time," he asked, "me going over there? I have tickets to travel this Saturday, so we can see together the finals."

"You are coming?"

"Yes, I told you that. Don't you remember?"

"Well, I'm not sure. I am too worried about my documents."

"But you can ask for a paper permit to the consul."

I laughed, which he didn't take very well. "I understand you might think this is funny," he said, "but the U.S. Consulate is there to help you."

It wasn't funny, and I should've been able to express my predicament better, but what came out was a giggle. "This is *not* the United States," I said. "The American Consulate, maybe even the consul, are worried about what the government might do to them."

His silence told me he got my point. "All right, Edgar," he said calmly. "I'll talk with a friend who knows people in Justice...the Justice Department. I'll bring you a letter, or a permit, so you can come back here with me when I return."

Something in my father's tone told me he had understood me well enough to think that perhaps my phone was bugged. "Don't worry, Edgar," he said. "I'll be there by the weekend. And don't you worry about picking me up at the airport—I'll get a taxi."

"But I can go and..."

"Just stay home, with your friend. I will see you soon, Edgar."

My father having used my name three times in a row was astonishing. In the scale of family worries, that would rank higher than crashing a car or getting a girl pregnant. We were in the territory of having murdered someone and needing to get rid of a still-warm body.

Incredibly enough, but not so much for my teenage self, I hung up the phone upset that my father was coming to rescue me.

2

After checking my fridge's leftovers and figuring it was Friday, we'd settled on making scrambled eggs. More than a day had passed since our escape, and we were still uncertain about what to do. Most of that time we had been sleeping, but the parts when we were awake didn't help much, and a sense of urgency built as the sun rose behind the still-closed shutters.

Warmed up by an abundant plate of toast and eggs, I told my friend I had decided we could get some useful information from Cristina. She should know whether Rafa had come back, and he could help us to devise a plan of action. I didn't want to talk with Pocha Venturino, not after seeing her with D'Agostini. Julian kept smiling as he cleaned our plates, probably thinking on a joke about the liking I had developed for Rafa's pretty girlfriend. I just ignored him.

Cristina was surprised by my call; it was as if my week-long absence had made her think I'd lost interest in Mariana. I didn't enlighten her about the time we'd spent on the other side of the fence and tried to remain outspokenly worried, stressing that nobody we'd called or talked to knew anything about Mariana's whereabouts.

"What about Rafa? Do you have any news?"

"He was able to...he's out now," she said. Her tone suggested she was worried about her phone—or mine—being listened to by the police. She was obviously trying to backpedal from any open statement. "He's spending time with friends...in Uruguay," she added, so I wouldn't believe her. But her point was clear—Rafa had returned, somehow escaping custody, and she knew where he was.

"Oh, I see. And Anibal?"

"Have you heard about Alemann?"

"Who?"

"The Secretary of Farmlands. His house was bombed during the game with Peru. A big mess; I think only his wife was hurt in the explosion."

"Is that..." I stopped, realizing she was talking about what Anibal and the Montoneros had been doing.

"Isn't that awful?" Cristina tried to keep the conversation going. "Such senseless violence. And during the World Cup! Anibal is very distressed; he wants only to watch the finals."

"The finals?"

"Yes. Argentina's game with Holland for the title. This Sunday."

"Oh, I see."

"Where have you been? On Mars? How do you not...?"

There was silence. We all learned from it. Cristina probably got from the stillness that we'd been forcefully secluded—*disappeared*—for a while, thus being possibly the only people in the entire city who didn't know about the game. Perhaps the guys who knew why and could be monitoring her phone—and mine—were covering their mouths not to laugh out loud on the line.

"You know," she said, "I'm sure that we can all get together and watch the game...there's a lot of interest around here."

I got the message. The plan was on and they'd try to interrupt that transmission. I thought just how much it could change the country if everybody saw a high military officer explaining—to the world—the nightmare we had a chance to see firsthand in the city's hellish underbelly.

"Yes. Sure, Cristina. You just tell us when and where, and we'll be there."

"Even if you make it by the half-time, it'll be plenty interesting."

"But we can...we'll make it for the start of the game."

I understood. The halftime. Best time to address the obsessed population as they watched the game. Best also because, if Montoneros ended the game-watching completely, the Argentines would never forgive them.

Cristina also liked talking with me, and we chatted a little longer, about her last exams and how well she'd passed them. I contributed my imagined harsh tests at the Gorostiaga School for the Supremely Accomplished. I just wanted to keep hearing her voice for a few more minutes, the soft vowels and that beautiful Mediterranean intonation of these Italians who spoke Spanish with each other.

I was happier after the call, with a feeling of being in a good track, getting to be able to do something about Mariana.

What I didn't know was that the next time I saw Cristina, we would all be in mortal danger.

* * *

We finally decided, insanely as usual, that we were going to get to Martínez as the Montoneros brought him to the sparkling-new television complex, known as *ATC—Argentina Televisora Color*, a color version of the old, state channel, *Canal 7*—and somehow, more-some-than-how, trade the officer for Mariana.

At first, we drew a blank about how to get into *ATC*. And then, we developed even more doubts, as we didn't know how the Montoneros were going to interrupt the World Cup finals' transmission. We persisted at this random brainstorming for hours and over countless cups of coffee I kept making at regular intervals. I had a huge supply of purple packages of the fancy Bonafide brand

and found the noise and smell when I ground the beans soothing.

Julian had triggered his vast imagination and started to concoct a plan, a fantastic adventure in need of some reality. Under my stern gaze and encouragement to measure our risks, he came up with the idea of getting some detailed plans and maybe contacts inside the *ATC* administration, to gain entrance past the police guards. He knew some guy, who owned an audio equipment store on Rivadavia Avenue, and used to have an import and export business that had collected him trade-related connections, a network reaching all over the city and even into the military's hierarchy—meaning he knew military men in power, political and criminal crooks, and mixed breeds who were both crooks and thrived inside the military. With such powerful contacts—a word Julian kept repeating—his so-called "friend" might be able to gather for us blueprints and up-to-date information on *ATC*'s futuristic buildings, which sprawled over a large field near the riverside.

The description he gave of a very fat and very pompous Don Marcelino Buscaglia prompted in my mind the Italian-sounding Argentine word that epitomized those on the fringes of truth and power—*los chantas*.

In all languages, there are slang words that immediately conjure up a complete archetype that's hard to translate—or doesn't easily match—the premade human stereotypes of other countries. The *"chanta"* was one of them, and hearing about Don Marcelino and his egregious doings, I remembered the many Argentines I knew who'd always say, when confronted with unknown or impossible subjects, that they had friends in high places who knew the answers to each and all cryptic matters. These *chantas* would always be up-to-date in all subjects thanks to hard-to-find books they and only they knew about, and they had influential acquaintances with unpronounceable names and composite job-titles Kafka would have wanted to steal for his books. They would use these fake personal connections—and the fake knowledge stemming from them—to win all arguments and debates.

Unfortunately for my truth-slanted mind, *chantas* were endemic at the time, a by-product of a society for which truth was a relative concept. Like everybody else in Argentina, these pseudo-experts were just trying to sort out the mixture of lies and facts a corrupt system had strewn all around their world.

As I heard Julian talk endlessly about Don Buscaglia, I was reminded, with every one of his exaggerations, calls to unprovable external authorities, and appeals to the expertise our subject had as per some gossipy source, that my own best friend was an outstanding member of the species.

3

Don Marcelino Buscaglia's shop was small and composed almost exclusively by shelves holding boxes presumably containing audio components from famous brands. Other than a couple of large speakers and a professional Pioneer turntable set on an empty wood rack, it could have been a postal office.

Just before talking with us—he didn't recognize Julian at first and for sure didn't know me—Buscaglia turned down a customer because he wanted to see what he could buy with a wad of cash. "If we open the wrapped box, you'll have to buy it," said Don Marcelino in a matter-of-fact voice, and then in so many other ways that the potential client raised his hands in an I-give-up gesture and left. For me, used to the American ways of trying and returning many of our purchases, what I had witnessed made no sense.

I wasn't very happy trusting this character with our destinies and thus spent the wait criticizing his appearance. He was a portly middle-aged man, with somewhat feminine manners and poses. He didn't (yet) wear a toupee but had combed his hair over his shiny cranium. His shirt was dirty, and the tie's knot poorly done, perhaps allowing air to get inside and refresh his ballooning chest.

When it was finally our turn, Don Marcelino kept pacing behind the counter and treated us as if we were policemen who'd asked him about his known connections with organized crime. Well, maybe we had.

Only Julian could manage to get something concrete from a sleazy character like Buscaglia. He maneuvered the massive shop owner until he surrendered, reeling him like a big fish. He waited at times for an answer, and other times he pushed Don Marcelino verbally and in an almost physical manner. Julian chased Buscaglia along the counter, while keeping his elbows on top of its glass cover, seemingly ready to grab the man's arm. I'm sure Julian would have slapped the guy before letting him hide from us in the backroom.

Don Marcelino searched nervously in his drawers—his wet handkerchief in hand, always in motion to clean perspiration—and finally found a black notebook, quickly starting to search its pages. His handwriting on that archetypically secret notebook was both unreadable and microscopic, and Buscaglia seemed to have trouble reading it. By then, his face looked like an advertisement for a soda drink; hundreds of crystalline droplets covered the convex surface of his cheeks.

Finally, our cornered interloper gave us a name and a phone number. Buscaglia's "friend" was a mid-level official who worked under a certain retired colonel Barbieri, the president and effective *interventor* of Argentine's newfangled color-TV channel. *Interventor* was a powerful-sounding name for the military appointees who took over civilian institutions to ensure—mainly to themselves— that the unruly, incompetent citizens didn't keep messing them up. Lots of bureaucrats dreamed of these cozy jobs, full of perks and bribes dispensed in order to obtain essential permissions to air programs or print magazines.

Apparently, Julian thought the name we had been given was quite enough. I was rather expecting to get directions to a complete map of the transmission complex, not just an administrator's blessing to tour the facility. But we got what we got, and it would have to be enough to get past the goons at the door.

* * *

As soon as we were back to the apartment—it was a cloudy day with one of those characteristic Buenos Aires lead skies I supremely hated—Julian got entangled in what, at first, I thought was going to be a single call, but turned into multiple ones to people working in the periphery of our contact. The calls were for background purposes, he explained, with one of his all-knowing smiles.

Julian was pleased with how the plan was taking shape, but to me the shape it was taking was murky and unrealistic. After we got into *ATC*, we would intervene to stop—or threaten to do so, thus gaining some leverage—the Montoneros' plan to hijack the final game transmission. And this should, somehow, lead to a later exchange of Martínez for Mariana. The how of this was still in the works, as in between we'd be trying to control a band of armed revolutionaries.

I also started to develop problems of my own. I had realized that we will be trying to get into *ATC* the upcoming Sunday, June 25, the date set for the finals between The Netherlands—it was still Holland for us—and the field's remaining competitor, Argentina. And Weston Senior might show up to take me to the game.

My father could be coming to Buenos Aires to witness a funeral (mine) rather than a sports festivity. Or to confront my complete disappearance from this world, as was the style of the times.

That was enough. I had to get out of the apartment. I left without telling Julian where I was going.

4

I was looking up and didn't see him coming. The English surprised me first, even more than the familiar face.

"Would you like to have a cup of coffee?"

I answered in a reflex— "*You!* Aren't you in the business of trying to destroy me?"

"Not today. Today we'll have a truce—and coffee."

He was wearing a gray outfit that merged him into the day's quasi-monochromatic tonality. In just an hour it'd be night.

He had been waiting for me.

I had been waiting for *me.*

We had been waiting for each other, maybe for an incomprehensible eternity of twisted time.

* * *

The café at the other end of Plaza Lavalle was narrow and full of dark wood, specifically designed to please the hordes of lawyers who run around that corner of the city during the day—the Palace of Justice confronted the long but fragmented park. It was a somber coffeehouse, especially in the approaching dark and when I was readying myself to talk about subjects best left to Ray Bradbury or Stephen King.

To avoid confusion on what follows, let me still call my inter-loper "the man" without forgetting who he really was.

My anger was not going to be tamed with coffee. "Why are you trying to talk to me?"

"We are kind of lost, and *we* need help."

"We? Don't you know what you're doing?"

"No. Not anymore."

"Why?"

"You have...changed things."

"Me? I thought you...well, you know, *me*. All right, whatever goes."

He smiled. It was all a big mess. "Believe me," the man said, "I understand. I didn't know why I was selected by the...let's call them aliens. They're really us, but after thousands of years in space, we don't resemble humans anymore."

"And what do they look like?"

Silence. He was considering how much he was able to tell me. "Let's forget I said that. The point is they were also out of options, and sending me back was a last, desperate ploy. Assuming I'd be able to figure what has to be changed."

"Hopeless."

"Well, yes, you're right, as I haven't figured out yet what you— well, what *I* have done wrong. Whatever it is that I did, it has to be important enough to make them send such a large..." The man stopped in mid-sentence.

"A large what?"

He thought carefully before answering. "A ship, a massive ship that flew me through time. You have heard about it...this much, I remember. The meteorites."

"The newspapers are now saying it was only one."

"Aftereffect."

"What?"

"After...well, consequences of the changes you've made. And of my trip."

"My changes? And, of my trip? You are not making much sense."

"Time travel is confusing. I'm sorry. First, you did make a substantial change—this adventure of yours in the bowels of the military. That, I haven't experienced before," he said, and I stupidly blushed. "So now, we are both in unfamiliar territory. But let's try to explain the other thing—about time travel—something basic that I did understand. When you send someone back in time, and forget for now the how, which I don't...when you send and add the atoms of a person to the past, this changes the whole universe, and thus nothing is like before. If you plugged a new human being in the past, and even if that person—in this example it'd be you—if he doesn't do anything, he is still changing the initial conditions that led to the future from when he was sent. He does change a little the departure point and his own arrival; and so, now the same person is sent from a slightly different point in the future..."

"And, I guess, he then creates a second change in the past. And a third...oh, my God!"

"Yes, the very mess we have now here, with a battalion of 'Mes' running around with different agendas." The man thought for a second, and then smiled again. "I'm glad I was so sharp in my youth." He waited to see if I smiled, which I did, and then said, "It took me a while to figure that one out."

"But wait," I said. "Didn't the aliens, you know, our descendants, know this?"

"Yes, they did. They predicted a Gaussian distribution of arrival and departure points..." He saw my lack of understanding and rephrased, "What I meant is that there'll be hundreds of us arriving and leaving at different points, a true tribe of us, coming to the past to correct a single mistake. I, myself, have seen over a dozen extra Edgars searching for you in the city. I'm sure there are more of them, some way back, when you were just a child. Perhaps many UFO sightings have come from my trip."

"Sorry, but I still don't get it. If you go back and change something, anything, wouldn't you end up in a completely different future?"

He smiled and then fell silent again. When he spoke, a weight was lowering his body as if he carried a backpack. "I didn't want to tell you this, really anything that might alter your future. But what the hell, we are already in enough trouble; the next time you see another traveler, he might end up killing you. This, and I mean the idea of a single timeline, which could contain many paths to the future, is—well, it's going to be—your, our idea. Your contribution, for what you will...." He stopped at mid-sentence and peeked at the shadowy park outside.

I thought about my vision of winning the Nobel Prize. But the many copies of me trapped in the past was an idea hard to grasp, maybe too much for any not-yet-future-alien human. "Wait," I said, getting him to look up. "So, you're saying that you can create several presents, all at the same time?"

"Yes, you got it."

"That's insane—like a science-fiction story."

"Reality has a way to exceed fiction."

"But then, it doesn't matter what you—what I can change. There will be all these other presents running wild...I'll never succeed."

"Well, you are right, but only in part. If you change the right event, whatever it is, none of this will have happened. The entire distribution—and my colleagues trying to kill you—will collapse, vanish, and the future humans will never get the idea of sending me back in time. Good for me, and good for you, of course."

"But we don't know—you and me—what has to be changed."

"Correct. We don't."

"Then, we are doomed."

"There's always the future."

"I had the impression that that is already being questioned."

"I am, apparently, quite smart."

"Not enough."

"Maybe barely enough—I do have hopes that you, or better we, will survive."

I didn't ask him, which I'd regret later, if he could come back to his own, my own, time in the future. I just repeated, "Maybe."

"So, at least I've taken you from hopeless to maybe. A good day's work, isn't it?"

This time, I smiled and offered to pay for a second round of coffee. He declined but ordered it anyway. "One last thing," he said, when the waiter had left, "something you need to know. Be careful with the bubbles."

"You know about them?"

"Yes, and I'm telling you not to get cozy with them. You can rely too much on their predictions and mess up everything." I started to talk, and he stopped me. "They are machines that can show you alternative futures. These might not be the correct outcomes, or the only ones. Worse, they take you away from your own thinking and thwart any hunch you might have about what to do. You, and only you, must decide what to do. You are the captain of this ship."

I saw pride in him. This was why they had sent him back. The gods had punished me with the eternal task of fixing the worst I'd done when young. I had turned into a tragic mythological hero, one who was cursed by our ultimate fantasy: traveling back and changing something for the better as we, in our arrogance, thought it should've happened.

"Don't worry, Edgar," I finally said. "I'm ready to sink with the ship."

"Edgar?"

"Yeah, I know. When I say it, it sounds weird."

"This, this whole thing is supremely weird."

I got the last word in— "Amen," I said.

He didn't answer.

It was night, and I should be going back.

I left the café refreshed, as my meeting with my elder advisor— let's call him that—had led me to believe there were many copies of me around, at different points in time. I had made a deal with the Devil and created a battalion of Edgars, who were trying to right my wrong.

My human life was like a beautiful butterfly, which lived for a day but stayed in the universe's memory, like an echo that lasts forever. Maybe dying didn't matter anymore.

5

That Sunday was a cold, cloud-covered day, and we had to dress in jackets and scarves, perhaps not the slickest of clothes for our plans. Julian had packed another of his duffel bags, this one also with no personal markings but colored in a glaring green tone—he was saddened about having lost the dark one at the *Cóndor* detention center, which he kept calling "our" prison.

Julian went over the bag's contents at least fifteen times before abandoning the task. He'd put in there some decent rope, duct tape, and scissors—and of course, the gun we had kept in my apartment, still loaded and ready for only the greatest of emergencies.

The morning went by at an excruciatingly slow pace—we had an appointment at one in the *ATC* station—and we reviewed once more our visibly incomplete plan. I was supposed to distract our host before crossing past the security post, while Julian hid the bag near the outside fence, to be later recovered. It was a stretch to think this would work, but we were being optimistic and ignored the many difficulties we could face.

As for our verbal passes from *Interventor* Barbieri's underling, they were coming from a very high official, so we were to be shown everything and let loose to prowl around the campus. Our story was that we were preparing a school paper about Argentina's TV industry, and our families had contacts in the States, who would distribute it internationally. A good lie, enticing as it made the military look great to the world, having built the futuristic TV station in record time.

According to our cover, we had dressed under the jackets with the most school-like attire we could find—black shoes, gray pants, and charcoal sweaters, plus solid-color burgundy ties over our best white shirts. Julian wore one of my scarves, to hide two nasty neck bruises, courtesy of our stay at the *Cóndor*.

We arrived at Figueroa Avenue and stationed ourselves on the steps of a nearby building, reviewing the information Julian had collected about *Argentina Televisora Color*. It was an amazing sight. The complex had four blockish buildings containing the studios, and a massive labyrinth of offices and storage areas that formed an underground complex. To top it off, there was a little artificial lake on the roof, with an island at its center, which supported a huge transmission tower that rose well above the roofs of the hangar-like cubic buildings. From the outside, it resembled something NASA would build to store space rockets.

After entering *ATC* by the front door, we took all the time in the world to chat with the three guards—security was tight with the coming game—while we waited in an immense entrance hall for the appropriately late functionary to come and validate our credentials. Julian kicked the treacherous bag to a corner, so the policemen didn't see it before he got to hide it. He showed great acting skill playing the studious guy who was proudly writing a most amazing story about *ATC* and how the government—the *military* government—had created such an awesome place. I was less ambitious and played the smart, shy foreigner entranced by the opportunity to visit a monument to the country's accomplishments.

I guess everybody was thinking about the game—soon to start, at 3 p.m.—and didn't care much about us. At some point, Julian disappeared, and I tried to chat in my best Spanish with the security boys; one of them practiced what he'd learned of English at school and was all smiles with me. Nobody bothered to ask for Julian—who was likely rushing to hide the duffel bag—delighted as they were with the American kid, who was trying to manage a decent Argentine accent and failing comically at that. They kept teasing me and joking about my not-so-Argentine pronunciation, wanting me to say chicken, *pollo*, over and over. Apparently, I was stressing both "l's" too much, like a Spaniard, instead of running over them with a sound resembling "sh-h" that made the word sound like "*poh-shoh*." They welcomed Julian back in the middle of their crying laughs, granting him a complicit nod.

When the functionary finally came, he immediately started to drag us around, lurching forward with a sense of imperative command. We were wasting his time, especially on that very special Sunday.

He rushed us along a huge central hallway and its countless intersecting corridors. First, we crossed the main campus, near the technical segments of the plant, and then we made a sharp turn right, in the vague direction of the lake above. Barbieri's underling—who talked softly and had a long, almost unpronounceable name, somewhere between Italy and Greece—didn't care much about what we saw or learned in our fast-paced tour of the facility, which probably took altogether less than twenty minutes.

The place was modern, but it had been built with the modernism of a military bunker. As we approached the lakeside and the administration site, I saw an angled wall of external windows that for some reason reminded me of my favorite spaceship—the *Jupiter 2* of *Lost in Space*. There was a cafeteria nearby containing what, perhaps more now than then, resembled a tribute to early environmentalism. They'd left uncut a tree from the original grounds, which went through an opening in the roof, surrounded by glass panels; it looked like a small cell in a zoo, the monkeys missing. Remarkably, you could see the *ATC* transmission tower from that opening.

I remember these odd details from *ATC* perhaps because my mind was trying not to get worried with what would happen next. It was impossible to monitor the streets from deep inside the massive building, and we could be missing the feisty arrival of the Montoneros.

Buscaglia's friend, the tour-giving functionary, soon got tired and left us to our own devices, with a final hand wave and an indication that we could get coffee and some cookies in one of the offices. There were preparations going on all over the complex to celebrate the night's epic transmission. He obviously implied with this farewell that we had to leave after our snack break, but as soon as we got free of the annoying man, Julian pushed me into a narrow corridor that ran in the opposite direction of the room we had been pointed to.

We ended up inside a small conference room, undecorated and unfinished, as perhaps a large part of the building would remain until more precise functions were given to all its quarters. There was a slight smell of paint, which nauseated my now empty stomach.

I could have used those cookies.

6

"What should we do?" My voice sounded tense, as if someone were pressing on my vocal chords.

"For now, wait."

"But we can't see what's going on from here."

"I know. We'll need to find a window that looks at the avenue, Figueroa Alcorta."

"Why that side?"

"Elementary, my friend," said Julian, smiling. "The Montoneros aren't going to sneak in unseen. They *will* try to crush the security post—the one over the main avenue."

"Okay, I'll give you that. Now, how are we going to search the offices for a window without being seen? There's a lot of police making rounds. You saw them downstairs."

"They are morons."

"Morons with guns. It doesn't take much wit to shoot a gun."

"It takes precision, which they don't have."

We had reached one of those points in our conversations where we both backed off. I was feeling trapped, and of course, we were. I also needed some air, and told Julian I was going to the restroom; he thought it was fine if it didn't take me long.

As soon as I left the room and closed the door, I felt as if someone had dropped me near the top of Mount Everest. I had been feeling bouts of anxiety since we escaped the detention center, but this one was worse. I couldn't breathe, and my heart was beating so hard and fast I put a hand over my chest as if trying to contain it from exploding. Back then, nobody talked about panic attacks—attributing them to asthma or daily stress—and so I didn't think much of it at first, until my legs turned soft and I began to sweat profusely. I leaned against the wall and felt a faintness that scared me even more; I fought not to lose control while losing it more and more.

I made it to the restroom at the end of our hallway. Inside, my head didn't seem to find the right equilibrium position above my center of gravity, and its weight started to pull me down, the floor now another wall that was tilting up. I staggered to the sink and splashed water on my face until my shirt's collar was soaking wet.

I finally collapsed, my back pressed against the wall, my butt harshly bumping on the floor. For a minute or two, I contemplated the urinals and stools from that odd perspective—the floor tiles were new, clean, and shiny—and I wondered if my mind would momentarily shut down.

I didn't faint—at least, I don't remember it—but did start to cry, and like they say, it did me some good. I was in a great deal of trouble, and it was time to accept it. I heard my own sobs as if they were coming from speakers attached to the bathroom walls.

Showing again that I couldn't get any relief from my personal angst, no matter what I did, I came out of the restroom to find myself in front of a police officer.

This was the kind of ultra-clean, never-before-in-the-streets, just-out-of-the-package policeman. He had a gun in a holster but exuded an air of informality, more office-like than his peers at the *Cóndor*. This guy was so far from the trenches he reeked of relaxation. My tension and recent tears were so apparent that I saw a gleam of pity in his eyes, just before training kicked in and he rested his left hand on his belt's weapon.

7

The policeman addressed me as if I were even more of a child than I looked, "Boy, what are you doing here?"

"I—I'm in a tour, with...." Unfortunately, I couldn't remember the name of our official tour-guide.

"This is not an accessible area. Do you know where we are?"

The truth was simple enough. "No."

"I'm going to take you under custody. Are you an Argentine national?"

This other truth wasn't going to help me or be welcomed. "No. I'm a visitor. From the United States."

"A *gringo*? And Yankee also?"

I would have needed a whole hour to clarify what those words might have meant, and, even if I'd had that much time, it wouldn't have taken us any closer to cordial terms.

My ideas about where to go from there were certainly a lot more complicated than what the short but stout police officer was thinking. For him, I was just a problem to be handled; but for me, there was a chance he could be helpful for our general plan.

As I turned around, I saw Julian in the hallway, carrying an aluminum chair and looking like a trainer ready to dominate a lion. The guardsman nodded and signaled Julian to move closer to the wall—and to forget his awkward chair-aided menacing stance.

At that moment, something clicked in my mind. Perhaps I was all cried out, or low in patience, but my blood suddenly boiled, and I found myself bathing in adrenaline—the first time in my life it had invigorated me rather than act as a freezing spell.

I decided, well not decided but became aware of my desire to do it, that I was going to attack the police officer. I took the policeman by his shoulders and somehow whirled him toward the wall—we both spun around, and I swear his feet left the floor for a second. The guy kept his left hand on the gun, but as I stared directly into his eyes, I saw emotion blending doubt with fear, perhaps as he considered how likely it could be for a teenager to strangle him.

He had very deep brown eyes and completely black, shortly cropped hair. His thin complexion had been compensated by a lot of weight training, and I could see the man's pectoral muscles crowding his logoed shirt—it said ATC, and in smaller type *Custodia Policial*, Police Custody—and two thick arms with hands that could have easily crushed mine. There was, however, something simple about the guy, the clear spirit of someone who had sought in the police force respect and a way to climb out of the economic abandonment so many suffered in the supposedly prosperous city of Buenos Aires.

I wasn't going to gauge his eyes after all, and, when I spoke, my voice came out strained. "The Montoneros can help me to rescue my girlfriend," I said. "Those sons of bitches want to stop the transmission of the game tonight."

For some reason, I felt as if I were living out a movie scene. In a movie, the guy would have believed me, and we would've run together to save my Mariana. But that wasn't a movie. The policeman regained his composure and pushed me away, hard enough that I bounced against Julian.

"You two are coming with me," he said. "And *you*," he added, pointing to me with a surprisingly big revolver. "If you touch me again, I'm going to shoot you...I'll *kill* you."

His expression had changed from fearful and startled to a shade of demonic possession that wasn't coming from any training at police headquarters. It was clear I had done something to greatly offend his machismo and he was regretting not having shot me when I'd first grabbed him.

We were led to another room, probably so our guard could consult his superiors and decide what to do with us. Likely, we would go back to be detained—with luck, a step above being *desaparecidos*—rather than being shot on sight as the terrorist operatives would be.

Julian was keeping himself together much better than I was, and he started to talk with the policeman as if we were taking a stroll, still sightseeing to get a feeling of the facilities. He asked the guy, "What's your name, Officer?"

"Joaquín Rodríguez. And keep quiet."

"You know, what my friend said is true."

"What?"

I was ahead of them, but from the side I saw how the policeman's gun swiveled a little toward Julian. My friend still managed to remain calm. "About the Montoneros. They are coming tonight."

"We know," said Rodríguez.

"You do?" Julian sounded, and was, very surprised. I jumped a little, between steps.

"We've known for some time. Your friends are going to be shocked."

"They are *not* our friends," said Julian, with a tone that showed some teeth.

"Then, how do you know what the young *gringo* said? About..."

"He told you," Julian interrupted, with enough energy in his voice that we all stopped, two steps short of an open door and our destination. "They kidnapped his girlfriend and want to exchange her for a military officer."

Julian had said this with so much conviction it took me a few seconds to realize it was more or less the opposite of what had happened, and that I had had a part in twisting the story toward this more useful direction. We wouldn't want to tell Rodríguez that Mariana had been taken by his very high-level superiors. The lie was strong, it had emotion, and it affected the policeman. We all stayed in silence for a few seconds.

"I understand," he finally said, "but can't let you leave. I'll pass the information to my boss, so they know about the girl. For now, you'll wait here until I come back."

In two seconds, we were inside the room and Officer Rodríguez was gone, but not before locking the door from the outside.

At least the room had a table and chairs, but not much else except for a cheap wall watch, which immediately handed us a piece of unwelcome news.

It was two o'clock. One hour until the game began.

8

Julian was sitting with his head down over crossed arms, completely desolated. I kept checking the room's clock, unforgivingly ticking over the silence. I felt my life was losing meaning with the passing of each minute. I had to do something, but that something wasn't known, even to the highest powers of my universe.

I heard the door opening. I didn't know who was on the other side, if the policeman had brought company and more guns. In a couple of swift movements, I took a foldable chair and waited behind the opening side of that door.

It was Officer Rodríguez, alone. He took two steps inside before I smashed his back with the chair. Two coffee cups and their contents funneled out in a swirling explosion of coffee drops, barely missing Julian. For a second, I thought I'd killed Rodríguez. And, worrisome to me even then, I didn't care at all. For me, he carried the sins of his brethren.

Rodríguez barely moved on the floor, his legs spread and his body looking like a swimmer frozen while jumping in a pool.

I guided Julian out of the room, while he mumbled his disbelief about how I had acted.

"What did you expect?" I said. "We were trapped."

We reentered the long corridor with a vague idea of where we could find the complex's entrance. Making it back there meant moving between the *ATC* studios and along their central corridor; very soon, we saw an exit to the outside. Julian forced me to get out and then drift alongside the buildings to where he'd left the green bag. He insisted we needed the gun—I couldn't argue with that.

We were in a fenced open space, right next to the broad avenue, Figueroa Alcorta, which was surprisingly busy for a Sunday afternoon. Everybody was rushing home to see the game.

I was the first one to notice them. Across the street, on the edge of the immense park, named after neighboring Uruguay, two cars had parked leaving little space between them. One was a truck, which could have been a military transport, if not for someone with little artistic taste who'd painted it bright red; the other was a blue Jeep-like vehicle, known back then as an *Estanciera IKA*, which had a hard top and backseats, making it into an early form of SUV. I considered several possibilities, coming from my experience with the Montoneros, like their inclination to make transports look indistinctly civilian, and concluded that these two vehicles were theirs.

Julian, always the contrarian, was watching the military standoff. Four cars were parked on the *ATC* side of the street, so evenly and broadly spaced no set of Argentine drivers could be held responsible for leaving them in such well-organized distribution. Only the square minds of policemen or military operatives would think such a chess-like arrangement of civilian cars—two of them Ford Falcons, to top it off—could be the result of casual behavior.

The board was set. The question was who would make the first move.

I was startled when Julian suddenly spoke. "I'm sure Martínez is in one of these cars. We need to get him...they will kill him after he talks on the air." That was the shortest—and so far, clearest—statement of Julian's plan. Without Martínez, there would be no Mariana.

Julian must have thought he was invisible, because he reentered

ATC by another side door and headed straight to the front desk. I was stunned by his blatant carelessness but also by the absence of police guarding the channel's entrance. The trenches had been moved outside.

We exited *ATC* very slowly, as stiff as if someone had added lots of starch to our garments. I was counting my steps and thanking God—any god available on that Sunday's countrywide holiday—for each foot I'd put up front without seeing the front of a gun pointed at me. Julian walked ahead, and I imagined he'd be whistling as we made progress toward the sidewalk's edge.

Suddenly, I felt the eyes trained in all these guns, and rushed to catch up with Julian before he started to cross Figueroa Alcorta. Reviewing the situation from the high point of time, this was a critical error. We were heading to the middle of a battlefield, and it was too late to escape.

I saw a guy jumping off the back of the red truck, carrying a sizeable rifle. Another man opened the driver's door, and a gun was propped forward, beyond the door's edge. I remember clearly the metallic sound of more than one of the Falcon's doors opening.

Julian turned to me with wide-open eyes and then started to run. I followed.

We didn't make it to the other side of Figueroa Alcorta. A car suddenly erupted into the avenue from *ATC's* side street—Austria was its name, I think—where it'd been parked against the traffic. It put itself across the avenue, so with the coming green light nobody would go forward. Several people were shuffling behind us, possibly pointing their guns to our backs.

Then, Julian fell. It was a spectacular roll and he ended up lying flat, spread on the pavement like a snow angel. I almost stumbled on his legs and fell over him.

He was hurt, and I could see a dark, browning spot growing on his now dirty gray pants, just over the knee. Even in my semiconscious state I was sure it was blood.

9

I checked my friend's wound through a gash on his pants—a long superficial cut, by a culprit I couldn't identify with the distracting chaos around me. He had also sprained his knee in the fall. I was ready to leave the green bag behind but thought of the first-aid kit Julian had stored there, and of our gun, in that order.

The Montoneros had stopped both directions of traffic, cleaning up a gap on the asphalt; this unleashed a barrage of beeps and yells, extending way back in the avenue. It was a momentary dam on its flow and it couldn't last. Perhaps that should count as an unforced error on their part.

Some of the Montoneros' soldiers had a uniform, but quite a few non-uniformed people were pointing guns from behind cars that weren't theirs, away from us and in the non-police side of the street. At least that's what I saw, while trying to prop up Julian on his sole functioning leg. My eyes were focused upfront and not on the officials who might have been pointing the remaining guns toward us—really through us, trying to reach the armed forces stationed across Figueroa Alcorta.

I glanced back once and saw a dozen policemen behind cars. But I kept pressing forward with Julian, trying to keep him steady. It was hard to move with my friend, as he couldn't bend his left leg. Something about our clumsiness might have excluded us from the proceedings; two Montoneros passed on either side of us, just before kneeling with their scoped rifles. We would be spared so long as we could get out of the way quickly enough.

We completed the crossing of the paralyzed avenue and left the pending conflagration behind to enter the park. Even as I deposited Julian across Tagle Street, on the steps of a building's fancy entrance, I knew I'd have to make my way back through the fighting troopers and into *ATC*—and figure out how to stop the Montoneros and save Martínez.

We were in a somewhat unstable position, since a lost bullet could travel straight from *ATC*, across the open gap of the park, and hit either of us. I found some gauze in the bag and stopped the leg's bleeding by applying pressure with my hand. Julian might need stitches later, and a good sterile cleanup; I had to use medical tape on top of that mess to secure the compress in place. Not a terrible situation, but he wouldn't be able to keep going much more.

I left Julian alone, moving with confidence but still worried that bullets would start flying any minute.

And they did. First, a single gunshot. Then, a couple more from afar.

The cacophony of beeps suddenly went quiet.

Watching it from the corner of Figueroa Alcorta and Tagle, the standoff occupied most of the broad gap between the avenue's sidewalks. It was like a giant public diorama of a modern-day battlefield, down to cutouts of cars and posted riflemen. The only movement was at the level of eyes being focused on their targets. Many cars had their doors open; their passengers had taken off.

Perhaps the different dangers that were present at that conjunction of evil had ways to cancel each other, or I was too numb to be impacted by the impending doom, but soon I was looking for the equivalent of a river's point of crossing. A straight path approach, taking a beeline for the door, seemed impractical—all the guns had a focal point I must cross to get back to the *ATC*'s doorsteps. Just a tiny doubt or a sensitive trigger, and I'd be gone, taking a number of souls with me.

Before I could conclude my observation, the decision was taken away from me. Just across the street and walking casually like there weren't any signs of upcoming combat, there was a stout fellow with a black jacket and matching turtleneck.

The man. Me, ahead by many years, and right now also taking the lead over the entire ensemble of crazy gunmen facing each other from either side. The man was strolling, unseen, into the TV station's entrance.

So, I, the teenager Edgar, had no choice but to take a stand and start crossing the stalled avenue. The beeline approach, after all.

As I moved on the side of the blue Jeep, now parked at the midpoint of the avenue, guys from either side looked at me as if insane—I was, of course—and one of them cursorily pointed his rifle at me, as a warning about not getting in the middle of the shooting gallery. I was tempted to obey, but then I saw, far away in the downtown side of the avenue, a line of military trucks. They were surely loaded with soldiers and guns.

There was no time for reflection, and I pressed on forward. My unexpected rush might have made me somewhat invisible, since both bands ignored me. I was just a kid carrying a sport bag, who seemed to be lost on his way to the gym. The green bag was protecting me more than the gun inside could.

I had no idea where the man was going and what he intended to do. I knew what the Montoneros were trying to do—the good that might come from a public shaming of the Junta—but I wanted them to fail, if only in a way that would force the exchange of Mariana for Martínez. A clear goal, but one I might not be able to accomplish without Julian.

I sprinted to reach the *ATC* building's entrance—a metallic portable fence now lay across it—while the bag kept hitting my sore back.

I didn't make it to the security point's door. Just as I jumped over a toppled section of the barrier, a great force snared me. I tumbled in the air, my legs having decided to land on their own. My body spun, and I crashed against glass, just short of the entrance's revolving doors. I had hit the glass with my back—very painfully.

I looked up, afraid of what I'd see. But it was Rafa, my good friend Rafa, the hulking Montonero. He had a bruised eye whose discoloration made it look greenish but not long ago it might have been purple-black.

10

"What are you doing? What the hell...?" Rafa actually had said *"qué demonios"* and made me smile. He'd been listening to my angry rants about the Montoneros.

I answered with a resonance of that anger, "I'm here to stop you, guys."

Now, it was Rafa who was smiling. *"You?"*

"Yes, and let me go." My arm was getting numb under his grip.

"I saw what happened with your friend."

"Julian?"

"I left him with Cristina. She'll take him to wherever he's safe."

"You brought Cristina? Are you crazy?" I couldn't help but sound protective about his girlfriend, but Rafa didn't say anything. "I need to get in," I said. "If you can help me, come with me."

"They are already inside."

"What...who?"

"Anibal, with Martínez. They entered through the side post, in Tagle Street. The whole thing outside is a distraction."

"But the police—those trucks—they'll catch them."

"It's all under control. We have people dressed like police, forcing a detour of the military help. We knew they would call them."

"God, you're *all* crazy." I couldn't express how stupid their plotting seemed to me, the way they were pointlessly risking lives. Like we weren't risking ours.

"Yes, they are all crazy. I'm leaving the organization as soon as this operation ends."

"And you think they are going to let you go?"

I'd just sounded like a character from *Godfather*. Rafa didn't answer.

I knew then that Rafa would go down swinging.

"Let's go in," Rafa finally said, a shadow crossing his face. "We don't have a lot of time. We're going to get Martínez, and then Mariana. If we don't get the bastard, they'll kill him." He didn't say that this would rend Mariana dead too.

Rafa had obviously come to the same conclusion I had.

We were in this mission together.

* * *

Inside, we were counting the seconds, and everything looked very different to me, as if a light shone from within each object; it was like being under the influence of a drug. The enormous tiredness I had, combined with the heights of an adrenaline surge, crossed my wires and made me see the world through bright magnifying glasses. The central *ATC* corridor, all glass on one side, was now a subway station in a distant future. Everything, *every* single thing, was now wonderful and unique—even the junk strewn over the office desks I could see through the windowpanes.

I got a hold of myself. "Rafa, we should be going."

"We don't know where Anibal and the crew are now."

"But we know where they're going. They need Martínez in front of a camera. The sports' studio, that's where."

A gratifying silence conceded my point, and we were on our way.

The deep inner corridors also appeared very different. Before,

I didn't look at them with the frame of mind of a thief, carefully storing information to guide me through. And I had not asked our guide where the game's transmission was going to happen, when Julian and I had that idiot all for ourselves. But Rafa was more decisive and dragged me along the longest hallway we could find. Noise could be heard ahead.

At least it wasn't gunshots.

* * *

The tension in the last thirty minutes before the game was high enough that *ATC* workers were being propelled to walk faster, think harder, and in general be oblivious to their surroundings. Someone could have paraded an elephant and been ignored by everybody.

We were a weird duo, but nobody noticed us. Rafa was huge and looked like a heavy weight boxer dressed in civilian clothes after losing by K.O. As for me, I had fallen more times than I could count, and my dressy gray pants now resembled a close-up photograph of some impure marble. My jacket's zipper was broken and there was a tear on my sleeve, probably a leftover of forcefully carrying Julian after his fall. But I could have been in shorts and the passersby would think I was in a soccer—football, I won't ever get it right—youth league.

We kept wandering between people so focused on their tasks they resembled ghosts—or perhaps, *we* were the ghosts—until suddenly Rafa shook me from behind. It was a powerful shake, and I stumbled over a small black bench behind me. Even before I raised my eyes, I thanked God for having him on my side.

"There they are."

Four people were approaching the end of a long corridor, almost invisible in its semidarkness. One of them had a big beard—I guessed that was Anibal—and another was in undescriptive dark-green fatigues; that one for sure was Martínez, on his forced way to the podium. The last two were likely help and carried long weapons. The *ATC* people were obviously used to seeing guys with guns as part of the daily background and nobody had sounded an alarm.

Things started to move quite fast. Rafa rushed toward the Montoneros—Anibal recognized him and made a conciliatory gesture. But before anyone in his group could move, Rafa pushed one of the armed goons, who fell and toppled Anibal. Shocked, the other armed Montonero tried to stop Rafa—an impossible task, as Rafa was twice as big as him—and only succeeded in hitting the floor face-first, just two steps away from me.

Across the sudden American football scramble, I saw something that horrified me. Hands tied behind his back, Martínez was running away.

I jumped over a couple of legs and was in pursuit.

I saw the man emerge from one of the corridors and immediately sprint for Martínez. I couldn't possibly catch up with the colonel before he reached the outside trail, but I could at least try to tackle myself, so neither of us—present or future—would get hold of Martínez. Trust that Rafa would get the colonel later, as I could now only stop the man from killing Martínez, and thus wrecking everything, finally and completely.

I was cutting my distance to the man, as he trailed Martínez, when I crashed into Officer Rodríguez, who grabbed me with a strength that left no doubt I wasn't going to have time to explain myself.

Oblivious to the risks, I swiped his left leg away from the inside—a clean *Ouchi-Gari* move, spontaneous and above my judo level—and he fell with his butt on the floor, hitting his head very hard on the wall.

I was free, and then I caught a glimpse of the man climbing the stairs at the end of our hallway. Before I could think a single thought more, I was rushing to the same stairs.

11

The stairs went partially out of the building in order to reach the roof. There was something peculiar about how they were connected but I can only remember a flash of yellow light coming through an opaque glass window. I guess my memory has been affected by what followed.

I opened a heavy, clunky door set over cement, just to find a gun pointed straight at me. I hadn't thought that the man could be armed.

"Move very slowly, nothing sudden." The man's gun got even closer.

"Why are you doing this?"

"What do you mean? You know what's at stake."

"No, I really don't," I said, and gave a step closer to the roof's guardrail. The gun followed me, but the man remained immobile. "All this stuff about changing the future sounds farfetched."

"Not so much. They sent me here to fix it, didn't they?"

"There's that, of course."

"And the only way to fix it is to eliminate the problem that originated the twist in time—*you.*"

"Me? And why not you?"

The hold he had on the gun relaxed a little, followed by

something that could've been taken as humor. "Well, I'm the one they've chosen to be the time-traveling killer."

"So, this is what my life would be, being turned into a criminal? Why don't we stop this, right now?"

"It's too late. And when you die, I'll disappear, and all of this will be normal again."

That was one possible solution—one I did not particularly like—but I refused to consider it as the only one. Since I'm telling you this story, you can assume I have survived. But time travel is a tricky business, and we might be now in any number of alternative universes where I wasn't killed that afternoon. So strong was the will of the Edgar I was confronting, I'm sure in more than half of those Earths I would be dead.

* * *

When death looms, one tries to pay attention to anything but her. It was sunset time, on a Buenos Aires-strength gray day. I could see the disk of the sun behind the clouds, every minute turning redder. I would have loved to see its bright face for one last time, not that disappointingly cartoonish silhouette.

"Why didn't you try to stop Rafa? Why me?"

"Good question. You are the source, of all trouble. Also, they won't succeed."

I wasn't surprised that he knew—we weren't talking about psychic premonition. He, or one of them, and me, we both had been on that roof hundreds of times.

I hadn't said anything for a while—didn't have any thoughts left. Then, one came. "It's all right. I understand, agree."

"You do?"

"I have to die for this to end. But..."

"But what?"

"You must assure me that...that Mariana will live."

His face didn't reveal any new emotion. "I can't. As soon as I kill you, I might not exist anymore."

He was right. I was asking the wrong person for help. I looked in the direction of the *ATC* tower, thinking of Rafa and how dumb I had been leaving his protection to chase this crippled version of myself.

"Over here," he said. "Kneel down."

My time to die had come. Suddenly, my world turned purple and I saw all possible outcomes of the moment at once. One possibility survived.

Why not?

In an unexpected movement, and as I passed near the man on my way to the final spot, my two hands grabbed his wrists and I shook the gun off an unprepared hand. It fell down at a surprisingly large distance, like a heavy toy being flung away.

A short fight ensued, with me having the clear advantage of youth and desperation. I twisted his arm and made him fall hard on one knee. I tried to kick his balls but, in my rush, I missed and hit hard on his right-side ribs. He winced, but was stronger and quickly forced my arm around his body—some martial arts training I still didn't have—making me roll over forward and land flat on my back.

I had enough time to stand and scramble to get to him as he moved away, but not enough to stop him from grabbing the gun. Again, the thing was in enemy hands and pointing at me. Its barrel seemed bigger this second time.

I was done, and this time there wasn't any need for dialogue. I walked backwards, and approached the guardrails with my hands raised, thinking about jumping. He guided me to kneel and face the horizon over the city's edge.

The sun had crossed the line of buildings inland. It was near sundown, and a boring one at that, barely suggested. I would have liked something different for my last day on Earth. I assumed my submission stance, feeling the roughness of the hard floor on my knees, and put my hands crossed over my back. I didn't want to give him the pleasure of thinking I was praying out of fear.

The last seconds of my life lay ahead.

The clock kept ticking.

It was the sunset, and my world was also coming into darkness.

12

I didn't know what one's supposed to think when facing death—even wondered if I should have asked before for suggestions and of whom. After a few seconds, the tension gave way to curiosity, and I turned to perhaps face that last flash of light.

The man was frozen, gun pointed to my head, but he had his face turned sideways, away from me. The reason was our old friend, Mister Officer Rodríguez. He was standing next to an access door, holding his very impressive pistol, also aimed at the man's head. The almost perfect linear alignment of those weapons was slightly comical. I didn't think at the time that it could mean I would get not one but two bullets straight into my brain.

I was the one who broke the conjunction of arrows pointed in my direction, slowly moving farther into the building's terrace, and then sprinting for the other exit. I was lucky it was open, as I hadn't considered that, being a different one, it could've been blocked, locked, or otherwise inoperative—after all, this was a very haphazardly finished building, even by Argentine standards. Since the two men were still threatening each other, I got away unscathed while the man now kept his gun directed back to Rodríguez. I had gained some experience in darting away from trouble, and my swift moves gave me a few extra seconds to pick up my abandoned duffel bag. After jiggling the door's handle around, I entered a dark space containing another set of stairs.

I wouldn't see Officer Rodríguez ever again, but that simple guy had something very good in him, and, even if he'd tracked me down out of a sense of duty, he'd ended up saving my life.

I ran like crazy, not just down the stairs, but in the direction of the complex's front doors. I'd had enough adventure for any single day and wanted to escape outside and disappear, run away from any future contact with either the Montoneros or the Argentine military. I passed flying through the long corridor with the tilted windowpanes, my eyes fixed on the street I could see through the entrance's windows.

The panorama out there wasn't much different from the standoff present when I'd entered by the main door. Rafa had been right—the military trucks never made it to *ATC*—and, in the absence of reinforcements, there was only sporadic shooting between the opposing teams. A new truck, presumably Montonero, was stationed on the avenue's midpoint; the people inside it were very busy funneling in shooters who had become isolated.

I wanted to leave but couldn't stop thinking that if the Montoneros took over *ATC*, I would never see Mariana again. I rested my hands against the front glass pane, unable to enter the revolving door and finally get out. Completely overtaken by grief, I began to hit the glass with my fists, as if begging for someone to let me out.

To be weighed against all the moments when my courage had faltered during those trialed weeks, I spun on my heels like a runner who'd touched the turn at mid-race and began to run in the opposite direction, deep into the complex.

On a hunch, I used the side exit and entered the outside garden, near *ATC*'s transmission tower. A shooting was going on across the station's pond. I heard shots from up high—one of the Montoneros was perched at the top of the station's tower. To this day, I don't know if that man was seeking the high ground for their attack or had a technical reason related to controlling the transmission from up high. It didn't matter much for him.

I'd never seen a man's head blown up—only on the film about JFK's assassination—but a second later, the Montonero was falling from the tower and splashing a big swath of water from the artificial pond. It was like a scene from a medieval fight, with men falling from the castle's ramparts into a dark moat.

I couldn't have been reached by the wake of the gunshot detonations, but I did fall backwards and against the outside windows, as if I'd been hit by one.

"Stop," I heard a loud, decisive voice, just behind me. I stopped, grabbed by fear.

As I turned back and away from the windowpane, I realized I knew that voice. It was Anibal, walking toward me with Rafa, another combat-dressed Montonero, and a guy with his hands handcuffed behind his back—Martínez. Close up, the colonel was both good-looking and foreign-looking, with glossy sandy hair and striking blue eyes; it was as if they'd hired an American actor to play his part.

"You will be coming with us," said Anibal. I noticed then how he was holding a gun parallel to his leg. Something in Rafa's posture—a glimmer of submission, rare on him—told me that the gun had been pointed at him quite recently.

I tried to say something, anything to quickly learn what was going on, before we were sucked again into the bowels of the Montoneros organization. "Didn't you guys have to reach the back end of the station to stop the transmission?"

Anibal flashed whatever is the exact opposite of a smile. "It was rigged," he said. "They knew we were coming; there were too many of them inside. We're going back, to the fridge."

"Fridge?"

"*Sí, la heladera,*" answered Anibal, his anger weighing down every word. "Go on. Move!"

I saw the gun rise and started walking. I guessed silently that the "fridge" was a kind of safe house, a secluded place where they could rethink their plans. I just kept marching ahead, toward the street.

Almost within a single breath, I had transitioned from hero to escapee to prisoner.

Before crossing the *ATC* entrance for another uncertain destination, I saw the time on an office clock—it was three in the afternoon.

The game had started.

13

I entered the chaos outside together with the Montoneros. I was now with them and we had acquired a prisoner who was one of the military's own. We were behind the backs of maybe ten policemen, all likely with orders to kill us.

Two of the cops shifted positions to point their guns at us. The junior Montonero who was holding Martínez on my left had no better idea than to raise his gun. He was shot in the chest at once, and for a second, I was sure the bullet had gone through him and into Martínez. But the sneaky bastard moved around the falling trooper and started darting toward a parked Ford Falcon. Rafa wasn't armed, but Anibal immediately shot two of the cops.

I should have run and hidden myself, but the idea of losing Martínez—and thus Mariana—was too much to bear. Since the rest of the policemen were seeking protection from the crazy shooter behind their lines, nobody used a weapon for a few seconds, giving me enough time to reach for Martínez and pull him down by the handcuffs they'd set on him. He flinched and stumbled sideways, falling over the closest car to us—a small brown sedan, probably a Renault—while I covered his body with mine.

Then, as I touched Martínez, something blinded me.

* * *

I have experienced the burdens of time much more than other mortals. And so, I'm fluent on the unexpected twists and turns the linear road we all believe we are on can take. The simplest way to explain what happened then is to say that the future barged into the present, all at once, flooding my mind.

I saw an elder Martínez, climbing the stairs of what looked like an old hotel.

I had a vision of a sandy beach, which I knew held a great secret.

I also became aware of the existence of immortal aliens, who had visited our world and left untold numbers of their machines. Machines with powers over time and space that exceeded the ones we'd ascribed to our own gods.

Martínez was connected with that future, although I couldn't see how. And this future was also connected to me, and to the man.

I was connected to Martínez, as much as I was to the man.

* * *

It had been just an instant, but it felt as if I'd been floating in space for ages. Martínez crashed against the Renault's trunk and I fell over him. We slid down over the car's rear bumper.

Anibal took it upon himself to defend us, and he started to shoot from the corner of our car; his friends at the truck chimed in. The barrage of gunshots that followed acted as a shield, and we made our way toward the group waiting at the truck's back. A couple of shots grazed the pavement like thick lines made with black chalk.

As soon as we got behind the truck, I endorsed Martínez to them with a pat on the back—I was still holding him with the other hand, by his handcuffs. Anibal looked at me with something close to approbation—the only time I ever saw him direct a little respect to me.

Anibal was already standing inside the back of the truck. "Just get up here," he said. "We *are* leaving." He grabbed Martínez by the shoulders, and the colonel seemed smaller next to him.

I spoke with surprising strength, "What are you going to do with him?"

I thought Anibal was going to slap Martínez. "We're screwed," he said, "and if we cannot get this prick on the air, I'm not much for keeping him."

Martínez shivered at that, and I did too.

"You should keep him," I said. "We still need him."

"Keep him? Why? Climb the damned truck. You should be glad we're taking you with us."

Rafa, who until then seemed stunned by our escape, put a hand on my shoulder. "He's right," he said. "We need Martínez to get Mariana back."

Anibal's expression was inscrutable. "Mariana? She knew the risks she was taking."

"No, she didn't," said Rafa. "And we can still exchange the son of a bitch for her."

Our stand was getting precarious, and two more gunshots highlighted how we were in a battle zone. "Stop it, Rafa," said Anibal. "Are you guys coming? We must take off."

"I'm staying," I said. They both looked at me as if I were speaking in tongues.

"You what?" Anibal pushed Martínez inside, into the hands of other Montoneros.

"I will find another way to get Mariana."

Rafa interrupted, "I'm going with you, Anibal." And he started to climb the truck's fender. But his recent wounds made him unsteady, and Anibal had to grab his arm to stop him from falling backwards.

"You are coming with us, too," said Anibal, pointing a finger to me.

"Let Edgardo go," said Rafa.

"I'm not letting anyone back who..."

"Let him go."

Another bullet went beyond mere sound and hit the truck's side, just centimeters from my body. No time for arguments. "Okay, Edgardo," said Anibal, "you're on your own."

Two guys raised the back door of the truck in a single movement, and I was left alone in the middle of the huge avenue. Rafa had left the green duffel bag next to the truck, and I had the presence of mind to pick it up before I started to run.

14

I had some Argentine *pesos* left in my pocket, so I took a taxi. The lights of appliance stores were the only memorable thing from my trip back to the apartment. Each lighted windowpane had a TV set tuned to *ATC*'s showing of the game. The few people still on their way home were transiently glued to the glass, some so close it seemed they wanted to cross into the green paradise the screens were showing. Everyone wanted to be in the stadium.

I can see that scene of people window-watching the game repeating *ad infinitum*. Maybe I saw all those Rockwell-esque gettogethers, but I'm not sure. My mind was chock-full of too much failure, violence, and a great deal of hopelessness, to be worrying about sports.

* * *

My apartment door opened, and I was immediately the center of attention. I had reached a private World Cup watching party I hadn't been involved in planning.

I had completely forgotten Julian and Cristina, but there they were, very cozy in my living room. Cristina opened the door, wearing a white apron with flowery designs, which I've probably had in the kitchen but would never wear. Julian was spread all over our longest armchair, now placed in front of the last-time-I-saw-it-was-in-the-bedroom TV, only suffering from a hurt foot and clumsily applied bandages.

And, between my friend and Rafa's girlfriend, my father stood undecidedly in his huge black overcoat, looking like a Nazi SS officer in his winter coat. He automatically started to walk in my direction.

I was stunned and didn't know what I'd say to him—but I oddly thought he had aged more gracefully than I will. Then, the insanity of all this took my breath away.

I don't remember well what happened next. My father wanted to know if I was Okay. Cristina wanted to hear from me whether Rafa was okay. Julian wanted to know what had happened inside *ATC*. And I wasn't in a mood conducive to explaining things to any of them.

But I do remember grabbing Cristina's hand as she tried to take my sodden jacket. Maybe it was seeing her bright green eyes, or the shapely body insinuated behind the apron, but something shook my defective decision mechanisms and I said that I needed to chat urgently with her, about some private communication from Rafa. I proceeded to drag her through the living room and into the privacy of our sweet-smelling kitchen. I had to elbow my father to get him far enough away to close the door behind me.

Overwhelmed by the warmth of the kitchen, I followed with my nose the recent history of its oven. Cristina had been making meaty *empanadas*, and the stove's gas fires had recently fried some *buñuelos* filled with a sweet concoction. Obviously, when the going gets tough, the Argentines get cooking.

Cristina and I remained still for a few seconds, holding each other's hands. She finally released hers to briefly caress my cheek. "Are you well?"

"Yes, a little sore but...Rafa's okay too."

"He told me about *Cóndor*. You two, with Julian, are...as crazy as Rafa. True head cases."

"We were just trying to make it there, so we could find Mariana—we were late. She wasn't there."

She grabbed my hand again, with a lot more force this time. "You and me. We got the short straw."

"I don't understand."

"We are stuck with the people we love—and the danger they seek. It'd be easier if we wouldn't be so attached."

"But I..." I was going to say something about her being more tied to Rafa, when I realized why Cristina felt so close to me, and why I was feeling that strong attraction to her. In her eyes, we were the same.

Mariana and Rafa. Both were in the Montoneros. Both were the love of our lives, lives that hadn't had any other before them.

Now, I was the one who grabbed and pressed her hand, making her flinch. She was right. We had the same kind of absurd dream. And we were the same kind of idiotic dreamers, the kind who feels entranced by the exotic bad girl—or bad boy—who has a heart of gold. And then we get trapped with them for the long haul, trying to remake them into a less dangerous species, still with the golden heart intact. It was just another quixotic dream.

It has taken me a long time to put it in words, but now I can say it: you can't change those people. And you can only keep the good heart if it's sustained by being involved in an overriding cause. You take the cause away, the power of being a rebel, and the violence will show somewhere else. I was too young back then to figure that out.

The time for prolonged silences and holding hands had ended, and Cristina wasn't ready to get more personal with me. "You too," she said, "you've sacrificed so much for Mariana. And you are not giving up, not even when you're up against stubborn jerks like Anibal." I could see something like pride about me in Cristina's eyes. "Rafa can't stand him," she added, "but he keeps going along and does whatever Anibal tells him to do."

I knew that Rafa wasn't much more than a good follower, the rest added by Cristina's affection for him, but I still tried to make her feel good about her choice. "He's a good guy, Cristina. He risked his life for me."

"Thanks, Edgardo. I do hope he comes back unharmed from this adventure. He keeps telling me this is the last time—it's always the last time—and then he'll cut ties with the Montoneros. But something else always happens and my little soldier is called back to the front lines."

"It will end at some point," I said, feeling the absurdity of my own words. For people like Mariana and Rafa, it never ends. Rebellion is too strong a drug to leave without unbearable pain.

I almost fell into Cristina's arms. My father had barged inside the kitchen, and I was hit by the door's swinging edge. I do remember her warm cheek touching mine for a little instant of consolation.

It was the last time I'd be in physical contact with Cristina. After that night, I never saw her again.

15

My father usually occupies all the available space for himself, and the kitchen suddenly felt small. Cristina drifted away to check her *empanadas*.

"I can't wait all night," he said. "We need to talk."

"I'm just—don't know if they've told you." Cristina's glimpse in my direction suggested that no, my adventures had remained private. They'd likely been masked by a barrage of typically Argentine white lies, which could lubricate any unexplained mystery, whether it was Julian's leg or my disheveled appearance.

"I brought you this." My father put a brand-new U.S. passport in my surprised hands.

"Oh, this's great. Thanks for..."

"Do you know how hard it was to get this? I'll be owing favors to Henry forever. He had it brought to me at the hotel in a diplomatic attaché."

It took me so long to figure out his comment that I missed my opportunity to show the appropriate astonishment. My father had been referring to the Henry Kissinger, who had been visiting Argentina for the World Cup, while palling around with the military Junta. I should've said something about my father moving mountains for me, but I was just too out of it to say anything thoughtful.

The kitchen's heat was getting to good old Daniel Weston. He started to struggle opening his shirt's collar with one hand. I knew that soon I was going to get the brunt of the storm my father was brewing.

Perhaps it helped that I was admiring the new and sharp passport—mine had been battered on my last trans-European trip—like it was a shining work of art, concrete but reminiscent of the latest hyperrealism emanating from Andy Warhol. I even took it to my nose, trying to better smell the ink-and-plastic aroma of the thing, and that sort of pleased my father.

"I'm glad you like it," he said.

"Thank you, Dad. I know you went to a lot of trouble to get it for me. Now, I am…"

"Now, what you are is coming with me. This is over."

"This?"

"This stupid adventure of yours, staying down here to study. It's not your country—was your grandmother's, but not ours. And it's getting downright dangerous to live here."

"I know," I said, really agreeing only with his last comment. I didn't have time to argue how I had wanted to know about the country just to keep alive what was left of my mother or explain that that was the real reason behind my extended stay in Buenos Aires.

Because, at that precise moment, the TV exploded, and Earth momentarily stopped its rotation.

"Goooool! GOOOOOOOOOOOOOOOOOOOOOOOOOOOOOOOO OL."

* * *

The commotion of the goal—and its tangible reverberation in the seismic waves that rambled outside—drew me and my father through the kitchen door and to the TV in the living room. At almost forty minutes into the first half, and after many failed attempts from either side, Argentina's unstoppable goal-maker, Mario Kempes, had fallen after moving gracefully between two members of the opposing team, but not before pushing the ball in an incredible straight line toward the goalpost's net. It was a great beginning for the host country but, like animals sensing danger, Buenos Aires and its people went back to move uneasily in their places. After the great collective outburst, silence fell sharply over the entire city.

"This is great," said my father, pointing to the screen. "But we've missed the game by being there. And you, you haven't answered me—are you coming back? What are you going to do?"

"It's that..."

I didn't want to say no, because even when I knew I was in danger and should have left the country ASAP, I didn't want to leave Buenos Aires. The possibility of a very long public argument with my father stopped me; I lacked the energy for any more verbal fighting.

Julian waved to me from the edge of the armchair, trying to get permission to enter the conversation— "Where are you going to go?" He had sat, and I saw his leg protruding beyond his folded trousers; it only had a puffy gauze pad. He wasn't in as bad a shape as I'd thought.

"I—my father wants me to go back to the States."

"Now?"

"Yes, *now*, Julian," my father said, burning my friend with a power look. "This is a family matter, not any of your...."

Julian tried to say something, but just stared at us.

"I've spent a lot of time getting your passport." My father was again holding the thing as if it were a hundred-dollar bill. "You are coming home with me—then, we'll decide if and when you can come back."

"I'll do what I want."

"You are a minor and will do what I..."

The phone rang, next to Julian, and he almost flipped back over the armchair's backrest. I thanked God for the intervention.

Julian managed to grab the phone's handset and answer. "It's Rafa," he said.

"I'll take it," said Cristina, appearing out of nowhere. She grabbed the handset by its twisted cord, pulling it away from Julian.

While Cristina tried to talk without being heard, I used the break to fish out my peace offering—the razor set—for my angry father.

Cristina was still talking when I came back. And the football match continued, now near its half-time break. The TV was showing different views of what looked like the same scene—people running, with either orange or light blue-white shirts, somewhat uncoordinatedly over a grass field covered in confetti. The players moved toward one or the other goalpost; it didn't matter which one. It was a timeless scene, primeval for that culture.

After a few minutes, full of Cristina's affirmative head swings and the repeated Argentine equivalent of "Really?" I decided to interrupt before we spent an hour letting her catch up with her boyfriend.

"What is he saying?"

"What?"

"Rafa—what's going on? And, where is he?"

"He is in *Constitución*."

"Where?" That was an incredulous Julian.

Cristina waved her hands around, as if she were translating from Turkish. "Constitution Station," she said, "well, near there, that's where they'd meet to discuss plans."

"And?" Even when dealing with Cristina, I was losing my temper. I had no patience left.

"He's saying that they *are* going to exchange Martínez for Mariana."

"Who? Who's that?" My father had been momentarily distracted while opening the paper-wrapped gift, which he hadn't even acknowledged to me.

"Don't worry, *Señor* Weston," said Julian, mixing up his English. "It's something good, very good. We're helping a friend who was kidnapped."

"*Kidnapped? Edgar, what are you involved in?*" My father's English merged almost coherently in that disjointed conversation.

"No, Father," I said. "It's nothing. They are going to rescue her."

"This...*es realmente loco*," said my father, back to his wobbling Spanish. "I can't believe you are mixed up with criminals." My father's speech fell into a moment of silence, while he contemplated the razor. "This reminds me," he said, "of something that an army friend used to say in Korea: I know that you have good intentions, Edgar, and that she's a friend, but what would pass for good intentions can be wrong-headed ones."

I was still coping with the message from Rafa. Cristina had hung up the receiver. Julian was trying to stand on his two feet.

In any other array of circumstances, *Señor* Weston's comment would've mixed with his previous admonitions and been forgotten immediately after. But for whatever combination of the reigning planets, the comment hit me right between the eyes.

I was ready to grab that passport from my father's hand and finally leave.

And then I wasn't.

What passes for good intentions can sometimes be wrong-headed ones.

Yes, my father was right. One can never be sure whether what looks good is not a matter of deception. What's that they say? The road to Hell is paved with good intentions?

Yes, sometimes good intentions can be bad intentions in disguise.

It flashed over my mind, oh so very quickly. Maybe I was wrong. Maybe the man was wrong. Maybe all the powers of time were wrong.

I can't explain it in a linear fashion, but I realized that I had to intervene.

I was the only one who could possibly know what to do. It was the last thing I would have wanted to do, but suddenly there wasn't any other way than forward for me.

PART VII

Time Unchained

1

I don't know how I convinced everybody that I should be present at the exchange—at least, watch it from a distance and be there when they finally released Mariana. Mine were meaningless arguments, but the weight of my personal odyssey gave them a power no logic could muster. Their inner truth came from being certain that I had a role to play in the Argentine version of Russian roulette the Montoneros would play against the paramilitary, pseudo-police monsters who had Mariana. But I was nevertheless surprised by how everyone around me kept silent when I spoke; my bruised face and battle-scarred clothes were speaking beyond my words.

By the time I had managed to collect my things and reassure my father—and Julian—that they didn't need to come with me, the game was well into the second half, still 1 to 0 for Argentina.

It took some time to extract from Cristina a more precise address for the exchange—Rafa had been strangely vague about the plan. When Cristina said Rafa had told her the exchange would happen on a short street named after Copernicus, that sent all of us to search for our copy of the *Filcar* maps for Buenos Aires.

I also asked for a few minutes off to think in my room, pleading with my interlopers that I had to work out my problems alone. For the break I'd requested, I had meant I needed time to uncover where I'd left the green bag with the gun, check to see if it was loaded, and hide it in my jacket's pocket.

* * *

I was hurriedly walking the streets of an empty city, where every person was either watching the last minutes of the game or trying to check on it from those who were. The streets were deserted in the stretch before reaching the grandiose Avenida Nueve de Julio. Even the usually crowded traffic of the enormous multi-lane avenue was now barely trickling by, and most cars carried Argentine flags.

As I walked north on the Nueve de Julio, I saw a truck heading in the direction of the city's immense decorative obelisk, *El Obelisco*, a predictable bull's-eye for the potentially explosive get-together to be had if the home team pulled off a triumph. The occupants of that truck were all dressed in shirts in the striped white-and-blue of the National Team, but many of these were placed over sweaters and puffy jackets, to cover bodies from exposure over the long night awaiting them. The truck was draped in Argentine flags but, so far, it was alone on its march.

I was in a dark mood, and such a preemptive display before a real victory seemed to me both vainly hopeful and incredibly arrogant. But this was Argentina, and escaping from reality was the other national sport.

I stopped at the sole newspaper kiosk I could find open and asked the attendant—who was following the game by radio—what was going on with the score. The Dutch had tied, with a goal just a few minutes before the end of the match; they had missed a defining goal by hitting the Argentine goalpost. They were now going into a supplemental period.

If Argentina won, the truck I saw might have been the first of hundreds to reach the downtown. Maybe these fans were smarter than others, and they were going to get the best spots for the after-game celebration, which would be epic.

I wished the best for the local team, to get the first world-level victory for a country that had sacrificed so much time and treasure for the sport. It was not a rational thought, and I was painfully aware of the reasons for contradiction, but I was collecting the waves of good wishes coming from the city's collective spirit, from every living soul born in the land.

I could feel that spirit rising. It was a goddess who was hard to please, and it might still need some sacrifices to warrant a victory. I was there to stop her from getting what she wanted.

I hadn't seen a single taxi, and now my original rush to get to Cortada Copérnico—a one-block-long "cut" street, supposedly not very far from *Argentina Televisora Color*—was conflicting with the need to save my energies for battle. I was going to keep walking briskly until I found a taxi or made it there. The whole distance I had to cover was less than 30 blocks, and I thought I could do it in less than an hour.

I wasn't sure how long it would take me to reach my target. But I was certain that nothing would happen until the game ended— military and Montonero alike, they'd all be watching it—and never before the result was known. Nobody would sacrifice being there during those potentially historic minutes, the Argentine's equivalent of a moon landing; and then, after the end, the invasion of the streets would offer a great deal of cover for any illegal activity. I smiled thinking that an alien ship could land, and nobody would notice it.

I couldn't see any cars—the flow of vehicles had receded like the ocean before a tsunami. And if that tsunami hit the city, it was going to be huge.

My smile disappeared as soon as I reached Libertador Avenue and turned to look back for one last time toward the obelisk. I was being followed by two men.

I started to accelerate my steps and touched the gun for a measure of security, though I wasn't going to start a shooting. I pressed ahead, with the idea of losing the presumed policemen as I skirted the darker edges of the expanse of Recoleta Cemetery and jumped into Plaza Francia. Images of the city and my own recent past crowded my mind. I didn't want to end up in another detention center, and I finally understood why in so many movies the gunman decides to go down shooting rather than be captured.

The city of Buenos Aires is a grand metropolis, and it has numerous parks and large woods all along its coastline, each peppered with fountains and monuments. I was moving next to the thankfully well-illuminated Avenida del Libertador and, on my left, the parks and the city itself sloped up as if the ground had been pushed by an invisible giant. Part of these slopes followed the old coast from the nineteenth century, before the village grew immense and spilled over the river.

I was having these history-laden thoughts when my pursuers felt closer and I switched directions, turning left and into a park's lawn. Going inland wasn't the greatest of ideas, but it surprised my relegated entourage—whoever would be doing such low-level surveillance work, and on that night, was the definition of a bottom-of-the-barrel choice.

To complicate matters, and just as I'd gained an extra half block of distance from them, there was another goal in the overtime, obviously from Argentina. It's no wonder I knew of it immediately, as the suspended collective breathing gave way to pervasive hollering in buildings, clearly heard in the streets, as it poured from the many windows kept open even in the cold evening. The cheerful yelling was followed by car horns and the distant explosion of what I was sure was gunfire.

The two men were trying to close in on me, perhaps trying to take me into custody and get on with the celebration. I was ahead by almost a block and slowed down to surprise them. They did stop, possibly thinking I had not seen them. I calculated for a few seconds all my current possibilities: which way that weirdly-named *Copérnico* Street should be, if they knew I was going there, and whether I would be more protected when I reached it. I cursed for not having taken anyone with me—Julian, even with his leg, or my father, a large manly body.

I then wondered if I knew enough of that corner of Buenos Aires, and wasn't sending myself into another closed-down, cut street, of which there were many in the oldest parts of *Palermo*. Or perhaps into the arms of another party who might have been searching for me while making a tweezer formation with the first.

They were just twenty meters behind me when I darted, running across a roundabout at the top of a hill and in the direction opposite of the one I wanted to take.

Into an unknown, dark street.

2

For once, the city took care of me. I can't remember where I walked during those last few minutes of the protracted chase. But I did feel the release of tension breaking over the city, instantaneously flooding it with cars and their beeping horns. And then, there was the widespread yelling, from thousands of lungs, and a soon-to-be characteristically South American clamoring produced by the clanging of aluminum pans, some of them being banged from the heights of very luxurious buildings. I couldn't imagine the chaos that would be descending onto the poorest suburban neighborhoods—isolated from Buenos Aires, as the police had closed all city bridges—and the human explosion that would shake the epicenter of each and all city-wide outbursts, the obelisk on the intersection of Nueve de Julio and Corrientes.

Argentina had won, unlikely but definitively enough, and for a second all the barriers in that society vanished. I imagined people like those I'd met at the *Cóndor* center, both captors and detainees, hesitating about if to hug one another, while everybody confusingly cried overwhelmed by the depth of emotion, the great cheer for one's country. Believers and unbelievers of all causes were united in a long second of happiness.

I was sure my pursuers were very angry with me for robbing

them of a once-in-a-lifetime moment of collective triumph. If they had gotten me then, I would have been a dead man.

In my rush to get away, I had ended up on an avenue I didn't recognize. I saw a corner park ahead, on the opposite side, which now I think was Plaza Mitre. At the time, with the streets so crowded by people, traffic was at a standstill, saturated with trucks full of celebratory human cargo, but also packed with cars as large as station wagons or tiny as Fiat 600s. They all carried families and friends, everyone waving hands, and some sounding whistles or banging saucepans. A huge vertical drum—what in Argentina's folklore is known as a *bombo*—was being pounded, and it sounded loud enough to make me wishfully think of earplugs.

But I was still being pursued, whether or not I could see them. I jumped forward to hide behind a car, the always-black monstrosity known as a *Kaiser Carabela*—those sedans would have taken a cannonball without a scratch—and tried to stay low to make it hard for the policemen to see me.

I then caught a glimpse of them. Dark jackets, one of them leather, and pants too formal to be a good match for their shoes. Add, of course, a short haircut and perfectly shaved facial hair, a mix that screamed police out of their daytime uniforms. They might have been conspicuous in the crowd, but that didn't make them any less dangerous. One woman tugged her kid against her skirt—she knew. We all knew they were all around in the city, especially at night.

And on that night, I was privileged enough to have two of them assigned just to me. My private nightmare.

I decided that the only way out was to do something crazy. I mounted a moving pickup truck, fighting with two fellows in football costumes, their team shorts worn over jeans to cover their legs from the cold. They were not so happy about being pushed aside, but it was a night of victory and they let me stay.

The two policemen saw me and started to run toward the truck.

We were approaching a turn, and I climbed over the truck's rear door, its wood so weak I thought I'd break it. The first two guys I fell upon shoved me sideways, but I still managed to sneak toward the street side.

I jumped out of the truck and the force almost made me roll over the broken tiles that covered most of the sidewalk. As soon as I could raise my sight, I smiled—the two policemen had also climbed the truck from its rear, and they were now fighting their way among the people it carried, trying to find me.

An oddly palatial stairwell came away from the sidewalk. And a tiny park stood just across that street and near the avenue. It all led to an elevated street, which ran away from what had to be Las Heras Avenue. That was exactly what Cristina had described for me. I was looking at the most perfectly triangular, full-size block in Buenos Aires, perhaps anywhere in the world.

I was at the doorstep of Cortada Copérnico. Destiny had delivered me where I should be. It was simple, and I wasn't going to argue the mysteries that this implied. There were too many to worry about them.

I just couldn't be anywhere else.

3

¡Oíd, mortales, el grito sagrado...!

Hear, mortals, the sacred cry! The beginning of Argentina's National Anthem took me by surprise. On the upper floors of a nearby building, someone was playing an old record, scratchy and perhaps more real because of it. It was the sound of a solemn celebration in a poor public school without a piano. But it had the power of entire Argentine cities as they stood up to sing it.

I stayed hidden under a balcony, oddly shivering with emotion. I was feeling the pride, coming from all around me, and it overwhelmed me, as if I had entered a sacred space.

The three cries of freedom reverberated across the elevated street:

¡Libertad! ¡Libertad! ¡Libertad!

And then I heard the words that have come to symbolize my entire quest to set the world right again.

Oíd el ruido de rotas cadenas...

To hear the noise from broken chains...

The sound of broken chains. As the verse was being branded in my memory, I recall that it surprised me how the order of those words followed more the English usage—in Spanish, it should have said *cadenas rotas*, not *rotas cadenas*. It was as if the nation was speaking just to Edgar Weston.

And for me, it was the chain of time that had to be broken, the ceaseless coming to be of the minutes I was finally ready to break at its weakest link. That was my sole mission, perhaps my last mission. To hear the sound of those chains breaking.

The anthem was reaching its emotional conclusion, which now I don't seem to be able to write too well in English, but to me it sounded like:

...May the laurels be eternal, those we knew how to obtain...
...*those we knew* how to obtain.
...Crowned with glory we are to be living,
or we swear that with glory we'll die...
Or, we swear that with glory we'll die!!!

I was there, on that night which will be forever remembered in Argentina as both triumphant and ignominious, and I was ready to hear a sound of broken chains that was bound to its origins. Once more, for a country that wasn't mine. I was to fulfill its deepest purpose and thus recreate it.

And I was also attempting to free mankind from those who wanted to remake it for some dark purpose.

I knew that much, not really a whole lot, but there was only way to find out the rest.

Go ahead and cut those chains.

4

After seeing two vehicles suspiciously parallel-parked away from the sidewalk, I decided to start walking along Copérnico. I moved very carefully—the blue Jeep-like *Estanciera* and an apple-green Ford Falcon were likely loaded with secret policemen.

I was walking on a glass floor, and below me there was a hell of time, eternity and destiny, all contorted in a terrifying landscape.

It seemed to be early for the exchange—I didn't see any distinctive vehicle from the Montoneros—and the *Estanciera* was stirring inside with anticipation. Even when I couldn't see anyone under those weak streetlights, I was sure the two huddled groups were busy getting ready. I saw in that an opportunity and ran across the street's gap like hunted prey; with belabored breathing, I hid behind the *Estanciera*.

My heart was beating so hard it forgot to keep an even rhythm. I had realized Mariana could be on the other side of that car's door. I extended my arms and touched it with the tips of my fingers.

A few unremarkable minutes went by. I visually inspected each of the cars parked along Copérnico. It was very odd how the street was abruptly cut by the stairwell; cars could only come, park, and leave, but they had nowhere else to go. It was a true metropolitan *cul-de-sac*, and the lack of traffic made it perfect for a protected retrieval. I would later learn that those few irregular blocks and interrupted streets, including the remarkable triangular block, were known as *"La Isla."* And it was called an island because it rose in elevation and floated over the rest of Buenos Aires, isolated from its infernal drivers.

I was stranded on an island, a true castaway.

A truck, large and dark, arrived and parked at the farthest end of Copérnico. I felt movement inside the *Estanciera* and was ready to move around it to see more, when an invisible hand pulled me back. I looked over my left shoulder and there he was, the man, with another turtleneck sweater, light blue just like an Argentine flag.

"You," I said.

"Yes—you."

"What are you doing here?"

"I thought to go out and celebrate."

"And, where's your...?" I lowered my voice, realizing how close our heads were to the car's windows. "Did you bring your Argentine pullover? Finally, something patriotic." My joke didn't seem funny enough after I'd said it out loud.

He probably thought the same. "Argentina owes me, you and I, a lot of our lives, which it has stolen for free."

"Can you leave me alone? I'm going to..." I was thinking how close I was to Mariana.

"No, you are not. I'm still around."

"You are, I see, but are you alone?"

"Yes, nobody else here who wants to kill you. You seem to be doing a fantastic job all by yourself. Maybe the 'masters' won't see the need to intervene anymore."

I ignored him for a moment to peek around the rear of the *Estanciera*. The Montoneros—it had to be them—stood on the back of their truck. I could only assume they'd secured Martínez and were readying him for the exchange.

"I know how hard it is going to be to change the outcome," the man said. "And you know this much too. It might not be possible to change it, to save Mariana."

"But it can be changed. Or, what the hell are you doing here—all of you—and why did they send you?"

That apparently did hit home, and he gifted me with a few precious seconds of silence. I didn't have the strength to take another peek around the vehicle. I was too nervous and worried, and with reason, since one or the other group of thugs could easily see me.

"What happened to me back then," the man continued, "it was awful. I came here too late, when they were already doing the swap. I tried to save Mariana, and I did, but then Rafa started to shoot, and Anibal gunned down Martínez. One of the policemen then fired back and killed Mariana."

Even when I had figured this out already—Anibal cheating to kill Martínez—the thought of losing Mariana froze me. From up close, I could see the enormous burden on my old self, how much he'd suffered after trying so hard to save Mariana.

All for nothing—that could soon be my curse.

But the thing that struck a chord with me from the man's words was how he had come too late to the exchange. I had not been late to the party and, at least, that was a difference.

I sprung up, forgetting the nearby crew in the *Estanciera*. I pushed aside the man, and his arm graced my back as I moved away. Over the years, I've come to think of his touch as kind, a goodbye of sorts.

My decisiveness lasted all but an instant. The two groups had begun to move. The Montoneros first, starting to walk glued together as an entourage—perhaps five men and Martínez hidden within the group's core. One of the bearded ones was Anibal Reinoso.

Then, the doors of the other car—the Ford Falcon—suddenly opened and three men came out, two of them holding a thin figure in puffy clothing, hooded in a way that reminded me of the *Cóndor*. It had to be Mariana.

The *Estanciera* on my side turned out to be full of police non-participants, and only the two who were sitting on the street side opened their doors and exited. One of them headed to join the others; another remained next to the rear driver's door, blocking my path.

I didn't know what to do, and then I saw something that made my heart skip a beat. After appearing above the stairwell's horizon, and quickly passing by the entrance's Romanesque statues of two children holding a flower vase, Rafa had started to walk the opposite sidewalk. He was surely armed, with the gun which would trigger the confrontation. Behind him, Julian was making some tentative steps with his hurt leg, as he clumsily tracked Rafa.

I might have been late again. Perhaps, I just didn't know it yet.

5

As I stood, I saw a policeman in front of my spot, his silhouette filling the gap between the blue *Estanciera* and the Ford Falcon. I couldn't get past him, and to make matters worse, the exchange had already started: three of the government agents were walking very slowly toward the other end of the street.

In a reflex move, I extended my right hand as if trying to touch Mariana's head. And then the world changed in front of my eyes.

I could say that a colored veil fell over my sight, and it was as if I were suddenly wearing tinted glasses. But it's not so simple to explain, and whatever color I was seeing was not the same as any of its versions in my remembered past. We use words like violet, purple, oxblood, or burgundy to describe those in-between hues; but the reddish, bluish, and something else's cast that had descended over my world went far beyond those parceled names. Like all perceptions, it was a private feeling, and I can't describe it beyond saying that, as I moved, there were a myriad additional versions of it, and their superposition made them into a color for which there is no possible name.

Even more than the color, what took me by surprise was that I had somehow moved past the standing policeman—perhaps through him rather than around his back—and now I was standing, or perhaps floating, over the midpoint of Copérnico. It wasn't that time had stopped, but rather that its movement had become skewed, as our reality appears to shift when a master magician makes a sleight of hand that seemingly violates Physics.

I had been propelled outside of time.

Two large spheres had appeared, suspended in the air, and that wavering color was more intense at the demarcation of their edges. After a hesitation that might have been swift or lasted a million years, I noticed how the bubbles' placement was not random. One was just between me and the group escorting Martínez. The other floated just ahead of the policemen who were carrying Mariana by either arm; not strictly between me and them but clouding my line of sight.

I didn't wonder anymore what these alien devices were doing there—they had been sent to either guide me or confuse me—and I knew that I was the only one who saw them. I was being affected by them, suspended outside of myself and witnessing time with its windows opened into all manner of alternative futures.

Then, something happened, and the tower of cards started to collapse.

* * *

At first, I didn't see Rafa run. He left Julian behind and started to move in a straight line to the group holding Martínez. Perhaps I wouldn't have left my nirvana if Rafa were the only one risking it all to capture the notorious officer; but then, Julian tried to catch up with him, clumsily running on his almost busted knee.

Perhaps because Rafa was feeling the presence of Julian behind him, he suddenly stopped his sprint and tried to get to his own gun. They both ceased to move, standing just at the other side of one of the ruddy bubbles.

Undeterred by both seeing and not seeing the passing of time, I willed myself to peer with body and soul into both bubbles.

I might have spent another million years tunneling through them, dwelling in their self-contained universes, as I got to see the many ways the game could play itself out to the end. But then I came back, an astronaut of time, probably just a fraction of a second after I'd left. My mind had seen too much, and it couldn't hold it inside. I don't have any natural memories of what I saw, just a kaleidoscope of shattered views, a billion instants only minutely different from each other.

* * *

A sudden movement across the street was what brought me back. Julian had somehow rushed past Rafa and was extracting a very large revolver from his jacket—someone had given it to him, as I still had ours with me.

One of the policemen—the one not holding Mariana by her arm—broke with his group and rushed toward Julian. In his dash, he crossed over the bubble on my right and made it vibrate, like a huge soap bubble being shaken and bent by a burst of wind.

On the other side of the street, Anibal had started to raise his gun and aimed it toward Julian. I could barely see him over the iridescent reflections of the other sphere. Somehow, I was watching through both bubbles at once, as if having two independent sets of eyes.

Julian might have perceived the policeman approaching him, because he darted ahead while still trying to point his gun. This was too much for his knee, and I saw him tilt forward in an angle that guaranteed a very hard landing. As Julian fell, a gunshot exploded on my left, and I got to see the bullet's trail as a purplish line darting between the ends of the sidewalk.

I must have finally known then what to do, because I lurched into the sphere on my right. It felt like falling in a dark well, full of freezing-cold water. I had a stabbing pain in my heart and almost bolted over, but a sense of what had happened reached deep into my brain.

The other bubble had vanished. Not knowing exactly why, I had made my choice. I'd thought that I had to save Martínez, and only then Mariana; that this would solve my impossible problem. Instead, I'd chosen to run for my fallen friend.

The pain in my heart stayed there, and I was barely able to breathe as I approached Julian.

But the policeman had reached him first.

6

I wanted to confront the policeman, but then I saw the gun on his left hand, protracted and making a straight line with its barrel to Julian's head. There wasn't enough time for a plea of rationality: I had to act.

I moved to my right and behind the guy's back, trying to stay away from his gun. I then grabbed his shoulders and rotated him in a swift turn to my left, luckily deciding to put my own left leg out front and block his movement. With his knee now being locked by my extended leg, he kept rotating away and his feet left the ground.

From afar, it would seem as if I'd attacked the policeman with some artful *Aikido* move. He fell forward, twisted in the air, and crashed with his face on the pavement. I heard his gun hitting the ground and skittering away.

The sound of the guy's body splashing on the asphalt, and a concurrent moan, convinced me that I wasn't going to hear more from him.

I probably should have stayed with Julian and propped him up, but my strange orbital perception of the world got me to consider something else.

The policeman who had been holding Mariana's right arm detached himself to start confronting the Montoneros up the street. And, since I'd just taken care of the third member of that party, there was only one man left to contain my girlfriend. This made me scramble in the opposite direction I'd taken before, crossing back through the same spot where I had exited a now invisible bubble.

Did I cross again through one of the spheres and not see it? How many of them were around?

The Montoneros had formed an attacking lineup and were still approaching the now small group of one that held Mariana. Anibal was in front of them, his gun hard to pinpoint as it was perfectly aligned with my sight. He was decisively approaching the scattered group of military men—and I had a purple flashback of seeing the Montoneros kill all of them, and then Martínez.

I caught a little glimpse from around my back of Rafa trying to approach Julian from the side. But I was moving too fast to turn, trying to swerve my way to avoid becoming an easy target.

Also, the guy who still held Mariana had a gun pointed to her head.

I couldn't be in all those places at once, and my goal of protecting Martínez might have already failed.

Everything was still moving, slowly and in flux. I wouldn't be able to avoid a crushing end, where those I cared the most about would get hurt. I felt the revolver inside my pocket, its trigger very close to my finger.

There was an explosion, and the side of my jacket was torn open in an instant. The blast expelled a cloud of smoke, and a splash of red spread on the policeman's ribcage. I must have hit something important, because his body collapsed instantaneously, releasing Mariana with enough force to make her fall forward.

I didn't even look at the fallen guy and rushed the last remaining steps before reaching Mariana. I put my free hand on her shoulder, very close to the hood that covered her head.

I wanted to help her to get up, remove the hood, and hug her, to sink into the warmth of her face. But the encounter behind us was deteriorating into a much deadlier shooting. Anibal and a Montonero friend were already firing against the group held up in the two unmarked military vehicles. I felt the vibration of the gunshots, and, as I turned, witnessed the births of a dozen holes on the door and back side of the green Ford Falcon. Invisible hammers banged one of the cars, and bullets ricocheted to implode another one's windows.

I saw Rafa near a fallen Julian, who was grabbing his knee in pain. Rafa's gun still pointed toward the group that held Martínez. He was going to kill him, and everything would be in vain.

Someone who wasn't exactly me took a gun out of my jacket's pocket, pushed Mariana aside, and with a swift movement directed the gun's barrel to Rafa.

I can't remember what I was thinking when I shot him.

7

After the booming explosion from my weapon, a wave of noises hit me as much as its blast's wave. I heard echoes of barked orders about stopping— *"¡Pará!"*—or moving away— *"¡Movete, Juan, para allá!"*—but I didn't know who was addressing whom.

Rafa was suspended in the air, and his gun was drifting away still sustained by his hand. He looked like a swimmer getting ready to take a plunge on a black sea of asphalt. It wasn't clear where I had hit him with a shot meant to be grazing, but the small stain on his jeans suggested that I'd missed valuable arteries.

He was falling now, for me slowly, but probably as fast as gravity got to pull him down.

One of the Montoneros had seen Rafa point his gun toward Martínez. Even before I shot Rafa, that Montonero had aimed his weapon at him. There was another bang, and the bullet silently crossed the street and approached Rafa.

But Rafa wasn't there to receive it. My shot had made him fall fast enough to miss the bullet by the width of his head.

Julian, still stumbling behind him, was not so lucky.

A starburst of dark mist burst out of his belly.

I didn't need a medical degree to know that, in a city paralyzed by a national victory, and standing right in the middle of an ongoing battle, my friend was as good as dead.

I was still trying to get back to where Mariana was standing, but some soul-bound magnetism drew me to reach Julian as he lay face down on the ground. Rafa was now recovering his stance, though standing on the one working leg, and he hadn't seen what happened to Julian behind him. He was attempting to seek cover in the entrance of a building.

The battle was raging, and one of the parked cars lost its rear windowpane with a shattering collapse. More of the military men who had been hiding in the blue *Estanciera* were getting out and shooting back at the Montoneros up the street. These previously courageous gunmen were now shuffling to reach the back of several cars, while still trying to recompose and return fire. At least everybody was busy enough to ignore Mariana and me.

I retraced my last few steps, and after so much, I grabbed Mariana's hand.

It was clear that Anibal wasn't going to surrender Martínez. He was controlling him with a neck chokehold while shooting sporadically toward the policemen closer to us.

I started to drag Mariana away from our more exposed side of the street. Three policemen I hadn't seen before had started to sweep the street with fire from their automatic weapons. The Montoneros decided to quickly move back and toward the other end of Copérnico; they were corralled, even when still holding their trump card, Colonel Martínez.

But then, as we approached Julian's body, my mind shut down, and I don't know any more particulars about the shooting that went on mercifully away from us.

* * *

I'm not sure how it was that I talked with Julian so much, or even if I actually did it, but after Mariana and I turned him around, and saw the blood on his battered school sweater, a helmet of silence covered the three of us and the gods granted us a minute of peace. Like most humans, we had a genetic predisposition to share the last few minutes any one of us spends on Earth. Mariana was crying, and I tried to talk with Julian while holding his hand.

"Julian..."

"I'm sorry," he said, his voice contaminated by a gurgling sound. "I should..."

"Don't worry. Don't...."

"You've made it."

"You should not force...made it?"

"You did it...got her." Julian smiled straight at Mariana, as if we were friends chatting in a café.

"Yes, I did."

"You are *lucky*, Edgardo...you..."

I noticed how he had mixed the English word *lucky* in his choppy Spanish speech. It was our private language, our tribe's perfect brew that had allowed me to always understand him.

"Julian, please. Stay awake."

"It doesn't matter. I couldn't do—what you did."

"I *didn't* help you. I should have..."

"No, that's not what I said. You did. You walked away."

"Away? From what?"

"From time, life. Everything."

And he was right, I had done just that. I wasn't sure anymore that was even my time, or my life. If any of it was real; if we'd ever get to die in that house of mirrors.

Julian had said something more, which I'd missed. He then asked me, "Is all of this real? I saw...those huge violet balls, like alien things...is it real?"

"Yes, it is."

"I saw them once...when I was little," Julian said. "They were what—what started the weird thoughts...my sickness."

I couldn't believe what I'd just heard, but the world was exploding close by.

It would take me years to understand that I wasn't the first.

That they had tried this before.

"Just remember me," he added. "I tried...to fix things...."

You did. More than I could.

With those mumbled words, my best friend had expired and left me alone with his epitaph.

He tried to fix the world.

And I should too. So, I stood up, told Mariana to seek refuge in a building's entrance, and started to walk toward the commotion at the other end of the street.

I finally knew what I had to do to fix the world.

And I was, finally, ready to die trying.

8

I have rewritten what happened in those few minutes over and over and for many years, and in the process, collected enough experiences to fill volumes. This comes both from the uncertainty I have about what saved my skin, and the feeling that, paradoxically, this same insecurity might have been what saved me.

I was still walking toward Martínez and Anibal, completely decided about rescuing the colonel, but also completely undecided about who I was going to shoot. Martínez represented the great evil that had possessed the country since who knows when, and he owed everybody a stay at the *Cóndor*, suffering the same fate his capture had imposed on Mariana. But Anibal was also guilty—all killers are, no matter their well-thought reasons.

I saw that one of the Montoneros was raising his gun in a way that suggested I was going to be its next target.

Anibal pulled Martínez closer to his chest and pointed his own gun straight at me.

I stopped. Raised the arm that wasn't holding the gun, as if trying to surrender.

But a preternatural intuition was telling me this was what I should do. That I had the power.

There was a purple explosion nobody but me saw.

The world ended in that instant.

* * *

I was inside the bubble and outside the universe. What I could see on the street was happening between two beats of a second, but for me that second could have lasted indefinitely.

I had been told the purple spheres were akin to machines, sophisticated calculators that could be used to study the universe's clockwork. But, as I stayed there, with my left arm still raised, I had an eerie thought—even now it makes me shudder—that maybe the bubbles were like windows, and I was now stuck in an elevator between universes; my actions would be what decided whether I could step out and find the same world I'd left or land in a completely different one.

It was possible that all the other worlds out there were illusory, creations from machines vastly more complicated than the spheres.

The bubbles were the tentacles of these Machines, their reach as they explored time.

And, if something had that kind of power over the universe, why not twist it to its own ends?

Why not become God?

I wanted to hurt Martínez, but I also felt that I had to liberate him to end the nightmare. Freeing such an evil man was unthinkable, as I'd been told over and over by whoever had tried to change the outcome of that already insane night. Even as my hand rose, and the gun pointed to the colonel, I knew I was being manipulated. A lot of what I'd thought during my ordeal of the previous weeks could have been the whispers of the Machines, suggesting me that I kill Martínez.

My finger started to slide over the trigger, compressing it farther back. The gun's aim had settled on the colonel's head. Whatever force had guided me to that moment was trying to make sure I killed Martínez.

But with that, I would be forever tilting the scales to ensure the eternal servitude of mankind to masters we would never be able to overtake.

In a moment of desperation, I made a gesture with my left hand, hoping I still had control of the bubble.

I opened the gate.

The man came inside, jumped in like a madman. He pushed me, hard.

I tried to push him. He pushed again. I fell.

We floated, grabbing each other.

We floated outside of the world, together.

We floated outside of all worlds, outside time.

I was suddenly being propelled out of the bubble and crossed a surface as icy as a distant planet.

The street was a rough landing spot.

I could still see the sphere, but I was now sitting astride on the floor, my hands supporting my torso from behind.

I didn't have the gun with me anymore.

There was a loud bang that echoed back from both sides of Copérnico.

Time was resuming its course.

I couldn't see anymore inside the sphere. It resembled a huge purple bowling ball, with a web of scattered lightning tattooing its surface.

Anibal had been hit in the shoulder. Martínez was free and lurched forward.

I hadn't been able to move my body enough to stand up when the bubble exploded in a purple firework more intense than the sun.

Nothing had been illuminated in the real world.

The bubble was gone.

The man was gone, forever.

Time had resumed its course.

The future had been changed, and I hoped it was better than before. That was my hope—for the good of the world.

* * *

I stood up as the policemen reached Colonel Martínez—Anibal remained on the floor, and I thought he was dead. Martínez then moved quickly over Anibal's legs, and the Montonero made a slight movement trying to catch him, while still clutching his pained shoulder. Well, at least he hadn't died—we didn't kill him.

I realized that my ankle hurt badly, and I wasn't going to outrun either of the fighting groups. I was a standing target for their guns.

I tried my best to limp in the direction of Rafa and Mariana. I wasn't sure what they had seen or how long I had been away in limbo. Mariana was kneeling on both of her knees, close to Julian. Rafa was next to her, still alive and with one of his hands resting on Julian's shoulder.

Rafa seemed completely recovered from my tangential shot, and when he saw me coming, pointed at me. He was really signaling toward my back, making me turn around to assess the danger. And there was plenty left.

The two Montoneros who were still around carried Anibal with them. They were rushing to get to the other end of our street, where their truck was ready to leave.

The policemen, however, were coming in my direction with a still-tied-up Martínez. The colonel didn't seem to be able to lift his head and look up.

Suddenly, one of them noticed our group. The policeman raised his gun, prepared to fire. I thought his weapon was pointed straight at me, but he might have been trying to hit Rafa, the larger target.

I got to reflect with irony on the vanity of life, on my adventure ending with me shot dead out of a warrior's pity. Then I heard a voice; it resonated in the now empty street.

"Let them go. The kid just saved my life...he shot that son of a bitch."

Martínez's commanding voice stopped the policeman immediately. He lowered his gun and made a sign to the *Estanciera* and its driver, who made it screech while backing up from parking; the vehicle swerved in such a rough turn it came close to tumbling sideways. The driver stopped just long enough for the two thugs and Martínez to get in and close the doors.

The *Estanciera* sped along Copérnico and away from us, passing very close to the Montoneros as they were climbing into their truck. Then, it disappeared in the night.

I walked the last few steps to the lifeless body of my friend.

As soon as I kneeled between Mariana and Rafa, a deadly tiredness started to take over my body. I felt the cold of the night and burning pain coming from my ankle. My hands were cold too, and I wanted to keep them in my pockets, but I managed to reach out and touch the increasingly pale cheek of Julian.

I would have wanted to cry for my friend, but what I did was to turn toward Mariana, raise her chin with my numb fingers, and kiss her.

Her lips were even colder than mine, but soon we would both be trying to warm up each other.

Someone, in the receding night, cheered loudly for the Argentine team.

POSTSCRIPT

I have spent many empty weekends organizing my journals for those two cold months in 1978 and turning them into something close to a novel. They collect the memories of my troubles and the extraordinary events surrounding them. But I also want to give a sense of how my life unfolded after that fateful night of the World Cup final.

None of the things I thought would happen actually did. My best friend had been killed senselessly, perhaps because I'd saved a war criminal from what over the years we would come to see as necessary justice. Many like Martínez would escape punishment—small consolation for my loss—but I still feel plenty of guilt for what I did, which shows up in my frequent attacks of anxiety. It is, I know, the price I pay for losing what could've been the most precious thing I had.

A true friend. My forever missing brother.

I was, and forever will be, alone with the result of my actions. Some power, a principality whether true or artificial, godly or evil, had saved me but exacted the price of my friend's life. I had solved my problem, only to be left alone in contemplation of the inscrutably dark side of a miracle.

The mess caused by the death of Julian confused my interactions with my father. He felt responsible, I'm not certain for what, and thus adopted a protective attitude I took to mean he considered me damaged goods. This brought further deterioration to my already weak connection with any family I had left.

A few weeks after the World Cup, the Venturinos took off to go in hiding from the military. Mariana, unexpectedly, decided to go with her mother. And I can't blame her; I hadn't been the good company I wanted to be and was a ghost of the person I'd been before I met her. We said our goodbyes, of all places, in Café Las Violetas. I returned her bracelet, almost intact, and as she looked at it, I felt trapped in a loop of time, back at the beginning of our story together.

I saw her take a bus and knew I might never see her again.

A girl with a long swath of black hair, standing on the steps of a *colectivo*—that was my last memory of Mariana.

And then, it was all like a dream. How I decided to leave Buenos Aires and live with relatives in Philadelphia. The way I finished high school pretty much alone. I was, as usual, the best student, and won plaques, medals, and diplomas, rediscovering a love for science and the universe. I tried, through those years, to forget what had happened. But I couldn't, and I didn't.

I was the science weirdo, but whenever someone tried to bully me, I looked at him hard—*very* hard—and he always walked away. I never had to fight again; I had acquired the eyes of a killer.

I knew that I was one.

Even after leaving for the States, I wasn't really living my own life. Years went by, and I saw their passing by a window, always thinking—second-guessing myself—that I had something to do with the events of Argentinean History.

In 1982, the military—still in power—took the country to war with the British over some forsaken islands. The economy kept crashing and rebounding in short cycles that destroyed most local businesses, and after much infighting, a democratic government was elected in 1983. For once, I was happy about something. To my amazement, the subsequent years didn't bring back the boots to power. Other than the ebbs and flows of political discourse, which being Argentine-strength implied occasionally violent swerves, history moved forward in relative peace. Many of those responsible for the *desaparecidos* killed in the '70s were judged, although most were never seriously punished.

I kept shuttling between the States and Argentina, as I first attended college at MIT, and then got a Ph.D. in the Physics program at Stanford. It's a miracle how well I did with my studies, considering that my mind has been forever bound to this lousy Buenos Aires apartment.

Still, my Ph.D. thesis in non-conservation of time symmetries (from high-energy particles, to be precise) won a major international award and was considered a revolutionary generalization, and the greatest advance in our understanding of time since Einstein.

A Swiss newspaper jokingly reported on my award's aftermath that, secretly, I might have been working in a time machine.

Clearly, I didn't find that so humorous.

* * *

Buenos Aires, July 2, 1995

I think that I saw *the man* yesterday. It brought me an unbearable level of anguish to think he might be around again. I can't possibly tolerate another mission spurred by a new twisting of time. I fear that, exposed to another awful choice, this time I'd take the wrong path.

I haven't been able to sleep well since the encounter. I feel something eating away my soul, the same pain that has kept me coming back here all these years. The feeling that I am an armless Atlas, who suffers the weight of history on his shoulders without the means to hold it.

* * *

Tuesday, August 1, 1995

The man stopped by at the pharmacy last Thursday—I was there buying my regular medications. He said that he's back to help me; that I can't stay in this timeline after next year. Something big is coming, he said, and it will change the world. He didn't say—or didn't know—what is coming.

He insisted that we should travel together to northern Argentina, to meet *them*. And he tried again to explain how the Big Machines are trying to take over the universe. He then insisted, trying to convince me, that there is—and there will be more—opposition. A war like no other is going to ensue. *A war in time.*

I said no—no way, actually—I'm not going.

What I didn't tell him is that I can barely leave the Córdoba Avenue apartment these days. That angst more powerful than my will is crushing me against these walls, a little more each day.

That this may be the last time I can gather the energies to travel south.

The man said he will help me. I got distracted a second and he was gone. Now, I think it was all a hallucination. Maybe everything I have seen is.

* * *

Thursday, August 10, 1995

I must add some final notes before I store this manuscript in a safe place, pack my old charcoal bag, and leave the apartment for good.

The man was right—he will help me.

He showed up this morning, in a taxi. Amazingly, this happened while I stood by the main window of the apartment's living room, watching another gray day.

I still can't believe what happened next. The other door of the taxi opened, and Mariana came out. So beautiful, like she was taller, and her black hair had turned shinier. She showed me a smile that made me feel the world was beginning again.

The most beautiful smile I have ever seen.

She looked at the man and then smiled again, straight at my window. They both pointed toward the same spot, a place around the corner I couldn't see from the upper floors.

And then, I knew what they were trying to tell me.

They were both pointing, like a compass, to the North.

(SIGNATURE)
EDGAR (DANIEL) WESTON

Editor's Note

Dear Tom:

I include here, in this quite bulky package, the manuscript (MS, in our parlance) I have been working on for over twelve years. As you know, I'm no longer employed by Conglomerate Publishing, but I'd like you to take a look and see if, with some more editing, we can find it a home. I still feel there's value in this MS, not just as a first novel from the author, but also as something more than that, a realized dream or something else. What it is, I can't really put my finger on. As usual, my musings follow, and they can get very intense. Be forewarned.

    The book—if we can call it that, even after so many revisions—was found in an apartment near Nueve de Julio Avenue, long time after the place was abandoned, foreclosed, and sold to new owners. The original owner, Daniel Weston, was a retired CEO from a big pharmaceutical company in the Midwest, a distinguished fellow who died from what nowadays we'd call depression after the sudden disappearance of his son, a promising physicist. Mr. Weston kept blaming the Argentine government, and the military leadership, even way past the point when they had anything to do with governing the country. Insofar as I have been able to gather information about him, he didn't know his son Edgar had written the piece.

I assume the MS would have been lost if the city's court hadn't decided to sell the apartment after the country's monetary crisis of 2001. The new owners removed a large drawer set from inside a closet and found a secret safe. The MS was inside; no note with it, no introduction, and about 600 pages of typed text, probably coming from a longer handwritten version I don't have. Since our old friend and bossy editor, *Señor* Patrick McQueen, knew one of the tenants, he got a first copy (the original is now in an unreachable trust back in the good old *Estados Unidos de Norteamérica*) and, after he fought for a while with the convoluted journal-like style of the text, did what he does best and passed it to me for fixing. He actually gave it to me in person, in one of those cloak-and-dagger meetings we used to have at *Librería Rodríguez*, while he shopped for American paperbacks. And, also not so rare for the old man, he added an imperative—with his customary four-letter-word cursing—that I should complete the cycle, fix it, and publish it.

That was almost twelve years ago, in 2002. I wouldn't be writing to you if I hadn't reached an impasse of sorts with regards to this monster. Let me give you my reasons, and please, don't think I have lost it.

* * *

I first approached the piece as a teenage rambling, the inventions of a youngster who wants to be a writer. He apparently went back several times over the writings, adding dialogue and chapters to break it up. It still felt halfway between a journal and a novel with strong magical realism themes. This should have been enough to convince me it was your run-of-the-mill first novel, an amorphous thing like most of them. But there's something else here, a lot more than I can understand. That's what I want to tell you about, so you

413

approach it with some care.

First, the author disappeared under mysterious circumstances, in August 1995. I discovered with horror he did so just after signing the MS's last page. My guess is that he placed the entire copy in the safe and moved the armoire to cover it. I couldn't find any coincident police records, or newspaper notices suggesting he was killed after a mugging or something like that, a very possible fate for a foreigner living alone in the '90s Buenos Aires. Also, I couldn't believe those characters he imagined—the girl, Mariana, maybe, but *the man*, please—had come to rescue him just before he wrote the final page. He was taking heavy antidepressants, antianxiety meds, and who knows what else, so perhaps he became manic and left the country for parts unknown.

Second to consider, a lot of the history in his accounts is, for the most part, real. I was able to dig up the name of an Anibal Reinoso, a member of the Montoneros organization, who was killed in 1979 during a raid at the outskirts of the city. And there was a Colonel Martínez, of some note as a professional torturer and for-hire mercenary, but nobody knows much about him, and anyway, he disappears suddenly in 1992. It's now common knowledge that there were many detention centers (*à la* Nazi concentration camps) in 1970s Argentina, and one of them was near San Juan and Boedo, as the story suggests. But there are no surviving records of an *Automotores Cóndor* center in *Floresta*.

And, of course, I couldn't find any mention of the terrorists' attack on ATC (*Argentina Televisora Color*) on the day of the World Cup finals, or of the huge traffic jam it supposedly caused.

Unfortunately, this had taken me to the part that has been torturing me for the best part of a decade. It has to do with the information pertaining to those meteorites Edgar mentions, which supposedly fell just before the World Cup of 1978, in Southern Bolivia, near the limits with Argentina. The newspapers of both countries quickly dismissed the impact (deciding it was just a single crash, after scattered reports of two) and kept saying it couldn't possibly be UFO-related.

To make it even more unreal, every single mention of the meteorites in the MS is *verbatim* from real newspapers and magazines of the time.

The official story (the press was totally under the control of the military) disregarded several UFO sightings that week, ignoring the two reports of twin impacts spaced for over a day. The press just ran with the story of a single meteorite taking off clean the top of a mountain in that remote region, the rock conveniently getting buried so deep inside the ground it was not feasible to dig it up. The repeated statements about NASA scientists coming to the site, and the following denial they'd ever come, made me uneasy. I have seen coverups, and the whole thing stinks of being one.

I must agree with Edgar that there is no rational explanation for two meteors hitting the same spot two days apart. It's so abhorrent to logic, I can see how it was dismissed outright by the press. His contention that those were UFO pieces traveling in time is of course insane—while being attuned with his own imaginations—but it does make more sense to me than the government's hiding of the facts.

This takes me to the part that has made me hold on to this MS for so long. The area in the north of Argentina and southern Bolivia, where the meteorite (or meteorites) fell, has come to be known as the Bolivian Roswell. Many sightings of UFOs have been made there over decades, to the point it has spun a whole cottage industry. Believe me, if I could, I would have just left you a little final footnote about this, but I must go on. Please don't think I'm crazy. I have read a lot about this region and spent several summers in northern Argentina to verify the facts. So, friend, please hear carefully what follows; it's in your purview to decide if you'll take this MS and consider it—with my considerable edits, and yours to come—for publication by Conglomerate.

In August 17, 1995, just a week after the MS ends, there were a couple of great explosions in Joaquín V. Gonzalez, a minor town in the very north of Argentina. A few days later, a search party found a huge gash in the top of a mountain (2,200 yards long and 700 yards wide, if I'm allowed to be precise) but no plane wreckage was ever discovered. Stones around the site had been pulverized to white ash, and trees were missing or scorched all over a large swath of land.

Perhaps another meteorite?

This would be still explainable by science, but there was a further event—witnessed by about 30 people—in the same town, on November 25, 2009, about fourteen years later. A bright cigar-shaped object showed up before midnight, hovered over Joaquín Gonzalez, drifted south and then disappeared. The town lost power for hours.

Did you ever notice how if you slice a flying saucer you get a cigar-shaped outline? Yes, I'm starting to think in time-traveling UFOs, or may be time machines that look like UFOs, with only slices of them we can see appearing in our timeline, in dates apart by many years. And then, perhaps, pieces of them (their landing gear?) might have ended up scattered over time but in the same place.

Please don't think I'm imagining things, at least not yet. And keep reading me, to the end. Like old times, as if we had a few drinks on us.

I wouldn't feel so confident that perhaps Edgar's story is closer to being a troubled memoir than a fictional tale, if it weren't for this last bit: I took those UFO sightings, all in the corridor running from Salta in Argentina to Orán in Southern Bolivia and tried to plot them. It gave me just scattered points over the page. Yes, they did have a general NW-SE direction, but only formed an elongated cloud on graph paper. *And so, what?*

Geodesic lines, dear Tom. The traces a path makes over the

surface of Earth. Planes follow them to shorten their flights. I took a big spherical Earth globe and placed the dots from all the sightings in the region, plus the original meteorite strike in 1978, over the globe's curved surface. And they all neatly line up, creating a perfectly continuous line.

It is as if an object had first crashed, and then maybe taken off, following a simple flight plan. But it flew over a span of 30 years or more. We, mere humans, saw it while trapped in the stream of time as isolated sightings of objects that were moving in higher dimensions. The ones in which *they* trawl across time.

Yes, I am this crazy. I can't hide it, as this story has done something to me.

Anyway, and to end this craze, I can't stop thinking that a great deal of this tale might be true. That Edgar Weston might have done some—or all—of what he told us in his journal. And if he did, the world we're now living in is a wholly different place.

I just can't help but to wonder, almost every day, where Edgar is now.

Or, if you think about it, WHEN.

(ILLEGIBLE SIGNATURE)
Richard Meredith, Senior Editor (Emeritus)
Conglomerate Publishing, Inc.
Buenos Aires, (CABA), May 14, 2014

ACKNOWLEDGMENTS

This book has been with me for years and it had not one but two beginnings in my own life. One day in early 1978, I was in Buenos Aires and crossing the downtown avenue that faces the Argentine National Congress, when I was almost run over by a light-blue Ford Falcon—not unlike those in this novel—that carried secret police with their guns out the windows and pointing to the streets. A few months later I would be there again, in that same corner, this time celebrating the country's victory in the Soccer World Cup.

I have always wanted to come back to that insane moment of extremes and change something—anything—to avoid all the pain that military dictatorship inflicted on innocent Argentines. Over the years, and even from abroad, the story kept growing. While working on another book, I found out about the two meteorites— and yes, all the news and stories mentioned in the book about two, and then maybe one, meteorites hitting a mountain near Argentina just before the World Cup are not fiction. This fantastic event slowly added to the tale's layers of time travel and the characters' deliberation about their own sanity, beyond my original plan of writing a romantic Young Adult novel.

Books are also what happens when we are busy writing other books.

Many great writers have given advice during the development phase of this project, including Marcy Dermansky, Karen Anderson, and David Payne. Copy-editing was provided by both Karen Anderson, from the Writers' Workshop of Ashville, and Christine Singleton, from Word Works Editorial Services. Carina Cortese—author of the play *Afterimages of the Disappeared*—has lent me her extensive knowledge of the period, in part gained by interviewing people involved in the resistance; she also allowed to borrow books and tapes from her considerable research library. And my wife Laura Voglino—whose relatives, the Lizasos, were persecuted for generations by the Argentine military—read early versions and provided information about the workings of the Montoneros organization.

I should also thank the places where the research for this book was carried out: The New York Public Library at Bryant Park, with its wonderfully helpful managers of the Stephen A. Schwarzman's Building newspaper collection; and the Argentine National Library in Buenos Aires, which unearthed for me period magazines with striking pictures of soccer matches and mountains destroyed by meteorites. And I especially thank Juan Trofelli, senior administrator from Argentina's Public TV, *Televisión Pública Argentina*, the present form of the book's ATC, *Argentina Televisora Color*, for a wonderful and in-depth tour of the building and studios where some of the novel's climax takes place. The meteorite might be real, but the takeover of ATC is pure fiction.

I am lucky to live in one of the most active writing scenes in the United States. Excerpts of this book were read in our North Carolina's Triangle area open mic events, including Raleigh's So and So Bookstore series of authors and readers (organized by Beth Browne, Alice Osborn, and Suzanne Crain Miller) and those hosted by the Orange County-Durham Chapter of the North Carolina Writers' Network (led by Ron Jackson, Sheila Callaham, Anne Anthony, and Linda Janssen in its various incarnations). Also, I want to acknowledge the always excellent and fine-tuned criticism by Durham's own writers group—initiated by Eric Meier and now led by the indefatigable Jonathan Giles—and the help of its long-term members: Peter Barber, Shawne Baines, Susan Emshwiller, Kelly Kandra, Leah Silverman, and Samantha Sweede. I feel privileged that some of our state's best writers agreed to read a pre-publication copy of the book: Heather Bell Adams, Gregg Cusick, L. C. Fiore, Padgett Gerler, Miriam Herin, Leslie Tall Manning, and Kathryn Watson Quigg. Of course, I can thank all these friends, writing coaches, and sources, but after so many revisions, the final form and its mistakes are all mine to regret.

Finally, and above all, I thank my wife, Laura, who encouraged this unusual project and accompanied my karmic journey from scientific writing to fiction. She has helped me to realized what this story I've been writing for so long truly is: a new Don Quixote.

Suggested Readings

The bibliography about Argentina's 1976-1983 military dictatorship is immense and continues to develop even today, thanks to the efforts of organizations that want to keep the memory of this tragedy alive. I just include here a few general titles from my shelves, their English editions available through online sellers and many university libraries.

Crassweller, Robert D. (1987) *Peron and the enigmas of Argentina.* W. W. Norton & Company, London and New York.

Dinges, John (2004) *The Condor years. How Pinochet and his allies brought terrorism to three continents.* The New Press, New York.

Gardner, James (2015) *Buenos Aires: The biography of a city.* St. Martin's Press, New York.

Gillespie, Richard (1982) *Soldiers of Peron. Argentina's Montoneros.* Clarendon Press, an imprint of Oxford University Press, Oxford, England. Revised edition published in Spanish (2008) by Editorial Sudamericana, Buenos Aires.

Lewis, Paul H. (2002) *Guerillas and generals: the "Dirty War" in Argentina*. Praeger Publishers, Westport, CT, and London, England.

McSherry, J. Patrice (2008) *Incomplete Transition. Military power and democracy in Argentina*. Authors Guild Back-print.com Edition, iUniverse, Bloomington, IN. Originally published by St. Martin's Press, New York.

Poneman, Daniel (1987) *Argentina: Democracy on trial*. Paragon House Publishers, New York.

Skidmore, Thomas E., and Smith, Peter H. (1989) *Modern Latin America*, Second Edition, Oxford University Press, New York.

Wynia, Gary W. (1986) *Argentina, illusions & realities*. Holmes and Meier Publishers, Inc., New York

The one book I want to mention that's only available in Spanish, but captures better than any other Argentina at the time of the 1978 Soccer World Cup, is:

Gotta, Ricardo (2008) "Fuimos Campeones: la dictadura, el Mundial 78 y el misterio del 6 a 0 a Perú" (*We were champions: the dictatorship, the 78's World Cup, and the mystery of the 6 to 0 win over Peru*). Published in Buenos Aires by Edhasa, Barcelona, Spain.

ABOUT THE AUTHOR

J. D. (Jorge) Cortese is a scientist and educator by training, and a writer out of a passion for communication. He has written regularly for a widely-read scientific newspaper—*The Scientist*—and served as at-large editor for educational magazines and large publishing houses. Winner of awards for both science and teaching, he is also the recipient of the prestigious award of The Writers' Workshop of Asheville for literary fiction.

After extensively pinning a world map, the author and his itinerant wife have found a home in North Carolina's Durham. His two children remain closer to New York, a city he misses as much as Buenos Aires, Shanghai, and Paris. All these places keep appearing in the dream worlds of his stories, as much in the now as in distant futures. When not at his desk writing, he feeds his two lifelong passions, photography and table tennis.

If you read and liked this book, please consider contributing an honest review in *Amazon*, *Goodreads*, or any other social media book source you regularly visit. The author posts news about his writing in Facebook, Twitter, and his author's website at: www.jdcortese.com

The addresses for these social media connections are:

Facebook: www.facebook.com/jorge.cortese.9
Twitter: www.twitter.com/JorgeDCortese
Goodreads: www.goodreads.com/author/show/18446927.J_D_Cortese
Amazon: www.amazon.com/author/jdcortese